My God & Saviour

BY Kenneth John Marks

Fideli
Publishing

Nabal and Joshua

When we were God's enemies he demonstrated his own love for us in this: Christ died for us.
(Romans 5: 8 & 5:10 combined)

Author's note: This fable was written to illustrate what it meant for our loving God to die on the cross for us miserable sinners, even though we were alienated from Him. For we, by our very nature, were His enemies until He saved us.

During the time when kings reigned in Israel, there were two men who lived in a little village in the hill country of Samaria. Their names were Nabal and Joshua.

Nabal was the village's wealthiest man and most powerful citizen. He had thousands of head of oxen, donkeys and camels, and his fields yielded so much grain that his barns and storehouses could not hold it all. As befitting a man of Nabal's station, his house was a palace, made of kiln-baked brick and polished stone, with many rooms filled with plush furnishings. He had a beautiful wife who loved him and many sons and daughters who were devoted to him. Yet he got little pleasure from his wealth, or from the love of his family, or even from his position of power.

You see, Nabal feared neither man nor God, nor had he ever felt true love for anything or anyone. Rather, his soul was filled with hatred, rage and greed. He was exceedingly miserly; his temper was legend; and he was utterly ruthless. If someone got in his way, he would not go around him but would shove him aside with a vile oath and a curse. And Nabal especially hated the poor: he spat into their cups if they dared raise them to him. No one who received such treatment would dare object, though, because Nabal could visit terrible consequences on the complainer. When Nabal walked the streets an aura of fear surrounded him. Children ran and hid and adults avoided him if they could. If they could not, however, and he chanced to look them in the face (which was not all that often), what he took from their expression to be the deference and respect due him was nothing but their consuming loathing of this man clothed in his delusion.

Joshua, on the other hand, was a man of modest means, who lived in a small house on the outskirts of the village. He had a loving wife and many devoted sons and daughters whom he loved and to whom he was devoted heart, mind and soul. Joshua loved and feared his God and walked in His ways. Joshua was righteous in God's eyes and had found favor in His sight. Therefore the LORD had poured out many blessings on His beloved child.[1] Joshua and his family never wanted for anything. His house was full of love and laughter, and they lived happy and contented lives. Joshua had also been given great skill in working with iron, bronze, stone and wood, and he was one of the foremost artisans in Israel. Therefore the work of his hands was greatly prized and he earned a good living by his craft. He also gave much because he had a heart after the LORD's own. His offerings greatly exceeded the tithe that was required by the Law of God,[2] and he never turned away the poor and needy. This wonderful man was especially kind to the children of the village. They would flock to his workshop, and none would ever leave without an animal figurine, skillfully carved out of stone or made of small scraps of iron or bronze, or a small chariot made of wood with wheels that turned without making a sound. Because Joshua was good and kind and was one of the wisest men in all Judah, he was well loved and highly respected by the people.

It came to pass on one beautiful day that Joshua was walking down the main street of the village, carrying under his arm a chest made of a fine hard wood with a rich dark grain. It had been stained and polished until it gleamed. The sides had several Psalms carved into them, all praising God. The top had been inlaid with gold, silver and many precious stones in wonderful designs. In Joshua's mind, this chest was his greatest work. But it had been very expensive to make, and he had had to borrow heavily to complete it. Nevertheless, he had risked much in the hope that his work would find favor in the eyes of the one for whom it had been so carefully and lovingly made. For, if it did, the profit from its sale would allow him to feed and clothe his family for many months. He would also be able to purchase the raw materials he needed to earn a living for the whole next year.

It was these thoughts that gave Joshua a dreamy look as he gave thanks to the LORD his God for His goodness, confident that his ambitions for his family would be realized. As Joshua walked along, many of the villagers stopped him to admire the chest. This greatly pleased him because he was on his way to deliver it to the wealthy merchant who had commissioned it.

The carpenter was startled out of his reverie by a great commotion, caused in part by the constant snapping of a whip followed by a loud report

---

[1] When LORD in all capitals is used, it denotes the Hebrew equivalent of YHWH or 'I AM'. We transliterate His name in English as Jehovah.
[2] See Leviticus 27: 30 – 32 and Malachi 3:10.

as it struck home, and also by shouts and curses. As he looked around to its cause, he saw only that a great crowd had gathered some distance away on the far side of the street.

When Joshua had pushed his way through the crowd, he saw that Nabal was standing in front of a small cart to which a small donkey was harnessed; that the cart was loaded with Nabal's wife and oldest son as well as with several large sacks of grain; that Nabal was furiously striking the pitiful creature with a leather whip, apparently because she had not moved along as quickly as he would have liked (for he was an impatient man); that in his haste, Nabal had forgotten to remove the hobbles he himself had placed on her, which was obvious to all who were standing silently by; that the poor little creature was jumping and squirming and flinching horribly with each blow; that her head bowed lower and lower; that her ears were pinned back as if in shame; that her eyes were blinking and watering from the terrible pain; and that she was whimpering pitifully. And, finally, that the violent man was cursing with the vilest of oaths the poor defenseless creature *and God* at the top of his lungs.

A great wave of rage broke upon Joshua's soul.

As Nabal prepared to strike the animal once more, his hand suddenly stopped in midair. He felt a terrible stab of pain from his wrist down through his forearm and into his shoulder. For the outraged carpenter had grabbed Nabal's wrist in a terrific vise-like grip. The vile man also heard gasps of surprise and consternation from the crowd. But Nabal was so overwhelmed with shock and astonishment that anyone would presume to interfere with him, all he could do was turn and stare dumbly at the trembling carpenter. He absentmindedly dropped the whip to the ground, where it landed harmlessly at his feet in a cloud of dust.

Seeing that he had gotten Nabal's attention, the carpenter released his hand, and Nabal's arm dropped uselessly to his side. Joshua whispered into Nabal's ear, "Can you not see that this animal's feet are still hobbled? Therefore stay your hand against her." Gritting his teeth now, the carpenter continued, straining with all his might to keep the disgust he felt from souring his tone of voice. "And it would be good for you to get quickly on your knees, right here, before the LORD your God and pray that He forgive you for your cruelty to this helpless creature, as well as for the terrible oaths with which you have defiled yourself."

Now this rich and powerful man was not used to being brought to account for his actions, especially before the entire village. To think that he should actually bow before anyone, especially before a God whom he did not acknowledge or fear, well, that was an outrageous affront. In his mind it would be like casting human filth at the great monument of pride he had erected to himself. Consumed with fiery rage, Nabal struck Joshua a great blow to the face.

God's beloved son tumbled backwards. He lost his grip on his precious wooden chest, and it fell to the ground. As Joshua staggered further backward with the force of the blow, he stepped on the chest, shattering it into many pieces. Losing his balance entirely, the carpenter fell backward over its remains and landed flat on his back.

Nabal shouted with laughter at the sight, but as he looked around exultantly at the faces in the crowd, his laughter died. The vile old man was shocked by what he saw. For as the crowd looked from him to Joshua, who was just now picking himself up off the remains of his work, it was clear by their expressions that their fear of him had been replaced by one of open hatred, anger, and repugnance, all these damning him in their vehement accusation; whereas their looks at the carpenter were filled with love and caring and sympathy. Nabal even imagined that he saw reproof in the eyes of his little donkey as she looked over her shoulder at him and then down at her fallen rescuer.

Nabal cursed them all, but with exceptional vehemence, even for him, because of the shame and humiliation he felt from those looks of theirs. How he hated this! As the thirst for revenge filled him, he gritted his teeth and clenched his jaw at Joshua, who was slowly coming to his feet.

On the other hand, as the carpenter surveyed the wreckage of his livelihood and then looked around at the crowd, then at the donkey, and then at Nabal, his thoughts were not filled with hatred or a desire to take revenge. They were, rather, filled with sorrow and pity for this poor foolish man who had defiled himself and everyone else. Joshua's heart also went out to the unfortunate little creature whose back was red with the welts from the blows she had suffered. God's beloved servant began to pray that the LORD would be merciful and forgive this vile man his terrible sin against his God and this helpless animal. He also prayed for forgiveness for all these people who had stood silently by and watched it all.

When the villagers saw Joshua's expression, they forgot Nabal for the moment. Instead, they saw the accusing finger of the LORD Himself pointing at them. As they looked into Joshua's eyes, they saw their own shame, and they all blushed to the roots of their hair. They knew that in their silent acquiescence to Nabal's brutal treatment of his helpless animal and to his vile cursing of God, they bore his guilt as much as he.

But Nabal's feelings of shame and humiliation were abruptly pushed aside by his hatred and rage. It was not long before he stiffened his neck, straightened his shoulders, raised his chin and glared into their faces, his jaw clenched. Nevertheless, they did not look away from him as they used to. This enraged Nabal more. To deflect their awful stares he shouted, "What do you think you're looking at? Get away with you all!" Their fear of him quickly returned, and they all flinched back and dropped their eyes to the ground. "And as for you," he said, pointing at Joshua and then at the shattered chest at his feet, "you got what you deserved. Never cross my path again or you shall rue the day you were born!" Nabal sealed this curse by spitting at his victim's feet.

As the crowd dispersed, Nabal cursed and ridiculed them. He avoided Joshua's continuing stare, however, as Nabal, with shaking hand, took the hobbles off his animal. How the vile man hated that he could not stop that loathsome tremor!

Freed, finally, from her restraints, and at the lightest touch of her cruel master, the little beast got quickly underway, faithfully pulling the overloaded cart, despite the many painful stripes she had borne.

Joshua did not take his eyes off Nabal until he had turned a corner.

In the days that followed, Nabal took his vengeance on God's servant. He went to each of the merchants in the village and to all the carpenter's customers, and he warned them that they were to have nothing to do with Joshua, nor were they to buy anything made by him, or they would suffer the consequences. Since Nabal owned much of the farmland around the village as well as many of the buildings where the people lived and worked, his threats were taken seriously. Everyone knew that he would certainly ruin anyone who displeased him, as he had done many times before—as he was intent on doing to Joshua.

Nabal's vengeance had its desired effect. Since Joshua was no longer able to sell his work, this wonderful and gifted artist and faithful servant of the LORD was reduced to shoveling animal dung to try to earn enough money to clothe and feed his family. Also, since he had borrowed much to make the ruined chest, he had to sell what he could of his own possessions to satisfy the demands of his creditors. Yet after Joshua had sold nearly everything he owned, except his tiny house, there were still many debts, and the fear of foreclosure was great in his household. His wife and children by their accusing and furtive glances gave him the impression that they were wondering whether he might have to sell them into slavery in order to pay.[3]

Because his family was suffering, Joshua asked himself, did they not rightly blame his thoughtless act as the cause? In his affliction and grief, he prayed to the LORD of heaven:

> "O LORD, how have I offended thee? O God, if I have offended thee in any way, you know that I truly repent in my heart, and would offer any sacrifice to atone for my sin. But LORD, how could I stand there and do nothing while that unfortunate man beat that harmless creature and shouted his vile oaths against you? Maybe I could have chosen a better way. I know that I was filled with rage and it blinded me for a moment. If I have offended thee by an act conceived in my anger, forgive your humble and devoted servant.
>
> "O LORD, do not let my failing cause my family to suffer. Rise up in your mercy and compassion, O LORD, and help us all that we may have enough food and adequate clothing to survive the winter that is now hard upon us, and help me earn enough to pay my debts.
>
> "May the God of my fathers Abraham, Isaac and Jacob forbid that we be forced to sell ourselves into slavery to do so.
>
> "I know, O LORD, that this affliction comes from your hand. But I also know that you are my strength and my redeemer, and that in your faithful love and righteousness, you will come to our aid. For your love reaches to the heavens. Your faithfulness is greater than the mighty mountains. As I stand before you, I testify that I have forgiven Nabal for his sin against me; therefore I know that my sins against you are also forgiven.
>
> "Hear the prayer of your servant, my LORD and refuge, and come to our relief. Shower us with your loving kindness, grace and mercy, and let your will be done."

---

[3] It was not unusual in those times for people to sell their children into slavery to pay their debts. Nor was it unusual for creditors to take children forcibly as payment.

Now the LORD greatly loved His faithful child, and He heard Joshua's prayer. He sent out His Holy Spirit to move among the villagers, who loved and pitied Joshua but who were afraid to show him mercy publicly for fear of Nabal. At the LORD's prompting and despite their fear, the villagers all secretly contributed money toward the payment of Joshua's debts, so that after a few weeks they were completely paid. Thus did the LORD make His faithful servant and his family safe from the threat of slavery. Also, from time to time, someone would come to Joshua's house, but stealthily in the dark of night, to give food, clothing and fuel. In this way, the LORD provided all that Joshua and his family needed to survive the winter.

Still, Joshua and his family were openly shunned by the village, and they lived in loneliness and grief. This persisted through that winter and well into the spring.

It was on a particularly warm day, after Joshua had left the stable where he was working and was walking along the same street where he had had his altercation with Nabal, that he heard something strange. Looking up, he saw that one of the villagers' carts had come loose from its moorings and had started to roll down a steeply sloped street toward Nabal. But the man was loading his own cart and was so absorbed in his work he was unaware of his danger. As the cart, which was rapidly gaining speed, bore down upon Nabal, Joshua quickly ran toward him. He arrived just in time to push Nabal out of the way before taking the full force of the rampaging cart on himself.

At first Nabal was confused and disoriented. Anger flashed in him because he had been shoved rudely aside. But when he realized what had happened and saw his enemy lying at his feet, crushed, gasping for breath and dying, he was dumbfounded with shock. How could this man, whom Nabal had so cruelly and unjustly misused, have saved his life at the cost of his own?

Immediately the Spirit of the LORD came upon him and his heart was crushed with grief and shame. Kneeling down beside his rescuer and cradling his head gently in his lap, the now repentant sinner wailed with grief, not only for the evil he had done to this fine man, but also because of all the wicked and cruel deeds he, Nabal, had done.

How he loathed himself!

The foolish old man cried to the sky, "O what have I done? O LORD, please take me instead." Nabal looked into the face of the dying man through his tears and begged, "If you can possibly find it in your heart, forgive me for the terrible things I have done. Ask of me anything and it will be yours, even my worthless life in trade."

7

Joshua smiled. "Be at peace with God," he replied. "He and I both forgave you long ago. So then let your heart be filled with His faithful love. Do not weep for me because I go now to be with my God. I hope that I will see you there when He requires your soul of you." Joshua coughed up some blood; then he gasped loudly, as if he were trying to pull back the breath that was quickly leaving him. "You may do one thing to ease my mind, if you would," Joshua said faintly.

"Of course, my friend, of course," Nabal replied eagerly, gently wiping the awful red mucousy fluid from Joshua's cheek and chin with the hem of his cloak.

Joshua said, his words almost too faint to hear, "Please take care of my wife and children." After carefully wiping a strand of hair away from Joshua's face, Nabal kissed his forehead with all the tenderness he could muster; then he took Joshua's hand and kissed it too, whispering in his ear that he must certainly do this very thing. Joshua's mind now at ease, he praised the Name of God in a surprisingly loud voice. Then he died.

Joshua's soul was immediately taken up into heaven accompanied by the Archangel Michael himself, where there was great singing and rejoicing, as he fell into the waiting arms of his loving heavenly Father. What joy there was in heaven that day!

And Nabal, by the grace of God, repented of his sinful ways. He and his whole house became devoted servants of the LORD their God. Because he no longer lived the life of a fool—for his name in the Hebrew tongue sounds like the word for "fool"—the LORD gave him a new name, Joel, which means "the LORD loves".

From that day the people of the village were amazed at the change in him. Some said it was as if the evil spirit of Nabal had died in Joshua's place and that Joshua's righteous spirit had come to dwell with them once more. While Nabal lived, no one in the village or the surrounding countryside ever went without food, shelter, or clothing. And he did see to Joshua's wife and children. He humbled himself before them, bowing low to the ground and begging their forgiveness, tearing his clothes and throwing dust on his head, loudly weeping and repenting. He also took them into his home, showered them with his wealth and loved them with the same selfless devoted love that he now showed his own wife and children. And he served the LORD his God with love and devotion all the rest of his days.

Abraham and Isaac

Sometime later God tested Abraham. He said to him, "Abraham!" "Here I am," he replied. Then God said, "Take your son, your only son, Isaac, whom you love, and go to the region of Moriah. Sacrifice him there as a burnt offering on one of the mountains I will tell you about." (Gen 22:1 – 2)

Author's note: We've just seen a person sacrifice his life for someone who hated him, much as God sacrificed His life for us when we hated Him. But what does it mean to give up something else that is even more precious than your own life—the life of your only child—as a service to God?

Early one spring morning, while it was still dark, Abraham awoke with great excitement. It had been sixteen years to the day that Isaac, his only son, the love of his soul and the light of his life, had come to him, as the LORD had promised. Today they would prepare a great feast to celebrate the day Isaac was born.[1] Abraham rose, and after kissing his wife Sarah, who was still sleeping soundly, he left the tent quietly. He did not want to wake her because he wanted time to be alone with God. As he left his tent, he looked up into the clear cold sky from which a vast array of stars winked gaily down at him. Imagining they were the eyes of the host of God's angels, he smiled back at them. He was doubly glad that the day promised to dawn beautifully.

Abraham took one of the glowing coals from the firebox and lit a fire. As he sat in the quietness of the camp and the little fire crackled into life, he reflected on how the gracious Hand of the LORD his God had blessed him and prospered him, and he considered all the good things God had done for him.[2]

For when the LORD God called Abraham out of the land of the Chaldeans, He had promised to make him a great nation, to bless those who blessed him, to curse those who cursed him and to bless all the people of the earth through him. Five times before the birth of Isaac, the LORD had appeared to him and promised to give him and his descendants all the land he set his foot upon, from the Nile to the Euphrates.

---

[1] Scripture does not reveal Isaac's age at the time this story occurs, but the story has the feel of a young man who relates to his father as a teenager would.
[2] The story of Abraham begins in Genesis 12 and goes through Genesis 25: 11.

Abraham raised his eyes for a moment to look around at the vastness surrounding him. He smiled when he considered that his son Isaac had been born to him when he was a hundred years old and Sarah was ninety. *How amazing*, he thought, chuckling.

Abraham's smile faded, however, when he recalled the hard times that had come when he had not fully trusted God. There was that time in Egypt when he had lied, saying that Sarah was his sister. Pharaoh had taken her into his house, but God afflicted Pharaoh and his whole household with serious diseases. Then there was that time just before Isaac's birth when he lied again about Sarah to Abimelech, king of Gerar, and put the king's whole country in danger. Abraham realized that every time he had doubted God, he had sinned, and it had gotten him, his family and others into trouble. Nevertheless, the LORD God, the faithful God who knew him as a friend, delivered him.[3]

Abraham chuckled again, raised his eyes to heaven and gave thanks to the LORD.

Now all of God's promises to Abraham had been very specific, saying that Abraham's own offspring would inherit this land. But when he and Sarah entered the land, he was seventy-five and she was sixty-five, well past the age of childbearing, and they had no children. Abraham believed God's promises, certainly; but he wondered whether all this might come through one of his servants who would be his heir.

Abraham then recalled how God had affirmed the Promise by saying:

> "Do not be afraid, Abram. I am your shield, your very great
> reward. A servant in your household will not be your heir,
> but a son coming from your own body will be your heir." [4]

Abraham, whose name means the Father of Multitudes, looked up into the night sky as he recalled God's words:

> "Look up at the heavens and count the stars, if indeed you
> can count them. So shall your offspring be."[5]

---

[3] As regards God considering Abraham His friend, see Isaiah 41:8.

[4] Genesis 15:7 – 21 tells of God's first covenant with Abraham. Abraham was originally named Abram. His name was changed by God in Genesis 17.5

[5] Genesis 15: 1 – 5 paraphrased for brevity.

As he did on that night, the old man marveled at the milky whiteness of the sky teaming with stars, filled with awe. God also affirmed this promise by making a covenant with Abraham, sealing His promise to give Abraham the land.[6] How wonderful that was. He smiled at that thought. How wonderful, indeed!

Yet at that time Abraham was well over eighty and he still had no children. Abraham blushed as he recalled how he and Sarah had tried to make God's promise come true by having him go to Hagar, who was Sarah's servant. But her pregnancy and then the birth of Ishmael had caused no little grief for him and Sarah. How foolish that was, Abraham thought. And awful too! For he had had to send Ishmael, who was then a teenager, and his mother away when Isaac was born. Awful!

Staring sullenly into the fire, Abraham shook his head slowly and sighed heavily. He had doubted God and tried in his own wisdom to force God's promise to come true. As usual, nothing but trouble had come from it. For what was probably the ten thousandth time, Abraham went to his knees and repented of his lack of faith on that day and on those other days.

As God's friend got off his knees and sat back down, he looked into the sky again and then around at the land. He thought about all the times he had trusted and obeyed the LORD God and watched as the blessings poured down from heaven onto him and his family. Abraham bowed his head and gave thanks to the LORD for being faithful, despite his occasional lack of faith, by raining down blessings on him because of the LORD's own faithfulness. And he thanked his God for giving him the heir that He had promised.

Then Abraham looked back at the tent where his son Isaac slept, and his love for the boy brimmed over in his heart and poured into his soul. What a miracle it had been that Isaac was conceived by him when he was one hundred and Sarah was ninety; a son, who, by the promise of God Almighty, would receive this tremendous inheritance. Abraham again scanned the surrounding hill country. As he thought about Isaac, little arrows of sweet pain shot through him—from overwhelming joy, borne of the most ardent hope, to the utmost thanksgiving, delight, and fulfillment that can be imagined by anyone who has had the greatest desire of his heart granted.

By this time the first rays of dawn had begun to gleam on the horizon, and there were no clouds. *Yes, indeed,* Abraham thought, *this day will be glorious. How appropriate to the occasion: my son's birthday.*

---

[6] Genesis 15: 7 – 21 tells of God's covenant with Abraham.

This sent his mind back to that equally glorious day many years ago when the LORD had come to him and said of Sarah, "I will bless her and will surely give you a son by her. I will bless her so that she will be the mother of nations; kings of peoples will come from her."[7]

Abraham recalled how he had fallen on his face, though he had laughed with this thought in his heart: *Will a son be born to a man a hundred years old? Will Sarah bear a child at the age of ninety?* The LORD heard his laughter, of course. He said, "Sarah *will* bear you a son and you will call him Isaac."[8]

Staring into the sky again, Abraham laughed out loud when he recalled how, in response to his laughter then, the LORD chose the name Isaac for his son because it means, "He laughs." The old man's laughter grew louder because he knew that the LORD, his Friend, had laughed with him that day.

Just as God said, one year later, the LORD did give Abraham a son. His *son.* O joyous, joyous day!

Isaac's father was now laughing so loud he was afraid of waking the camp. In his heart he still heard his wife's joyous cries when Isaac was born to them. He could still hear the celebration in the camp as they feasted on the sacrifices they had made to the LORD their God in thanksgiving for that day. A son was born to Abraham. O *hallelujah*! Praise the LORD!

A bird's song began to wake the camp. *It's such a beautiful song,* Abraham thought, *like the one that plays in my heart when I think of my beloved wife and son.* Just then Sarah came out of their tent and started to bustle around. She waved to her husband, and he waved back and smiled, immediately returning to his musings.

Abraham recalled the very first time he had held his son in his arms and saw the tiniest of fingers and toes and heard the sweet little cry of hunger. Then there was that day when Isaac said his very first word. Abraham was *absolutely* sure he said "Abba" (Daddy). He had teased Sarah about it then, and they both laughed at his good-natured joking.

How Abraham's heart filled with love as he watched Sarah, the very best of women, bustle around!

---

[7] In Genesis 17:15 God changed Abraham's wife's name to Sarah from Sarai (which may mean "princess"). Based on the LORD'S reason for giving Sarah her new name, it could either mean "Mother of Nations" or "Mother of Kings". In Genesis 17:16. Scripture indicates that this happened about one year prior to Isaac's birth.

[8] Genesis 17: 17, 19 (portion). The italics are mine.

Then there was the day Isaac took his very first steps. Abraham could still see his son's little arms waving up and down like the wings of a bird learning to fly, Isaac's little hands holding onto one of his tiny toys, but with such a terrible grip, as if his life depended on staying on his feet.

And there were the years Isaac grew into a healthy little boy and then into the young man he was today. There was that day when young Isaac went into the fields with his father for the first time to tend the flocks. Abraham recalled the glowing joy he felt when his son learned to use a sling and bested the other boys in the camp competitions. Abraham especially loved how Isaac became the darling of the entire community. The old man smiled as he recalled watching the little (and now not so little) girls follow his son Isaac everywhere, adoring every step he took, and how Isaac was so gentle and good with them, and how they *all* worshipped him. Abraham's son!

One of Abraham's favorite memories was of the day Sarah was grieved because one of her favorite little ewes had been slain by a stalking wolf. Isaac, then a boy of thirteen, went out and killed that wolf and brought its fine gray-brown pelt, completely cured, to his mother as a gift. Warmth filled the old man as he remembered the glow in Sarah's eyes as they beamed down first upon her son and then at the beautifully groomed pelt. It still lay next to their bed; and Abraham treasured his wife's tender expression when she looked at it, the outpouring of a mother's love that came from a heart bursting with joy. Yes, Isaac made Sarah's heart glow too.

Abraham gave thanks that Isaac had grown tall and straight like the great Mamre trees under which the Promise had been made. Clearly the LORD's hand rested on his son, for not only had Isaac grown strong in body, he had also grown strong in his faith and had come to love the LORD God as his father did.

The camp had fully wakened now and everyone was scurrying around, lighting fires, preparing the morning meal, going out to the flocks, milking the goats and the like. The old man especially loved this time of the morning. Abraham got up and went over to his wife and embraced and kissed her. Sarah blushed because there were many eyes on them, but she did not mind. Then Isaac came out of his tent. Though the boy was in a hurry to get out to the flocks, he came over to his father first and embraced and kissed him warmly. The old man smiled as he watched his son disappear over the rise.

Abraham looked up and frowned. The sun had risen fully, but a few dark clouds were creeping over the horizon and there were more on the way. The wind suddenly kicked up, and God's friend became troubled. Abraham wondered if the sudden turn in the weather was a sign of something else that might darken the day.

But as the day wore on and preparations for the celebration of Isaac's birthday became more feverish, everyone forgot the clouds and the wind. As the sun began to set, Sarah and her servants and many of the women in the camp were still busily preparing the feast. It would be unusually large tonight because many had been invited from the surrounding country to celebrate with them.

Meantime, Abraham had gone out to be with Isaac, whom he had sent out to help his foreman in one of the far pastures where some ewes were lambing. Abraham had wanted to make sure Isaac stayed out there because he wanted the feast to be a surprise. Late that afternoon, before the old man headed back to the camp, he pointed to one ewe that was starting to give birth and admonished his son, "Make sure you see that she has finished before you come home!"

The boy nodded and waved gaily at his father as he went back to tending the ewe.

Now on his way back to the camp, the LORD called to him, saying, "Abraham."

Abraham bowed low to the ground, bathed in the shining light of the LORD and said, "Here I am."

Then God said, "Take your son, your only son Isaac, whom you love, and go to the region of Moriah. Sacrifice him there as a burnt offering on one of the mountains I will tell you about."[9]

Abraham froze. He slowly rolled to a sitting position, struck dumb with shock and despair. Isaac's father sat there motionless for a good long time, hardly able to breathe. He could not believe what he had heard. His heart pounding now, hot grief burning in his breast and sweat pouring down the sides of his face, Abraham asked himself over and over, How could this be? How could this be?

A wave of yearning and loss poured over Isaac's father. He could still barely breathe, though he understood that the LORD had every right to demand the life of his son. For everything was the LORD's, and if the LORD intended that Abraham have only these few years with his son Isaac, so be it. And they had been such glorious years. (Heretofore dammed up by paralyzing despair, tears now gushed out of the old man, flowed down his

---

[9] The dialogue comes directly from Genesis 22: 1 – 2.

cheeks and dripped off his chin.) How many men had been so blessed by the love of the LORD as he? Yet … yet, what a hard, hard thing this was for him to bear.

Trying to see beyond his act of obedience, the image of Isaac's body burning in the flames came to him. His son's future also flared up and disappeared like a blade of dry grass thrown into that awful blaze. In desperate hope, the trembling old man thought, *Surely the LORD will not take his life.* Recalling the Command, he reasoned, *Even if God does take his life, surely He will raise him up from the ashes of the fire, for how else could He keep His promise of making me the Father of Multitudes?*

Now, as always at times like this, Satan was close by. Seeing Abraham struggle with all his might to find the strength to obey the words of God and seizing this opportune moment, Satan entered Abraham's mind and said to him, "Surely you don't think God will really raise him from the dead, do you? You know the only reason God wants your son's life is that He is jealous of the love and devotion you have for him. He would have you take Isaac's life so that you will not love anyone but the LORD your God." The old man flinched upward suddenly and glanced at the sky.

Thinking he might have struck sympathetic a chord in Abraham's breast, Satan continued boldly, "But if you spare the life of your son, what will the LORD do? Really? Has He not said that He will make you a great nation through Isaac? Come to think of it, how can a God of love, a God who claims to be your friend, really expect you to slaughter your own son?"

These words stabbed at the weeping man because he had already considered them. As the urge to give in to Satan's tempting words welled up in him, Abraham recoiled, asking himself how many blessings had God blessed him with when he obeyed, and also what bitter harvest had been sown in disobedience?

Realizing that he truly loved his Sovereign LORD more than anyone, even his only son Isaac, Abraham said to himself, "Surely the LORD has commanded this hard thing of me for a good reason. And maybe it's true that I have placed my devotion to my son above that to the LORD my God. Maybe Isaac has been an idol to me." The old man quickly stopped and huffed out loudly, staring at the sky, "Well, that is not true, of course." Abraham nodded firmly. "Nevertheless," he continued, "how can I disobey my God?" Because of Abraham's faithful spirit, the Spirit of the LORD entered him with great power. Abraham's faith firmed up, and the Father of Many stopped weeping and thrust his fist into the air. "Let it not be!" he shouted at the sky. "I will surely do this thing that the LORD has commanded me. God forbid that I should offend Him in any way."

Defeated, Satan fled back into the darkness, cursing God and His servant Abraham with all his heart.

Meanwhile the LORD's faithful servant set his face to do the thing God had commanded. Abraham rose from the ground, dusted the burrs and brambles off his robes, set his chin and straightened his shoulders. Then he returned to the camp where the preparations for the feast had just been completed. Heavy as his heart was, he resolved not to let anyone know what he was about to do. Not even his wife Sarah. *Well, until after the feast, at least,* he thought, *for she must surely be told.*

The sun was setting when Isaac and all the men returned to the camp. As Isaac came over the rise, everyone shouted a greeting, acknowledging his birthday. Isaac stared around at them all, first in surprise and then with great joy.

The LORD's friend embraced his son before the entire camp. Then he shouted, "Let the celebration begin!" But in Abraham's heart oppressive despair had crushed to death any joy he might feel. It would take three long days and nights to get to Moriah; and these, Abraham knew, would be the worst days of his life.

Late that night, when Isaac and the camp had retired, the LORD's great servant went into his tent to be with his wife. How he hated the awful news he had for her! His resolve not to weep but to be strong and resolute for her was quickly dissolving in caustic grief.

When Sarah noticed the heaviness in her husband's face, she said, "My husband, why are you so sad? Did we not have a great feast in honor of our son's birthday?"

Abraham gently touched her cheek. "Today, my little dove, the LORD our God commanded me to offer up our son as a burnt offering somewhere in the region of Moriah."

Sarah gasped with fear and sadness at this awful news. Her heart crushed with despair, she grabbed at her chest. She looked over at the wolf's pelt lying next to her mat. Seeing that her husband's eyes had followed her and seeing his tears, she buried her head in his shoulder and her grief wailed through a storm of tears.

"Surely you must have misheard Him?" Sarah said after several minutes, still sobbing. She probably hoped that she could persuade Abraham that he had misunderstood the command of the LORD.

"No," he said softly, "there was no mistake. The LORD, with a wisdom I cannot pretend to know, has required the life of our son." As Abraham caressed Sarah's heaving back, he set his chin and said, "And He shall have it!" After this, Abraham tried as best he could to comfort this wonderful woman and devoted servant of God—the life of his soul—as she wept bitterly on his breast.

Early the next morning, Abraham got up, but very slowly because of the terrible weight in his heart. He saddled his donkey and gathered two of his servants and his son Isaac. They all went into the forest to cut wood for a burnt offering.[10]

When they had finished and had started on their way, Isaac looked at his father with loving eyes and said, "Abba, where are we going?"

This look from his only son pierced Abraham's heart deeply. Without flinching, he said softly, "My beloved son, the LORD our God has demanded a burnt offering of us. We are going to Moriah to obey Him."

The young man had never had reason to question his father's wisdom. Though they had no ram, or ewe, or goat, or even a dove with them to offer to the LORD, Isaac accepted this answer without question.

As they rode, Abraham glanced at Isaac from time to time, who inevitably caught his look and smiled an adoring smile back at him. The old man had to look away, pretending that he had gotten some dust in his eye. When this happened he could not help but reflect again upon the days before his son's birth and upon all the blessings the LORD his God had showered on him. Nor could he stop thinking about all the hopes and dreams he had had for Isaac.

Many times during the journey he prayed silently, "Dear LORD and Almighty God, I do not pretend to know why you have demanded the life of my son. I do not pretend to be able on my own to do this thing you have commanded me to do. Nevertheless, as you have always blessed me with many great blessings, and because you are merciful, give your servant the strength to obey this hard command." Then, despite his heavy heart, the LORD's friend would praise God for giving him Isaac, if only for these few years. His only son!

On the third day, Abraham looked up and saw a hill in the distance. Seeing that this was the place God had commanded, they stopped and

---

[10] Genesis 22: 3.

Abraham said to his servants, "Stay here with the donkey while the boy and I go over there. We will worship and then we will come back to you."[11]

Abraham took the wood, bound it up into a bundle, and placed it on the back of his young son, while he himself carried the burning embers in the fire pot and a knife reserved for the slaughter of the burnt offerings.

Isaac looked up to the place where they were going. He was puzzled because they still had no lamb or other animal to sacrifice. He turned back to his father and said, "Abba?"

Now with each step the old man's heart had become heavier and heavier. Nevertheless, doing the best he could to disguise the overwhelming sadness in his voice, Abraham said, "Yes, my son?"

"We have the fire and the wood, but where is the lamb for the burnt offering?"

Abraham, barely able to control a sob, said, "God Himself will provide the lamb for the burnt offering, my son."[12]

As Abraham said this, he and Isaac continued to the crest of the hill the LORD had shown Abraham. When they reached it, the old man began building an altar.

As Isaac watched his father, he was becoming increasingly puzzled because there was still no sacrifice. Recalling what his father had said, Isaac thought that perhaps the LORD would rain a lamb down from heaven, or that maybe one would come bounding, unsuspectingly, through the bushes. So the boy decided that he would look for any sign that a lamb or goat or ram might be lurking about and went off a little way into the brush to search for one. A little while later, after Isaac had been wandering through the brush, he heard his father call to him.

Isaac ran through the bushes and into his father's arms. Then he said, "My father, I am sorry to have wandered away, but I thought the LORD our God might provide a sacrificial lamb by having an animal wander by and come to us through the bush. I had even thought that as you completed arranging the wood on the altar, one might run and jump right into your arms so that we could do as the LORD our God has commanded us." The trusting boy smiled at his childish fancy and embraced his father.

Abraham looked away. He could no longer restrain his tears as the image of that unsuspecting lamb came to him, who was now nestling in his father's loving embrace.

---

[11] Genesis 22: 5.
[12] Genesis 22: 6 – 8.

Seeing the tears on his father's face and realizing that he himself had just come running through the underbrush and into his father's arms, Isaac felt a sharp chill cut through him. Nevertheless, the boy asked his father gently and timidly, "What is it, Daddy? Surely we will find a sacrificial lamb in the brush."

His father replied, his voice quivering with despair, "Oh, my beloved Isaac, how the laughter has ceased for me! The LORD our God has commanded that *you* be that sacrificial lamb."

Isaac, with the Spirit of the LORD upon him, sought to comfort his father. "So be it then. Blessed be the Name of the LORD. For from the LORD do all things come, and all things are the LORD's, even my life. Do not grieve, my father, for we serve our God, even until death."

These encouraging words pouring out of his young son and over Abraham's soul were like a healing salve to the wound in the old man's breast. And Isaac stood steady as a rock before him.

Abraham bound Isaac lightly, took his beloved son in his arms and gently helped him onto the altar. He took out the knife and, with a trembling hand but a steady heart, raised it to strike the life out his son. But as God's great servant went to plunge the knife into Isaac's chest, his hand would not move, try as he might.

Then the Angel of the LORD called to him from heaven, "Abraham! Abraham!"

Abraham felt the knife leave his grasp, as if it had been taken forcibly from him. Staggering around, trying to stay on his feet, he answered, "Here I am." His legs were so weak the old man sank down to the earth next to the altar, sweat pouring off his brow.

"Do not lay a hand on the boy," the LORD said. "Do not do anything to him. Now I know that you fear God because you have not withheld your son, your only son."[13]

Though Abraham's heart rejoiced, his hands and knees were shaking so badly he could barely stand. He had to struggle to his feet. He had just begun to untie Isaac when the young man said, "Look, my father, in the bushes."

Abraham then noticed that a ram, which they had not seen before, was stuck in the bushes a few yards away. After freeing his son, and with Isaac's help, he took the ram out of the bush and offered it up as a burnt offering.

---

[13] Genesis 22: 11 – 12.

God's faithful servant named that place "The LORD will provide". To this day this mountain is known by that name in the kingdom of heaven.

The angel of the LORD called to Abraham from heaven a second time: "I swear by myself, declares the LORD, that because you have done this and have not withheld your son, your only son, I will surely bless you and make your descendants as numerous as the stars in the sky and as the sand on the seashore. Your descendants will take possession of the cities of their enemies, and through your offspring all nations on earth will be blessed because you have obeyed me."[14]

It came to pass that about two thousand years later the LORD our God had a Son by a virgin named Mary. He walked the earth for about thirty-three years, teaching and proclaiming the Good News of God's blessing to all the nations of the earth. Then our LORD, also known by the name the Anointed One who saves His people, or Christ Jesus, who was also a son of Abraham, was given to us as a holy sacrifice of atonement for our sins by His heavenly Father.

---

[14] Genesis 22: 15 – 18.

from there.[7] The whole crowd was murmuring such things, shaking their heads.

Until a really strange thing happened. A dove came flying out of the sky—it had seemed to come out of nowhere too—and landed on Jesus' shoulder. All the crowd noise ceased. I'll never forget looking up into the sky, though as I think about it now, I don't know why I did. Anyway, I recall seeing the heavens part and a voice like a clap of thunder come down from a gap in the sky: "This is my Son, whom I love; with him I am well pleased."[8] I felt chills run all up and down my body. I remember looking over at my sisters, whose eyes were as wide as cooking pans, and who were looking back and forth from Jesus to me, clearly astonished. As you can imagine, we were all astonished, though no one else seemed to have seen the heavens open but me. Well, I saw it, no matter what my sisters say. We all heard the voice, though. Make no mistake about that!

Then what happened next was really remarkable. After Jesus came up out of the river, He came right over to my sisters and me. I can still remember all the eyes in the crowd following Him. We started to rise, but He motioned for us to remain seated. Then the very LORD of the Universe, as we eventually came to know Him, squatted down in front of us, looked my sisters and me right in the eye and smiled. "Lazarus of Bethany," He said, "I am going into the desert shortly. But now I need a place to stay."

I laugh now as I recall watching my sisters jump to their feet, chattering wildly, blushing and smiling. They immediately took the LORD by His hands and pulled Him away from that place and to our animals.

Well, as I think about it now, it was Martha who was doing most of the talking, really. Mary, who was the quiet one, just smiled and blushed for all she was worth.

Jesus was chuckling too as He looked over his shoulder at me while I scrambled to keep up with them. How they laughed and (Martha) talked His ear off as He followed them. I also recall that I had brought an extra donkey that day, but if you had asked me why, I would not have been able to tell you—then. Now I know the answer, of course, but that's an altogether different story. Most of you who know the LORD as we know Him would know the answer also.

---

[7] This saying about Nazareth was common among the Judean Jews, who scorned anyone from that village.

[8] Matthew 3: 17.

Well, we got back to our home in Bethany later that evening, and we all had a wonderful meal together. We talked and talked well into the evening. I chuckle to think that even Martha was silent long enough to let the LORD get a word in edgewise. Which He did; long enough to tell us all about Himself, where He came from—both His human birth place and His eternal place of authority, seated on the very throne of God—and about His ministry here on earth.

When He told us that stuff about eternity, we were stunned to silence—well, for a moment at least—until we started wondering what all this meant for our people who had been oppressed by occupying powers for five hundred years since our captivity in Babylon. We were all speaking at once for a while—which, as you may know, is not uncommon when you have two energetic sisters and you, yourself, also tend to some degree of loquacity—until the LORD started talking again, and we all listened to Him in intense *silence*. That was such a wonderful evening!

(Though I may poke a little fun at my sisters from time to time, they were wonderful women. For from the time they were children they had loved the LORD their God and had served Him faithfully. Therefore it should come as no surprise that they were our LORD's most devoted servants. When He came to stay with us, Martha, God bless her heart, could not get enough of fussing over Him; while Mary could not get enough of *listening* to Him.)

In the two years or so that followed, Jesus made it a point to stay with us here in Bethany whenever He came to teach in Jerusalem. You see, though He was the God of Abraham, Isaac and Jacob come to dwell with us and then to save us Jews from our sins, many of the leaders were hostile to His teaching, so the city itself was not the safest of places for Him. Despite this, we felt, maybe a little pridefully, that He would always be safe in our home. I guess this was because I, I blush to admit, was an elder in the town and was well respected by all the town's inhabitants, and we were always entertaining high-ranking muck-a-mucks from the city.

Now shortly before the LORD our God died for us all, two incidents occurred which astonished me, and will probably astonish everyone who ever hears of them. It's about these that I want to tell.

The first occurred after I had fallen very ill.

Poor Martha was beside herself. She had even stopped working—and talking—long enough to sit by me and hold my hand as I lay on my bed. And Mary, blessed Mary, hardly ever left my side. She sang to me, bathed me, kissed me and told me it would be okay. She was the most loving sister a man could ever want. They both were: two more loving and devoted nurses a man never had than these two, who loved me with all their hearts.

How they fretted, too, because the LORD had gone north across the Jordan River, and He had been away for some time. Jesus had gone away from us because it was well-known among the people that some of the priests and Pharisees and many other leaders of the people wanted to put Him, their very Eternal Saviour, to death.

Can you imagine?

Nevertheless, I remember my sisters pooling all their money—well, all that I knew of at that time—to hire a man to ride across the Jordan to find Jesus and tell Him I was sick. I can still remember Mary and Martha sitting by my bed, then going to the door to look for the LORD, and when He did not appear, coming back to me and saying over and over again, "If the LORD comes, He will heal you, Treasure."

Of course I knew that He would. I also knew that He was in grave danger from some of our leaders and that coming to me would put His life in jeopardy. I did not want that then, and I told them so. Oh, how they scolded me. I can't help but laugh, but only a little now, as I remember the looks on their faces. How I love those two!

As I got worse and started to slip away, you can't believe how Mary and Martha wept and carried on. They kept wringing their hands, wondering where the LORD was. Though He did not come for me then, not once, ever, did they question His love for or devotion to us. How proud of them that makes me. I tried to comfort them by assuring them that I was going to be with our LORD as He exists in heaven and that I was not afraid. But they, bless their hearts, did not want to lose me, even though they knew what I said was true. And maybe I did not want to go to be with our God all that much then. For, truth be told, I thought I would miss my sisters too much to enjoy being without them, no matter where I was or in Whose Presence I was basking.

I was so foolish!

Well, after a sickness that lasted some weeks, I died. After this I can only recount to you what my sisters told me later.

After they had stopped weeping, they lovingly prepared my body for burial. That very day! You know how they do: they smear precious oil all over your body; put a lot of expensive perfume on you—makes you smell like, well, I don't know what all—and then they wrap you in linen from head to toe. Then they took me to our family tomb, which was a cave dug in the wall of a valley outside of town, and they laid me in it and had a large stone set over the entrance. You see, grave robbers weren't all that uncommon in those days, and I had been buried with my favorite necklaces and bracelets; and they were worth a pretty *denarius*, let me tell you![9]

After this, the whole village came to our home to mourn my passing. I guess that gave Martha plenty to do, what with feeding them and all, and I hope it helped her with her grief for a time. At least she had plenty of company to talk to.

Well, about four days later, Jesus came back into town. Our LORD knew that I had died, of course, but He had waited purposefully so that He might come back and do a work that would astonish the universe and glorify His Father at the same time. My sisters tell me that He wept bitterly when they met Him. He loved me, you see.

I can just imagine the look on Martha's face when the LORD commanded that the stone to my tomb be removed. She hated bad smells; that's why our home always smelled to high heaven with incense and perfume and what all. She knew that after four days in a hot tomb, my body would not have been in the best of shape, to say the least. Nevertheless, she obeyed our LORD.

All I remember about that time is that I was resting in a peaceful place. I heard singing. I think I saw the Glory of God shining down on me because the place was full of light. There were angels too, I think, although I don't really remember this experience very well.

Then, suddenly, I heard the LORD's voice call to me, and I felt as if I were being pulled away by some violent wind. I also remember being carried on its flapping wings for a brief time. Then I remember my eyes opening and staring up at the ceiling of the cave. I also remember that there was light all round me. Now if it had been up to me, I might have lain there for a while. I might even have rolled over and gone back to sleep. (Martha always used to scold me about that because I loved to sleep, and she had to pull me out of bed some mornings.) I did not have that luxury, however, because I felt a hand pull me to my feet and then several hands shove me along and out of the door of the tomb.

Next thing I remember I was blinking in the bright sunlight. I couldn't see for a moment because it blinded me. The hands kept pushing at me, and I remember wanting to shout at them to stop because my legs had been wrapped so tightly in the linen cloths that my feet could hardly move. But shove me they did, and out of the cave I popped, or stumbled, rather, almost

---

[9] A *denarius* was a silver coin weighing about 5 grams. Matthew 20:2 implies that one *denarius* was equal to a day's wage.

falling on my face! I'll never forget the looks the people standing near the cave's entrance gave me. The crowd must have numbered a thousand.

I heard my friend Jesus say, "Take off the grave clothes and let him go."[10]

Then my sisters came up to me and smothered me with hugs and kisses. Martha never stopped talking, of course, laughing and hugging me at the same time. While Mary, bless her heart, just caressed my cheek with tears in those beautiful eyes of hers. I wanted to cry for her because she was so filled with the joy and thanksgiving I saw in them.

Finally, there was my friend, Jesus. He embraced me too. Then He put His arm around my shoulder, and we walked back to my home where we had the feast of a lifetime.

I don't think I've ever seen Martha so happy: she got to feed at least a hundred people that night, and she talked a blue streak the whole time. I know she was really happy because she didn't yell at Mary this time, though Mary had been sitting at our LORD's feet and listening as He taught us, while Martha worked her fingers to the bone, as she was always wont to say.[11] How happy we all were!

I was especially happy because my sisters, especially Martha, could not get enough of hugging and kissing me. Nor did I have to lift a finger around the house, and she even let me sleep in. Well, for a few days, at least.

Then there was the second incident, which, I am sure, was as equally glorifying to God as raising me from the dead was, His displayed-for-all-to-see awesome power notwithstanding. It concerns something Mary did for the LORD. To tell of it makes me so proud of her, I feel like I'm going to burst every time I recall it.

After a week or so, Mary came to me and said, "Lazarus, considering what the LORD Jesus has done for us, I want to do something for Him."

I could not have been happier, considering how much He had come to mean to all of us. So I said, "Well, Treasure, whatever seems good to you, go and do it." But she seemed hesitant. I took her by the hand and sat her down and stared into her eyes, but she looked away from me and bowed her head in that way that she does. She was blushing too. It's an especially endearing way she has about her when she has certain deep feelings of love come over

---

[10] John 11:44.

[11] Lazarus is referring to a separate incident earlier where Martha complains about Mary listening to the LORD while she worked as recorded in Luke 10: 40 – 42.

her. I knew that she was thinking of our LORD, so I said, "Darling, what is it?"

She beamed a beautiful smile at me. "I've saved up some money out of the wine from our field and other things."

Now both of my sisters were the most industrious of women, but Martha had a noisy way about her, bustling and bumping around, talking and laughing and carrying on—how I love her for it!—whereas Mary tended to be quiet, austere and reflective. She generally glided quietly around the house like a joy-filled sigh. She happened to be referring to a small field she had bought near town where she had planted a vineyard, which the LORD our God had blessed so greatly that we needed ten men to harvest the grapes. The wine from those grapes was terrific too!

She and Martha also had a little shop were they employed several women who spun and wove cloth and sewed woolen garments, and they also dyed them. Both of these enterprises provided us with a handsome income. I thought I knew how much income, but Mary had scrimped and saved out of her earnings, so much and so quietly, no one had any idea how much she had accumulated.

Until she brought out from under her cloak a rather large purse and set it in my hands. I opened the purse. There were fifteen *aureii* in it! I looked up at her with wide eyes and an open mouth, and she blushed again. It was a big enough sum to feed a large family for a year![12]

I was astonished, needless to say, and I stammered, "Mary. This money. Where?"

"My darling brother," she answered, turning beet red, "I have saved it out of my own share of our income. Now that the LORD says He is going away from us in a little while, well, I want to do something for Him. You know how He said He's going to die and be resurrected. Well, I want to do something for Him to prepare Him for his brief burial trial."

Mary had been referring to a conversation we had had the day Jesus raised me from the dead. He had spoken well into the night of what was eventually going to happen to Him. We were astonished. I didn't think that any of us understood what He had meant. But Mary had, as I think about it now. It's always the quiet ones that surprise you, isn't it?

So what could I say but, "Well, my heart, go and do what you must, and the LORD be with you."

---

[12] An *aureus* was a golden coin worth twenty-five silver *denarii*.

We embraced and she kissed me again for what was probably the thousandth time since that day. But I had no idea what she had in mind.

Several days after that, about six days before Passover, which we Jews celebrate each year to honor the LORD our God for saving us from our Egyptian oppressors, Jesus was given an honorary dinner at a friend's house. It was going to be a big to-do, so we could not have it at our small house; and since our friend had a big wonderful place, we all went over there.

Martha did all the planning and cooking, of course. I don't think this man's servants knew what hit them because she descended on that place like a storm off the Great Western Sea. They survived her well enough, though, and the food was excellent. The wine, which came from Mary's vineyard, was terrific. And we all had a good time.

As we all ate and drank and chatted, Mary left off serving and disappeared for a moment. Only I seemed to notice this, though, because Jesus was telling us wonderful stories and everyone was captivated.

When she came back she was carrying a large, beautifully made alabaster jar. She had also let her gorgeous hair down so that it flowed down her back and all the way to her waist. We were all amazed because respectable women never let their hair down in public, and Mary was especially modest and respectable. And beautiful, I must say, with her hair down like that.

So we all stopped speaking as she came up to our LORD, weeping. Her hands were shaking too. He turned to her as she knelt next to Him. I'll never forget the look on her face as He lovingly caressed her cheek and she pressed His hand close to her and held it there for a moment. Nor will I ever forget the looks on all the rest of our faces, either.

As Mary opened the jar, the room was immediately filled with the sweetest of scents. It was spikenard, the most expensive of perfumes imaginable. Then she did an absolutely incredible thing. She said, "LORD, this is for you for what you've done for our house and for my brother." She smiled over at me briefly before taking the jar and pouring most of the perfume over Jesus' head. She then poured what was left on his feet and took her lovely hair and wiped his feet with it. As she did this she was still weeping and her tears mingled with the perfume. How wonderful this was! How touching!

As I remember this incident, two things especially strike me. The first was that during all this time the LORD never took His eyes off her. I get goose bumps thinking about it. The LORD our God, for this briefest of moments in the history of the universe He created, had eyes *only for my sister*. Isn't that just terrific? The second was that there were actually some cries of indignation that such a vast sum of money should be wasted on this frivolity instead of being spent to help the poor. Can you even imagine?

Jesus would have none of it, of course. When Mary finished, He took her in His arms and embraced her in front of us all. Then He turned to the crowd, still with one of his arms around my sister, and said the most wonderful thing: "Why are you bothering this woman? She has done a beautiful thing to me. The poor you will always have with you, but you will not always have me. When she poured this perfume on my body, she did it to prepare me for burial. I tell you the truth, wherever this gospel is preached throughout the world, what she has done will also be told in memory of her."[13]

Mary immediately left us and went home. Though she went away weeping, I think it was for joy. It was certainly not for any shame that she had let her hair down in front of all these men, or for having "wasted" a whole year's wages—you can absolutely bet on that. Nor can I find the words to express how proud I was of her, especially when the LORD reached over to me and took my hand warmly in His, smiling into my eyes.

Well, that's all I've got to say. Except that now, my sisters and I live in the presence of this same Jesus and will continue to do so for the rest of eternity. How glorious it all is! And I know that Martha could not be happier because she has the most attentive audience to listen to her. It seems that God's angels have an almost unlimited capacity to listen, which Martha is certainly making the most of, let me tell you!

---

[13] Matthew 26: 10 – 13.

A Sinful Woman

Now one of the Pharisees invited Jesus to have dinner with him, so he went to the Pharisee's house and reclined at the table. When a woman who had lived a sinful life in that town learned that Jesus was eating at the Pharisee's house, she brought an alabaster jar of perfume ...
(Luke 7:36 – 37)

Author's note: This scene has always touched me deeply. Also, many believe it to be a different incident from that described in the story of Lazarus just related, though there is some debate on this point. Be that as it may, I've come to realize what a noble spirit it takes to humble oneself before God as this woman did. Note that the name I've given to the woman is fictional; her name is never mentioned in Scripture.

Salome had always been a bad girl. At least, that's what her father kept telling her as he repeatedly raped her. Maybe it had been that she had struggled so intensely to defend herself. Not to say that a man can't be put out a little when someone who's about a quarter his size and weighs less than a quarter than he dares to kick and bite and scream when he's brutally attacking her. Oh no, not to say that at all. Still, he seemed to be overstating the case a bit. Though I don't think her brothers thought so when they also brutalized her and beat her for not giving in to their every desire, or for not moving fast enough to serve them at mealtime or at any other time that suited their fancy.

It might not seem too surprising, then, that Salome grew sullen, uncommunicative and angry; that hatred filled her soul to the brim; and that it vented itself against everyone who came into her life. Against men especially.

It happened that when Salome was a young woman of about thirteen or so, her father sold her to a man in a neighboring village for a few shekels of silver. She might have brought much more. For she was strikingly beautiful and very desirable. Even at this young age she had acquired a woman's body. But she was not manageable at all. Rather, she was more like a wild animal than a human being.

At least, that's what this man must have thought as he tried to beat some sense into her, but to no avail. For one night, when he was beating her mercilessly, she grabbed a knife and stabbed him in the heart. The man died instantly.

She then ran from that village never to be seen by its residents again. Since he was known to be an especially brutal man, the very scum of the earth, as his neighbors put it, they were more than willing to let things lie. To tell the truth, they were happy that he was dead, and since the girl meant nothing to them, they did not pursue her.

There were many more men who came into her life after this. It did not take long for a man who had seen this striking beauty who was unmarried and obviously in need, and who offered to take her into his home, to find out how she hated him. Therefore as she was passed from one man to another, most of them treated her badly, but for no better reason than that she hated them all and let them know it. Beatings did nothing to faze her. Nor did starvation. Not even attempted acts of kindness, though they were few and far between. Nothing did. After a month or so, she found herself back on the streets. Most of these men were lucky to escape with only the minor wounds that her kicks, bites, and knife cuts left them.

Now in those days, a woman had nothing if she was not married. Therefore, Salome did whatever it took to survive. A survivor by nature, she did not let this small female handicap deter her, and she became a cunning outlaw. She stole, she begged, and she sold her body to anyone who'd pay. Since she was also as clever as she was ruthless, she managed to avoid the authorities.

As time passed, Salome became one of the most successful prostitutes in Judah, and she became quite wealthy. She was well known to all the people, and they shunned her, at least by day. But being one of the most beautiful women in Judah, whose reputation for sexual skill was legend, many of the same priests who openly scorned her by day did not hesitate to pay her handsomely for her services by night. Despite her success, Salome might have died brutally in her sins had she continued on the lawless path she had taken. Eventually she would have met a man more brutal, more cunning and more ruthless than she, and he would have killed her. Certain events intervened, however, that dramatically changed her life and eventually saved her immortal soul.

One beautiful spring day, Salome happened to be traveling in the district of Galilee. She had heard that a prophet from God was preaching and teaching among the people. She could not have cared less about any god. Still, the stories about the prophet were so unbelievable she decided to search him out to see if he was really as "wonderful" as the people said.

On the way, as she was carried along in her luxurious litter, she reflected on the rumors she had heard. Since he was a man, he was corrupt; there was no doubt in her mind about that. Salome smiled and nodded. How was it then that he did all the miracles the people talked about? She frowned and shook her head. Rumor had it that this prophet had turned six very large stone jars of water into wine at a wedding party in Cana, here in Galilee.

She almost choked on her laughter at this crazy tale. Wine indeed! Bending over in mirth, she thought, *How I wish I had been there. Gallons and gallons of wine!*[1] *How wonderful!*

She stopped laughing suddenly. The rumors had been persistent, after all. She had also heard over and over again that the prophet had miraculously healed many diseased people and cast out many demons. At this thought, Salome's expression turned sour. Though she did not fear any god, she believed that the Jewish god existed, as did his nemesis, the devil. She knew that the devil had demons as servants, as Jehovah had angels to serve him, because she had participated in various demonic rituals with certain clients. She had seen what these servants of evil could do to a person. She knew about demons, all right!

Salome shuddered. The thought that some human being could command demons and evil spirits with impunity brought beads of perspiration to her brow and made goose bumps rise all over her. But coming back to herself, she forced these thoughts out of her mind. What am I doing, she wondered? I almost scared myself to death. She tried to laugh at herself, but strangely she could not manage even a chuckle.

As they neared the Sea of Galilee, she passed by Capernaum, a small village resting on its northern shore. Near the village was a large well. Feeling thirsty, because her mouth had gone dry as dust with imagining that demons were stalking her, Salome ordered her bearers to stop. Her chief bodyguard offered to get her a drink, but since the day was beautiful and the breeze cool, and since there was no one else there at this hour, she decided she'd draw the water for herself.

As she stood there drinking the fresh cool water, a young man approached the well.

He had obviously been traveling for some time because his hair and beard were matted with dust and dirt, and his face and hands and arms were soiled as well. He also looked quite poor because his clothes were ragged. Still, he was a man, and she hadn't had a man in a while. Why not this one?

---

[1] The New Testament equivalent of a gallon was about 8 *sextarii*. In John 2, Jesus turns turned from 960 to 1,440 *sextarii* of water into wine (6 stone jars of between 20 and 30 gallons apiece).

She'd done worse. He wasn't that bad looking, after all; he was young; and he looked strong. Several lewd thoughts involving this young man occurred to her, and a smile creased her lips.

Until he sat on the rim of the well near her, looked up into her eyes, smiled and then said, "Mistress, could you get me a cup of water?"

What?

All the hatred for men she had ever felt welled up in her in violent outrage. She spat at his feet and growled, her voice rising in volume with every word, "Who are you, you filthy wretch, that I should serve you?" Screaming now, she continued, "Get you water? You must be kidding me. I'd rather wallow in a trough with all the pigs in Judea and Samaria than do that." With that she threw the cup at his feet and stalked off, leaving him sitting on the side of the well.

But as Salome started back toward her litter a weird feeling came over her and her anger began to subside. Though she had vowed with all her strength not to look back, she did anyway.

And there was the young man looking at her with the kindest eyes possible. There was no hate there. There was no urge to take revenge on her there. His expression was all serenity—no anger darkened it in the least. Salome knew how to spot those awful emotions in men's eyes, all right, and they simply were not there.

Then what was it that she saw there?

She could not say as she stared back at the young man for a few moments. Salome got into her litter, and, with an oath, urged her bearers to leave that place.

No, indeed! Salome could not have answered that question had she had a thousand years to think about it. For what she had seen in his eyes was love! For her!

The next day, word spread throughout the village that the young prophet was walking along the sea. Salome decided that she'd go and see what this was all about. Hoping to hide her identity she donned the plainest robe and most worn sandals she had. Then she went out to find him. She rode her litter down to the seashore and stopped it at the edge of a large throng of people, which blocked her way. She got out and headed toward the crowd, ordering her bearers to remain behind.

There were thousands of people milling around, and she could not get a good view of the prophet because they had completely surrounded him. Setting her jaw, she entered the crowd and tried to push her way through. She had started to make some progress when the crowd stopped suddenly. She was caught in such a tight press of people she was unable to move. Suddenly, they all turned away from the sea and toward a slope of a hill nearby. This sharp turn left Salome back where she had started—in the rear—and she cursed loudly. So loud was the murmur of voices, however, no one seemed to hear her.

The crowd walked for some time and started to climb the slope. She became increasingly irritated as these "smelly peasants" jostled her and brushed rudely by her. She wished she had brought a few of her bodyguards with her, especially because she was still wearing some expensive jewelry and was worried about the thieves—pickpockets as we would call them today—who loved to work situations like this. Nevertheless, she set her jaw again and pushed rudely by the people in front of her so that after a few minutes she found herself walking in the front of the crowd.

When Salome broke through, what she saw astonished her. For there was the young prophet in front of her, his back turned to her, healing a little girl's broken arm. He then cast a demon out of another little girl. (The skull-piercing shriek it uttered as it was thrown back into hell shook her to the marrow of her bones!) After this, he healed the flow of blood in a grown woman, who went away weeping for joy. Then he turned and looked right at her. Right into her eyes! And smiled warmly at her. She almost fainted: it was the same young man she had spat on yesterday.

Salome staggered back as he turned away from her and continued to walk up the side of the slope. She felt faint and nauseated. Her heart burned in her. And a new emotion she had not felt since she was a very little girl welled up within her. Shame! She felt this slimy thing crawling around in her gut for the very first time in her adult life. With that came the sting of guilt and remorse. Then she caught a glimpse of herself as God saw her, and she began to weep. Hatred, the idol she had always worshipped, quickly rose up in her and urged her to leave this place—to run! But for the first time she could remember she did not give in to it. As she struggled to throw off its awful temptation, she realized that she simply could not turn away from this young man. She felt compelled by a force she could not identify to go on, to see what he would do next.

When the young rabbi got about half way up the slope he stopped. Salome noted that there were twelve young men staying very close to him. *These must be his disciples everyone keeps talking about,* she thought.

She noticed that two of these men in particular seemed to be watching her. This made her very uncomfortable, and she tried to avoid their stares as best she could. This was a new sensation to her. She had never been cowed by a man's stare before. Fortunately, as the rabbi found a rock and sat down upon it, the young men turned their faces toward him and sat down at the young prophet's feet. Salome breathed a sigh of relief and faded back into the crowd, hoping it would hide her from them. Then she sat and waited for the multitude to settle in.

Despite her self-consciousness, she could not resist the urge to get closer to the prophet. As the young man waited for all the people to find their places, Salome got on her hands and knees and crawled toward him. She could hardly believe she was doing this. Every once in a while, the two young men would look back at her. When they did, she stopped, averted her eyes and sat as still as she could; but when they turned away, she crawled closer. When she had gotten about fifty feet or so away from him, she stopped directly behind the two young men, sat cross-legged on the ground, lowered her eyes and waited. Because of her excitement and eager anticipation, she was hardly able to breathe. She could never recall feeling this way.

Then something happened that caused her heart to skip a beat. The young rabbi looked around at them all and then down at his disciples, who smiled up at him adoringly. Salome could see that from even this distance. Then he looked RIGHT AT HER! He smiled and gave her a little nod in greeting.

Salome wanted to cry again. She felt like a child, totally humbled and fully exposed, as if she were naked in front of all these people. Strangely enough, she did not care in the least as the young man continued to smile warmly at her. Suddenly she knew what that look in his eyes was. And she let the tears flow this time. It was all she could do to wipe them away fast enough so that she might be able to see into his kind eyes, and to control her sobbing so that she might hear what he had to say.

The young man (Jesus of Nazareth, she heard someone in the crowd say) stood and surveyed the crowd for a moment. Then he turned his eyes toward her and, staring at her, began to speak:

> "Blessed are the poor in spirit, for theirs is the kingdom of heaven.
> "Blessed are those who mourn, for they will be comforted.
> "Blessed are the meek, for they will inherit the earth...."[2]

---

[2] Matthew 5: 3 – 5.

Jesus spoke for some time. Many people murmured astonishment at his teaching. Some reacted angrily. When the young rabbi got to the part about the hypocrites who love to be seen praying in the streets and the synagogues, a priest, who had been sitting near Salome, got up, uttered a curse and stalked away. But the young woman, enthralled beyond her ability to tell, struggled to stuff down her sobs so that she might hear every word.

Salome had heard a lot of self-righteous pious blathering in her time. Some of her clients were the very best at it. But these words, coming from this kind young man, had no sense of falseness about them. Therefore each one of them penetrated her heart as if he were shooting them into her chest with a tightly strung bow. And Jesus' eyes never left her the whole time. At least, that's how she remembered that day for the rest of her life.

When he was done, the crowd got up slowly and wandered around, hoping, it seemed, to talk to him, or, failing that, to maybe get a brief chance to touch him. But Salome could not find it in herself to move. She gave in to her shame, guilt and remorse, and began to weep. Sobbing heavily, she kept her eyes bent toward the ground, too ashamed to look anyone in the eye, especially this wonderful young man, whom she had come to love with all her heart.

Bent over and weeping quietly now, her heart breaking with guilt and shame, tears running down her nose and dripping onto the earth, a strange thought came to Salome: she must look a mess. Imagining what her tear-stained face and puffy eyes must look like, her sobs stopped and she smiled. As the image pressed itself into her consciousness, she started to chuckle. Then she laughed because she had always prized her beauty above everything else. She had often had terrible nightmares about growing old and ugly. Right now she could not have cared less how she looked. She laughed harder, wiping away her tears and then her dripping nose with the heels of her hands.

A shadow suddenly loomed over her. She looked up and saw that Jesus had left his disciples and was standing over her. She tried to stand, but he waved his hand, palm flat, and she stopped. He got down on his haunches in front of her, looked into her eyes and smiled.

She could not believe it. This young man, who was obviously a great prophet like Elijah, had humbled himself so that he might look her in the eye. Then he did another astonishing thing. He opened his arms to her, and she shot into them and melted into his embrace so fast she could hardly believe it.

She bawled like a baby this time, not caring how she must appear to everyone around her, all pride having melted away in the kind warmth of Jesus' embrace. And as he held her gently, she found that she actually enjoyed his fatherly touch. She had always hated having a man touch her when she was not in control. But not now. And she understood immediately why. He wanted nothing from her. Rather, he was giving something precious to her with his touch, a sensation she had never experienced before.

After a few moments Jesus let her go. As Salome sat back and looked into his eyes, he said, "Young sister, you have led a very hard life. You have been much abused." She nodded, wiped her eyes, sniffed and tried to smile. With sympathy and kindness radiating from his eyes, he said, "Yes, you have been much abused. Yet you have also done many bad things. Is this not so?"

Without hesitation and with no desire to justify what she had done, she murmured, "Yes, Father." She did not know why she had addressed him as she might have addressed God, if she ever prayed, which she never did. But she had.

Salome glanced away from Jesus for a moment as memories of all the awful things she had done flooded into her mind. But her eyes slowly, inevitably, came back to his. She was astonished that the shame she felt, though awesome in its power, had not had the power to cause her to run from him. Rather, it had caused the very opposite. She had turned back to him. She *had* to look him in the eye. She had to confess what she had done. Nor did all the evil done to her come into her mind to justify her actions. When she thought about this later, she was amazed that she could not seem to find excuses for herself, even if it were to deflect Jesus' piercing stare.

She looked back at him and in a firmer voice, she repeated, "Yes, I have done many bad things. Even murder, Father."

Jesus touched her shoulder lightly and said, "Yes, Daughter, I know. But know this: your God loves you and desires that you repent of these things." He put his hand to his breast when he said "your God." Noticing that little movement of his hand in what would normally have been an inconsequential gesture, she found her mind fixing on it, wondering what it could possibly mean.

So fixated on Jesus' hand lying on his breast was she, it took her a few seconds to recover herself enough to find the words to answer. When she did, she answered truthfully, "No, Lord, I do not know about such a god." Her hand rose, as if of its own accord, and gestured toward him. She lowered her hand. "I have always been a bad girl, you see. How could anyone, much less the God of Abraham, Isaac and Jacob, love a miserable wretch like me?"

Then the young rabbi did another astonishing thing. He rose to his feet and extended his hand. "Well then, come, follow me, and you shall see."

Doubt and wonder now crowding out her guilt, Salome timidly took his hand and rose. Then, wonder of wonders! she not only held his hand briefly, but she raised it to her lips and kissed it tenderly. He smiled, nodded and then turned and went back to his disciples. A few moments later they left that place. Salome walked quietly some distance behind them, not wanting to get too close, still pulled along by the undertow of her swirling shame and guilt. And she still felt her hatred pounding mercilessly at her insides.

During the next few weeks Salome followed Jesus everywhere he went. At first, as she heard his teaching and saw all that he did, her guilt and shame for her sin intensified. She needed some relief from the pain it caused her, but she did not know how to get it because her pride was a terrific goad to her. She could not bear to ask anyone for anything, much less the God of the Universe for forgiveness for her awful sins. She just couldn't! Nevertheless, as she continued to follow Jesus around and listen to his words, her stubborn pride began to melt away.

One day, she went to Bethany because she knew Jesus was staying there with an older man named Lazarus and his two sisters. She found herself walking past their home many times, hoping to get a glimpse of him. She never dared go to their door because she suspected they would have known about her.

It happened that after a week or so, as the older sister was returning from the market, she saw Salome looking longingly at her door. The matron stopped, turned, approached her and asked if she wanted to come in. Salome blushed furiously and shook her head rapidly. Not willing to take no for an answer, the woman took Salome's hand and pulled her toward the house, saying, "Oh, come along anyway." It was so kindly done and with such a good-natured smile, Salome allowed herself to be led into the house, despite the fear rising in her.

When Salome saw that Jesus was not there, she was disappointed. On the other hand, since no one else was there but she and the woman, who had introduced herself as Martha, Salome allowed herself to relax a little. The gray-haired matron had the young woman sit down at a small table and placed before her a goblet of wine, a bowl of fruit, a large plate of fig cakes, another plate of cheese and one piled high with bread. All this while Salome, with wide eyes, kept saying, "Please no, Mistress, I'm not hungry. Really!" To no avail, of course. Then, for a moment or two, Martha and the girl stared at each other quietly over the table.

Martha then tried to put her guest at ease as best she could, engaging her in casual conversation. The kindly matron talked about the house, the weather, about the Pharisees and how foolish they seemed; she talked about anything and everything. Many of her statements where gaily punctuated with, "Don't you think?" or "I'll bet you've seen the same thing."

But Salome sat quietly and shook her head uncertainly. Had she wanted to respond otherwise, she would not have been able, because the question had barely been shoved out of the way by a big sigh and a chuckle before Martha began a new topic.

Now as the kind lady talked she also laughed. At first Salome did not know what to make of this loquacious, friendly, jovial, good-natured woman. No one had ever been so relaxed around her, or had had such an accepting open attitude toward her. Therefore as Martha laughed and talked and pushed at her guest's knee, the girl relaxed more. She found Martha's funny stories about her sister Mary and brother Lazarus increasingly entertaining, especially because Martha often made herself the butt of her own jokes. Though Salome tried to resist Martha's charming manner, she could not help but chuckle from time to time, hiding her smiles behind her hand as best she could. Seeing this, Martha pointed at her and laughed harder.

This wonderful woman was so full of mirth and cheerful good nature that after a time she had completely captivated the girl. Eventually Salome gave in and laughed heartily too. At one point, the two women were laughing so hard they had to hang onto each other to avoid falling off their chairs onto the floor.

After they had finished one particularly good laugh, Martha took a deep breath, wiped her eyes with the hem of her apron, sat back and looked deeply into the girl's eyes.

In response, Salome did something she never did (well, except for that time on the mountain). She blushed. Like a young girl she blushed; not for shame, but for the same reason she had when Jesus smiled at her: Salome now knew what totally accepting and nonjudgmental love was. She knew that this wonderful woman loved her—a complete stranger, really—though Martha must have heard about all the bad things Salome had done. And this had kindled such wonderful warmth in the young woman's breast, it vented itself through the pores of her skin and turned her face red with its heat.

Bowing her head, trying with all her strength not to let on that her will to resist Martha's love was crumbling, Salome felt tears coming to her. And she never cried, either (well, again, except for that one time on the hill near the

Galilean sea). As Martha's love bathed her in its bright soft light, the final bits of Salome's pride melted away and she allowed herself to weep openly.

The kind elderly woman opened her arms to her. Totally vulnerable and helpless now, Salome knelt beside her, laid her head on her ample breast, and sobbed uncontrollably. Martha held her close and petted her gently. "There, there, it'll be all right," she said over and over as the girl sobbed and sobbed.

After Salome had calmed down somewhat, Martha told her another story: how she and Lazarus and Mary had met their LORD. At that mention of God's name, Salome's head shot up. But she laid her head back down again as Martha told her how happy they were that day to have taken Him into their home and into their hearts. Then she told the now quiet girl how Jesus had come to Israel to deliver His people from their sins. "That's what the name 'Jesus' means, don't you know," Martha said, shooting a finger into the air.[3] And then she told her what a difference putting their faith in Him had made in their lives.

Martha stopped speaking suddenly and leaned back. Salome leaned back too and smiled, expecting another funny story. But Martha said instead, "What am I telling you this for? Of course you must know Jesus already."

Salome replied softly, "No, Mistress, I don't." She got slowly off her knees and sat back in her own chair, wiping her eyes and smiling bravely.

When Martha's head jerked back in surprise, the girl amended her assertion to say, rather, that she did not know him all that well, really, though she had met Jesus on the side of a mountain in Galilee. And at a well near Capernaum. But she only whispered that last admission.

"Well," Martha said, seeming perplexed, "that's strange, because the LORD God of Israel talks about *you* all the time. We've all noticed you hovering around, don't you know?" Martha nodded for emphasis, but she was smiling that comfortable, winning, endearing smile of hers at the wide-eyed young woman.

"What?" Salome answered, a terrific thrill shooting through her. Unwilling to savor the joy she felt and a stranger to the sweet pain it brought to her, she insisted that that was crazy. God doesn't talk out loud to people anymore; such things had not happened since ancient times.

At this Martha laughed gaily, slapped her thigh and reminded her that she, Salome, had talked to God herself. On that very mountain. In Galilee.

---

[3] The name "Jesus" is Greek for the Hebrew equivalent, "Joshua", which means "the LORD saves."

Martha chuckled loudly as Salome sat back—eyes impossibly wide now, her mouth making a large "O" as she fanned herself.

Martha looked over at the table and took the plate of fig cakes and stuck it under Salome's eyes. Martha nodded encouragingly. The girl took one, but only to be polite.

Still unwilling to fully give in to this very kind woman, and, nibbling absentmindedly on that fig cake, Salome reluctantly admitted that certainly, on several occasions, Jesus had actually claimed to be God, but that she did not think anyone actually believed him. (Salome interrupted herself to look down at the fig cake and her eyebrows went up. It sure was good!) Looking back into Martha's smiling eyes Salome thought, *But here's this woman who does believe. How strange.*

Well, Salome then conceded—accepting a cup of wine from her hostess absentmindedly, at first sipping it gingerly but then taking a big swallow (it was so very good!) and then eagerly grabbing another fig cake from the plate that was again held out to her—that Jesus was certainly the greatest prophet of the time. And … well … yes, he did have miraculous powers, which everyone had seen. And he had certainly gotten her to start thinking about herself. Salome then sat up straight, wiped her eyes again, and brushed the crumbs off her robe. (Blushing and looking stealthily up at her hostess from beneath her brow, Salome reached across the table to take just one more fig cake.) The girl then said emphatically that no, she did not really believe that Jesus was God's only son or God Himself, for that matter. She thought, rather, that this was just a preaching tactic Jesus used to get people's attention. "Nor do I think that anyone else has really believed in him," Salome concluded, her mouth full of fig cake.

This stopped Martha for a moment. But it wasn't long before she recovered enough to smile delightedly into Salome's eyes as the girl grabbed *yet another* cake. A few more moments passed. Martha then punched Salome playfully on the shoulder and said that she'd better believe that Jesus was God because it was true. And more than that, that Jesus was in fact the Messiah sent from God to deliver all Israel from its sin. "Meaning my sins," Martha said. After a long pause, she added, poking Salome in the knee, "And yours too, young lady!"

Salome avoided Martha's eyes, lowering her head humbly, thinking how this woman troubled her, but in such a nice way. After a moment or two she raised her eyes and smiled back. She blushed *again* as she covered her mouth to muffle a little burp that had erupted unexpectedly.

Just then Salome heard voices outside the front door. She jumped up and hastily thanked her hostess for her hospitality. She quickly grabbed another one of those wonderful fig cakes and rushed out the door, brushing by a very beautiful woman and an older man, who were approaching the house. Begging their pardon, she bowed her head, wrapped her veil about her face and left them standing there open-mouthed with surprise.

Salome did not look back as she ran to her litter, jumped aboard, closed the curtain and with a loud command was swiftly carried back to her own village. Upon arriving she ran into her large house. Its stone floors were polished to a high shine and its walls and roof were supported by the finest cedar beams; it was also filled with the finest furniture and many precious items of gold and silver. On entering, she told her servants not to disturb her, and she went into her most private room where she often withdrew to be alone. She drew the curtain that covered its entrance and sat down to think about all that Martha had told her. She took out that last fig cake and smiled warmly, nibbling at its edges, thinking what a wonderful woman Martha was and wishing with her whole heart that she could be like her. Maybe even that Martha and she might be best friends. But a tear came to her eye: that would probably never happen she concluded sadly.

Salome thought about what Martha had said about Jesus. She recalled all the miracles he did. This brought to mind the time he shouted at some angry priests who had taken up stones to stone him, saying, "If you don't believe that I am He, believe the miracles which speak for me."[4]

In that moment, Salome's eyes went wide, and she realized finally that she had indeed been in the very presence of God; that it had been the very LORD of the universe who had knelt before her that day and taken her in His arms, and who had offered to forgive her of her sins. Then and there. Because He loved her. Amazing!

When Salome recalled that day at the well and the awful things she had thought about Him and said to Him and then reflected on all that she had done in her life, she wept again. She looked around at her opulent surroundings and considered how wealthy she was and all the things she had and how she had acquired them. This thought came to her suddenly: *How many souls have I destroyed to get all this; how many men have I compromised?* The number was staggering. Then she thought, *I must find a way to get His forgiveness for all I have done, and I must find a way to*

---

[4] A combination of the verses John 10:25 and 10:38.

return His love. For the first time in her life, she got on her knees and prayed, which she did all that night and well into the next morning.

She had fallen asleep briefly when she was awakened by the sound of one of her servants entering her room. He started back when he saw how red-streaked and puffy her face was. But then she did something that astonished the young man—she smiled at him, rather than barking or snarling at him for disturbing her.

He breathed easier and approached her slowly, bowed low before her and said softly, "Mistress, I'm sorry for disturbing you, but we all were worried about you."

She waved off his apology, saying that she was all right. But her tone of voice revealed that she did not really believe her servants were concerned because she had always treated all of them very badly.

Understanding her reaction, the young man went to his haunches to look her in the eye and said, "Mistress, as you ordered, I have found out that there will be a reception for this Jesus fellow you talk about all the time at the home of Simon the Pharisee." Salome's head came up suddenly. She wiped her eyes and smiled again. A little nonplussed by her lack of anger, and also by her seeming eagerness at the mention of the Nazarene's name, he added hastily, with a tremulous voice, "But, Mistress, many of our regular guests will be there."

He then stood slowly, confused more by her non-aggressive—no, even compliant—body language, than by her seeming willingness to leap into danger. He was worried because she had recently become a fanatic about Jesus. And he was concerned that she might put her life in danger if she went to Simon's house where many powerful men from the temple, many of them her clients, would be. Though she did not seem to understand this, he knew fully what it might mean for her. And he cared because he loved her, although he never dared show it in any way because he was terrified of her.

Then she did another astonishing thing. She sat back on her haunches and held out her hand to him. He looked around furtively to see if anyone else might have entered the room. Seeing that no one had, he took her hand and helped her to her feet. His heart skipped a beat when she smiled at him, put her hand gently on his forearm and wept. When she fell into his arms and sobbed on his shoulder, he forgot to breathe for a moment or two.

After a moment she pushed back from him and looked with her tear-filled eyes into his. "Claudius, I have treated you badly in the past." He started to protest, but she interrupted him. "Yes I have too, and I want you to know that I am truly sorry."

Young Claudius did not know what to say. Yes, she had slapped him and kicked him a couple of times, and she had yelled at him times without number. But she had never done anything really bad to him. She paid him very well, and she had come to trust him, which in his eyes was the next best thing to demonstrating any real love for him. The young man loved being her servant and being there to take care of her, though quietly and unobtrusively. He loved the way she had come to rely on him for nearly everything, though he did not think she realized how much she depended on him. Therefore, doing the only thing he had ever known how to do, he asked, "Mistress, is there any way I can help you?"

She replied with amazing sincerity, "Yes, my good friend, there is." The lovesick young man could not ever have expressed in words how wonderful it made him feel to hear her utter that endearment. She left his arms, went over to a large chest and pulled out a large leather purse. She handed it to him. "Go to the market and buy absolutely the best scented oil you can find. Then bring it to me. Be quick, for I desire to do something for this Jesus fellow, as you call Him." She chuckled when his eyes widened as he looked into the purse. After watching his lips move as he quickly estimated what it contained, Salome laughed, saying, "Yes, Claudius. It's a lot of money. Over four hundred *denarii*! That ought to buy a pretty nice perfume, don't you think?"

He bowed to her and said breathlessly, "Yes, mistress. A whole year's wages should buy the best perfume in the entire Empire." Looking into her smiling eyes, he laughed with her as she nodded at him.

He said, "Mistress, if I may. Please do not be offended, but ..." She smiled into his eyes, and with a motion of her hand indicated that he should continue. "Well, Mistress," he continued slowly, "this is about all the cash you have left. You have not taken a client since that day by the lake up north. And expenses have not fallen off. It's not that I'm worried about myself, you understand." Her bright smile indicated that she understood. Her kind look confused him for a moment. He stammered, "But ... but ... what will you live on, my ..." He had started to say "love" but stopped himself abruptly. He said instead, "... er, my lady?"

She put her hand on his cheek and inclined her head. "Well, I can sell all this." She waved around at the house and its expensive furnishings. "After that, well, I don't know, my friend. I may need to ... to ... call on you to help me. Would you be willing?" She had bowed her head and waited, half expecting him to laugh at her because that is certainly what she deserved.

Salome had always known that Claudius loved her. She had seen this as a weakness and had hated him for it, and for no better reason than that she despised herself deep in her own soul and could not understand why anyone would dare love her. Before she had met the LORD at the lake, she had loved to toy with this young man's feelings, to goad him and tease him, especially when she was entertaining her guests. This was, in her mind, one of the most egregious sins she had repented of last night.

As Salome thought about it, she was amazed that Claudius had never wavered in his love for her. This gave her a glimmer of understanding about what self-sacrificing love meant. It again affirmed for her that what she had seen in Jesus' eyes those many weeks ago was this kind of love, the kind of love with which God loved her. She also found, to her surprise, that she had come to love Claudius in return. She realized that her feelings for him had deepened in the past weeks as he served her without complaint, though she had taken no clients and their income had gone to nothing. Salome had, in fact, come to love him desperately. She was afraid to show this to him, though; afraid that he might laugh at her and throw her love back at her, as she would have at him had he dared to express his feelings to her—before. But today, the look in his eye and the touch of his hand gave her hope that he would not.

Would he be willing? Claudius was astonished at first. Then he became giddy with joy. He knelt at her feet and kissed her hand. "I would plow a six oxen field with my bare hands, if necessary, to serve you, my lady."[5]

Salome's heart swelled with joy. She laughed gaily and tugged at his hand. "Well, I don't think that will be necessary. I have not told you everything about what I own." His eyes widened with astonishment, and she laughed again. "Now go. And be quick. Then I want you to come with me to hear Jesus speak. You might be surprised at what you hear."

Claudius scampered to his feet, kissed her hand again and ran off to do her bidding.

That evening Salome and her young man went to Simon the Pharisee's house. They did not go to the rear entrance where the servants entered, however. She knew that they would not admit her. They knew who she was, and they did not want her there to embarrass the master of the house or any of his influential guests.

---

[5] A six oxen field was the amount of land six oxen could plow in a day.

Rather, she waited stealthily near the front entrance as the guests arrived. When Jesus and a few of His disciples arrived, she and her friend followed Him to the door. As He reclined at the table along with the other guests, she went up to a guard, took out an *aureus* coin and bribed her way past him. Salome and Claudius quickly stepped into a small room next to the front entrance. She handed the jar of perfume to Claudius and began to unpin her hair.

Her friend said, "My lady, what are you doing? Are you going in there like that? In front of everyone?"

As her hair cascaded shamelessly down to her waist, she looked up at him with tears in her eyes and said, "Yes, my love. I thought I could march in here and give this gift to our LORD, but something has changed my mind. There is something else I must do. Will you please help me?"

As her tears flowed, Claudius nodded and took her veil, her sandals, and then her linen cloak as she handed them to him. When she was done, she resembled a common servant girl. Her undyed tunic was made of coarse wool cloth, the same one she had worn at the lake that day. This time, however, she wore no expensive jewelry. She took the jar from her friend and before turning to enter the room, she went up on tiptoe and kissed his cheek. As his hand went to his cheek, she put her free hand over his, held it there for a moment, and then squared her shoulders and went into the room thinking, *It is because of God's love for me that I do this very hard thing.*

As she entered everyone stopped speaking. She looked around the room and saw many familiar faces. Their hostile stares made all her bad deeds come rushing back to her, bringing with them humiliation and shame she would have never thought she could endure. This was not because of her attire or for her lack of decorum in front of these powerful men or because of the way they looked at her. It was because her LORD was looking at her with the kindest and warmest eyes she could have imagined. That day back at the well came to her, adding to her shame, as if all the guilt of her sin were condensed into the awful thing she had thought and the words she had spoken that day to her God.

As they murmured and pointed at her, she approached Jesus timidly, knelt down in front of Him, bowed her face low to the ground at his feet and began to kiss them. As her tears wetted His feet she wiped them lovingly with her hair. Then she opened the jar and began to pour the perfume over his feet. She was weeping audibly now as she continued to stroke his feet gently with her hair. After she had emptied the perfume jar onto his feet, she looked up into His kind face and said, "Oh, LORD, I am so sorry for what I said to you that day. I am so sorry for everything I have done. And I want to ask your forgiveness. Now I know that there is a loving God in heaven, just as you said that day." Then she bowed low to the ground at Jesus' feet.

There was a lot of grumbling all the while. Salome could hear things like, "What is this prostitute doing here? Doesn't the rabbi know that she's a sinner? If he were a prophet like he says, he would know what kind of person is touching him. And look at how shameless she is."[6] The loudest among them was the host of the party, Simon the Pharisee, whom she knew *very well*.

Jesus glared at them, silencing their grumbling immediately. He turned to His host and said, "Simon, I have something to tell you."[7]

Simon blushed deeply as he looked around the room. He knew that Jesus had heard his grumbling. Clearing his throat, Simon answered in a small voice, "Tell me, Teacher."

"Two men owed money to a certain moneylender. One owed him five hundred *denarii*, and the other fifty. Neither of them had the money to pay him back, so he canceled the debts of both. Now which of them will love him more?"

Simon cleared his throat again, looked around the room for a moment, and then replied, "I suppose the one who had the bigger debt canceled."

"You have judged correctly," Jesus replied. He looked down at the prostrate young woman before Him. He said to the red-faced Pharisee, "Do you see this woman? I came into your house. You did not give me any water for my feet, but she wet my feet with her tears and wiped them with her hair. You did not give me a kiss, but this woman, from the time I entered, has not stopped kissing my feet. You did not put oil on my head, but she has poured perfume on my feet. Therefore I tell you, her many sins have been forgiven—for she loved much. But he who has been forgiven little loves little."

Simon had nothing to say in response, but he could tell by Jesus' look that He knew what a hypocrite he was, and he instantly resolved to do everything he could to have this man silenced.

Jesus knew, of course, that He had made another enemy. He then turned to the weeping woman, lifted her eyes up to His with a finger under her chin

---

[6] Paraphrase of Luke 7: 39.

[7] This conversation between Simon and Jesus is recorded in Luke 7:40 – 43. Some words have been added to aid the flow of the narrative.

and said to her, "Your sins are forgiven. Your faith has saved you. Go in peace."[8]

Salome rose, kissed Jesus' hand and then His upraised cheek, and left.

The sound of a great deal more grumbling followed her out the room, but she did not care. Joy filled her as she left, even more so when she found Claudius waiting for her and looking at her with admiring eyes. She fell into his outstretched arms, and after they had embraced, he put his arm around her protectively and led her out of Simon's house and back to her home. She did not take her eyes off him the whole time.

---

[8] Luke 7:48 combined with 7:50.

Nathanael

[Jesus said,] "If anyone comes to me and does not hate his father and mother, his wife and children, his brothers and sisters—yes, even his own life—he cannot be my disciple. And anyone who does not carry his cross and follow me cannot be my disciple... In the same way, any of you who does not give up everything he has cannot be my disciple."
(Luke 14:26 – 27, 33)

Peter said to [Jesus], "We have left all we had to follow you!"
(Luke 18:28)

Author's note: As Jesus said, serving God faithfully often requires great sacrifice. Though very little is known about the life of Nathanael Bartholomew, his character in this story is based on the sixth apostle,[1] who was called a "true Israelite" by the LORD and who appears in John 1 and John 22.

On a sunny afternoon in a grove of fig trees near Bethany, a small village less than an hour's walk from Jerusalem, a young man was seated on a small stool beneath one of the trees. He was oblivious to the warmth of the day and to the whispers of a gentle breeze that played through the leaves, nor did he hear the scuffle of little footsteps sneaking up on him. For he was bent over a scroll, studying the following passage from the Vision of Isaiah the prophet:

> To the law and to the testimony! If they do not speak according to this word, they have no light of dawn. Distressed and hungry, they will roam through the land; when they are famished, they will become enraged and, looking upward, will curse their king and their God. Then they will look toward the earth and see only distress and darkness and fearful gloom, and they will be thrust into utter darkness.
> Nevertheless, there will be no more gloom for those who were in distress…

---

[1] See Mark 3:16 – 19 for a list of the apostles.

> The people walking in darkness have seen a great light; on those living in the land of the shadow of death a light has dawned ...
>
> For to us a child is born, to us a son is given, and the government will be on his shoulders. And he will be called Wonderful Counselor, Mighty God, Everlasting Father, Prince of Peace. Of the increase of his government and peace there will be no end. He will reign on David's throne and over his kingdom, establishing and upholding it with justice and righteousness from that time on and forever. The zeal of the LORD Almighty will accomplish this.[2]

There are many more words in the passage, but Nathanael had focused on those quoted above, as if they were highlighted for him by a supernatural light. He closed his eyes, raised them to the sky and thought, *How true of my people. Roaming through the arid land of our sin; enraged; distressed; full of darkness; famished for the truth. Oppressed by our Roman occupiers. Oppressed by our own religion and its hundreds of rituals and miniscule laws. If I could get that appointment I've worked so hard for, I might be able to change all this. Nevertheless, I praise you, O LORD, knowing that you will come and throw off the burden of our oppression. How I long to see the fulfillment of this, O LORD. How I long to ...*

He was startled when two hands suddenly covered his eyes and a giggling female voice said, "Nathanael? Guess who!" There was more giggling as the owner of those hands pulled him close and he leaned back into her.

He said, "Well, let's see," but with a contemplative air as he leaned back further into her and placed one of his hands over hers. Stroking his beard thoughtfully with the other hand he said, "Pontius Pilate?"

A giggle and a "Noooooo," was whispered into his ear. Nathanael could feel her body quivering with anticipation. She loved to play these little games, and he did too.

"Hmmmmm. How about Herod Antipas?"

A hearty laugh and another, but louder, "No, silly!" followed that too.

He exhaled loudly and said, "Well then, I'm stumped. I guess I'll have to gueeeessss ..." He paused long enough to feel the tension build up in the

---

[2] Isaiah 8:20 – 22; 9:1a – 2, 9: 6 – 7.

girl's arms; then he pulled her hands away from his face, spun around to face her and said, "YOU!"

With a piercing shriek, the young woman, whose name was Abigail, jumped back and laughed a deep belly laugh. But when he opened his arms to her she ran into them.

After they had embraced a few moments, she pushed away from him, leveled her eyes and pointed at him. "Oh, I am really sure I sounded like that old bullfrog Herod." He laughed with her, but he nodded convincingly, and she pushed at his chest, saying, "You!"

Abigail looked adoringly into his eyes, put a hand to his cheek and thought, *When are we getting married, Nathanael? I have loved you since I first saw you, a young awkward boy just arrived from Galilee. I know you love me. Why are you so hesitant to see my father about this? Could it be money?*

Nathanael understood that look from this exquisite girl. How he wanted to marry her! But he was still in training; he was a man of only modest means, and she was very wealthy—at least her father was. Nor could he bear the thought of not being able to bring something to their marriage, something more than just himself. His training would be finished soon, however. He was well known for his knowledge of the Law and was making a name for himself. And he was hoping for that appointment to the Ruling Council.[3] (Well, there had been talk at least. In his heart of hearts he was sure he was going to get it. He blushed at the presumption.) If he got the appointment, then he might be able to do something about the miserable state of his country's government. And this would make Abigail proud of him.

Such idealistic thoughts were all well and good. Still, Nathanael did not want to wait too long. After all, to have Abigail's heart made him the envy of every young man in Judea—at least everyone he knew.

For her beauty both inward and outward was breathtaking. Her exotic almond-shaped hazel eyes sparkled keenly with intelligence; her heart-shaped face radiated a stunning smile like the gleam of some heavenly jewel; her olive-colored skin was almost without blemish, except for an enticing little mole just above the corner of her mouth. Then there was her long neck, curvy body, tiny wrists and beautifully shaped hands. It all came together like a stunning cloak woven by Eternal Hands to adorn the innate kindness

---

[3] This body was also called the Sanhedrin. It was the ruling council of the Jews which enforced their oral laws as well as the written Law of Moses contained in the first five books of the Bible.

and industrious but gentle nature that shone through that wonderful garment; and it gave her the air of an angel—an angel who had been single-minded in her love and devotion to him. O how Nathanael thanked the LORD for her!

Nevertheless, as the young lawyer caressed Abigail's cheek and she closed her eyes and leaned into his touch—her adoring smile becoming brighter yet, amazingly enough—he thought that he might be able to wait a while longer.

Ignoring the question in her eyes for the moment, he said, "So, Treasure, what brings you all the way out here?"

"I've been looking all over for you. I thought I might have to have Micah go all the way to Cana to fetch you."

She pointed to a large chariot in which a well-dressed young servant stood waiting for her. It was an exquisite vehicle harnessed to three large white horses, indicative of its owner's great wealth. Nathanael's eyes followed Abigail's finger, and he laughed at her exaggeration. For Cana, his home in the district of Galilee, was a good day's fast ride north of Bethany. He waved a greeting at the young man in the chariot, who replied with a nod.

Abigail was laughing too as she added, "Daddy wants you to come over tonight to sup with us." She stopped and put a finger to her lips. She looked around, sighed, leaned close to him and whispered, "I'm not supposed to tell you this, but there will be some important men from the Ruling Council there." She raised her hand to the side of her mouth as if she were revealing to him the cleverest of strategies and said, but a little louder this time, "So act surprised or Daddy will kill me!" Then she giggled and pushed at his shoulder.

Nathanael felt a rush of pride go through him and his heart soared. Here it was, everything he had ever wanted: this lovely wonderful girl who adored him, and now a position of authority on the Ruling Council. *Now I can make a difference,* he thought, trying to suppress a victorious smile, but not very successfully. "Well, then," he replied, "how can I refuse?" She laughed with him, understanding his self-satisfied expression.

Then she bowed her head, and her body language told him that there was something else. He took her hands in his and asked, "So what else, my princess?"

"Daddy's wondering if you are ever going to ask him ..." she looked at the ground and then back up into his eyes, "... ask him. Well, you know what, you hard-hearted man, you." She had tried to sound exasperated, but all she could do was laugh at the absurdity of calling him hard-hearted, the kindest man she had ever met.

Nathanael laughed also and teased, "Just Daddy?"

She blushed deeply and bowed her head again, looking furtively up at him from beneath a rose-colored brow.

"I'm sorry for teasing you, Abigail." He sighed and lifted her chin with a finger. "You know that I need to finish my training, Princess. And if a certain position is offered, well ..." The young woman strained forward a bit. He grinned at that eager look on her face and said, "Then we can get married."

She punched him in the shoulder. When he went to kiss her she pulled away, but just far enough so that he had to make an effort to get at her. When he did, he pulled her to himself and kissed her passionately. She pretended to resist him for a few seconds, but then she returned his kiss fervently.

When they parted, she pushed him away in mock exasperation, trying to hide a smile that would not relent from giving away how much she had enjoyed this. Affecting anger, she scolded, "Oh you! Kissing me like that!"

She looked away for a second and then looked back with a truly stern expression this time. "You know very well that you are highly regarded by your colleagues; that you are one of the most sought-after teachers in the city; and that you are almost certainly going to be offered that *certain position*." Her voice had gone low for emphasis and she had pushed again at his chest. The young man blushed and bowed his eyes humbly.

She decided to tease him back. She put a finger to her chin and added thoughtfully, "Weeellll, if you're worried about being poor, you know Daddy thinks the world of you."

Nathanael's eyes shot up. This intelligent, discerning young woman had hit too close to home for his liking. He did his best to remain inscrutable. To no avail, though. Abigail had caught that little motion of his eyes and she chuckled at his discomfort.

Abigail put a hand to his cheek, looked into his eyes, and teased again, "Aha! You are worried about being poor, aren't you?" Nathanael scuffled the ground with his toe, looking at her from beneath sheepish brows. "You know very well that there's an opening and that they will ask you," she said. "That must be why they are coming tonight." Nathanael relented, nodding humbly, his color deepening. Loving the tease, she added, "Well then, you can come live with us if you are worried about supporting me. Daddy has plenty of money, you know." The young woman laughed heartily at the look on Nathanael's face.

For he did indeed know. Abigail's father Benjamin was one of the wealthiest men in the Roman Empire. Seeing that glint in her eye, he said, "I know, Dove. I know." He sighed loudly. Then he got a certain glint in his own eye. "Is there any doubt in your mind that I love you?" He took a deep breath before adding, "Dumpling."

Abigail stopped laughing abruptly and bridled. She was tall for a woman and larger boned than she would have liked; and like many beautiful and naturally slender women she was always concerned about her weight. But that was perfect, as she well knew. As she had looked in her mirror that one last time before coming to find him, she had been quite pleased at what she had seen, her opinion reinforced by that very admiring look he was giving her. And there *was* that teasing glint in his eye. Nevertheless, she folded her arms against her chest and leveled her eyes at him. "Nathanael Bartholomew, I am not a dumpling!"[4] She turned away from him and pretended to pout.

"Sorry, my beautiful treasure." he said affecting a contrite tone. "Of course you are not a dumpling. You are, rather, a veritable wraith, a stalk of wheat, a reed, a mouse, a sparrow, ... a ... a ..."

Abigail turned back abruptly, punched him hard in the shoulder and cried through a chuckle that had forced itself up through her throat, "Will you please stop?"

He put a hand to his mouth to try to hide a smile, but not very successfully. He then rubbed that spot on his shoulder vigorously, and she gave in to a smile in response. Seeing this, he laughed. Then she laughed. When she could not stop laughing, Nathanael held her close to him and tickled her for good measure. With a squeal and a shout of "Hey you!" she pulled away and tickled him back. After this they laughed together until tears came.

When they had quieted, she wiped her tears away and answered his question. "Of course there isn't any doubt in my mind that you love me, *you!*" she responded, her eyes glowing with the love *she* had for him.

"Well then, I am grateful for your father's willingness to provide support for us, Treasure. But I want to bring more than a warm, and, it must be admitted, a very loving, body into our marriage. I want to know that I can support us both. And I want you to be proud of me."

She had melted a little at the words "very loving". But then she scowled and cried in a gravelly voice, "Oh, you *man* you!" trying her best to make herself sound angry, but not very convincingly. "My daddy says you're one of the best teachers in all Judea, and that you have knowledge of our Law

---

[4] Nathanael is thought to be the apostle Bartholomew listed in Matthew 10:3, Mark 13:18, and Luke 6:14 and also mentioned in Acts 1:13. The patronymic "Bartholomew" means son of Ptolemy or *Talmai*, its Aramaic equivalent.

that is second to none. Look at you. Not yet thirty and going to be offered a seat on the Council. I am so proud of you right now I could burst."

Though she had grown up in the comfort of extraordinary wealth, she had convinced herself that she would be willing to live in a pauper's shack with him. It must be said that she was quite proud that he did not covet her father's money and the power that would come with it as many other young men might have. She gazed at his face with quite the admiring eye, indeed!

Nathanael said softly, "Thank you, Abigail, my treasure. It won't be that long, you know, and then we can get married." She smiled brightly at him and sighed.

"Hey, you two," came a call from a short distance away.

The young lovers looked up and saw that it was Philip of Bethsaida, one of Nathanael's closest friends.[5] He was smiling broadly at them both as he climbed up the gentle slope toward them. Abigail liked this young man, especially because he always cast such a respectful but admiring eye at her, today being no exception.

She said, "Greetings, Philip."

The young man greeted her with a smile and a nod as he came up to stand beside his friend. He then took her extended hand gallantly and kissed it chastely. She giggled and squirmed delightedly before snatching her hand away coyly. She shined a look at him that suggested she was not particularly displeased by this show of respect for her and appreciation of her beauty.

"Greetings, Philip," Nathanael said gaily, taking his hand. "To what fortuitous turn of events do we owe this pleasant visit?"

Chuckling a little, Philip said, "There's somebody I want you to meet."

Abigail understood this to be the end of her conversation with her husband-to-be. She bowed graciously to them both and said, "Well, I can see you two have business together, so I'll go." Nathanael took her hand as if to restrain her. Appreciating the gesture, she squeezed his hand. "Remember this evening, Darling!" she said, pointing at him. He nodded. She turned to the other young man. "Well," she said, "I'll leave him in your hands. Keep your eye on him. And make sure he's back here by sunset!" She had issued these commands so forcefully both men laughed.

As she started toward the waiting chariot, but before she could get too far away, Philip managed to tear his eyes off her long enough to ask his friend, "When are you going to marry that exquisite girl? If you don't, I will."

---

[5] Bethsaida was near the lake in the district of Galilee, about 20 miles northeast of Cana.

Abigail looked back at her blushing lover and laughed appreciatively. Then she mounted her chariot, blew a kiss at Nathanael, waved at Philip, and with a motion of her hand, the chariot leapt forward and sped toward the city.

Nathanael cleared his throat as Philip grinned up at him. Brushing off the discomfort Philip's knowing look gave him, he asked, "So, who is this somebody?"

Philip grinned broadly. "We have found the one Moses wrote about in the Law, and about whom the prophets also wrote—Jesus of Nazareth, the son of Joseph."[6]

Nathanael made a face and chuckled. "Nazareth! Can anything good come from there?"

"Come and see," said Philip, laughing.[7] "He claims to be the one mentioned in the scroll." He pointed to Nathanael's scroll. "He claims to be the Son of the Living God, Nathanael!"

Nathanael mused, "You know, we get so many prophets claiming to be someone. And they all say they are going to free our people from their bondage, but nothing ever comes of it." Philip nodded sympathetically. "Remember that nut Thaddeus who got himself and his four hundred followers killed by the Romans? Then there was the rebel Judas the Galilean during the census. He was killed too."[8]

Philip said, "Yes, he was." Then he said, "But Jesus is not like them. He speaks not of our oppression by the Romans, but of our oppression by our sin and by our religious leaders. He sounds a little like John the Baptist and all the true prophets in this regard." Philip pointed again at the scroll and needled his friend with, "Jesus has about as much use for Israel's religious leaders as Isaiah did, that's for sure."

Nathanael, true to form, bridled at this implied slur of their rulers. He was a patriot; he loved his country and respected his rulers, even if their government was a mess. Philip, no less the patriot and also true to form, had always claimed that it was their own rulers, especially the priests and Pharisees and not the Roman occupiers, who oppressed their people. This had been the cause of some disagreement between them. Nathanael smiled

---

[6] For Moses' prophecy, see Deuteronomy 18:15 – 18.

[7] The part of their conversation, starting with "We have found ..." and ending with "Come and see," is from John 1:45 – 46, with a few words added for the sake of the narrative.

[8] See Acts 5: 36 – 37 where Paul's teacher, Gamaliel, also mentions these two troublemakers.

nevertheless, understanding that his friend was teasing him and that Philip, as concerned about his oppressed people as he was, meant well.

As Nathanael stared at his friend, his thoughts turned to Philip's description of Jesus. *If this Jesus fellow is not concerned about the Romans,* he wondered, *what kind of prophet is he? All the prophets say clearly that our Messiah will come and liberate us from our oppression at the hands of foreign occupiers of this land.* This brought to mind the passage he had just read, "… of the increase in his government and peace there will be no end." Then he thought, *All the prophets say this except for John the Baptist, who hardly ever mentions the Romans. But why should we follow another John the Baptist? And if this Nazarene is the Son of God, what does that mean?* He glanced away from Philip and looked dubiously down at his scroll. Nevertheless, as he thought more about it, his curiosity started to grow.

He relented and asked, "So then, where is this Jesus of Nazareth?"

"He's at that place near the Jordan River where John has been preaching. It's not far; I have a chariot waiting. We can be back well before *sunset*." He had emphasized the time of their return by raising his voice to mimic a woman's voice and fluttering his wrist.

Nathanael laughed. "Then let's go see him. But what am I going to do with this?" He waved at his precious scroll.

"Bring it. There's no time. Jesus is set to head back down to Galilee and you don't want to miss Him. I'm going with Him and I want you to come."[9] When Nathanael hesitated, Philip said, "I know, *this evening*." Nathanael sighed. "Well then, come meet Him," Philip insisted. "Then you can decide. Or you can come down tomorrow. I'll leave a message with your father in Cana."

Nathanael nodded, rolled up his scroll, secured it in a large leather pouch and sealed it tightly. Then they went down to the chariot Philip had waiting.

It did not take them very long to reach the place by the Jordan River where Jesus was, across from the ancient city of Jericho where the river widens a bit. Upon their arrival, the two men dismounted quickly and walked through the woods. They eventually found Jesus sitting near a small fire with two other men, neither of whom Nathanael had ever seen. As Philip and his

---

[9] The Judean Jews saw things in terms of elevation, not in terms of north verses south. Since Jerusalem is on a hill and represented the spiritual center of their faith, the Jews thought of going up to Jerusalem and going down from it to everywhere else. See, for example, Mark 3:22.

friend approached Jesus, He looked up at them and smiled. Nathanael was immediately captivated by His smile.

As Nathanael continued to approach the young rabbi, Jesus rose, turned to the other two men and said, directing His hand toward the young lawyer, "Here is a true Israelite, in whom there is nothing false."[10] He held out His hand to the blushing young man, who took it but averted his eyes modestly.

Confused by feelings that were cascading through his heart so loudly he thought everyone must be able to hear, Nathanael choked out, "How do you know me?" He was blushing much more deeply now at the admiring stares of Philip and the other two.

Looking at the sealed leather pouch, Jesus answered, "I saw you while you were still under the fig tree before Philip called you."[11]

Astonished, Nathanael looked around at them all, and they all nodded slowly. He felt the leather pouch at his side. Recalling Philip's claim and the prophet's words he had read, he declared, "Rabbi, you are the Son of God; you are the King of Israel."[12] He bowed low to the ground before Him.

Jesus took his hand and brought him to his feet. "You believe because I told you I saw you under the fig tree," He said. "You shall see greater things than that." He looked around at them all; then He turned back to Nathanael. "I tell you the truth, you shall see heaven open, and the angels of God ascending and descending on the Son of Man."[13] They all shook their heads, their eyes wide with wonder; their mouths open in awe.

After a moment, one of the other young men stepped forward. Smiling at the still awe-struck young lawyer, he said, "Greetings, Nathanael. I am Simon son of Jonah from Capernaum, and this is my brother Andrew."

Nathanael took their hands in greeting, saying, "Greetings, Simon. Andrew. I am Nathanael Bartholomew." He noted that they smelled of fish—and it was none too pleasant.

Jesus opened His arms to Bartholomew and embraced him. He said, "Welcome, Nathanael, son of Talmai."

---

[10] Jesus' greeting is from John 1:47.

[11] Nathanael's question and Jesus' answer are from John 1:48. Note that being "under the fig tree" is thought to be an idiom used at the time to denote the act of studying and meditating on the Word of God. Jesus indicated by this that He was clearly able to see into Nathanael's heart as well as being able to see him as he studied the Word, though Nathanael had been a few hours' fast chariot ride away.

[12] John 1:49.

[13] John 1: 50 – 51.

With this the young man was put completely at ease in his LORD's presence. He also felt as if Jesus had known him his whole life, which He had, of course! And he marveled at the change in the atmosphere surrounding them. Before he had been bowing at the feet of the King of Israel and the Son of God. Now he regarded this man as he would his oldest friend, one from whom he would never hold back anything—one in whom he could confide everything.

Philip put his arm around his friend and motioned with his free hand toward Jesus. "He's something, huh."

Nathanael could not seem to find his voice immediately. He looked around at them all, wide-eyed, and tried to answer—his mouth moving but no sound coming out. As Philip, Andrew, and Simon Peter watched the young man's struggle they started to giggle; and as Nathanael's mouth continued to open and close soundlessly, their giggles turned to laughter, though they bowed their eyes and covered their mouths. After about a minute, the young lawyer laughed too, staring at Jesus and pointing at Him. Then Jesus began to laugh with him, and they all laughed for a good long time.

When they finished, they sat around the fire, and Jesus taught them. He told them how the Kingdom of God was at hand and how He had come to be a Shepherd for His people. He told them how the Good News of God's salvation would free His people, who were oppressed by evil.[14] He gave them examples of how that evil had infected the rulers of their people. He told them how the righteousness of the Pharisees and Sadducees was false righteousness. He spoke of their hypocrisy—noting how they laid heavy burdens on the people that they themselves would not lift with a little finger and how they loved the places of honor in the banquets and to be called *Rabbi*—and how they had nullified God's law by their traditions.[15]

Jesus had been staring at Nathanael the whole time and this made the young lawyer uncomfortable. He had also become a little angry, especially when he looked over at Philip, who was nodding at him and smiling. But he couldn't really quarrel with what his King said. Nathanael had seen it all but had refused to acknowledge it, for he had always thought this could be fixed.

---

[14] In John 8:32, Jesus says, "And you will know the truth, and the truth shall set you free." This comes after a long discourse on the evil in the hearts of men, especially in the hearts of many of the Pharisees.

[15] Here are several examples, among many, of Jesus' teaching on this theme: Matthew 6: 1 – 16 and 23: 2 – 7, Luke 13: 14 – 15, and Mark 7: 9 – 13.

Men of goodwill could always find a way. Then again, suppose they were not men of goodwill. Certainly Jesus' words implied as much. What could Nathanael say? Well, he had nothing to say. A lover of truth, he listened quietly and soaked it all in, until the sun got lower in the sky and the young man looked nervously in its direction with increasing frequency.

Jesus, knowing the reason for his discomfort, peered into the young man's eyes and said, "So, Nathanael of Cana, I know that you are zealous for freeing your people from their oppressors." Nathanael nodded and glanced over at Philip, who bowed his head and smiled. "Well, then, come and follow me, and I will show you their salvation. We're leaving tomorrow for Galilee—your home. You will see an amazing thing there."

The young lawyer was confused. What of the Ruling Council? What of all his plans? What of Abigail? Was his King requiring that he throw all this away? What a hard thing that would be! Still not sure what Jesus might say in response, he said, "Well, Lord, may I go and tell my betrothed and her father? We have plans, you know." His voice trailed off as he looked into Philip's exasperated face.

Jesus said, "Well, yes I guess you do!" Turning to Philip, He said, "Be sure to bring your friend here with you when you come."

Philip smiled brightly and nodded, looking expectantly at Nathanael.

How can He be so sure that I will come? the young lawyer wondered, struck by Jesus' confident tone.

Jesus said, "We will leave around the third hour."[16]

Nathanael nodded and hurried off with his friend. They got back to Nathanael's tiny home as the sun was just touching the tops of the hills. As Nathanael dismounted, he said, "Philip, can you wait for me? I need to get cleaned up. All this dust, you know."

"Of course," Philip said, amused by the dreamy look in his friend's eyes as he followed him into the house. When they got in, Nathanael unpacked his scroll and laid it lovingly on a table. Then he went in to wash. Meanwhile Philip unrolled the scroll and began to read.

When Nathanael had completed his washing and changed into a beautiful cloak, the hems and collar of which were embroidered with blue and gold thread, Philip looked up at him and asked, "So, what are you going to do?"

---

[16] The ancients thought of the "day" as extending twelve hours from sunrise to sunset. The "third hour" is commonly thought to be around 9:00 a.m.

Nathanael slumped down into a chair near the tiny table where Philip had seated himself. "I don't know, my friend. I have had my heart set on helping my people and on righting the wrongs visited on them by our rulers."

Philip shouted gaily, "Aha! So you agree with me!"

"Not so fast, you," his friend rejoined, chuckling. "I agree that we could be better run as a nation. I agree that some things have crept into our law that should not be there." But as Nathanael thought about Jesus' words, his increasing unease about the honesty and sincerity of his leaders was betrayed by his tone of voice; and that knowing look his friend was giving him annoyed him.

To change the subject, Nathanael said, "What if I do chuck it all and wander the countryside with Jesus? What will Abigail think? She has her heart set on me being the big man on the council, you know." They laughed. The young lawyer looked up at the ceiling and said thoughtfully, "I don't think she has ever understood why I wanted to be on the Council in the first place. I've always thought that if I could get a seat, I might be able to change something. I am not so foolish as to believe that change won't come without struggle. Still it can come!" He pounded the table.

Philip chuckled. "That's what I've always liked about you, Nathanael. You're such an idealist." His friend blushed. "But get with reality here, my friend. You know as well as I that to change our rulers would mean shearing their power away from them like a man shears a squirming sheep." Nathanael laughed nervously. "You know very well that that isn't going to happen." Nathanael sat back and stared at him. "Just as our LORD said, they love the place of honor. They love to be seen standing in the synagogues praying loudly; or to wear their expressions of pain when they fast so that everyone will know; or to be loudly praised when they throw a few of their thousands of *denarii* into the alms plate and then shake their robes and walk away, as if giving a little bit of money were really going to help the poor souls of this city."

Nathanael nodded reluctantly with each assertion.

Philip sighed and looked out of the door of the house and into the street where several poor, shabby people were walking, their heads bowed and their shoulders bent. "No," he continued. "See those people out there?" Nathanael's eyes followed his. "They live in fear every day of their lives because they're afraid that they might do or say something that our rulers ..." He raised a cautionary finger and interrupted himself, "... not the Romans mind you ..." Nathanael nodded. "... that they will say something that our own *Jewish* rulers will find offensive and bring them before that very Council of yours to punish them."

Following those paupers with his eyes, Nathanael mused quietly, "They seem like a flock of sheep wandering around aimlessly, looking for a shepherd."

"Yes, they most certainly do. But their Shepherd has come, and you have met Him." Nathanael nodded slowly, cautiously. "So now, my friend," Philip continued, "do you really want to be on that Council?"

Nathanael stared at him but did not respond.

His stubbornness annoyed Philip. He pointed a warning finger at Nathanael. "Look, you! It will corrupt your soul. You won't make a difference there. On the other hand, with Jesus—serving Him—you can really make a difference. Come with us tomorrow."

Nathanael sighed and said, "I hate to think that these men are really as bad as all that, though." Philip grunted with exasperation. The young lawyer motioned toward the door. "How do I explain all this to Abigail? She's never known want or fear. Her father is very powerful and influential with our leaders, as well as with the Romans. She won't understand me chucking it all away. She might think I'm rejecting her. She might even think that I'm a traitor to the Law she loves."

Not knowing what to say immediately, Philip stared at his friend. Then, reflecting on what he knew about Abigail, he said, "Oh, I don't know about that. Remember what a terrific woman she is." Nathanael smiled a relieved smile. "She will certainly be disappointed, of course." Nathanael's smile vanished. "But she'll come round, just you wait," Philip concluded.

Nathanael put a grateful hand on Philip's shoulder, but he replied, his heart sinking, "What if she doesn't?"

Philip sighed. "Well, my friend, that's certainly something to consider. Remember how the LORD took Ezekiel's wife from him?"[17]

"Yes, I recall," Nathanael said softly, a tear forming in his eye. He had always found that story to be incredibly sad; and he had always held the prophet's faithful service to God, despite this, to be the highest example of commitment, worship and faith. He knew also that this was what it meant when the Scriptures referred to someone as a Man of God—someone who served God no matter what the personal cost. He had always wondered how

---

[17] Ezekiel 24: 15 – 18.

he might react in similar circumstances. Now, he realized, this very test might be upon him.

Understanding what must be going through his friend's mind, Philip said with a truly heavy heart, "Well, Nathanael, you will have to decide how important serving God is to you." He patted his friend on the shoulder and said quietly, "I think I know what you will decide, though." Philip sat back and watched as his friend wrestled with his thoughts.

A few more seconds passed and then the clack of chariot wheels and of horses' hooves could be heard without. The two young men looked up to see two well-dressed servants standing at the door, smiling.

Nathanael knew them, of course, because they were Benjamin's servants; but to him they were very good friends whom he loved. Cheered by their friendly smiles and wiping a tear from his eye, he smiled in return. "Well, Jonah, Micah," he said, "I see that you have come to fetch me."

"Yes, master," they replied, concerned by his tears. But when they saw the open scroll, they assumed that he had been especially moved by something in it. Hoping that he might share this insight with them, they looked down at the open scroll. "Master Nathanael," one of them said, "what have you been reading? Teach us."

The young lawyer smiled again. How he loved that these young men hungered and thirsted for God's Truth, as he did. He wished that he could sit and spend hours with them. But not right now. "I'm sorry, my friends, I cannot." he said. Their faces fell in disappointment. But when he said, "I think someone is waiting for us," they smiled knowing smiles at each other.

Nathanael cleared his throat and turned to Philip. "Do you want to come?"

Philip extended his arms, hands palms out. "No thank you. This is for you, my friend. I'm staying safely here."

Nathanael said, "Thanks a lot. *Friend*!" He and Philip laughed. Seeing the puzzled looks on Jonah and Micah's faces they laughed harder.

When he was able, the teacher said to them, "We're laughing because I may have some news for your mistress that none of you will like right away." Their faces went white, thinking he would reject her. "No," he hurriedly added, "it's really ... er ... ah ... wonderful. I met the Son of God today. In the flesh."

They covered their grins with their hands, shifted their feet and bowed their heads.

"Really! I did."

They nodded agreeably, looking at each other, their smiles wider now.

"Well, you'll see." Much amused by those looks of theirs, Nathanael patted Philip on the shoulder and said, "Well then, my friend, I guess we're off."

He motioned to the two young men. Jonah and Micah accompanied him outside, nudging each other while looking at Nathanael out of the sides of their eyes. They stood aside to allow him to mount, which he did, and they rode off quickly to the house of Nathanael's beloved Abigail.

Benjamin's house was a palatial dwelling made of the finest cedar beams and kiln-baked brick, finished with polished stone, and filled with the very best furniture and carpets, all made by noted artists and craftsmen. The trio entered through a small foyer where Nathanael left his sandals. A young male Egyptian slave, who was carrying a basin of water and several towels, immediately ran up to him and knelt down to wash his feet.

The young man, seeing Nathanael hesitate, said, "Please, Rabbi, allow me."

Nathanael, blushing at the form of address, said, "Of course, Heco. I wouldn't want you to get into trouble."

The young slave laughed dismissively as Nathanael sat and allowed him to wash his feet. He would never "get in trouble", of course, because his master was the kindest man in Judea, or so Heco thought. Nor was he ashamed to wash Nathanael's feet because he had come to love and to greatly admire him—though they rarely spoke, but only because the young servant was exceedingly shy and humble.

When it came to Nathanael's teaching, however, the young Egyptian was not shy. Heco had always listened attentively when Nathanael taught, which the young lawyer often did at Benjamin's request. But Heco only heard it from behind a curtain, or when standing quietly nearby, his head bowed, waiting to be called into service. Though he could neither read nor write, he was an intelligent man, and in Nathanael's teaching he was convinced that God's salvation could reach even lowly slaves like him.

For example, he recalled how a few nights ago this young master had quoted the following words of the Jewish prophet Isaiah: " 'I, the LORD, have called you in righteousness; I will take hold of your hand. I will keep you and will make you to be a covenant for the people and a light for the Gentiles, to open eyes that are blind, to free captives from prison and to release from the dungeon those who sit in darkness.' "[18]

---

[18] Isaiah 42:6 – 7; the applicable teaching goes through verse 16, which is quoted below.

Well then, was he not such a man, the young Egyptian reasoned? Certainly he was a Gentile who lived in the blindness of ignorance. Had he not come from a society where the blind led the blind into worshiping darkness? Yes he had! Were his people not all prisoners trapped in dungeons of darkness? Yes they were! Had he not also heard how the Jews called themselves sons of God and how they called God their Father?

It was on that very night that Heco had secretly prayed to this invisible God—to this God who called himself, simply, I AM—and asked if the LORD might be pleased to accept *him* as a son. And for some reason, he knew that the Great I AM had heard him and that He loved him and valued him, despite his lowly station. As Heco reflected on these things, tears of gratitude ran down his face and dripped into the bowl.

Hearing his sniffling and seeing one of those tears drop into the basin, Nathanael stopped him, bent down to him and asked softly, "What is it, Heco?"

The young man sniffed, wiped his eyes and swallowed hard, barely able to choke out the words, "Young Master, may I ask you something?"

Jonah and Micah looked at each other and smiled. For Heco was a favorite of Nathanael's, so he would certainly not say no to *him*. They could feel their scalps move as they tried to turn their ears toward Nathanael to hear his answer, though they kept their eyes directed ahead as if they were not listening.

Nathanael, not fooled at all, glanced over at them before saying gently, "Of course, you may, Heco."

The young man wiped a tear from his eye and looked directly into Nathanael's eyes. "I heard what you said about the LORD being a light to the gentiles the other night." Nathanael did recall the lesson he had taught. Heco continued, "Since I'm a gentile, I with all my heart want to bask in that light. I hear how you Jews call yourselves sons of God. I want to be His son too." Heco looked away, blushing so deeply his face hurt. Fortunately for him, because of the darkness of his skin, the others could not perceive how embarrassed he was.

Jonah and Micah put their hands over their mouths and smiled. *How ridiculous!* was their thought. But when they saw the stern eyes of their teacher boring into them, their smiles evaporated, and they bowed their heads to avoid the look of rebuke he was glaring at them.

Nathanael had to admit, though, that this question had brought him up short too—for a moment. Up until now he had considered that passage a rebuke to Israel. Ever the Israelite patriot, he had thought that eventually, when the Messiah came, He would bring all people under the domination of Jewish rule. But as Nathanael considered the rest of that passage—"I will lead the blind by ways they have not known, along unfamiliar paths I will guide them; I will turn the darkness into light before them and make the rough places smooth. These are the things I will do; I will not forsake them."—a light dawned in him; and in that instant he understood that God's salvation would indeed extend to the gentiles also.[19]

It suddenly occurred to Nathanael that Jesus had not come as a conqueror of human empires, as his people had always been taught. Rather, Nathanael knew that this Son of God whom he had met, this Jesus, would conquer the very empire of Sin itself—the work of the devil's conquest of the world. He did not know how Jesus would do it—yet—but he vowed to think very carefully about this.

Now all these thoughts had occurred to the young teacher in less than several breaths' time. After that brief moment, he put his hand on the young slave's head and asked, "Have you prayed to the LORD your God about this and asked Him to show you His salvation?"

The young slave's eyes went wide and a bright smile flashed out at Nathanael. "Oh yes, Master. And I think He has heard my prayer, though I cannot say how I know this. But yes. Yes I have, with all my heart, Rabbi."

"Then He will," Nathanael replied firmly. "When the Lamb of God who takes away the sin of the world comes to you, you will know that your prayer has been heard." Nathanael saw Philip's face in his mind as he recalled their conversation on the way to the Jordan concerning what John the Baptist had said of Jesus. He wondered, though, why this particular name for Jesus—"the Lamb of God"—had come to him so suddenly. Yet how appropriate, he thought, to call Jesus, this kindest and gentlest of men, the Lamb of God.

Meanwhile, Heco had wiped his eyes one more time, thanked him and then continued his task.

For their part, Jonah and Micah realized that Nathanael was right: they had heard something they did not like—that even lowly alien slaves could become sons of God. But if this young rabbi said it, he whom they regarded as the picture of *veritas*, as the Romans liked to say, then it must be true. But they did not know what to make of this, and they blushed while staring into the knowing eyes of their teacher.

---

[19] The passage Nathanael recalls is Isaiah 42:16.

When the slave was done, he rose with Nathanael, thanked him again, took his hand and kissed it, but so quickly that Nathanael could not manage to prevent it, and ran off.

As Nathanael headed toward the main room, Abigail came rushing up to him, put her arms around him, kissed him and said breathlessly, "I'm so glad you finally got here, Love." She looked over her shoulder at Jonah and Micah with slitted eyes. "I thought they'd gotten lost or something." She knew how they liked to pester her "husband" to teach them all the time; and, she reasoned, this had been the reason for their delay, which had vexed her no end on this night of important nights to her.

The two men bowed their heads and cleared their throats; they were also trying to hide their smiles with their hands, but not too successfully as they glanced up at her from time to time.

Nathanael cleared his throat also. "Uhmmm, well, Precious," he said soothingly, "it's my fault we're late." The two servants admired him for his willingness to take the blame, if there were any to take.

"Well, you're here now," the girl said, brushing off his apology, but still looking with no little suspicion at Jonah and Micah. "Come, Daddy's waiting, as are our house guests. They are all anxious to see you. Come!" She pulled at his hand as he moved slowly forward. "Don't be nervous, Darling. It's okay. Rabban Caiaphas and his associates can't wait to see you."[20] She hid her mouth behind her hand, glanced briefly at the still smiling servants, assumed a conspiratorial air, and whispered into his ear, but loudly enough for everyone to hear. "I shouldn't have told you that the high priest himself is here." She sighed and continued. "Anyway, they've got an offer to make you, I think. Remember to act surprised, though." Nathanael nodded understanding. Then Abigail said, grabbing his hand, "So come, my very precious. Let's eat. I'm really hungry." She turned away from her servants with a toss of her head, as if she were flinging their snickers back at them.

As Nathanael was pulled away from them, he looked back and grimaced a smile at his friends, who fluttered little girlish waves at him, still smiling those annoying smiles of theirs. He could hear them chuckling even as he entered the dining room.

Standing in its center near the dining table and chatting quietly were four men plus Nathanael's host, Benjamin, a short, very fat man of fifty or so. He was bald on top but with a long graying fringe of hair and a full gray beard,

---

[20] *Rabban* or 'our teacher' is a higher form of the honorific *Rabbi,* which means 'my teacher'.

and he was dressed luxuriously in a fine blue linen cloak over a white linen tunic, wearing a four-stranded gold necklace and several large gold rings. The other men were priests, dressed in their tasseled linen cloaks and robes.

As Nathanael entered, the master of the house smiled broadly, raised a hand and announced in his gravelly voice, "Ah, here is the guest of honor. Nathanael, my boy, it's so good to see you." He waddled over and took the young man's hand. Nathanael placed Benjamin's hand to his forehead, then he kissed it, as his host gleamed with pride.

Nathanael said, "Father, it's good to see you too. Thank you so very much for inviting me to sup with you tonight."

"Not at all," the old man wheezed as his lungs worked hard to keep him upright and allow him the breath to speak at the same time. He turned to the other men. "I'm sure you know our high priest, Rabban Caiaphas, and also Rabbi Nicodemus, Rabbi Zacharius, and Rabbi Porteus."

Nathanael bowed a polite greeting toward each man and then approached the high priest, took his hand and kissed it. "It's an honor to see you once again, Lord," he said.

The high priest beamed. He loved the honorific. But it was right and proper, after all.

Nathanael caught his reaction and his eyes narrowed. He stared at the high priest for a few seconds before turning and greeting each of the other men.

The master of the house then turned an appreciative eye on his daughter, who blushed very charmingly and lowered her eyes modestly. He took her hand and gestured toward her with his free hand. "And, my lords, I'm sure you all know my beautiful daughter, Abigail."

For which warm and glowing praise she remonstrated with her father, "Oh, Daddy, please." A little glint in her eye indicated that she was not as displeased by this introduction as her protest might have indicated. They nodded at her and smiled. Annoyingly, Abigail thought, as they looked from her to Nathanael and back, as if they knew *everything* about the two of them.

Catching their knowing looks, the old merchant laughed, leaned close to the high priest and said, "You know my daughter will one day marry this excellent young man."

"Daddy!" Abigail cried, glancing quickly at all the men, and then looking back at Nathanael, but with such love in her eyes the young teacher felt his heart squeeze in his chest.

"I'm sorry, my treasure," the old man laughed, "but it's common knowledge how much this young man loves you, you know."

Nathanael allowed his gaze to linger on his beloved, and she blushed charmingly at them. It *was* common knowledge after all, and he was not ashamed of loving this excellent young woman. The marriage was merely awaiting the formality of a formal negotiation followed by a betrothal—and everyone knew that too. Desiring to put the love of his life at ease, Nathanael said, "Well, sir, maybe we can have that certain conversation sometime soon." Hearing Abigail's sigh, he looked at her and smiled. He knew in that moment that he would remember that one particular look she gave him until the day he died.

None of the other guests made any verbal comment, though their expressions spoke volumes. Nevertheless, Abigail was grateful for their graciousness.

Benjamin then said, "Well, I think dinner is ready. Can you smell it?"

Indeed, the wonderful smells of roasting lamb, nicely flavored with many savory spices, freshly baked bread and cooking vegetables wafted throughout the room, making everyone's mouth water.

Nathanael, laughing, said, "Well, it smells like lamb. I hope it's a big one because I could eat a horse." They all laughed. Suddenly, however, Nathanael wished it weren't lamb that was being served, though he kept smiling for their benefit.

Before they could take their places at the table, Abigail, who had assumed the role of the steward of the feast, gave two loud claps. Several servants rushed in and extended an alabaster jar of expensive perfume to each guest. This surprised the high priest, and he looked at his host with an approving eye. Benjamin smiled proudly. "It was my daughter's idea, Lord."

The high priest turned to his young hostess and said, "Well, we are very gratified by your attentions, young woman. I can see why this man of yours is the envy of everyone in the city." At this both Nathanael and Abigail blushed, but the girl was glad at the tender look her "almost betrothed" again gave her.

After this, the servants poured the perfume over the heads and onto the beards of each of the men; and as they did, the room was filled with the wonderful aroma of lavender and cinnamon, which blended splendidly with the aromas coming from the food. Then silver bowls filled with water were provided along with linen towels, which each guest used to wash and dry his hands.

After this, the host said, "Now, my lords, let us give thanks to God. Rabban Caiaphas, would you do us the honor?"

But the high priest said graciously, "You know, I think our young guest here should do this."

They all looked over at Nathanael, who nodded, opened his arms, raised his eyes to heaven and sent up a fine prayer of thanksgiving. But as the young man added pointedly, "Finally, LORD God, we pray that you will bring justice to our people," Caiaphas saw that Nathanael had glanced over at him when he said this, which irritated the high priest, though he could not have said why.

The others seemed to catch neither Nathanael's implication nor the high priest's discomfort as they said a loud "Amen!" They then turned to the dining table, which was square and sat low to the ground and was large enough to accommodate up to twelve guests. Around it, on three sides, were set low couches appointed with lush cushions; its open side faced the doorway through which the servants would enter to serve the meal. On it were set the finest silver plates and goblets, one for each guest.

As they approached the table, Benjamin motioned that the high priest should take the place of honor on the "highest" couch, situated on the right side of the open end of the table as you faced it.[21] Caiaphas had started to accept, but catching a flash from Nathanael's eye, he stopped and offered it instead to his host. Benjamin beamed a smile around the room and assumed the place of honor at the end of the couch by slowly lying down on his left side (but with many grunts and wheezes, taking a long time to do so).

Rabban Caiaphas then reclined with his head close to his host's chest— well, as close as he could reasonably get because Benjamin was almost as wide as he was tall. It irritated the high priest a little more that he had not taken the place that was rightly his. He looked again over at Nathanael, who had waved his hand toward Nicodemus, suggesting that he, rather than an unknown young lawyer, take the last place on the highest couch. The high priest found himself wondering what it was about this young man that nettled him. He was more unsettled when Nathanael, the guest of honor, took the lowest place to be offered tonight, the third to recline on the middle couch facing the open end of the table.

When they had all settled in, Abigail began directing the servants as they served the meal. They also set a plate of flat bread before each of the men. She then poured them wine. When they had all been served, she took some

---

[21] The designations of the couches as highest, middle, and lowest during a meal were based on the status they held for the diners; therefore the guests would recline on each couch in order of their importance.

food and wine for herself and sat demurely on the lowest couch, directly opposite her father, and waited for the men to begin to eat, which they did immediately. She ate hungrily, nevertheless, never taking her eyes off her lover, who smiled at her while glancing at the high priest from time to time, who, in turn, though speaking with her father, glanced frequently back at him. Abigail thought she saw a look in her young man's eye that was not all that admiring of the high priest. Rather, Nathanael seemed to be evaluating *him*, and she wondered what her beloved must be thinking.

Benjamin was first to address them. Looking at the high priest, he said, "Well, your lordship, it is certainly an honor to have you and your colleagues here." Caiaphas smiled and then looked over at Nathanael, who nodded back graciously. Encouraged by this wordless exchange, the host said, "You know, my lord, that Nathanael here is highly regarded in my home and throughout Judea as a teacher. As you can imagine, it thrills all of us to see that such important and influential men as yourselves have come to honor us and him this evening. We are glad at the wisdom shown by the Ruling Council that ..."

"Daddy!" Abigail interrupted. She stared reprovingly at her impetuous but well-meaning old dad and said, "Nothing has been mentioned yet concerning the Council."

The old man deflated instantly and cleared his throat. "Of course, Darling. You are right." He murmured quietly, as if to himself, "Nothing has been mentioned." Flushed with embarrassment, Benjamin looked around at all of his guests. But he was relieved when he saw their approving smiles, except for Caiaphas, whose face had turned toward Nathanael. It was certainly no secret that they all expected a certain appointment to be offered tonight, Benjamin reasoned. Nevertheless, he smiled acquiescence at his daughter.

Caiaphas turned back to Benjamin. "Well, my friend," he said, "we would be glad to obtain the help of such a talented and well-known young scholar as this in our deliberations." The high priest's colleagues all nodded eagerly at Nathanael, who smiled and nodded back, but not as convincingly or as eagerly as Abigail would have liked. The high priest went on to say, "As you know, being occupied by foreigners presents special challenges to us." There were many murmurs of agreement around the table, but Nathanael remained silent—much to Abigail's annoyance. "Yes, indeed," the high priest continued, looking steadily at the young lawyer, his jaw muscles flexing, "they bring a lot of pagan traditions with them that infect the people.

It's hard to keep our nation from being defiled by these gentiles who impose their laws on us willy-nilly without regard for our long-held traditions."

Nathanael's head went up and he posited, "Well, maybe God has sent them to us to humble us, to shake us up a little." The other men laughed as if Nathanael had made the funniest joke in the world, Caiaphas especially. Abigail laughed and clapped delightedly, glad that her friend was finally getting into the swing of things. She stopped laughing, however, when she noticed that her "betrothed" had failed to join them. Eventually the other men noticed the same thing and stopped laughing also.

With his smile fixed firmly in place and jaw muscles flexing more rapidly now, Caiaphas said, "Of course, you must be joking, young man."

Nathanael said, "No I am not," looking around the table at them all. He noted a certain pair of lovely hazel eyes staring knives at him, and he winced internally. He then smiled back good-naturedly at the high priest and continued in a relaxed tone of voice. "Well, my lord, I seem to remember how the LORD has sent occupying armies into our land from time to time in the past to wake us up. I was reading Isaiah today and ..."

"Why do you think we might need any waking up at all, my friend?" the high priest interrupted, looking around at his colleagues, his smile more like a tooth-filled grimace now.

Abigail slowly put her wine goblet down and stared at Nathanael. She wondered if her beloved could possibly be annoying the high priest on purpose. She certainly got that idea as the high priest smiled tightly at him. If this continued she could see their future together going up in smoke and she did not like it. How she wanted to take her friend aside and warn him! She had hoped to catch his eye by glaring at him, but Nathanael was so fixated on the high priest she could not. Setting her jaw, she resolved to take him aside and shake some sense into him as soon as possible.

Nathanael said, "Well, my lord, I was at the Jordan River today. You may know that there is a young man there ..."

Benjamin saw the same thing his daughter had. Hoping to rescue his future son-in-law from the pit he was digging for himself, and hoping to lighten the atmosphere, he interrupted, "Oh, yes, my lord. You know, John son of Zechariah, whom they call John the Baptist. It's amazing how the crowds flock to him. Why, he preaches the coming of the Messiah and ..."

His voice trailed off when Caiaphas stood and glared at him, a terrible jaw-muscle-filled grimace set firmly in place. Abigail exhaled a loud exasperated breath, though none of the men heard her because their attention was focused on their high priest and this upstart, this ungracious young lawyer.

But Nathanael smiled easily back at his host and said, "Yes, indeed, Father. The reason they flock to John is because he preaches that righteousness comes through repentance and humility, what we used to call faith, and not through slavish obedience to thousands of meaningless …"

"Take care, young man," the red-faced high priest interrupted, a finger shooting into the air. For John the Baptist also excoriated the priests and the rulers with every breath he took. He was certainly no favorite of Caiaphas or many of his colleagues. Not in the least!

This was why all the priests sat up as well and looked around at each other and then stared at Nathanael, wondering what he might say next. Nicodemus was especially interested. For he had gone out to see John the Baptist preach many times, but only under cover of disguise (of course). And strange as it might seem, he found himself agreeing with John that he and his priestly colleagues were the true oppressors of the people, not the Romans.

Benjamin happened to catch the exasperated look from his daughter, and he mouthed an apology at her and then looked around at his guests, wondering why things were turning out so abominably badly. What was the problem? He could not figure out why Nathanael had decided to irritate the high priest and what could have conceivably gotten into him.

He breathed a sigh of relief, however, when his soon-to-be son-in-law seemed to apologize by saying, "My lord high priest, I meant no disrespect at all. Please excuse me."

The high priest seemed to relax and Abigail exhaled heavily again, this time blessing her betrothed with all her heart. She smiled encouragingly at him, hoping that he would continue to humble himself before the embodiment of their future, who was still glaring at her beloved, though not quite as menacingly.

"Actually, I did not really mean John the Baptist, Father," Nathanael said apologetically to his host, who nodded back with relieved understanding. Everyone relaxed a bit more and smiled warily. As Nathanael took a drink from his wine goblet, the men began to recline again, though quite stiffly, Caiaphas not taking his eyes off him. "No, actually," he went on matter-of-factly, "I meant the Son of God, our Messiah who … "

He was interrupted by two of the men choking loudly on their wine, one aspirating a large plume of red liquid onto his neighbor. And by Caiaphas, who shot up so suddenly he dislodged a morsel of bread-wrapped lamb from

Benjamin's fingers and sent it flying across the table. It landed at the feet of a white-faced Abigail.

Nicodemus, on the other hand, turned his face away to hide a smile. He was also swallowing hard, hoping to prevent the loud guffaw roiling up in his throat from exploding into the room. Not out of disbelief. He had heard of this Jesus of Nazareth through friends; he had seen Him get baptized and he had heard John the Baptist's declarations concerning Him. Rather, he had wondered how his colleagues might react to the news of the Messiah's coming. How he loved it!

"**What?**" choked out an enraged high priest, amid the continued spluttering and coughing.

"Yes, my lords," Nathanael said matter-of-factly. "Our Messiah has come to us. Isn't it wonderful news?" He beamed around at them all as if it were such a no-brainer any idiot could see it, but maybe a bit disingenuously.

Caiaphas stood slowly. "What do you mean, the Son of God? The Messiah. That's ridiculous!" He was pacing back and forth now, looking around at his colleagues. When he could manage to swallow the bile that had risen in his throat, he choked out a dismissive laugh. "Everyone knows that when the Messiah comes He will bring a conquering army and rid this land of its pagan hordes." Rabbis Zacharius and Porteus—the latter rubbing furiously at the stain on his robe—grunted affirmatively. Nicodemus, having successfully, though with no little struggle, stuffed down his laughter, remained quiet.

His head going back and forth following the pacing high priest, Nathanael said, "Excuse me, my lord, you are absolutely right, of course. That is what we've always been taught." Caiaphas stopped suddenly and nodded forcefully at Nathanael; then he straightened his robe with two swift yanks. "Nor has this man," Nathanael continued, "come with any conquering armies that I could see."

"Who is this man of whom you speak, my son?" Nicodemus managed to ask softly.

"What possible difference can that make?" growled the high priest.

Nicodemus was mouthing the words "none, I guess" apologetically when Nathanael said, "His name is Jesus; He is from Nazareth and …"

"See?" squeaked the high priest, raising his finger again and smiling broadly in triumph, looking around at his colleagues. "That proves it. Nothing good can come from Nazareth." Rabbis Zacharius and Porteus laughed loudly along with Caiaphas.

"Except that the prophets have said that our Messiah will be called a Nazarene," said Nicodemus, but so softly that only Nathanael seemed to be able to hear him over the other men's laughter.[22]

Nathanael glanced over at Abigail. She was shaking her head at him, tears in her eyes. He wanted so very badly to take her in his arms. Nevertheless, he said, "My lords, please hear me out." They stopped laughing and glared at him. "I spent the whole afternoon with Jesus. He is truly the Son that Isaiah prophesied about." He went on to quote the passage of Scripture he had been reading earlier. "And since it says, '… of the increase in his government and peace there will be no end,' he must surely be the Messiah for whom our leaders have always waited." He glanced around at them all with a pleading look in his eye, hoping that they might believe. Then he made a decision. "He is going to Galilee tomorrow and has asked me to accompany Him."

"**What?**" cried Abigail, who blushed deeply as all the men turned quickly round to stare at her. She bowed her head and whispered, "I am so sorry, my lords, for interrupting you." With a dismissive wave of their hands they turned away from her abruptly. She wept quietly as she stared at her beloved, who seemed to be throwing their lives away as someone might throw out the contents of night bowls.

"Yes, *what,* indeed?" said the high priest, regarding this impertinent young woman through narrowed eyes, before turning back to Nathanael, who was staring at him, his chin raised slightly.

I'll wipe that defiant look off his face if it's the last thing I do, Caiaphas resolved before continuing. "Just *what* can this mean, young man?" Before Nathanael could answer him, he turned away to look at his colleagues, one of whom—Rabbi Porteus—was still rubbing fiercely at his red-stained robe. He cleared his throat loudly. Porteus blushed, excused himself, and then folded his hands meekly in his lap, his eyes raised (finally!) to his high priest. Caiaphas glared at him a moment before addressing them all. "You know, we had hoped that we might add a new member to our number tonight." They nodded obediently. He turned back to the still "defiant" Nathanael. "You realize, young man, that if you go chasing after this false prophet of yours, this so-called Messiah, we will have to reconsider our thinking on this matter." Nathanael opened his mouth to answer, but he was cut short when the high priest turned his back to him and spoke to his colleagues as if

---

[22] Matthew 2:23.

Nathanael weren't there. "Come to think of it, I'm not so sure that maybe we haven't been mistaken all along." He pointed back toward Nathanael, though he did not look at him. "Maybe it would be best for this young man to go on to Galilee if he loves this rabble-rousing Jesus person so very much." He nodded around at his colleagues, who turned to look at Nathanael and then turned back to him. Two of them murmured something unintelligible though it sounded like agreement.

Benjamin said, "My lords, please. Let's not be hasty here; why ..."

"Father, don't. Please," Nathanael interrupted. The old man deflated again and sank down on his couch, staring up at his son, his hopes and dreams for him and his daughter evaporating rapidly under the heated glares of the high priest and his colleagues.

Nathanael turned to the high priest. "My lord, you are quite right. *As usual.*" The inflection of his voice as he added this last and clearly facetious acknowledgement of Caiaphas' infallibility made it impossible to take it as anything but a gross insult. Two of the priests looked from Nathanael to the high priest and back again, dumbfounded. But rage filled Caiaphas to the point that he wanted to murder this young man where he stood.

"Yes, indeed," continued the young lawyer fearlessly, "it means that I will be going with Jesus to Galilee." Nathanael looked over at his betrothed, then back at Caiaphas. "It means that I will be going with Him wherever He leads me."

Staring at the high priest, whose expression left little doubt what he was thinking, Nathanael's mind was suddenly opened and these thoughts flooded into him: Jesus is certainly the Lamb of God that takes away the sin of the world; and what Isaiah said about the Messiah: "[That] he was oppressed and afflicted, yet he did not open his mouth; he was led like a lamb to the slaughter, and as a sheep before her shearers is silent, so he did not open his mouth. By oppression and judgment he was taken away,"[23] was true; therefore, Jesus was fated to die, and these men or men like them—the oppressors of his people—would be the ones doing the slaughtering.

Nathanael realized suddenly that where Jesus might be leading him could very well be to his own death, as had happened to the followers of Thaddeus and Judas years ago. This filled his heart with grief, but not for himself. Rather, it was for these blind men about whom the prophet also said, "Distressed and hungry, they will roam through the land; when they are

---

[23] Isaiah 53: 7 – 8.

famished, they will become enraged and, looking upward, will curse their king and their God."[24] What the young man realized, finally, was that they would refuse to be led to salvation. How sad it was.

Abigail could no longer contain herself. Weeping, she ran over to her beloved and said, "Think what you are doing, my beloved. Please don't throw it all away. Please."

Nathanael said, "My precious darling, I don't think I can undo what has already been done."

The high priest said, "Your betrothed is correct, young woman. There is nothing to be done now." He wrapped his cloak majestically about him and said to his host, "My thanks for your hospitality, my friend." Benjamin nodded back sadly. Caiaphas turned to his colleagues. "Let us depart, my brothers. And let us leave this young man to this Jesus of Nazareth and see what that gets him, since he is too good for the likes of us." He had snorted out that last gracious sentiment before turning on his heel and walking out, followed meekly by his three colleagues. Only Nicodemus looked back at Nathanael. His expression was filled with remorse and sympathy, as if he were regarding the remains of a dead man, whom, had he known him better, he would no doubt have loved like a son.

When they had left, only the sound of Abigail's weeping could be heard. Nathanael opened his arms to embrace her, but she pushed him away. She cried, "What have you done? For what? Some shabby man that's going to get himself killed, like all these 'prophets' that come to us all the time, claiming to be someone? How could you throw our lives away like that?" She punched him in the chest for emphasis.

With a tear in his eye, Nathanael said, "I didn't know that I was throwing away *our* lives, Dove. This man, Jesus, *is* the Messiah. Come and meet Him." She shook her red-streaked face at him. "Father," he said as he turned to his host, "please come and see Him. Listen to Him. He *is* truly the Messiah." Then Nathanael turned again to his beloved and pleaded, "Please, my treasure. Please."

But Abigail shook her head again and ran from the room, weeping loudly.

Benjamin followed her out with his eyes. Then he said, "My boy, she has had a shock. We all have." He sighed deeply. "Let's give her some time. Give me some." But there was something in his tone of voice that kindled

---

[24] Isaiah 8: 21.

bright hope in the young disciple's breast. The old man, seeing that look in his eye, said, "No, my son, I don't think you've heard the end of us yet." He held out his arms to Nathanael, who embraced his friend and wept for gratitude on his shoulder.

When the young disciple returned to his home, he found Philip waiting for him. The look in Nathanael's eye told the young man what he needed to know. Philip embraced his friend warmly, and they spoke well into the night of what had transpired at the dinner and of things to come. Nathanael broke into tears when he recounted Abigail's reaction.

Before they retired to get a few hours' sleep, Philip said, "I bet Abigail will surprise you."

Nathanael smiled, sniffed and took his friend's hand in gratitude. "I hope so. Oh, LORD God in heaven, how I hope so!"

The two young men left Judea the next morning with Jesus. Over the next several weeks, the Son of God went throughout Galilee, teaching in the synagogues, doing many miraculous works and preaching the Good News of the kingdom.

News about Jesus spread throughout the land. People brought to Him all who were ill, the demon-possessed, the lame and the blind, and He healed them all. His fame quickly spread throughout Judea and Samaria, so that large crowds not only from Galilee, but also from the Decapolis, Jerusalem, Judea and the further regions east of the Jordan began to follow Him.[25]

Nathanael and Philip were amazed, of course. Yet Nathanael always found himself looking forlornly into the crowds, hoping to see if "someone" might be there. But she never was. Philip, with a heavy heart, watched his friend go through this sad routine day after day. When he tried to console him, Nathanael merely smiled, wiped a tear from his eye and went on with the work Jesus had called him to do.

One bright morning Jesus and His disciples were walking along the shore of the lake in Galilee. Nathanael and Philip were following Peter, John, Andrew, and James when the crowd stopped suddenly. The two young disciples wondered why.

They saw that Jesus had stopped and turned to Peter and John. Over the roar of voices, they could barely hear Him say, motioning to the crowd, "I must speak to them." He turned away from the shore of the sea and strode

---

[25] This paragraph is based on Matthew 4:23 – 25. Also, the Decapolis was a large territory south of the Sea of Galilee and east of the Jordan River, which included most of modern day Jordan.

toward one of the hills nearby. Jesus said, "Let us go up there. There will be enough room for everyone." The young men obediently turned to follow Him and pushed their way through the crowd so that Jesus might make His way up the side of the hill.

As they walked slowly along, Philip watched Nathanael crane his neck and look around, as he did every day. Philip said, "I wonder what our Master's going to say."

"Don't know," came the absentminded reply, as Nathanael's eyes scanned the crowd intently.

As they began to climb the slope, Philip's heart skipped a beat, for a very plush litter borne by four dark, heavily muscled slaves had just set down a short way away. While he had never known Benjamin and his daughter to travel by such conveyance, it was clearly the property of a very wealthy person.

He was about to tap Nathanael on the shoulder when a young woman whom he had never seen stepped out and began to follow the crowd up the slopes. She was beautiful, certainly, and obviously wealthy, if her ride were any indication. Philip was surprised at her dress, however, for she wore a plain woolen robe and old worn sandals, not at all the type of dress he would have thought suitable to a person of such obvious means. *Maybe she's trying to be anonymous,* Philip thought, smiling at the absurdity of the thought. He was also perplexed by the way she kept her head down and made no eye contact with any of the crowd, while trying to slide obsequiously between them—not at all the way of wealthy persons who, in Philip's view, tended to pride and overweening arrogance.

As she got closer, Philip noticed that she looked as well-worn and tired as her clothing, and also that she seemed very sad. When she reacted angrily to the little bit of jostling she was getting, he nodded in understanding. He'd seen such flashes of anger, borne of ill-use and spiritual desolation, many times. He instantly knew that though she was wealthy she was also miserable, and his heart went out to her.

Philip nudged his friend. "Look over there."

Nathanael pulled his eyes away from the back of the crowd to see the woman still angrily pushing at the people around her. When someone tripped over her, he saw by her reaction that she had cursed him heartily. He turned to Philip and gave him a look that indicated he felt the same compassion for this woman that Philip did.

After they walked a few more minutes, they noted with interest that the young woman had made her way almost to the front of the crowd, so they made it a point to keep track of her. When they noticed that she had no eyes for anyone but Jesus, they looked back and forth between them. When Jesus healed a little girl's broken arm, they saw how the woman's eyes went wide and her mouth opened in wonder. When Jesus cast a demon out of another little girl and then healed the flow of blood in another young woman, they saw her begin to weep.

Surprised by her tears, Nathanael said, "You know, my friend, I don't think that one cries much."

"I think you are right, my friend," Philip replied softly.

Philip nudged Nathanael when he saw that a certain pair of Eyes had turned toward the young woman. The young disciples watched with intense interest as she realized that Jesus was looking at her and then jerked her eyes away and looked around, obviously wondering whether her LORD and God might be looking at someone else. They were intrigued when He smiled directly at her, and they were fascinated by how deeply she blushed and then lowered her eyes and covered them with a trembling hand.

Philip whispered, "Our Master seems to know her. And she Him. We know how He knows, of course, but I wonder about her?"

Nathanael said, staring over at the weeping young woman, "I certainly agree with you about Jesus." As the young woman looked furtively around and then submerged herself in the crowd, as if she were trying to find a hole to climb into Nathanael continued, "Our Master certainly knows everything there is to know about her, and from her reaction, that can't be all too good." Philip nodded as they continued to follow Jesus up the side of the hill.

Eventually the Sovereign LORD of the Universe found a low stone and sat down upon it, and the crowd began to settle in all around Him.[26] The air was filled with the sound of their murmuring voices, which made having a normal conversation difficult.

Philip and Nathanael watched the young woman seat herself. As she did she raised her eyes suddenly and caught them looking at her. They tried to smile a welcome at her, but she seemed disturbed that they had noticed her and avoided their eyes. Not wanting to make her more uncomfortable than she obviously was, they relented and turned their eyes back to Jesus, who continued to wait for the crowd to settle in. They sat down as well, but they glanced back at the young woman from time to time.

---

[26] As to Jesus being our Sovereign LORD, see Jude 1:4.

After a few minutes, while the crowd was still busy settling itself, Philip nudged his friend again and said, "Look who's coming." Nathanael turned and saw the woman crawling up the hill on her hands and knees. Philip added, "I don't think she does that very often, either." Nathanael muttered concurrence. After this the young men turned their eyes back to Jesus, who was now looking over their heads. They knew at whom He was looking. When He smiled at her, they turned to see the young woman go white with surprise and then break down and weep more.

They both turned back to Jesus as He rose to His feet. The loud roar of voices stopped suddenly and an eerie quiet descended on the hillside. Jesus opened His mouth and began to address the crowd, still looking directly over Philip's and Nathanael's heads:

> "Blessed are the poor in spirit, for theirs is the kingdom of heaven.
> "Blessed are those who mourn, for they will be comforted...."

They were astonished as they listened to Him. Nathanael turned with wide eyes to Philip several times. For his part, Philip could only manage to nod dumbly, his mouth partially open.

When Jesus was done, and the crowd began to rise, Nathanael turned to try to catch a glimpse of the young woman, but when he looked up he saw Abigail instead, standing behind him, weeping and smiling at him. He wanted to shout for joy and would have if he could have found his voice. As she ran up to him, he opened his arms, and she flung herself at him and kissed him several times, clawing at his back, and then nestling her head on his shoulder. After a moment they parted and looked into each other's eyes for the longest time. Meanwhile, Philip touched his friend on the shoulder, smiled and walked away, praising God for the joy he felt.

"I am so glad to see you, Beloved," Nathanael said, smoothing a strand of hair out of her face. "Come, Abigail, you must meet the LORD." When they turned, they saw that Jesus was sitting on His haunches and speaking to the woman Nathanael and Philip had been observing.

As the woman wept and then embraced Him, Abigail said, "He is truly incredible." She then said, pointing at the rock on which Jesus had sat, "I heard every word He said. It was amazing! I'm so sorry for doubting you, my love. So very, very sorry."

"You have nothing to be sorry for, my beloved. Nothing! Come, let's meet the LORD. Where's your father?"

She pointed down to a chariot at the base of the hill where her father sat along with Jonah and Micah. Nathanael waved and they waved back.

Abigail said, "This was much too steep a climb for Daddy, and the chariot would not make it either. He can't wait to see you and meet Someone else." She went up on tiptoe; her hand went to the side of her mouth, which she put close to his ear, and she said, "We've been here a week listening to Him." She tipped her head in Jesus' direction. He had left the young woman and was now speaking quietly with Peter and John.

Nathanael's eyes went wide, and he said with a bright smile, "Why didn't you tell me?"

Abigail blushed and lowered her eyes. "Because I was too ashamed of myself. Daddy was relentless, though. He insisted that I come up to you, so I did." Her blush deepened as she looked shyly up at him from beneath her brow.

This charmed the young disciple more than he could say, but he responded laconically, "I'm glad!" When her head shot up in surprise at what seemed such a tepid response, he shouted with laughter. He grabbed her around the waist, lifted her off the ground, and spun her round and round. She squealed delightedly, pleading that he put her down before he made a fool of himself. Which he did, eventually—put her down, that is. He glanced over at Jesus, who caught his look and smiled at him. Jesus then nodded at Abigail, and Nathanael chuckled at the delighted look in her eye as she smiled at Him bashfully.

"Let's go meet Him, my love."

She nodded eagerly; and with delirious joy they approached Him hand in hand. This was but the first step on the glorious path they would follow for the rest of their lives.

The Very First Evangelist

[Jesus] came to a town in Samaria called Sychar, near the plot of ground Jacob had given to his son Joseph. Jacob's well was there, and Jesus, tired as he was from the journey, sat down by the well. It was about the sixth hour. When a Samaritan woman came to draw water, Jesus said to her, "Will you give me a drink?" (John 4:5 – 7)

Author's note: Like a previous story, this one tells of a "fallen woman" whom Jesus met at a well and who turned out to be one of the great heroes of the New Testament. It seems that she was the very first person who led unbelievers outside of Judea to the knowledge of the LORD; hence the title of this story. It was written to honor this woman; to show my admiration for her. If you are not familiar with the account of her meeting with Jesus, it can be found starting in John 4:5. This story picks up after John 4:26, after the woman and Jesus have spoken at length about who He is.

Naomi was stunned, looking gape-mouthed at the young man sitting near her.[1] Here was the Messiah who had been speaking with her. The very Messiah Himself! She was filled with wonder. A crunch of a branch and the sound of voices caused her to turn away from Him for a moment. She saw the young men who followed Him, now coming back from her village. They were muttering to themselves and pointing at her.

She understood their looks. That any Jew at all would have deigned to speak to her was amazing because the Judean Jews scorned Samaritans. That a Jewish Rabbi would have bothered to speak to her was especially amazing because she was just an uneducated woman. But that her Messiah would be speaking to her personally, a sinful woman who was scorned not only by the Jews but also by her own people, was—well—it was too wonderful to imagine. And she had instantly loved Him because He had been so very gentle with her. Even when He confronted her about her sin—that the man she was living with was not her husband—He had been loving and kind about it.

As she stared into His eyes for a second more, she thought, "No matter what they think of me, I must certainly tell all of Sychar about Him." She

---

[1] The name Naomi is fictional. Scripture never reveals the name of the Samaritan woman in John 4.

immediately left Jesus sitting on the side of the well and hurried back to tell them all the Good News. She was so excited she forgot to take her water jar with her as she hurried away into the woods and back toward the village.

Since the day was hot, for it was around noon, and the meeting place was some distance away, Naomi stopped for a moment to catch her breath. She asked herself again, *What was this Living Water He kept talking about?* She smiled, thinking, *Well it certainly wasn't like any water you could actually drink from a cup. How stupid I was to think that.* She giggled at her "stupidity." When she had recovered her breath, she resumed her walk.

As Naomi walked along, several women from the village passed her on the way. She stopped to tell them the wonderful news—that she had met a great prophet from God who claimed to be the Messiah—but they passed rudely by without deigning to speak to her or even to acknowledge her. How that hurt!

How it always hurt. But what could she do?

It seemed that Naomi had always been an outcast of sorts. A few months after she was married, her husband had stopped loving her and threw her out of his home. No other man would marry her then, and a woman without a husband or a family to go home to was as good as dead in this day and age. To survive, she had lived with any man who would take her in, which was why she was scorned by her people as an immoral woman.

A tear came to Naomi's eye as she reflected on the hard days of her life and her loneliness and misery. *What a name,* she thought. *Who had ever taken delight in me?*[2]

Weeping audibly now, Naomi continued on her way. Perhaps Joseph, the man with whom she now lived, might be able to get the village's attention. She would tell him. Maybe he would believe her.

It did not take Naomi long to reach her house, for she lived on the farthest outskirts of the village nearest the well in a section inhabited by the poor and outcast. Her home was a small ramshackle affair with three small rooms: a main room, a partially walled off cooking area, and a bedroom of sorts. There were also a few goats that shared her and Joseph's shelter. Only the animals were there, however.

How frustrating!

How could she do this? Naomi had to tell everyone that the Messiah had come. But she hated to go into the village alone because the children threw

---

[2] "Naomi" sounds like the Hebrew for "my delight."

rocks at her and shouted obscene names. The men turned their backs on her, refusing to look at her. And the women! Well, their scorn was the hardest to bear because they all certainly understood what it was like to be an unloved woman thrown out of her home: the hardship and loneliness. Naomi would have thought that she might get some sympathy from them at least. She sat down on a little stool and buried her tear-streaked face in her hands, wondering how she might muster the courage to tell the village.

But as she recalled the wonderful loving eyes of that young man at the well, her fear of the villagers melted away, and her resolve to tell them the good news about Him hardened. She got up, wiped her tears away, straightened her shoulders and marched with a purposeful step into the center of the village.

As she entered the central square, the children, as usual, laughed at her and taunted her. They stopped, however, when they caught a certain look in her eye. They could tell that she was not going to quietly bear their insults this time, and they shrank back from her. This piqued the interest of a few of the men, and they turned to stare at her. They were not used to seeing her walk so confidently among them.

When she got into the center of the village she shouted at the top of her lungs, "Our Messiah has come to us. I have seen him!"

All the villagers dropped what they were doing and stared at her.

Turning slowly around, Naomi said, "Come out to Jacob's well and see a great prophet. He told me everything I have ever done. He claims to be God's Anointed One. Could it actually be?"[3] She stopped and stared into their eyes without shame. For the first time she could remember, she was able to look into people's eyes without feeling small, or insignificant, or hated. Rather, the hatred she had always seen in their eyes had turned to interest and wonder. How this thrilled her!

"How do we know she's telling the truth?" came a voice from behind the crowd that had gathered around Naomi.

She turned toward the voice, and the crowd parted to reveal an old man sitting on a bench next to his house. He was known as being spiteful, hateful, and also, as it seemed to go with these two laudable characteristics, as a very religious man. He was snickering at her, for he had always been one of her harshest persecutors. She took no particular umbrage at this, however,

---

[3] John 4: 29, paraphrased for the sake of the narrative.

because he persecuted everyone he deemed less holy than he, and most of the villagers feared him.

Undaunted, maybe because there were a few admiring stares coming at her from the crowd rather than the scorn she was used to, Naomi said quietly, but with a smile, "Well, Aram, maybe you might think about getting off that self-righteous old butt of yours and coming out to the well with me to see."

Everyone roared with laughter. Even the women were laughing because Aram was not popular with the town.

The leader of the village, named Jabez, came up to Naomi, laughing around at them all, extending a hand toward her. He was a kind, elderly man, who had always had sympathy for her and who had helped her in times of need. Since he had been the only one in the village to do so, Naomi loved and trusted him.

He smiled at her and then turned to the crowd. He raised his voice to them all. "Let's go out and see this man who claims to be the Christ come to us." He turned back to Naomi and said loudly, with a smile, "Won't that give the Jews fits? The Christ come to Sychar in Samaria instead of to Jerusalem?" They all laughed more.

With Jabez in the lead, many from the village went out to Jacob's well. There they found the young man of whom Naomi had spoken along with twelve other young men. They were sitting on some grass near the well, eating dried fish, barley cakes, and dates.

The villagers were all amazed when the young man rose quickly, walked up to Naomi, took her hands in His and smiled down into her eyes. The women looked at each other; the men blushed; and they all murmured among themselves. A clammy feeling of guilt oozed over them as they looked furtively around at each other, for the loving light in this young man's eyes, which shone brightly down on this outcast young woman, also illuminated the contempt for her they had stored up in their own hearts.

Jesus looked around at them all with those knowing eyes of His, and then He turned back to Naomi and said, "Well, my child, I see that you have brought your friends with you." He looked around at the villagers again, and they all felt their shame pooling deep red in their cheeks and foreheads. In that moment, they knew that what the outcast young woman had said was true. This man must really be the Christ, come from God—the Prophet that Moses had told them about.

In a burst of magnanimity she did not know she could feel, Naomi said, "Well, LORD, all that has happened in the past is of no consequence now that you are here. And how could I keep *you* all to myself?"

She smiled a forgiving smile at her "friends" but they avoided her eyes. How much more awful did they all feel as the LORD looked down at her, knowing and loving her more for what she had said for the sake of these "friends" of hers!

Jesus looked up again and smiled, as Jabez, whom He knew to be a truly godly servant, approached Him and bowed low to the ground at His feet.

The old man said, "Master, our sister Naomi told us that you are the Christ, come to save us all. Please, come into our village. We will prepare a place for you and your men here. Please come. Though we are not worthy, please come." Jabez began to weep, for he, as the leader of the village, had taken upon himself the shame for their treatment of their sister.

Jesus took Jabez' hand and brought him to his feet. "You have spoken well and truly," he replied. "Of course we will come. We have traveled far, and we would be happy to share your hospitality."

Because His back was to His disciples when He spoke, the LORD God of all creation seemed not to notice that they had shown some discomfort at the thought of staying in the village.[4] For from their youth they had been taught to look with scorn upon the Samaritans. But when they saw and understood what had transpired between their God and this woman, whom they knew to be a village outcast, and when they realized that the elder was weeping for shame at how she had been treated, they too felt shame at harboring the thought that it might be inappropriate for their LORD to stay with them. When Jesus looked back at his disciples, it was their turn to blush. With that glance, they knew that they were in for a little talking-to.

The LORD noticed that Naomi was squirming with excitement, so He turned to her. Seeing His encouraging look, she shouted, "LORD, tell them about the Living Water!"

Her eyes were so wide and her smile so broad that Jesus laughed, and everyone laughed with Him. Thinking that they were laughing at her, Naomi bowed her head and blushed furiously. But when one of the village women put an arm around her and embraced her, Naomi knew that they were not laughing at her at all. How relieved she was!

Jesus raised His hand and the laughter stopped. He held out His hand to Naomi, who was still blushing, but for a much different reason now, and she took it. Then He turned to them and repeated what He had said to her. "All of you come to this well every day to get the water that sustains your bodies."

---

[4] Speaking of Jesus as LORD of creation, John writes: "Through him all things were made; without him nothing was made that has been made." See John 1:3.

He pointed to Jacob's well with His free hand. Their eyes followed that motion and they murmured agreement among themselves. "But now the Gift of God is among you, and I am He, the Messiah for whom you are waiting."[5] He put His free hand on His chest, and their eyes returned to Him. "If you were to ask it of me, as this young woman has done ..." He laid His free hand lightly on her shoulder and she leaned into His touch, closing her eyes. "... I would gladly give you the Living Water she told you about. It is Water that will slake the thirst in your souls for all time, and it will become like a spring in you and well up to eternal life."

They looked around at each other, murmuring, "We want this Living Water."

Jabez said, "Then come, Master, and sup with us. Everyone, go quickly and prepare your homes to take in all these fine young men."

The people cheered when Jesus again agreed to come.

So they all followed Jabez and Jesus back into the town where He stayed for two days, teaching them about the Kingdom of God and preaching the Good News to them. During this time many of them believed His message and put their faith in Him.

---

[5] See John 4:10 and 4:26, where Jesus describes Himself as a "gift of God" and as the Messiah.

Mary and Joseph

In the sixth month, God sent the angel Gabriel to Nazareth, a town in Galilee, to a virgin, pledged to be married to a man named Joseph, a descendant of David. The virgin's name was Mary.
(Luke 1:26 – 27)

Author's note: There are many great heroes in the Bible, but one of the greatest by far, in my opinion, was Mary, the mother of Jesus. And following close behind her was her betrothed, Joseph, son of Jacob.

Mary paced rapidly around the room, hands joined at the palms, jerking them back and forth nervously. "Mary, my darling," said her mother Ruth, "you're driving me crazy. Why don't you sit down and relax?"[1]

Ruth was sitting at a little table in the main room of their tiny house. She wanted to smile because her daughter had always been so patient and level-headed. Seeing her like this—at the ends of extremity—reminded Ruth of herself when she was looking forward to marrying her husband, and it struck her as funny. But she did manage, with no little struggle, to keep a serious face.

Mary stopped her pacing and lowered her hands. "Oh, Mother, how can I relax with Daddy still talking to Jacob (Joseph's father)? What's taking so long? I wish this was over and we were done already." Her face crumpled into tears, suddenly. She fell at her mother's feet and asked, "Suppose Jacob does not want me as a daughter?"

Mary's look was so pathetic her mother had to look away to hide a smile that would not be denied. What a ridiculous thought! Why, Jacob had as much as jumped for joy when Ruth's husband had proposed the betrothal of

---

[1] Note that Mary's parents' names are never revealed in Scripture, nor is Joseph's mother's name, though his father's —Jacob— is revealed in Matthew 1:16. Also note that Mary's line of descent is not made absolutely clear in Scripture. Some think she was a descendent of David as was her husband. However, since Scripture says that she was Elizabeth's relative (Luke 1:36) and Elizabeth was a daughter of Levi, whereas Joseph was a son of Judah, they probably were not directly related. Others have disputed this. In this story I have assumed that she was not directly related to Joseph.

Mary to Jacob's son, Joseph. She said, "Mary, Mary, don't be ridiculous. Of course Jacob does."

Mary, apparently not convinced, said, "Well, maybe Daddy wants too much for the bride price." She got up and turned toward the door. "Well, I'm going over there right now to tell him I don't care what Joseph's father pays him. I want to be Joseph's wife!"

"Darling, stop! I don't know what's taking so long, but it's not that, I'm sure. Please, come sit on Mommy's lap." Mary's shoulders slumped and she obeyed her mother—as she always did. When she had nestled her head on her mother's shoulder, Ruth began stroking her lovely jet-black hair. She murmured into her ear, "That's better, Precious. It'll be over soon and you can go off and leave us and be with your husband, if that's what you really want so badly." Although Ruth had never heard the term "reverse psychology", she found that applying it in principal generally worked with her daughter.

Mary started up. "Oh, Mom," she replied, "you know how I love you and Dad." Ruth nodded and smiled, brushing a wayward strand of hair from her daughter's eye. "But I've loved Joseph ever since I can remember. I want him so, I just can't stand it." Mary smiled and blushed at the thought of being held in this grown man's arms, not as a friend but as his wife.

Ruth's heart warmed at seeing her daughter's desire expressed by that dreamy look on her face. "I know, Precious. I do know. Ever since you were a little girl, you have loved that fine boy."

How Ruth knew!

They had come to Nazareth from Bethlehem in Judea when Mary was a child of about seven, and they had immediately become close friends with Joseph's family. She recalled how Mary had taken to Jacob's nine-year-old boy; how she had always tagged after him; and how she had eventually come to love him in the way that a woman will love a man on whom she has set her heart.

With good reason, Ruth thought!

Ruth nodded reassurance down at her daughter, who had looked at her briefly before laying her head back on her shoulder. Then a smile and another little chuckle burbled up from Ruth.

Mary raised her head and asked, "What's so funny, Mom?"

"Well, Treasure, I was recalling those years when you and Joseph were children. I remember how you always said that you were going to marry him some day. I also recall a very frustrated little girl coming to me and crying her eyes out on my shoulder over that very same boy. How many times was that, now?"

"Oh, Mom, that was so long ago," Mary admonished her chuckling mother, blushing again.

Well, it had not really been all that long ago, Ruth thought, as she rocked Mary back and forth.

Ruth recalled how Joseph had always been a kind and godly boy, and she understood that Mary had sensed his nobleness of spirit, even at a very young age. Ruth had also admired him because he had always been kind to her daughter. He never said a harsh word to her. He never made her feel unwanted, though there were many times when he obviously would rather have been with his male friends but had stayed to play with her anyway. It had also been clear to Ruth that Joseph had not formed the same type of attachment to Mary that she had to him—because she was "just a girl." (Ruth's smile had come as she recalled the look on the boy's face as he said those words and how deeply this had frustrated her little girl.) Even as Joseph became a young man and Mary grew to young womanhood, he still didn't look at her with that type of manly adoration she longed for.

Mary too recalled all this as she rested in her mother's arms. It *had* been so very frustrating, passionately loving that boy (well, he was not a boy any longer!) and not having him love her back the same way.

But Mary also recalled how things changed suddenly when Joseph noticed (finally!) that she was no longer the little girl he had played with. It had happened last year, sometime after she turned thirteen.[2] She looked down at her curvy body and smiled. She could recall *that* day as if it were yesterday.

She had gone over to Joseph's house—to visit him of course—but with an excuse to borrow some grain from his mother. Mary had been a "woman" for some months, and her body had almost completely filled out into its current loveliness. Mary recalled with some embarrassment how, in preparation for her visit, she … well … maybe she put a little fragrant rose-colored cream on her cheeks and lips, but just a very little, after all; and maybe she wore her very best smock and her very best sandals.

(Mary blushed so deeply it hurt when she saw her mother looking at her with that knowing eye of hers, as if she were reading her thoughts.)

---

[2] It was not unusual in this culture for girls of thirteen or even younger to be betrothed. And there has been some speculation that Mary was about fourteen when she gave birth to our LORD.

Mary recalled hesitantly knocking on the door and how the joy of seeing *him* had overwhelmed her when he opened it. She had hoped that he would be there, of course, but she became so nervous that she forgot on what pretext she had come. She knew that if he asked, she would not have remembered, nor would she have had the courage to tell him the real reason.

Her self-doubt and timidity were seared away, however, when she saw a light go on in his eye, as if he saw her for the very first time. She recalled how her face heated up; how her whole body seemed to swell with warmth and excitement because of the way he stared at her. It was on that day that Joseph had finally come to his senses, as she liked to think of this change in him. Ever since then their relationship had taken a much more satisfying direction for her, leading to the discussions her father and his were having now.

"*How many* prayers has it been since that very first time you saw Joseph, my child?" Ruth's tone of voice climbed dramatically to emphasize the question as she smiled down into her daughter's eyes.

Mary laughed for the first time since her father had gone off to negotiate her marriage. "Well, Mom," she answered, "how many stars are there in the sky?" Both women laughed. Mary nestled her head on her mother's shoulder and sighed. "I've prayed that the LORD my God would grant me my heart's desire—Joseph—every night since that time." She raised her head and laughed brightly. "And now the LORD has. At least, I think He has." She frowned and looked toward the door, hoping to see her father return. Finally!

"Of course our LORD has, my child. Be patient. It'll work out fine." Then Ruth decided to tease her daughter. "Of course, if they can't make a deal, well, I'm sure there are many other young men who would love to marry you."

Mary leapt off her mother's lap, crying, "What?" Ruth put a hand to her mouth and looked away for a moment. "What do you mean, **if**, Mom?" Seeing Ruth's shoulders quivering, Mary exhaled loudly and said, "Oh, Mom, please don't tease me."

Ruth held out her arms and Mary sat down again. She punched her mother playfully on the shoulder, and they both laughed.

"Joseph will be the best of husbands," Mary said dreamily. "He's so good and kind. He's so devoted to the service of God."

"As you have always been, my child."

"Oh, Mom, please." Mary bowed her head humbly. Then she looked at her mother from beneath her brow. "Well, I can tell you that since that day, I have never thought of anyone else but him, Mom. I've kept myself as pure as the whitest white for him, you know." Ruth agreed heartily, very proud of her daughter in this regard. "You know that I've never even allowed him to kiss me on the lips," Mary added.

"I know, child. I think it drives him crazy."

Mary chuckled. "I do too. But he understands why. I don't think he'd respect me if I allowed him."

Ruth said, "Probably not." She smiled a knowing smile at her daughter

As if to give words to her mother's thoughts, the young woman leaned close to her mother and whispered this confession into her ear: "But, Mom, I have had certain desires. You know." Ruth feigned shocked outrage. Mary pushed at her shoulder. "Oh, Mother, please." Ruth chuckled and nodded understanding, one loving woman to another. Then Mary laughed a sparkling little laugh and whispered into her ear again, "How I wish we were married today!"

It was Ruth's turn to blush at the total, trusting honesty of her daughter's declaration of desire for her husband-to-be.[3] Then Ruth said, "You know the key test of whether we love God or not, my child?" Mary shook her head, suspecting she did know, but wanting to hear her mother's answer. "Well, it's how we show obedience to His will. It is how we handle those very appropriate and good desires God has given us. If we allow them to control us, we can sin. If we submit to His will, though, He never fails to bless us. That's why I think He has granted your prayer."

"And I am so thankful," Mary said, embracing her mother.

Suddenly her father came into the room. He nodded gravely at Mary and then at her mother. He didn't say anything immediately, however, nor was he smiling. Truth be told, he was *actually* frowning a little.

Alarmed, the young woman jumped out of her mother's lap and cried, "Daddy! What! Did he say yes? Oh, tell me tell me tell me." She had grabbed the lapels of his cloak. "Why are you not telling me?" she shouted when he did not respond.

Nathan, still looking at her gravely—though had she bothered to look closer, Mary would have seen the glint of a smile in his eyes—stood aside and extended his arm toward her. "Daughter, may I present you to your new husband." Joseph entered, smiling as broadly as was possible for one to smile. His father and mother followed him in.

---

[3] This is in accordance with God's word in Genesis 3:16: "... your [Eve's] desire shall be for your husband ..."

Mary blushed: Joseph had heard everything! But she did not care. Throwing her pride away, she shouted, "Yes!" as she ran into the young man's outspread arms. For the first time she kissed him passionately, as a wife might kiss her husband after a long separation. She did not hear the delighted sigh of her mother, or the chuckles of Joseph's father and mother, or those of her own father.

After the young couple had parted and were holding hands and standing *very close* together, Mary's father, still laughing, said to his son-in-law-to-be, "Well, I am glad to finally be rid of this troublesome young woman!"

Everyone laughed at the absurdity of that statement, especially coming from this man. For he never failed to praise his daughter's purity and godliness to anyone who would allow him that very great pleasure, nor had he ever failed to tell all who would listen how much he loved, adored and admired her.

After their laughter died down, he said, "All kidding aside, young man, you've landed the best of women, and I hope you appreciate her."

"Oh, Daddy, stop embarrassing me." Mary blushed quite charmingly as she looked carefully into her betrothed's eyes.

In response, Joseph put his arms around his young bride-to-be, embraced her and kissed her again, to many additional sighs.

Then, her eyes sparkling with mirth, Mary started jumping up and down in Joseph's arms, asking, "So! When are we going to be married? When when, when?" They all laughed again, and she laughed with them utterly without self-consciousness.

When he could take a breath, Joseph said, "Well, Darling, as soon as we can." He turned to his father and said, "Father, when?"

Jacob frowned. "Well, Son, her father and I thought it would be good to wait until Mary turned fifteen." That was six months away, and everyone laughed at the look on Mary's face.

Mary's father took his obviously frustrated daughter's hand. "Treasure, I know how frustrating this can be. But I don't want you to go into this before then. Please understand."

"Okay, Daddy," she sighed. She put her arm around Joseph and laid her head on his chest to let him know that if she had her way, their marriage would happen much, much sooner.

Joseph whispered into her ear, "It's okay, Mouse. I'm not going anywhere and neither are you."

She giggled at his little pet name for her. Hers for him was "Turtle" because she had accused him of being as slow as a turtle on that day when he had finally noticed her. When, as his excuse, he had accused her of being as quiet as a mouse and hardly as noticeable, they had laughed until their sides ached. How she loved it when he called her that!

She sighed again. Another six months! How could she manage to bear it, she wondered? But when she looked into her mother's smiling, sympathetic eyes she knew.

Now the day had grown quite hot by this time and the door was open. They heard a clatter rise outside, and they all went to the door to see what was happening.

Marching down the street was a crowd of angry people pulling an obviously pregnant young woman along with them. Behind her was a young man who looked angrily at her from time to time, though she kept her head bowed with embarrassment. Mary and Joseph and their families looked on, filled with sadness. For the people were shouting that the poor young woman had committed adultery and that she should be stoned.

Jacob said, "How sad that is when a woman lets her desires overcome her. I feel so sorry for her husband. How must he be feeling?"

How indeed, wondered Mary, who—nestled in Joseph's protective arms—felt him shudder. She looked up at him and saw that his mouth had formed into a thin straight line. Was he angry? Was he judging that poor woman? Well, probably not, because he was a kind and godly man. On the other hand, maybe he did not pity her as Mary did. She knew what it was like to desire a man to the point of distraction. Being a godly young woman, Mary had put herself in her place. Nor could she find it in herself to feel the crowd's outrage, though she did not condone in any way what the adulteress had done. She decided, rather, that she would pray for her tonight. Maybe the people would have pity on the young woman.

She tugged at Joseph's arm. "Please don't be too hard on her, my love," she pleaded.

Joseph smiled at her plaintive face and said, "Of course not, Mouse. I know how hard it must be for them all. Such a mess!" He added with a sigh, "If only people could control themselves."

Mary shuddered. She praised God with all her heart that she had kept herself pure for Joseph, and she praised her LORD that no one would ever be able to accuse her of coming to her marriage bed with any stain on her. Nor would anyone ever after that. Mary would rather die than be unfaithful to her husband. Much more, she would rather die than be unfaithful to her God.

Sensing her thoughts, her betrothed said softly, "That's one of the things I admire about you, Mouse. Because of your love for the LORD your God, you are just the best and purest of women. Next to your mother of course."

Mary glanced at her mother, who was also shaking her head sadly. She whispered into Joseph's ear, "But everyone can have a day of weakness, my love. Suppose I ... well, suppose I ..."

She was startled by the vehemence of Joseph's reaction, "I can't imagine that ever happening. Just as I can't ever imagine being unfaithful to you, who are the light of my eye."

Seeing how she had started, as if she were afraid, Joseph held her tightly. He said more quietly, "Well, Love, of course no one is perfect. But, that would be so out of character for you. I guess I was surprised you might even mention such a thing." He paused for a moment. Then he said, "As I think about it, now, however, I realize that you have never considered yourself as better than anyone else. You were merely putting yourself in that poor girl's place, weren't you?" Mary nodded and managed to smile through her tears. "There, there, Mouse. Don't be afraid. I'll never stop loving you; just as the LORD your God would never stop loving you. That's another thing I like about you—your humility. Of course. Now I understand the reason for your question."

Despite his soothing words, she wondered how Joseph might react if she ... well ... if she did. But then she knew that she would die before ever letting *it* happen. For it was precisely the very godliness of her heart that produced this determined thought, which, in turn, would prevent any such sinful desire from controlling this wonderful young woman's mind.

That night, Mary was kneeling next to her bed, confessing her sin and the sins of her people and praying ardently for the young woman—that the people have would pity on her and show her mercy—when suddenly the light in the room got blindingly bright and Mary started up.

There, standing before her, was the most magnificent being she had ever seen. He looked like a man, but the light seemed to adhere to him as clothing might. Then she realized that the light was indeed a cloak that covered his body from his shoulders to his ankles; his eyes flashed the bluest blue she could have imagined; he was beautiful beyond her ability to describe; and tremendous power seemed to radiate from him—power that bore down on her.

She fell face down on the ground in fear as the being spoke to her with a voice that sounded like a thousand rushing rivers. "Greetings, you who are highly favored. The Lord is with you."[4]

"Oh, please don't hurt me," she murmured, gasping for air, her heart beating wildly.

Suddenly she felt her heart slowing, her breaths coming more easily, and peace descending on her. When she found the strength to look up, she saw that the being's hand was receding from her shoulder, and that he was smiling kindly at her. She suddenly felt completely and utterly safe in his presence. She got back onto her knees and stared into his face, wondering, *What can he mean, the LORD is with me? Who am I that I should find favor with God?*[5]

The angel, for that is what Mary had decided he must be, must have been reading her thoughts, for he said, "Do not be afraid, Mary. You have found favor with God."

She nodded gratefully and got to her feet. With a wave of his hand, the angel indicated that she sit, and she did, on the side of her bed, her hands folded in her lap, staring at him, her eyes wide.

The angel approached her and went to his haunches before her to stare into her eyes. She reached out and touched his forearm. He was warm like a real man, but she felt a tingle go through her finger and it tickled. She giggled, putting that same finger to her lips and then lowering her eyes.

Smiling into her eyes, the angel said softly, "You will be with child and will give birth to a son, and you are to give him the name Jesus. He will be great and will be called the Son of the Most High. The Lord God will give him the throne of his father David, and he will reign over the house of Jacob forever; his kingdom will never end."

As the angel was speaking Mary had several confusing thoughts run through her mind all at once. The first was astonishment that she had been chosen to bear a son to the LORD her God. Amazing! Then, how could this be, since she was to be married to a mere earthly man? And the angel had not mentioned her husband Joseph. Why? Was he not to be the father? Of course not. God was to be the Father. This brought the image of that poor girl on the

---

[4] Mary's interview with the angel Gabriel is recorded for us in Luke 1:26 – 38. Some words have been inserted to aid the flow of the narrative.

[5] Luke quotes the angel as using *kurios* the Greek word for "supreme authority." Mary has translated this in her mind as the word for Jehovah which is how the Jews referred to their God

street to her mind, and unutterable sadness washed over her—how would she explain giving a son to Joseph, but one not conceived by him? What would he say?

Hoping against hope that her earthly husband might be involved in this somehow, hoping for an answer that would calm her confused and fearful heart, Mary asked, "How will this be, since I am a virgin?"

The angel smiled, indicating to Mary that he must have heard her thoughts. "The Holy Spirit will come upon you, and the power of the Most High will overshadow you. So the holy one to be born will be called the Son of God." Seeing her eyes fall, the angel tried to cheer her up with: "Even Elizabeth your relative is going to have a child in her old age, and she who was said to be barren is in her sixth month. For nothing is impossible with God."

Mary understood Gabriel's intent. But she thought, *What will Joseph say to this? Child of the Holy Spirit? Oh come on! I mean, really! I wonder what that poor girl's husband would have thought had she said, "It wasn't my fault, darling. God did it."* Mary smiled despite her despair. Then she bowed her head. A tear ran down her cheek as this thought occurred to her: *What will my beloved think? Will he still love me?* She then remonstrated herself. *What a selfish thought that was! Of course, I am thrilled that God has chosen me. What an honor!* She straightened her shoulders. *Well, what is my earthly happiness compared to God's will?* Mary concluded.

Therefore, she wiped that tear away, looked straight at the angel and said, "I am the Lord's servant. May it be to me as you have said."

Clearly pleased with her answer, Gabriel laid an encouraging hand briefly on her shoulder and then left her in a blinding flash of light.

After considering what had happened for a few moments, Mary curled up in her bed and wept softly. A short time later, she decided that sorrow was not appropriate for the honor she had been shown. She got off her bed, knelt down and gave thanks to the LORD for smiling on her. She also humbly asked that He might speak to her earthly husband to help him understand what would happen. She asked because she knew that if Joseph heard it from the LORD Himself, he would believe and understand and would still want her for his wife.

She was convinced that the LORD had heard her prayer. She therefore knew that everything would be all right. Joseph would never stop loving her, nor would he cease to desire her. With that realization, her tears ceased and a smile crossed her lips. She realized that not only would she be the most blessed woman in the history of the world, but that after God's Son had been born, the LORD would give her gladly to Joseph, the love of her soul, and that He would grant them many children. Her smile broadened as confidence in the LORD filled her completely.

Then she stood and looked to heaven, opened her arms to her God and said in a loud firm voice:

> "My soul glorifies the Lord and my spirit rejoices in God my Saviour, for he has been mindful of the humble state of his servant. From now on all generations will call me blessed, for the Mighty One has done great things for me— holy is his name.
>
> "His mercy extends to those who fear him, from generation to generation. He has performed mighty deeds with his arm; he has scattered those who are proud in their inmost thoughts. He has brought down rulers from their thrones but has lifted up the humble. He has filled the hungry with good things but has sent the rich away empty. He has helped his servant Israel, remembering to be merciful to Abraham and his descendants forever, even as he said to our fathers."[6]

After this she got back into her bed and slept soundly, overwhelming joy filling her heart.

How the LORD loved her! And how He loved her betrothed, who He knew would react to the news in a much different but much nobler way than Mary could have possibly imagined. The God of Abraham, Isaac and Jacob was anxious to deliver the news to her betrothed as she had asked; but because all things must occur in their proper time, the LORD our God waited.

Some weeks passed. Nothing seemed different to the young woman. As usual, she and Joseph and their families met every day to eat at least one meal together. There was a great deal of joy in their homes. She blushed every time Joseph looked at her; she laughed sincerely at all of his little jokes, and even at her father's constant teasing. She even made little jokes herself. Everyone commented on how beautiful, how radiant she had become. That is, as if she were not already stunning, they said to her humble, smiling, lowered eyes. But they thought nothing of it, especially, having

---

[6] Luke 1:46 – 55.

attributed this change in her to the joy of being betrothed to this fine young man, whom they all loved. Which was true, in part.

A few more weeks passed, and one morning she awoke and stretched slowly, deliberately. How wonderful she felt! For a moment. Then her stomach turned. She felt nauseated. She knew! She had been late a week now, and she was never late. It had happened, just as the LORD had said. She needed to tell her parents and her betrothed. She was definitely with child.

So that very morning, as they were eating their first daily meal together, Mary said, "I need to tell you all something." They looked up at her. Joseph smiled and took her hand. She placed her hand over his, leaned close to him, and kissed him softly. By her proximity Joseph sensed that she desired that he take her in his arms, so he did.

She kissed him again and said, "A little more than a month ago, I was visited by an angel." The women gasped and the men grunted with wide eyes, nodding for her to go on. She nestled closer to her beloved. "Gabriel, which was his name, said that God had chosen me to bear our LORD's son." In a tremulous voice she told them all that the angel had told her. "I am with child even now," she exclaimed, turning a fiery red. The silence that greeted her declaration startled her. She looked around at them all anxiously. "Surely you can't be thinking that I …"

Joseph let her go and pushed her gently away from him. This frightened her. He said, "No, my little mouse, I don't think anything like that." She sighed with relief. "I absolutely believe you, my love. I would die before believing that you had done anything to dishonor me or our vow." They all nodded and smiled at Joseph. Mary's heart calmed more. "But what can this possibly mean for our union as man and wife? You are married to the LORD, now." Tears filled his eyes and a tremor came to his voice.

They were tears of such overwhelming disappointment and a tremor of such deep sadness, that Mary wept for him, even knowing what she knew. How she loved him in that moment! How sad he must be, thinking that she could never be his because he thought she was now the LORD's wife. She caressed his cheek and told them, while staring love into Joseph's eyes, what the LORD had told her, that it would be all right for them to get married after His Son was born.

Joseph said, sadness overwhelming him, "My darling, you will be married to the LORD. Who am I that I should step between you and Him?"

Tears rolling down her cheeks, Mary said, "No no no, my dearest treasure. The LORD our God told me that it would be all right. Really!" *Strange,* Mary thought, as she looked into her beloved's tear-filled eyes, her heart beating with fear, *Joseph believes that I will bear God's Son, but he can't seemed to accept that it will be all right to be my husband after.*

Joseph rose quietly. "I must go." Looking longingly at his weeping young friend, he cried, "How I want to be with you, my love!"

She sobbed, "Please don't go, Turtle. Please, it's going to be all right, really."

Tears streaming down his face, the godly young man said in a whisper, "You belong to the LORD now, my little mouse. To the LORD only."

He put his knuckles to his mouth and sobbed, as he had done as a little boy when his heart was breaking, which his beloved mouse noticed, *her* heart breaking also. Then he turned and left, Mary's sobbing pleas chasing desperately after him as he ran out of the door and into the street.

Joseph ran out of the village, into the surrounding countryside and up into the hills. He could not see precisely where he was going because of his blurred vision. However, once he got a hold of himself, he climbed to the top of one of the hills near the city, to a spot he usually went for solitude, a secluded place where he had gone many times to speak with his God.

He looked up to heaven and prayed, "O LORD, how destitute is the soul of your servant. I weep for the loss I have suffered. Yet I give you praise and glory because you have honored my beloved in a way beyond comprehension. I am so proud of her and for her. Yet, I have loved her so very much, more, even, than my own life. I have loved her for as long as I can remember."

Thoughts came to him of the little girl who had come into his life when he was a child. He recalled how he had loved her, even as a little boy, though he had not understood this feeling for some time. Of course while he was a little boy he had acted like she was a nuisance and had appeared to reluctantly tolerate her. But that was because of his childish heart and, truth be told, because of his childish fear of her femaleness and of its strangeness to him. Once they became the very best of friends, he had often thought of telling her how he felt about her. His innate humility and her exquisiteness and desirability as a woman made him afraid that she might reject him as a man, and he could not have borne that.

Well, maybe thinking that she might reject him—absurdly, as he now understood—was not that inexcusable after all because he was such a slow old turtle.

Joseph alternatively laughed and cried at the sound of the word, "turtle". He loved that she called him that. To him it communicated the depths of her love for him.

He then recalled that day when she had looked so extraordinarily lovely that he could not help but declare his love for her, and he recalled her wonderful response. (He blushed.) O how he had praised the LORD his God over and over for giving him the very dream of his heart that day! At least he had thought so. But no. It was never to be. His weeping intensified.

He knelt again, bowed his head and sobbed, "Well, LORD, who was I to think that such a wonderful woman as that could ever be my wife? Me, a nothing, after all. Just a lowly carpenter, a slow old turtle." Looking up to heaven, he said, "LORD, I give this wonderful woman to you with all my heart. She's yours now." Sobbing loudly now, his breath coming in loud gasps, he said, "That means we will have to revoke our vow. I will have to divorce her." How he hated the thought!

After he had managed to pull himself together and wiped his eyes to clear the blurry tears away, and when he had managed to swallow the last sob, he got up and started to walk back to town. He recalled the day of their betrothal and the specter of that poor, adulterous young woman and the outrage of the villagers. This stopped him for a moment. He leaned against a tree and stared into the sky. Well, Mary was pregnant also and not yet finally married. He wondered what these same people might say. Of course he believed that she had not been with another man simply because he was absolutely certain that she would never have allowed any other man to touch her. Why, she had never even allowed *him* to kiss her properly until that day. How frustrating this had been for him! A brief smile fluttered down through his sadness and landed delicately on his lips.

Only to quickly dart away as Joseph pounded a fist into the palm of his hand, saying "No!" loudly. There was simply no possibility that what she was saying was anything other than the truth, though the village wouldn't necessarily believe it. I mean, having a child by a spirit? They'll all laugh at her. She and her family will be disgraced. Joseph's jaw firmed up and he said out loud, "We'll have to find a way of doing this quietly. We'll send her away so that she can have the child away from prying eyes, pointing fingers, and gossiping mouths." He straightened his shoulders and walked with a firm step back toward Nazareth.

It was early evening now; the sun had just set and darkness, that thief of light, was now stealing all the color from the land. How dismal it was! The day had also been warm, and fatigue suddenly overwhelmed the despairing young man. Joseph slowly approached a tree, and with his weary heart weighing him down, he sat down heavily with his back to its trunk. He immediately dropped into a deep sleep, and he dreamt.

Joseph was walking in a beautiful place, full of blooming flowers and green grass. It was a lovely day and the sun was warm, but a delightfully cool breeze was blowing. He heard the sound of rushing white water nearby. He went over to the river's bank and looked down into it. The water tumbled and rolled violently. He knelt down, dipped his hand into the ice-cold liquid and took a drink. It tasted wonderful! Then he looked up and saw a man standing on the other bank. The man smiled at him as Joseph got slowly to his feet.

The man was immediately transformed into a being of surpassing brightness. The light radiating from him blinded Joseph, and he fell to his knees. He then heard the angel's voice saying to him, as if the rushing stream itself were speaking to him, "Joseph, son of David, do not be afraid to take Mary home as your wife, because what is conceived in her is from the Holy Spirit." Joseph knew that. But because of his fear, he had not focused on the first part yet. The angel continued, "She will give birth to a son and you are to give him the name Jesus, because he will save his people from their sins."[7] Then the angel abruptly left him.

Joseph started awake. He wiped the sleep from his eyes and looked around dumbly. He looked up at the dark clear sky. The angel's words came back to him: "Do not be afraid to take Mary as your wife." He jumped up, shouted for joy and turned to run home as fast as he could. Then he stopped suddenly. There was no moon and the ground was rough; it was hard to see the way and he did not want to fall and break something. That meant he would have to walk much more slowly than he would have liked. He laughed at the little joke God was playing on him.

It took more than an hour for him to make it back to Nazareth. After his parents had done with embracing him and telling him how frightened they had been, he told them about the dream. They shouted for joy and embraced him again.

---

[7] See Matthew 1:21.

Then his mother pushed him out the door and pointed him toward Jacob's house. She commanded, "Go over there right now and tell that young woman before she dies of sadness." He chuckled and ran over to tell Mary the news.

When he got there, the door was open and he saw his beloved sitting next to a table, her head resting on her arms; she was looking away from the door, so she could not see him enter. He could see by her trembling shoulders that she must be weeping. Her parents were not around, however, and he was glad, because he wanted to be alone with her. He tiptoed in and put a hand on her shoulder.

Her head went up, but she said without looking around immediately, "Daddy, please ..." She stopped when she saw who it was standing by her side. Her eyes got wide; she jumped to her feet and stared into his eyes. Joseph was struck by how red and puffy her eyes were and how tear-stained her face, and he loved her more in that moment than he could have thought possible. Then he held his arms out to her.

Her face lighting up with joy, she scrambled into his embrace, saying, "Oh, praise God, we were so worried about you. Oh, praise God, praise God. Oh oh oh, my beloved. Beloved beloved beloved." She kissed him passionately, as she had done that first time.

When they finished, Joseph, trying to catch his breath, said between gasps for air and his joyous laughter, "I was visited in a dream." He then told her what the angel of the LORD had told him.

She shouted for joy and hugged Joseph to her as hard as she could. Just then her parents came into the house. Seeing their daughter in her betrothed's embrace, they too laughed for the joy they felt. Then Joseph's parents joined them, and they celebrated the reunion of the two young people.

The next day, they made plans to send Mary to visit her cousin Elizabeth, who was staying in a small village in the hills of Judea. They wanted to get her out of town to avoid the inevitable questions. Mary had protested, of course, while looking into the loving eyes of her husband-to-be.

Joseph said, "It's a good idea. I will go with you. In my mind you are mine, now. Let's get the rabbi and make it official, Dad." Joseph's father heartily agreed.

So Joseph married his betrothed, but he was careful not to instigate any union with her until her Son, the LORD Jesus Christ, was born.[8]

---

[8] Matthew 1:25.

After that day, when she had fully recovered, they did come together, and aside from the glorious day of the LORD Jesus' birth, that night was one of the happiest of both of their lives. Needless to say, the LORD eventually blessed Mary and Joseph with many children in addition to their first-born son, Jesus.[9]

---

[9] Speculation that Mary might have gone to her grave a virgin is not supported by the scriptural accounts of Jesus' life. That she and Joseph finally had physical union is certainly implied in Matthew 1: 25. And the following passages testify that the couple had many children beside Jesus: Matthew 12: 46 – 49; and Matthew 13: 55 – 56, which mentions daughters as well as sons. The same accounts of many brothers and sisters are also given in Mark 3: 31 – 34 and Luke 8: 19 – 21. This also comports with what we know about that culture: for a woman not to have children was like being cursed; a fate for Mary that seems inconceivable in light of how the LORD loved her.

Behold Eternal Value

The law from your mouth is more precious to me than thousands of pieces of silver and gold.
(Psalm 119:72)

Author's Note: In my study of this wonderful psalm, this verse particularly captivated me. This little fable may shed some light on its application.

During the time when kings reigned in Israel and Judah, in a small village in the southern kingdom, there lived an elderly man named Jacob. He was a farmer and he was poor, as were most of the people in his village. Most years his family barely managed to eke out their living, tilling several small fields adjacent to their home. Despite his material poverty, Jacob was content because the LORD had blessed him with a wife he loved dearly and with many sons, daughters, grandsons and granddaughters.

Now Jacob was revered by the people because he trusted the LORD and served Him faithfully, and because he was always careful to carry out the commands of the Law. He was especially careful to bring the required tithes to the priests every three years.[1] He also gave generously to those who were poorer and needier than he. It was not uncommon for him to give his very last bead of sliver to a lame or blind beggar sitting beside the road.[2]

He did all this because he trusted in God to provide for his family. He always had. It is true that Jacob's generosity placed some degree of hardship on them; and it was not uncommon for Jael, his wife, to chide him during the especially bad times, asking, "If you give everything away, how are we going to live?" But old Jacob would simply smile and reply, "My dove, do we ever want for anything? Have we ever not had clothes to wear and food to eat? Have we not always had a house to shelter us from the wind and the rain?" Jael would have to agree because this was true. And she would also have to admit, if you asked her, that though her life with Jacob might be difficult, it

---

[1] Deuteronomy 14: 28.

[2] Before Judah was taken into captivity by the Babylonians, the common specie was the shekel, a weight of about 10 grams, usually of silver. One commonly carried a purse of silver beads or an item of jewelry such as a necklace, bracelet, or ring as money. Coinage was probably not common in Israel or Judah during this time.

was also fulfilling because he loved her, and he was completely devoted to her and their children.

Now Jacob was much sought after as a teacher of the Law, for he carried God's Word in his heart and meditated on it day and night, and he had been careful to teach it to his family exactly as the LORD God had commanded.[3] When this godly man was out on an errand or strolling through the surrounding countryside and praying, which he did often, it was not unusual for a shepherd tending his flock or a farmer gleaning his fields to call out to him to seek his counsel. (Many times they were struggling with some particularly difficult question of faith or with some family hardship, matters which Jacob could handle with delicacy, sympathy and wisdom.) Jacob would always stop, of course. Sometimes he would forget the errand he was on and stay the whole day; which exasperated Jael no end.

Now there had been a famine in the land for some time, and Jacob's fields had dried up for lack of rain. His family had managed to survive so far because they had been living on stored grain. But the stores were running short and they had little money to buy food in the market. Therefore Jacob decided to go out into the hills to pray for the deliverance of the land and his family, confident that the LORD his God would hear him and rescue them.

It was a beautiful spring day in Judah as the elderly saint walked slowly through the hills near his village, quietly praying this passage from one of the psalms of David:

> " 'One thing I ask of the LORD, this is what I seek: that I may dwell in the house of the LORD all the days of my life, to gaze upon the beauty of the LORD and to seek him in his temple.
> " 'For in the day of trouble he will keep me safe in his dwelling; he will hide me in the shelter of his tabernacle and set me high upon a rock.
> " 'Then my head will be exalted above the enemies who surround me; at his tabernacle will I sacrifice with shouts of joy; I will sing and make music to the LORD.
> " 'Hear my voice when I call, O LORD; be merciful to me and answer me.' "[4]

---

[3] Joshua 1:7 – 9 and Deuteronomy 11: 18 – 19.
[4] Psalm 27:4 – 7.

Perplexed that this prayer had not lifted his soul out of the depths of concern as it usually did, Jacob then prayed, "My soul is weary with sorrow; strengthen me according to your word."[5]

As he finished praying, he looked up and saw a dark opening in the side of the hill. *A cave?* Jacob wondered. *I've never seen a cave here before.* He stared dumbly at it. Had he been less taken by surprise he might have noticed that rocks that looked like teeth overhung the entrance, which made it resemble the mouth of a large beast. There was also a gleam of light coming from the opening. Not noticing the resemblance, however, Jacob said to himself, "I will go and see this place."

As the LORD's faithful servant approached the mouth of the cave, the breeze ceased suddenly and the birds stopped singing, as if the Earth itself were holding its breath. Jacob also got the strange impression that the mouth of the cave opened a little wider as he stepped near it. The old man stopped for a moment. But when a refreshingly cool gust of air wafted suddenly out at him from the cave and offered him a welcome respite from the heat of the day—and telling himself that he must be imagining things—he shook off any unease he felt and entered.

As Jacob's eyes became accustomed to the dimness, he saw a path leading deeper into the earth, bending to his left behind a wall of rock, obscuring the back of the cave whence that strange light emanated. As he stepped slowly forward and turned that gentle corner, an enormous cavern opened up. Piled on its floor was the most awesome treasure imaginable. Jacob staggered back, awestruck by the mountain of large polished gemstones, all of startling beauty—sapphires, rubies, onyx, chrysolite, topaz and many others. There were countless bricks of silver and gold and pieces of jewelry, decorative plates, goblets and flagons, all made of gold and silver and inlaid with more jewels. Standing as tall as the ceiling, its feet splayed out to each side of the cavern, Jacob thought that the mountain must completely fill the cave. Amazed at how everything sparkled and gleamed in the dim reddish light that surrounded him, he looked around, searching for the source of that light, but he could not make it out.

His eyes wide, trying to take this all in, Jacob realized that owning even one of these precious things would enable him to feed and clothe his family for years; that having a few of them would allow him to buy sheep, cattle, and great estates of land; that he would never again have to wonder how the

---

[5] Psalm 119: 28.

LORD might rescue him or his family from starvation. As these thoughts occurred to him, his feet seemed to move of their own accord to the foot of the mountain. He stopped and allowed his eyes to work their way slowly to its summit. Then he bent down and slowly picked up one of the stones. He held it up to the dull red light where it sparkled and shone with dazzling beauty.

He heard a scuffling sound behind him.

Coming back to himself, Jacob turned around abruptly to see a man standing behind him. He was dressed in rich purple robes; he had a severe face with jet-black mustache and goatee and piercing black eyes; and he had a crown on his head that shone with a wondrous light. Jacob turned to him, still holding the gem in his hand. Thinking that this man be the lord of this treasure, Jacob held out the stone to him. "Lord, forgive me," he said. "I was walking along the way and saw this cave. A light struck my eyes, and I came in and found this. I realize now that I have trespassed against you, and I am truly sorry."

He turned to put the stone back.

But the lord of the treasure said, "Behold, my son, stop!" Jacob turned around abruptly, clutching the jewel to his chest. The man waved around at the mountain of gems. "Whatever you desire here in this place is yours. You may take as much as you can carry. I have reserved this treasure for such faithful servants of God as you. Take what you wish."

Jacob turned slowly around and began to survey riches beyond imagining, his eyes wide with wonder. As he did, he reflected on all his years filled with bone-crushing labor and want, with pain and suffering. His wife's endless worrying over their poverty came to him. Of course, he reasoned, she had been right to worry. How could he not have realized it until now, he wondered? But all that quickly melted away before him at the promise of riches beyond his wildest imagination. Overwhelming visions of wealth and power began to flow through his mind. He saw palaces, nations, and all the people of the earth kneeling before him.

As Jacob tried to decide which of the stones he might take with him, the lord of the treasure said, maybe a bit hastily, but also quite sweetly, "Of course, there is only one little thing I would ask in return." He raised his finger into the air, a smile creasing his face.

Jacob could not quite be sure, but the man's voice seemed to echo through the chamber. Not with a human tone, though; rather as the snarl of a wild animal rising in volume briefly and then fading quickly away. Jacob also thought he heard myriad other voices carried on that echo, like eerie plaintive sighs, or moans transported on the desperate wings of unimaginable suffering. As these impressions blew through the old man's mind, his thoughts of grandeur evaporated like a wisp of vapor in a gale force wind. The little hairs on the back of his neck bristled; a terrible chill ran through him; and a strange leaden feeling filled his gut. He turned away from the mountain of treasure and dropped the stone at its owner's feet. He straightened his shoulders, narrowed his eyes and asked, "And *just* what might that be?"

The lord of the treasure's smile broadened. "Oh, *just* such a little thing that I am sure you will never miss as you enjoy all the wealth and power that all this," he waved grandly at the gems, "can bring you. All you have to do is to forsake the Word of your God and bow down and worship me." How sweet it sounded!

Fear and shame filled Jacob's heart, which, like flint striking a stone, kindled rage and indignation in the old man's righteous heart, and they burst into searing flame. Without hesitating, he sprang forward and scurried past the grasping arms of the man. Following Jacob from the bowels of the cave and echoing in his mind was a great roar of frustration and a loathsome hiss; also came the wailing of many tormented voices, saying, "Jacob, Jacob come back to us."

As Jacob cleared the mouth of the cave and emerged into the light, the panting old man also felt several chilly streaks flash down the length of his back, as if the claws of some great beast had swiped at him, just grazing his flesh. These immediately became rivers of perspiration that trickled from his shoulders down to his waist. This was a terrifying memento of the evil he had barely escaped, he thought later, as he reflected on this day. He was also convinced that an angel from God had grasped him by the hand and dragged him out of the cave.

After he had run some distance, he stopped to look back. At that very moment the jaws of the cave slammed shut, the rumble of falling rocks pierced the air and the cave was gone.

Jacob started running again, and he did not stop until his breath failed him. Gasping deeply, his knees shaking and his hands trembling, he got on his face before his LORD and prayed, "Almighty Sovereign LORD and Saviour, great is your compassion and faithfulness. How grateful I am that you rescued me from that awful place! I am ashamed to think that I could have for one moment considered taking a single piece of that loathsome treasure. I repent of this with all my heart. In your awesome love, you have truly saved your servant this day."

Sweat still pouring down his face, Jacob got up and looked around him. The sun had now dipped below the horizon, and its blood red light reflected off the clouds overhead. He shuddered, thinking that that could have been *his* blood. And he was amazed that he had been in the cave almost the entire day without realizing it. With that thought, he put all that had happened in the cave behind him and hurried on his way home, knowing that Jael would be worried.

When he arrived, it was very dark, and he found his family gathered around a table. They were weeping. When he entered they all jumped up and embraced him as if he had been gone a month rather than a day.

"What is all this?" he asked his wife, looking around at all the relieved faces staring back at him.

It took a few moments for Jael to let go of him, for she had embraced him and held him tightly. Tears running from her eyes, she replied, "When you did not come back this afternoon, my husband, we sent men out looking for you, but they could not find you. We thought you had been eaten by a lion or a bear." She smiled and caressed his cheek. "I am so glad you are back." Then, in an instant, her smile turned downwards into a frown. She said in a scolding voice, "Where were you?"

"Let me tell you, my treasure." Chuckling at the rapid change in her demeanor, he embraced her. She immediately forgot her anger and hugged him back. "First, I need water," he said, releasing her. "I am dry and parched with thirst." They hurried to get him a water skin, and he drank several deep draughts.

Jael said, "And you must be hungry too." He nodded. So she and several of her daughters leapt up to prepare a meal.

After Jacob had eaten, his family anxiously watching every bite, Jacob motioned for them to gather round. He told them that he had found a cave in the hills and had gone in to see what was inside.

"But, Abba," one of his sons interrupted, "there is no cave in that part of the hills." Many heads nodded in confirmation.

"You are right, Samuel, and there is no cave there now, either," he said with a forceful nod of his head and a stab of his finger into the air. They all looked at each other dubiously. "But there was a cave there this morning. It was the mouth of hell that had opened to me, though I did not realize it then." Many of the adults snickered quietly. The young ones seemed more than willing to believe him, but his oldest sons and daughters smiled patronizingly. Undaunted, old Jacob then told them about the mountain of gems and the man in the cave.

One of the teenage girls whispered, "I wonder if Grandpa hit his noggin on a rock or something." There were some loud shushes, while others argued among themselves about what this might mean.

"I am ashamed to admit," he continued, having difficulty making himself heard over their chattering voices intermingled with dismissive chuckles, "I say, I have to admit …" He was close to shouting now, a clear tone of aggravation sounding in his voice. They all got respectfully quiet. He said more softly now, "I have to admit that I had certain thoughts about that treasure." Looking at Jael, who blushed and bowed her head, he said, "I had certain thoughts about how it might make our lives easier."

His wife reached out to him, saying, "Oh, my husband, I know how much I …"

He took her hand and put his finger to her lips. "No, my treasure, it's all right." She embraced him again, a tear trickling down her cheek. "These thoughts were mine alone, my love," he said into her ear. She hugged him closer. "But when that monster suggested that I forsake my God and bow down and worship him, those thoughts flickered into nothingness like thorns in a flame." They all nodded seriously and smiled respectfully. Smiling in return, he said, "Yes, it's true. I know what it is to have true wealth." He held his wife away from him and kissed her. "Yes, my darling," he continued, hugging her back close to him. "I know what really matters in this life. It's not money at all. It is having you and my sons and daughters here. It is worshipping a God who has given us His word. A God who loves us. That is true wealth!" At least, they could all agree with that. "And in the next life, the treasure that lasts for all eternity comes not from worldly wealth. It comes from knowing this God of ours and His true salvation. As for that man and his false gold, I can't imagine bowing down to that!" They were all equally grateful that he had not.

Now despite the earnestness of his manner, not all of them were completely convinced of the truth of his story. As they retired for the evening, some of them were still smiling skeptically. Others were wondering a little more loudly than they intended whether he had suffered some sort of heat stroke in addition to that "knock on the noggin" proffered earlier.

Later that night, Jacob awoke to the sound of rain pelting his roof. He got out of bed and went over to the slatted window and opened it. As he looked up into the rainy sky, dully lit by a full moon's light glowing happily behind the clouds, he found himself enjoying the coolness of the moisture on his brow; and he praised God that He had brought rain to the land at last.

When he turned back to his bed, he saw something gleaming on the floor next to where he had draped his belt. He went over to it, bent down slowly, and picked it up. When he realized what it was, he loudly sucked in his breath.

This woke Jael, who said with a sleepy voice, "Husband, come to bed, and close the shutters. It's cold!"

He went over to his wife and knelt down in front of her. "Look, Dove!" he said, handing her a large oblong ruby stone, polished so that it gleamed even in the dull light.

She took it with lidded eyes. When she realized what it was, her eyes shot wide open and her hand started to tremble. She turned to her husband and asked, "How?"

Jacob laughed at her expression of astonishment, for he suspected that Jael had doubted his story, despite all her protestations to the contrary.

After that day, there was joy and celebration in Jacob's house and in the entire village, for Jacob sold the ruby for a thousand shekels of gold in Jerusalem, and he shared his newfound wealth liberally with the inhabitants of the village.[6]

---

[6] A thousand shekels of gold was a truly enormous sum in those days. It would have fed and clothed everyone in the village for many years.

No Ribbons for Tillie

*"You have heard that it was said, 'Love your neighbor and hate your enemy.'
But I tell you: Love your enemies and pray for those who persecute you, that
you may be sons of your Father in heaven ... "*
(Matt 5:43 – 45)

*Author's note: Tillie's character was inspired by someone I have known
personally. It's also true that the story of redemption through love cannot be
told often enough. Hence this offering, which bears a similar theme to one
already given, but which allows for how the testimony of a godly servant
might influence others who do not know God as their Saviour.*

There was a large crowd milling around in front of one of New York
City's most prominent hotels. There were also many television crews,
the reporters speaking rapidly, staring into their cameras.

"This is Mike Nunez, reporting for WXZY TV here in Times Square. It
is now 7:30 p.m. As you can see, a large crowd has gathered outside the
entrance to the large ballroom where Mr. Geoffry Mallik, scion of business,
billionaire philanthropist and noted Evangelical Christian will come to accept
the International Peace and Service award for his contributions to humanity. I
can tell you that we are all getting quite anxious as we await the arrival of ...
hey ... I'm busy here!"

Nunez had shouted at one of his competitors who had brushed rudely by
him with his cameraman in tow, trying to get a better view of the large black
limousine pulling up to the curb, another immediately following.

Shaking out his coat and giving the rude person a scowl, Nunez pasted
his smile back on and turned back to the camera. "That first car must be
Mallik's car." He pointed toward the limousine. "The second must contain
his security detail."

Immediately the cameraman focused on six very large men, clad in black
business suits who had emerged from the second car and began to make a
pathway through the crowd. Some did not bother to fully conceal their
weapons.

The reporter waved a hand at the men. "Well, it looks like it will be a
few moments before the guest of honor makes his appearance. So as we
watch and wait for him, I will tell you that Mr. Mallik is being cited for his
tireless crusade against the spread of the AIDS virus. It has long been known
that he has used his enormous fortune to set up foundations throughout the

third world, focusing principally on the continent of Africa, to fight this dreaded plague, which now infects over eighty percent of its population. That's why he is being recognized today. It is worthy of note that he has never been shy about admitting that his crusade has been motivated by his profoundly held religious beliefs, which have made him many enemies over the years. That's the reason for all the security. But his friends in the Evangelical community have labeled him the billionaire evangelist, the reincarnation of Billy Graham, who was a famous twentieth century evangelist. They say that Geoffry Mallik has tirelessly ..."

The crowd roared and drowned out the reporter's voice as the rear door of the first limousine opened. As Nunez turned and his cameraman focused on the car, a tall, dapper, handsome gentleman, graying at the temples and dressed in a tuxedo, emerged. As he stepped onto the curb, the crowd surged toward him. His men had to shove them aside so that he might make his way into the hotel. The WXZY reporter extended his microphone through the crowd and shouted some questions at Mr. Mallik as he passed by, but the reporter was shoved aside as the Christian billionaire was led through the crowd and into the hotel.

As Mallik disappeared into the hotel, Nunez cleared his throat and smiled sheepishly as he turned back to his camera. "I guess he's not answering any questions right now."

Inside, the dinner guests were assembling around their tables in the enormous room. The sound of their voices filled it with a low roar, punctuated from time to time by the clink of glasses being filled with ice water and the wrenching of chairs as the people took their seats. On the north side of the room, a dais had been erected on which a long table sat. In the middle of the dais was a podium prominently displaying the emblem of the International Community of Humanity—a large light blue oval in the center of which were the white letters ICH emblazoned over the outlines of Europe, Africa and Western Asia. To the podium's right and left were ten seats, and the room was filled with dozens of circular tables that sat eight people each. It was clear from the great throngs of people moving between the tables that there would not be a vacant seat for this event.

Promptly at 8:00 p.m., the guest of honor and his hosts began to file into the room, and the sound of voices dimmed as people turned to watch them enter. As they took their places on the dais and sat, Mr. Mallik sat two seats to the viewer's right of the podium. Then a short skeletally thin man from a West African nation noted for the affliction of its population with the AIDS virus, stepped up to the podium and stood for a moment surveying the room.

When the crowd quieted down he intoned in heavily accented English, "Ladies and gentlemen, welcome to the sixth annual International Peace and Service awards banquet. Please take your seats." There was a cacophony of chairs being moved and a swell in the sound of voices. When everyone was seated and had quieted down again, the host said, "Thank you. The meal will be served momentarily." He looked around the room again and the people followed his eyes to see that an army of waiters and waitresses, dressed in dinner dress, was preparing to begin serving.

The host said, "In respect of Mr. Mallik, we have invited a man of his own Christian faith, the Reverend Mark Jones, to invoke God's blessing on this gathering."

There were murmurs from the crowd as a graying thin man walked up to the podium. He looked at the upturned faces and said, "I've known Geoff for many years, and we both understand that there are many faiths represented here tonight. Nevertheless, we feel compelled to give thanks to the One whom we believe to be the God of the universe." The murmurs got louder. Unwilling to give in to the hostile faces in the crowd, Pastor Jones went on, "So please bow your heads to the deity you worship and follow me as we invoke God's blessing on this meal."

A short prayer was offered asking that God bless this time and that He shower His blessings on all assembled. Not all heads bowed and there were some frowns; but most of the owners of the frowns and the upraised heads remained respectfully silent until the man of faith had finished, saying, "In the name of your Son, Jesus Christ, we pray, Amen."

During the prayer, some had stood and started to walk out of the room, but they were gently restrained by their colleagues. Such rudeness to the honor of this man would be unspeakable, they said. The offended parties reluctantly sat back down, staring with narrow eyes at Mr. Mallik.

As the meal was served, there were still many murmurs from those who mocked the Name of God. Nevertheless, some of these were mollified by the excellent cuisine and the fine wine that had been served. These came from the hands of a famous French chef of one of the city's best restaurants, who had volunteered her services for the evening out of respect for Mr. Mallik's work.

When they were almost done eating, the African host rose. "Ladies and gentlemen," he said, "it is time to begin the ceremony." He looked at Pastor Jones and then at Mr. Mallik. "I am Muhammad Ngambe, and I too have known Geoffry Mallik for a long time. Therefore, it is my distinct honor to introduce him to you, though he needs no introduction, of course." Mallik seemed relieved. Mr. Ngambe, smiling at his blushing guest, said, "Having said that, I'm going to introduce him anyway." There was a smattering of laughter when Mallik, by a facetious wave of his hand, affected a bit of irritation with his friend.

Mr. Ngambe then gave a brief biography of a man who had risen steadily in business to become the largest shareholder of one of the biggest media conglomerates in the world—the United Christian Network. There was a smattering of applause, while others shook their heads, their eyes narrowing further. He went on to say how Mr. Mallik had given hundreds of millions of dollars to worthy causes. This time the applause was loud and was accompanied by many cheers, which were especially loud at the tables of the African delegates whose countries had benefited most from Mallik's philanthropy.

When the room had quieted, Mr. Ngambe continued, saying that this work was the result of Mr. Mallik's great faith in God. He was also careful to point out how Mr. Mallik always gave God the glory for his work. Some applauded, while others frowned. But when the black man mentioned how the work of Mr. Mallik's various foundations had been credited with saving millions of lives from AIDS-related diseases, loud applause followed again, especially from the African tables.

Having seen the many irritated expressions, which did not surprise Mr. Ngambe, since he knew that Christianity had many enemies in the room, he did not bother to mention that these same foundations had also brought the Christian Gospel to many millions, converting hundreds of thousands to the Christian Faith, as he also had been converted, though he still retained his Muslim name. As he went on at some length about the work of Mr. Mallik's various charitable foundations and their notable achievements, Mr. Mallik's head remained bowed modestly. Many in the audience could not help but admire his humility. When the host finished, the sound of polite applause filled the room.

Then Mr. Ngambe introduced the next speaker, the President of the ICH, who would present the award. A graying, elderly Swedish man, Dr. Bjørn Johansen, sitting immediately to the left of the podium stood. After the applause had died down, Dr. Johansen took out a large sheaf of papers and began reading his remarks introductory to the presentation of the award.

Now a curious thing happened as he was speaking. A young man, clearly a hotel employee, came into the room to the right of the dais and motioned an envelope toward Mr. Mallik. One of the bodyguards took the envelope from him, checked it briefly and motioned the young man away from the dais. He then slipped behind the dais and handed the envelope to the guest of honor.

The speaker was oblivious to all this, however, as he read on and on in a droning monotone, scarcely bothering to look up at his audience. Nor did he notice that no one seemed to be paying attention to him as the guest of honor opened the envelope, read from two small pieces of yellow telegram paper, and then pulled back abruptly as if he had been struck. Some hands went to mouths in the audience and many heads turned toward each other, whispering, keeping one eye on Mr. Mallik. Their murmurs were loud enough that they could not hear the speaker very clearly, but Dr. Johansen kept reading as if he were the only one present. And the voices increased more in volume when Mallik placed a hand to his brow and began to shake his head slowly.

After about ten minutes, the steadfastly oblivious elderly man turned to the guest of honor and motioned for him to stand and approach the podium. The audience noticed with some amusement that he did not make eye contact with Mallik.

Geoffry Mallik stood slowly, placed his napkin on his plate and approached, his head still bowed. Those closest to the podium could see that his eyes were red, and no one thought it was from the joy he might have gotten from his award. When he wiped his eye with a finger and turned away from the audience briefly, the murmur volume increased to a low roar. The still oblivious speaker raised a gold-rimmed placard on which words of praise and honor had been elaborately engraved and read from it, his voice reflexively increasing in volume to overcome the noise from the audience. All the while, Mr. Mallik stood quietly, facing the audience but staring red-eyed over their heads.

When the president of the ICH was done, he motioned to another man who approached the guest of honor and placed a large purple silken sash over his head and draped it over one shoulder slantwise and around Mr. Mallik's waist. It was quite beautiful. All the while Dr. Johansen had been looking straight ahead and smiling at the audience. A few in the crowd joked quietly that he had still not seen his guest, because he had not bothered to glance in his direction once during the entire ceremony. But when the smiling elderly ICH official managed to look into Mr. Mallik's eyes, his head shot up. He slowly handed the placard to him and then went back to his seat, his turn to appear unsettled as the guest of honor stepped up to the podium.

A hush fell on the crowd as Geoffry Mallik took several folded pieces of paper from his breast pocket with trembling hands, laid them on the podium and stared at them for a few moments. He then looked up at the audience and began with a quivering voice, "Let there be no doubt ladies and gentlemen, that I am greatly honored to receive this recognition for God's work in the world."

There were some murmurs and the narrowed eyes now superposed some thin-lipped grimaces.

Unaffected by these hostile stares, Mr. Mallik continued. "When I say God's work in the world, I mean God's work done in me through the work of His Holy Spirit. Therefore in giving me this gift, you have honored Him as well."

Many heads turned and now a few more grimaces darkened the faces in the crowd.

His voice becoming firmer now, Geoffrey Mallik continued, "You all know that I have never hesitated to proclaim the Gospel of my God, and that I have done it throughout the world. So you should not be surprised by these remarks. For without Him working in my life, none of this would have happened." He waved his hand over the placard, which lauded his Service to Humanity. The speaker looked down at some of the broader frowns and asked, "That is my right to believe, is it not? Whether you disagree, I am allowed that right, am I not?"

The murmurs quieted. Some faces got red, not with shame at their hypocrisy as one might think, but rather with outrage, their owners squirming in their seats.

Mr. Mallik sniffed audibly and dabbed at his eyes with a handkerchief he had hastily removed from his breast pocket. He looked at the letter that he had gotten and then at the other pieces of paper lying in front of him. "I came tonight with a short prepared statement. I did not think it necessary to bore you with a long-winded speech, since that has been done already." He looked slyly at his African friend, who laughed heartily. There was also some sympathetic laughter in the crowd.

"I want to tell you a story instead. It won't take long. I'm sure that every one of you here who has a loved one who has benefited from our work will come to understand why I feel compelled to tell it."

The black faces from Africa leaned forward in their seats and watched the speaker with eager eyes. Many others followed suit.

Geoffrey Mallik wiped at his eyes again. "This message I just received gives the sad end to that story, though. Let me quote." He took one of the pieces of paper and read, "Geoff, I was so glad to hear of your award. What a testimony to God's work you are! I am so proud of you. Remember me in your prayers. Love, Tillie."

There were loud murmurs now.

Then Mallik took the other piece of paper and, his voice breaking and tears streaming down his cheeks, he read, "From Aidous Hansen, Director, Christian Vision for the World in Western Africa, to Mr. Geoffry Mallik. Geoff: We are so very sorry to inform you that our wonderful sister Matilda Owen was brutally murdered last night in the village of Ngama. She was comforting several young women who had lost their babies to AIDS related diseases. They also died in the attack. They were hacked to death by machetes and then the hut in which they were staying was burnt down around them. Tillie Owen was certainly murdered because she was a follower of our LORD Jesus Christ. We included her message to you, which we found in the ruins, thinking you would like to have it anyway."

There were groans from the crowd, which stopped Mallik briefly.

When the noise died down Mallik said, "Well, they go on to speculate who murdered my very best friend in the world, but I won't share that with you." There were many muffled voices in the crowd, and many eyes glanced at their African host, who had shaded his eyes with his hand and had bowed his head because this awful deed had been done in his country. Meanwhile, Mr. Mallik looked down at the sash around his shoulders and murmured to himself, "How much more did Tillie deserve this little ribbon than I?"

When the voices in the crowd died down, Mr. Mallik turned to his friend and asked, "I believe you knew Tillie, didn't you Muhammad?" The weeping man looked up and nodded quietly, his eyes red and puffy, and his face streaked with glistening tear tracks. The speaker turned to the audience. "It's too bad that most of you did not know her. She is the reason I am standing before you today. It is she, much more than I, to whom this award is owed." He motioned to his sash.

"I first met Matilda Owen when I was in the third grade. We went to school together in a suburb of San Francisco in the U.S. state of California." He took a deep breath and bit his lip. He seemed to lose the thread of his story as he said, "You know, it's amazing as I think about it now how cruel children can be, sometimes. I guess murder, like that done here, is done by people who never outgrow this childish penchant for cruelty. Why did I say that, you wonder? " There were many nodding heads.

"Well, when I first met Tillie Owen I did not understand her. You see, she was what we would call today a special child; back then she was what we called "cripple" because she had been born with a mild case of cerebral

121

palsy, which caused her some trouble walking and sometimes with speaking. She was also what we might call today a gifted child; back then she was a retard to us because she was a slow learner. It turns out that she was dyslexic, but we did not understand dyslexia all that well at the time. She was certainly not mentally retarded; in fact, she was one of the brightest people I have ever met. She was also a gangly child and not pretty to look at by any means. Some even might have thought of her as being ugly." He lowered his eyes briefly. "What I did not know then, but have come to clearly understand now, was that many of us kids were afraid of her because her father was what we call now a fundamentalist Christian preacher. I was one of those kids."

Mr. Mallik paused and looked knowingly at certain frowning faces before saying: "We are always afraid of what we don't understand, don't you think? And that's why we want to kill it."

Murmurs filled the room, and some red faces got redder, their ugly expressions fully revealing how much they hated this man and his God.

Mallik took a deep breath and looked into the air. "But to God, as to me after I had gotten to know her, she had the most beautiful soul of any human being on earth. How do I know this? Well, let me tell you how.

"The kids loved to make fun of Tillie and taunt her. As she hobbled off the bus they would shout 'cripple', 'duck', 'slug', 'fanatic', 'retard' and other such things at her. You know who was shouting these things the loudest?" Choking in his grief, all Mr. Geoffry Mallik could do was point at himself, though the audience greeted this revelation with some degree of incredulity. "Yes, really. And much to my shame!" He sniffed and wiped at his eyes again.

"But you know what was amazing about her?"

By the audience's expressions you could tell that most all of them eagerly wanted to know, including many of those who had been the most outraged at his profession of faith.

"She never fought back or said an angry word to any of us in response." There were murmurs indicating disbelief. "No, indeed!" Geoff Mallik said flatly. "I learned later that she cried a lot, but she never let us see her cry. Rather, she would go into the girl's room and cry her eyes out. There were times when we would be sent home with notes from the principal, and I was certainly given "a good talking-to" by my folks. I didn't care all that much, of course, because it was fun to make sport of poor Tillie Owen. And we never got any threats of retribution from her or from her parents."

This was greeted by more looks of astonishment, to which he replied simply by nodding affirmation. The murmurs got louder.

"My parents did get a visit from Tillie's father one time, though. Tillie's parents lived a street or so away from us, as it turned out, though we had not met them before. Well, he came over and asked if he might see me, so my folks invited him in. They sat with me as he patiently explained his daughter's disabilities to me and to my folks by extension. He then asked humbly if I might show her a little more consideration. He never mentioned how much our taunts hurt his daughter, though. I said yes, of course, never really intending to let up." Mallik stopped, wiped an eye again and looked up; he then laughed out, "He even invited us to a Sunday service. He left a church bulletin with us. My parents graciously thanked him, of course, and promised that I would behave. He nodded and left. Of course that church thing went right into the garbage. My parents hated any form of religion, especially my dad.

"Now we had many athletic events for grade-schoolers in those days. Swimming was especially popular. I remember one time when we had a swimming meet, we were all in fifth grade, I think, and Tillie Owen had entered the girls' half of the meet. She was pathetic, of course, but she finished her first heat. Some of the other girls had dropped out because the heats were swum in lengths of one hundred yards. Not Tillie. She splashed and slapped at the water relentlessly until she finished. It must have taken her ten minutes.

"I got to watch the whole thing because I had finished my heat earlier. I think it was the first time that I allowed myself to admire her. I remember asking myself if I would ever have the guts to do something hard like that. You see, everything has always come so easy to me—I eventually won my grade level in record time—while all ol' Tillie could do was splash and flail away.

"I must mention that we all called her ol' Tillie because when she walked she scuffled along like an old lady." He sniffed again, and for the first time tears welled up in many eyes in the audience.

"After I received my first place award and was standing on the podium, they invited Tillie Owen up to give her an honorable mention for her heroic effort. I was surprised, as were the second and third place finishers. While they were laughing and making jokes, I remember looking at the smile on Tillie's face and the delight in her eyes. I also remember thinking that our prizes were not worth one tenth as much to us as Tillie's was to her. Nor was our accomplishment nearly as great. Of course, I did not have the guts to tell my friends that I admired her for what she had done. I knew that that would have turned them against me, and I could not have borne that!"

There were some loud sniffles from the audience now. Many of the women, and even a few of the men, had taken out handkerchiefs and were dabbing their eyes repeatedly.

Mallik looked down at his sash. "You know what I got for winning? It was a fancy purple ribbon something like this. Tillie's honorable mention was only a piece of paper." Many in the audience looked around at each other. Seeing that look, Mr. Mallik said, "Now that I think of it, if they had dumped a hundred such ribbons on her it would not have done her justice." People turned to each other and began to whisper among themselves. "I never admitted to myself how much I really admired her then," Mr. Mallik added. "But I'll shout it to the whole world now!" The whispers grew in volume.

Ignoring the noise, the speaker looked down at the podium and said softly, "Now that I think about it, the only winner in God's eyes that day was Tillie Owen."

Some heads nodded, and a few more eyes started to glisten. The whispers now seemed to fill the entire room like a gentle mist, a cloud of tears raining down sorrow and regret, as many in the audience recalled their own childhoods and maybe a few of the Tillies they too had known.

Geoffrey Mallik waited until the mist cleared somewhat before continuing. "Some time later, while I was in class, the principal came to the door of the classroom. He glanced at me and motioned for the teacher to come over to him. He whispered something to her, and she looked at me. I'll never forget the look on her face." He stopped for a moment and breathed out a deep breath. "She waved to me to stand and to come to her. I did, and she told me to go with Principal Martin. So I got my books and went with him."

He stopped for a moment. There were some nervous rustles in the audience and many squirmed impatiently in their seats.

"When I got to his office he sat me down in a chair, sat close to me, put his hand on my shoulder and said, 'Geoff, I've got some bad news for you.' I will always remember how sad that look on his face was, even as tears welled up in my own eyes. I will always remember those tears because I could not see his face very clearly as he said, 'It's your father. He, well, he ...' Mr. Martin stopped and looked at the ceiling as if he were searching for the word he needed, hoping to get it from something or Someone up there. Then he looked down at me with tears in *his* eyes and said, 'Geoff, your father died this morning. He fell dead all of a sudden. It was his heart. Just gave out, they say.' I don't recall what he said next because I had begun to cry. I do recall how he put his hands on my shoulders and said with a breaking voice, the sound of which I will always remember, 'I am so sorry, son. We'll get Miss Anderson to take you home.' Miss Anderson was the school nurse and one of the nicest ladies in the world. At least, that's how I always thought of her. So I allowed Mr. Martin to lead me to her office, and she drove me home. I was crying the whole way, of course."

There were more tears in the audience, and some of the women were audibly weeping and their escorts took them in their arms as the women lay their heads on their shoulders.

With a gulp, Mr. Mallik said, "I'll never forget that day. Do you know who I found to be with my weeping mother when I got home?" They all mouthed the word "no". "It was Tillie's father. He was holding Mom's sobbing shoulders in his arms. When Mom saw me, she left his embrace and held me to her, and we cried for a long time. Tillie's mother and some of the church ladies also came over and began to set plates of food on a table along with some of the neighbors.

"I guess I should mention that after Tillie's father visited us that first time, Tillie's mother made it a mission to become friends with my mother. And she succeeded. She even talked Mom into coming to church, which she did. In fact, she started going every Sunday. She'd drag me along, but I wasn't very fond of it at first.

"Well, after I had finished crying with my mom, I went to my room and lay on my bed and was crying my eyes out when I heard someone come in. I looked up and who do you think it was that had come to console me?"

Several hundred mouths formed the word, "Tillie."

Geoffry Mallik said, "Yep, Tillie. That 'ugly 'crippled' girl of eleven or so that I had so mercilessly teased and taunted sat down beside me and opened her arms to me, and I put my head on her shoulder and cried, my heart breaking. I'll never forget how she embraced me and held me close to her. I can still remember feeling the beating of her heart as she held me and murmured sweetness in my ear."

The audience wept more loudly.

"So after all the bad things I had done to her, and by extension, to her family, what did I get in return?" He looked around the room. "What *I got* in return was love and caring." He sighed audibly. "Needless to say, my attitude toward church people changed dramatically after that day, and I was more eager to go with my mother to Mr. Owen's church. After a few months, I accepted the LORD Jesus Christ as my Saviour. I was baptized about a year later." Looking upward toward the ceiling, he said reflectively, "How I loved that church and its people. I've never met better, kinder, godlier people than at Tille's father's church." He looked back down at his African friend, who smiled up at him, as if he too had known these wonderful people his whole life.

"It was during that time that I got to know Tillie Owen, and we became close friends. The very closest of friends. After this, there was no more teasing, of course. Especially after I got into a fight with one of my friends when he teased her." Mallik raised his chin and said, "And I beat him up pretty good too."

Some disapproving faces looked up at him, but the speaker said defiantly, "Got in a lot of trouble for that, of course, but I didn't care. After my father died, it did not take long for Tillie and me to become the best of friends. And if I ever needed any encouragement, Tillie was there to provide it." The speaker stopped and looked down at the podium. He said softly, "It seems so funny, really, that it was she, with all her limitations and disadvantages, who was encouraging me when it should have been I who encouraged her."

There were a few nodding heads.

"Many of you might be surprised to know that I came to love Tillie Owen. I have never loved anyone as I loved her. That's the reason I've never married. I eventually came to know that she had always loved me, though why, after all I did to her, I'll never understand. I came to believe that we loved each other with that kind of love that would normally have resulted in marriage." Many of the women smiled sadly. "We never married because she had felt God's call to be a missionary, and I could never have done that."

Some of the looks he got sent a message that could not have been clearer if "How sad for you, you poor man!" had been shouted at him.

"And another reason was …" He paused again and many of the people, especially the women, scooted toward the edges of their seats. "Well, it was because I never considered myself worthy of her."

Every woman sighed, smiled sadly, and shook her head slowly.

Geoffrey Mallik exhaled loudly and looked down at the little pieces of paper. "It bears repeating again. It's because of her that I stand here today. It was because of her belief in me that I was able to attain some modest degree of wealth." There were many groans. He ducked his head. "Well, maybe a little more than modest." There was laughter, but accompanied by many loud sniffles as well.

He looked down at his sash and took it off slowly. "Well," he concluded with a sniff, "when we were children, there were never any ribbons for Tillie. No, no ribbons for Tillie at all. But there will be one terrific reward that day when the very King of the Universe Himself bestows the greatest gifts of all on this wonderful woman—a Crown of Righteousness and the gift of Eternal Life. I can't wait to see it!"

Bowing his head solemnly, Mr. Mallik said, "This is how I will always remember Matilda Owen, and maybe some of you will too."[1] He looked up at the ceiling and said softly, reverently,

> "It seems that God has put His servants around the world on display at the end of the procession, like men condemned to die, and they have been made a spectacle to the whole universe, to angels as well as to men. They are fools for Christ when others consider themselves wise; they are weak when others consider themselves strong, and dishonored, when others much less worthy are given great honor!"

There were some very outraged faces in the crowd, but Mr. Geoffry Mallik took no notice as he continued.

> "For the sake of the LORD's work, they will eagerly go hungry and thirsty, and are content to remain clothed in rags and to be brutally treated, or to go homeless.
>
> "And they work so very hard!"
>
> "When they are cursed, they bless; when they are persecuted, they endure it; when they are slandered, they answer kindly. It seems that many consider them the scum of the earth and the refuse of the world. And many are murdered in return for the kindness they show others.
>
> "Such was Matilda Owen, dearly beloved of God, who loved Him and served Him with all her heart and soul."

Mr. Mallik bowed his head, slowly took his seat and rested his head in his hands. No one spoke. And even faces that had been outraged before, many of whom considered themselves servants of God, looked sheepishly around at some of their colleagues who had found the gift of Eternal Life by the Grace of Almighty God.

After a few moments of silence, Geoffrey Mallik rose and left the stage. Everyone else got up and left the room quietly.

---

[1] The following homage to Tillie Owen was inspired by 1 Corinthians 4: 9 – 13.

Healing the Blind

As [Jesus made his way away from the Temple grounds], he saw a man blind from birth ... Jesus said, "For judgment I have come into this world, so that the blind will see and those who see will become blind."
(John 9:1, 39)

Author's note: Except for raising the dead, which Jesus did on several occasions, the miracle He performed by restoring the blind man's sight was one of the most astounding. Like restoring and then raising Lazarus' corrupt body from the grave, our Sovereign LORD had to perform a creative act to give the blind man the necessary biological functions that would allow him to see. But that is only half the story. This man became one of the first great witnesses of Jesus' lordship to the Jews in Judea. I have always been impressed by the blind man's courage in the face of the withering fire of scorn heaped on him by the Pharisees.

Simon liked to allow the heat of the dawn to shine on his face.[1] So as the sun started to rise over the walls of the city, he turned away from the crowds marching up the temple steps to let it warm him. He had never actually seen the sun—he had been blind from birth—but he always imagined that it must be like those intense fires his mother would stoke in the oven as she was preparing to bake their daily bread. He imagined that it was crackling and burning furiously up there, somewhere in the sky, where all the stars were; where God lived—in heaven. Yes, Simon decided, maybe the sun was the fire of God's own oven, baking his heavenly bread each day. *I bet heaven always smells wonderful, then,* Simon thought with a chuckle. Chuckling more, he said to himself, "Mom always said I had a good imagination."

He sighed and turned away from the warming rays. He fumbled with his cup, and holding it in front of him, he called out to the passersby, "Alms for the poor. Alms for a poor blind man. Alms."

Simon had always had to beg for his daily bread. It was such a shameful way to make a living, though, and it made him feel awful. He hated that people pitied him and that they gave out of their pity. "Well," he mused

---

[1] The name "Simon" is fictional. We are never told by Scripture what the blind man's name is.

quietly, "maybe that was the only reason they could find to give. Why else would they? But who are they to pity me?" For, Simon reasoned, God had always been good to him; his parents were still alive and they loved him; his family had always had enough to eat and a roof over their heads; and he had his friend Nicodemus to watch over him and his family. "Praise God for friends like Nicodemus," Simon murmured to himself.

Now there was this great prophet of God who had come to Simon's people, a man from Nazareth named Jesus. The blind man heard him preaching and teaching in the temple on several occasions. He had even sneaked up to listen from time to time. Actually, Nicodemus had helped him up the steps, but Simon had been sneaking in his mind, nevertheless. He smiled at the equivocation.

And there was the time the young rabbi had gone into the temple and thrown out the moneychangers and bird sellers. What a ruckus that caused! There were certainly a lot of feathers ruffled that day; and they were not all dove's feathers either! Of course there was the yelling and cursing of the Pharisees and the temple officials, but only after the teacher had left. They did not have the courage to curse him to his face, of course. Cowards!

Then there was Nicodemus. A Pharisee too, Simon had to admit. But one of the very few decent Pharisees in Judea.

With this thought, Simon spat on the ground between his feet. The rest of them were all a bad lot. How he hated them! "They pile burden upon burden on our backs," he murmured to himself, "burdens they would not lift a little finger to carry themselves. Then, when we crumple to the ground, groaning under their impossible weight, they bring us before their Sanhedrin to flog us, or to put us out of the synagogue."

Simon shuddered. Being put out of the synagogue was almost worse than dying because you would be shunned; no one—well no Jew at least—would dare do business with you; and you and your family could lose everything you owned, including your home.

Nicodemus was not like them, though. He was kind and thoughtful. He always gave generously. Where one of *them* might put a *lepta* or two in Simon's cup (that is if they could be bothered), well, Nicodemus would put in a lot more than that![2] And almost every day too! Simon also knew that he

---

[2] A *lepta* was a small bronze coin minted by the Jews. The name implies 'the smallest coin imaginable.' Eight *lepta* equaled one copper *as*. Sixteen copper *as* equaled one silver *denarius*, which was a day's wage. Therefore it took approximately one hundred twenty-eight *lepta* to equal one silver *denarius*.

and Nicodemus were kindred spirits in that they shared outrage at the awful things perpetrated on the people by these evil men. Simon knew how this kind and godly man hated their evil ways.

Suddenly, out of the cacophony of voices and the scuffling crowd, Simon's thoughts were interrupted by the sound of feet approaching him. He could tell by their owner's distinctive odor who the person was, and he smiled. Clink, clink, went the sound of two large coins dropped into his cup. They were heavy!

Simon rattled the coins around in the cup. He said over the loud clinking, "I was just thinking of you, my friend."

Nicodemus answered, "Well, then, I can see that you are keeping your thoughts on good and excellent things." They both laughed heartily. When he could manage, Nicodemus cleared his throat and said, "I've put two *denarii* in your cup, my friend. If you don't have at least that when you get home, let me know."

Simon nodded. Stealing from the blind was not an unheard of crime in Jerusalem those days. "Thank you very much, my friend," he replied with a smile. "You are too kind to a poor beggar boy."

A loud sigh told him that Nicodemus was being modest, as usual; but Simon could sense that there was something else there too. This troubled the blind man. Ignoring this for the moment, however, he said, "No, you really are the kindest of men, allowing me to hear the great teacher teach. Well, I felt kind of important sitting among all you *really important people,* you know." Nicodemus chuckled at the sarcasm in his friend's tone of voice.

With a little pressure on the Simon's shoulder, Nicodemus indicated that he should make room for Nicodemus to sit next to him, and the blind man quickly scooted over.

A quiet moment or two passed, during which Simon could sense that this kind man was staring at him. The blind man had never seen a kind look, but he knew that that was the way Nicodemus was looking at him. This gave him the courage to ask, "Is something troubling you, my friend?"

Nicodemus sighed again, touched the young man's wrist lightly, and asked, "How is it that you can tell that I am troubled, Simon? Sometimes I think you see more than any of us." Simon blushed and bowed his head. "No, really," the kind, godly scholar continued, "the way you talk about the Scriptures. Your faith in God. Your comments as the teacher spoke were especially insightful."

"You're embarrassing me, you know. And it takes a lot of doing to embarrass a beggar, especially a blind beggar." Nicodemus did not laugh as

Simon hoped. Not to be denied, the blind man chuckled and grabbed at his friend's wrist, took it firmly and gently shook it.

Nicodemus laughed obediently. "Well, my friend," he said, affecting a jovial tone of voice, "at least I've accomplished something good today, then."

After they had patted each other on the back a few times Simon asked, "So, what's up?"

There was another deep intake of breath, and he felt his friend's body shift around a little. When Nicodemus spoke, it was obvious to Simon that he was not looking directly at him. The blind man imagined that he must be staring off into the distance.

"Well, my friend, I'm wondering where our nation is headed." He took another deep breath. A slight movement of Nicodemus' body indicated to the blind man that he was shaking his head slowly. "We have seen the greatest prophet of the age come to us," he said sadly, "yet by the way my colleagues are acting you'd think he was the devil incarnate."

Simon spat outrage on the ground in front of him.

"Yes, my friend, I agree," Nicodemus responded sympathetically. "The Sanhedrin hates this man and what he teaches. By extension they hate anyone who subscribes to his teaching. Think how much they'd hate someone who started to preach like him." Nicodemus sighed again. "You asked what's troubling me? Well, I guess I'm wondering what have we come to that we would actually talk about killing this man?"

Simon started. Killing? Killing a teacher and great prophet who could work miracles? He squirmed, his outrage building in him. He could sense that his friend had turned back to face him now.

"I can see in your face how you feel, Simon. Please don't speak of it too loudly. Maybe I should not have mentioned it." The blind man acknowledged this warning by touching his friend's wrist. Nicodemus, obviously relieved, said, "Remember! Be discreet, my friend. There are ears everywhere; and I'd hate to see you or your family get, well, get hurt, if you know what I mean."

Simon sighed through clenched teeth. "I do certainly know what you mean, my friend," he said. He knew that his friend was referring to his family and him being thrown out of the synagogue. "If I weren't blind," he growled, "I'd march right up to that cowardly lot of despicable men and tell them a thing or two, and the devil take the consequences." A shudder by Nicodemus made Simon backtrack. "I know, my friend," the blind man said, patting him on the shoulder. "I know. It's useless to fight them."

"You know," Simon mused, "we always talk about being oppressed by the Romans. I think that's an excuse our leaders use to cover up their own mendacity and pusillanimity. Who's oppressing whom here, anyway? It's not the Romans who flog us or put us out of the synagogue for daring to take issue with these self-righteous hypocrites." Heat rising in the blind man, his voice had also risen in volume. He could sense, by the sudden diminution of the noise of the surrounding crowd, that others were taking an interest in his conversation.

His friend's hand covered his wrist. "Please, my friend," Nicodemus urged softly, "do not speak too loudly. There are others ..." His voice drifted off ominously.

Understanding this, Simon whispered, "I know, Nico, I know. I don't want to get you into trouble, me being such a threat and all." Then he deadpanned, "You know how much trouble we blind beggars can cause."

Relieved by his humor, Nicodemus slapped him on the back, took his hand and squeezed it warmly. "Well, again, be careful," Nicodemus warned. "And remember what I said about those two coins. If I were you, I'd put them in my belt. Now!" Simon immediately took the coins and stuffed them into the purse in his belt. Nicodemus said forcefully, "Good!" Patting his friend's hand, he said, "Well, I need to go. It's Sabbath and there's a lot to do today. It's strange, isn't it, that we priestly types seem to work *hardest* on the Sabbath?"

Laughing, Simon answered, "I thought it was the only day of the week any of you 'priestly types' actually worked at all." Nicodemus laughed with him and laid his hand on his friend's shoulder. Simon covered his hand with his own and squeezed it gently. Then the godly Pharisee left him.

After an hour or so, Simon heard a commotion. He could tell that it was coming from the temple court above. He got up and hobbled over to the steps. Begging help from one of the passers-by, he was led up to the temple gate. Once inside he could just make out Jesus' voice above the voices angrily shouting and hissing at him. Jesus was also shouting, but only because he was trying to make himself heard over the crowd.

Simon slipped into the grounds and squatted down with his back to the wall as Jesus was saying, "As it is, you Pharisees are determined to kill me, a man who has told you the truth that I heard from God ..." The rest was drowned out by their shouting, until Simon could make out the words of another man shouting back, "We are not illegitimate children. The only Father we have is God himself." In the ensuing murmurs of agreement, the prophet responded, "If God were your Father, you would love me, for I came from God and now am here. I have not come on my own; but he sent me."[3]

There were many more shouts of outrage at this, and Simon could not make out the rest of what was said. Nevertheless, a chill had run down his spine at the young prophet's statement that he had been sent directly from God. And he was outraged that they wanted to kill Jesus, just as his friend Nicodemus had said.

Wanting to hear the young man's words more clearly, he stood slowly and carefully moved toward the sound of his voice. The people were so intent on the melee unfolding in the court, they did not seem to mind the blind beggar's squeezing between them. As he pushed by someone, he heard Jesus say, "He who belongs to God hears what God says. The reason you do not hear is that you do not belong to God."[4]

Simon murmured, "How true that is!"

Suddenly he was grabbed by the arm and an angry voice growled, "What are you doing here, you useless beggar? Get out!" Simon was shoved back through the crowd by a succession of men. As he stumbled backward he heard Jesus shout, "I am not possessed by a demon!"[5] By this time the blind man had been shoved perilously close to the temple steps, and he would certainly have fallen had not another man caught him and gently led him down to the street while muttering angry words about how their nation was going to the devil.

As the man led Simon man down the steps, he said, "I am so sorry for their rudeness, my friend. I do think it's getting dangerous here, though. You might consider moving a ways away. There's probably going to be a riot here soon." Simon sensed that his companion looked back toward the temple briefly. Turning back to Simon, he said, "Here, let me help you."

The blind man took his hand gratefully. He also got the definite impression that the man was young, maybe in his early twenties.

As they moved further away from the temple, Simon replied, "Yes, I think you are right. Thank you for your kindness. What is your name, Sir?"

"They call me Simon Peter. I am a fisherman."

"Well, that's my name too. Simon, I mean. I don't fish much, though." His young companion chuckled despite his desire not to. Smiling ruefully,

---

[3] John 8: 40 – 42 excerpts. The word 'Pharisees' has been inserted into the rendition of verse 40 to indicate to whom Jesus is speaking.

[4] John 8: 47.

[5] John 8: 49a.

the blind man said, "That man in there sure seems to rile the leaders up." Simon pointed back over his shoulder and then turned his face toward the continuing sounds of yelling and screaming.

"Yes He does, indeed. Have you heard of Him?" Peter responded.

"Yes. His name is Jesus and he comes from Nazareth?" Simon turned his face back toward his companion and said, "Well, that just proves that something good can come from Nazareth after all." His companion chuckled again. "They say he is a great prophet," Simon continued. He could tell by the young man's intake of breath and the way his arm moved that he agreed.

Which Jesus' young disciple affirmed by replying, "Oh yes, He is. And so much more."

As they walked Simon began to warm to his young companion. They spoke quietly for a few moments, after which the fisherman asked a strange question. "How did you become blind, Simon?"

Simon was not offended. Rather, he was impressed that this young man had the courage to ask. No one ever did, and Simon always thought that most of them did not care enough to find out, while others were too embarrassed to do so. Glad of the concern for him that had registered in the fisherman's voice, he replied brightly, "Well, Simon Peter, I was born blind." When Peter's hand squeezed his arm gently, Simon understood that the fisherman felt sympathy for him; but he did not mind. Rather, it endeared him to this kind young man all the more.

They had now gone maybe one hundred or so yards south of the temple. By the sounds of the voices shouting out prices and hawking goods, Simon could tell that they were near Ophel in the market district. He said to his companion, "This is fine, Peter. You had better get back to your master. It sounds like he might need some help in there."

The young fisherman laughed. "Can I tell you something?"

"Sure!"

"My master has them all exactly where He wants them. They don't realize that it is they who need the help." He laughed and the blind man laughed with him. Then Peter left him.

Simon walked slowly away, continuing toward the south-most end of the marketplace. As he thought about the goings on at the temple, he recalled the last words of the prophet he had heard: "… if anyone keeps my word, they will not taste death."[6] What an amazing thing to say! He wondered what it

---

[6] John 8:51 excerpt.

meant—not to taste death. Then he reasoned that since the Scriptures said that only God himself could grant salvation from death, Jesus must have been claiming to be God! He shuddered as another chill ran down his spine and along his arms. How he wished he had had the presence of mind to ask the young fisherman about this.

When Simon arrived at his destination in the market, he was greeted by Artemis, a young Greek, one of his closest friends, who helped him to a seat. Because of Nicodemus' generosity, Simon had the equivalent of two days' wages in his belt, so he did not want to beg anymore that day. He was content to sit quietly by his friend and listen to him and his colleagues as they shouted out their pleas.

Simon suddenly felt chilly. The day must have clouded over, he thought, because he could no longer feel the warmth of the sun on him. He gathered his cloak around his neck as he sat and listened to the pleasant sounds of buying and selling that engulfed him.

After another few moments passed, Simon heard the tone of conversation around him change. Suddenly people were running this way and that, and there was excitement in the air. It reminded the blind man of the atmosphere before a threatening storm. He sat up straight and faced the sounds coming at him. He turned to his friend and asked, "Artemis, what's going on?"

"I don't know, my friend. There is a crowd coming, though, and there's a young man at its center. He appears to be speaking to many of your priests."

Simon's heart began to beat quickly.

After a moment, Artemis got up, saying, "Now I recognize him. That's the young prophet everyone's talking about, Jesus of Nazareth. Let's go see him."

Simon muttered, "No thanks," and waved his friend on, though he was excited. He really did want to go over to Jesus and speak to him. He wanted with all his heart to find out what it meant not to taste death. He also wanted to ask him if he was really God. But recalling that incident back at the temple, he decided it was safer not to. So the blind beggar was left sitting alone by the side of the path, listening. He thought he could hear two familiar voices: one, the young fisherman's; the other, Jesus'. He heard the word "blind" a couple of times. They must be talking about him, he concluded. But why?

He heard the crowd approaching him and he could suddenly feel the warmth of many bodies. He sensed that there were many eyes staring at him.

"Master," the young fisherman said, "Here is Simon. He was at the temple too."

Then Jesus said, "Simon, son of Jonah, would you like to receive your sight?"[7]

Simon was startled, not by Jesus calling his name, but because the young man had known who his father was. How could he have known that? As Jesus knelt down in front of him and leaned close, the blind man could feel the warmth of the young prophet's body; it felt strangely like the sun's first dawning rays he had felt earlier this morning. The hair on the back of Simon's neck and along his forearms bristled suddenly. He was so excited he could not speak for a moment. But he could sense that the young rabbi was staring at him.

When Jesus touched Simon's wrist lightly, he said, "Well, Rabbi, I've never thought it possible that I might receive my sight. So I guess I've never considered it." He paused for a moment.

There were murmurs in the crowd, and he could sense by the movement of the young rabbi's body that he was looking back over his shoulder at the crowd. Simon got the strange impression that Jesus was smiling back at them.

Gradually warming to the idea of getting his sight, Simon said finally, "Of course. I hate begging. I hate being such a burden to my family. Oh yes, Lord, I would very much like to receive my sight. Oh, yes, indeed." He felt a sudden pang of fear go through him because he had addressed this young man as if he really were God!

When the murmurs got louder, the beggar wondered if the crowd shared his unease. But all the voices said was, "How's this possible? No one has ever healed a man born blind. Not even the prophet Elijah did this."

Well, that does it! This Jesus of Nazareth must not be God after all, Simon thought, discouraged suddenly, even as he could sense the young man moving closer to him. Then he felt Jesus spreading mud over his eyes.

After He was done, Jesus of Nazareth said to the blind man, "Go to the pool of Siloam and wash your eyes." Then He stood, turned and left the blind beggar, dragging the murmurs of the crowd along with Him.

Simon was stunned, but he dared not touch the mud. He felt compelled to rise, and he did. He turned to his Greek friend, who, by his distinctive and somewhat pungent odor, he could sense was standing close to him. He asked, "Artemis, will you help me get to the pool?"

---

[7] Jesus calling out Simon's name is fictional: He does not address the blind man by name in Scripture. Nor does Scripture tell us the names of the blind man's parents. But the following events are true as reported in John 9: 1 – 7.

The young man said, "Of course!" And off they went.

As they turned to go to the pool, Simon could tell that people must be staring at him because there was none of the usual idle chatter. And one other thing began to happen: he felt pressure surging behind his temples. He also felt a strange sensation unlike anything he had ever felt before: the darkness that had always surrounded him brightened in direct proportion to that pressure. He put his hands to the sides of his head as the pressure increased for a moment, only to subside quickly. But the light in his brain continued to get brighter every second. Suddenly it took on differing qualities.

Colors! Simon thought.

His hands trembling now, he began to perspire.

Seeing these changes in his demeanor, Artemis said, concern sounding in his voice, "Here, my friend, is the pool. You are about a cubit away from the wall."[8]

As Simon knelt down by the side of the pool, his friend added, "Are you all right, Simon, my friend?"

Too distracted to respond, the blind man dipped his hands in the water. The colors were dancing around so brightly in his head now, he felt the urge to shout at them to stop. Nevertheless, he managed to ignore this impulse as he raised his hands to his eyes and washed away the mud.

He opened his eyes slowly. At first everything was hazy, like looking through a fine mist. Then the shimmering surface of the water suddenly became clear. He could see a face looking back at him. He swiped at the face, ruffling the surface of the water. It was his face! He jumped up and shouted for joy. This startled Artemis so greatly he fell over backward and landed flat on his buttocks in a sitting position, his eyes wide, his mouth open.

Simon turned slowly around to stare at the sights around him. He looked up at the sky and around at the buildings, then at the people near the well. He looked up at the sun which was a hazy yellow-white ball shrouded by the filmy clouds overhead. He laughed because he had to shade his eyes from its still potent glare. He looked down at his hands and feet. He turned back to the well to look at his reflection again. He put his hands to his face, his lips, his forehead, his throat. Then he turned around to look down at his friend, who was still sitting at his feet, staring up at him, drool now running down his chin. Simon pointed at the wide-eyed young Greek and laughed.

---

[8] A cubit is about 18 inches.

Artemis rose and looked warily at his friend. The young Greek ducked his head, looked closely at his friend's face with squinted eyes, blinked a few times, put his hand near Simon's cheek, and asked, "Can you see me, my friend?" He gingerly touched Simon's forehead just above one eye with his index finger.

Simon grabbed that finger suddenly and shouted, "**Gotcha!**"

Artemis jumped and howled with surprise and yanked his finger out of Simon's grasp. He held his whole hand close to him as if it had been plucked from a burning flame.

Looking down at his hand and then back up at Simon, who was pointing at him and laughing, Artemis began to chuckle. Realizing how foolish he must have looked, he began to laugh. Then the two of them howled, hanging onto each other and pointing at each other. Simon grabbed his friend's finger again, and the young Greek pulled that finger away and said "**Gotcha!**" over and over, that is when he could manage between gulps for breath.

They did not notice the astonished expressions of the people, who had watched as the "blind man" and the young Greek embraced and then danced around in a little circle, still howling with mirth. When the two young men saw how the others at the pool looked at them, they laughed harder. Eventually all strength left them, and they sat down in the dust and laughed until their sides ached and they had no more breath left in them.

Suddenly, a voice called out, "Isn't that Simon, the blind man? He can see." Everyone oohed and aahed as Simon rose, nodding at the man who was pointing at him. The man ran off shouting, "Simon, the blind beggar, can see. He can see."

Everyone approached Simon. Some bent down to look into his eyes. Others reached out to touch him. This was quite annoying, so he and his friend swatted their hands away. Then they started back to the north part of the city.

As they walked, Simon turned to Artemis and asked, "This is going to sound really strange, my friend, but where do I live?"

His friend chuckled and answered, "Don't you know?"

"Well yes, I do. But I always relied on the sounds of the different streets and districts of the city. Now my mind is flooded with all this," he waved around at him, "and I don't know what to make of it. I can't hear anything right now, if you know what I mean, because I'm so busy seeing it all. For the first time. *Hallelujah!*" When Simon shouted out the praise everyone nearby turned and stared warily at him. He laughed again, but at nothing, it seemed.

"Well friend, let's go back to your home." In a fit of jocularity Artemis held out his still tingling finger and said, "Take this and I'll lead you home." Simon grabbed that finger tightly. Artemis added, "I'm sure your mother and father will be overjoyed at the news." Pointing at his friend, he said, "I do have to say, though, you looked better than ever with that mud in your eyes and all over your face."

Simon chuckled. "Coming from *you,* Artemis, that is quite a compliment."

With that tart reply, Simon gave his friend a look suggesting that he intended some degree of irony, for Artemis was far from being the best looking man in the world. Simon's friend quickly caught his meaning, and he again howled with mirth. He bent backwards and then forwards and slapped his thighs many times. Simon laughed too. Hanging onto each other, laughing as they went, they stumbled along toward Simon's home.

When the "blind man" arrived at his home, his mother had her back to the door. She was on her knees praying to her God, so she did not hear him come in. Simon put his finger to his lips and tiptoed into the house behind his mother. He put his hands over her eyes. Artemis covered his mouth to stifle a giggle. Simon's mother started up and her hands went to her eyes, covering her son's hands.

"Guess who."

"It must be you, Jonah," she replied, thinking that it was Simon's father, "but it sounds like our son Simon." She ripped his hands off her eyes and said, turning quickly around, "Jonah why are you playing such a silly ..." Her voice trailed off and she gasped when she saw that it was her son who was smiling down at her and *looking at her.* "Oh my," she exhaled loudly. "Oh my," she breathed out again slowly, tears forming. Simon stepped back a foot or two and nodded in confirmation of what his mother saw but could not quite believe. "How?" She asked, putting her hands to his forehead, to his eyes, to his cheeks and then falling into his arms and weeping for joy.

Simon patted her trembling shoulders several times. He looked over at his friend, who raised a certain finger to his eye in a joy-filled salute and then left them out of respect for their privacy.

Simon pushed his mother away from him. Looking into her eyes, he said, "There was a man named Jesus. He put mud on my eyes. Now I see." He let her go and danced a little turn for her.

His mother cried out, "Wait until your father sees this, why ..."

She was interrupted by her husband's voice shouting, "His father has seen it, Martha; what a glorious day!" He ran into the house and embraced his son, and they all danced with joy.

One of Martha's friends happened to peek into the house. "I was wondering what all the commotion was about, so I'd thought I'd ..." Her voice trailed off when she saw that Simon had been healed.

The woman and Jonah asked in unison how Simon got his sight, and he repeated his story. For the rest of that day and well into the evening more of their neighbors came over. Soon the house was crowded with people. Simon must have repeated his story several dozen times that day, and he kept telling them what a great prophet this Jesus must be. They all nodded in joyous agreement when Simon told them what Jesus said to the Pharisees in the temple about them not belonging to God. They also continually remarked how no one, not even the prophet Elijah, had restored sight to a man born blind. How marvelous it was!

By the morning of the next day, which was the second day of the week— a day on which the Jews' Ruling Council generally met— word got out that a blind man had been healed, and that he had been healed on the Sabbath. It also got out how he was singing the praises of a certain Jesus of Nazareth.

As Simon and his folks were eating their morning meal, they were interrupted by a clamor outside. Everyone in the house turned to see that a crowd had gathered, and by their faces, they could see that some of them were not happy. In particular there were several scribes from the temple, men who worked directly with the Sanhedrin, who seemed most annoyed. Simon also recognized one man in the crowd as the one at the well who had gone off shouting about Simon's restored sight.

Simon went out to meet them with his arm around his mother's shoulder and his father next to him. The man from the well pointed at Simon. "See, I told you. He got his sight." There were murmurs, many of them decidedly unfriendly. One man said, "I don't believe you. He only looks like the blind man." Another said, "No, brother, I've seen him many times outside the temple gate. This is the man, I tell you." Then the man from the well said, "I saw him hobble up on the arm of this man." He pointed to Artemis, who had just arrived. "Then he washed his eyes, and when he was done he could see. This is the man!" There were more murmurs from the crowd.

One of the scribes stepped forward and asked with an angry scowl, "How, then, were your eyes opened?"[9] His tone of voice as well as his expression indicated that he found having to ask about this perplexing thing distasteful in the extreme.

---

[9] John 9:10.

Suddenly Jesus' words at the Temple came back to Simon about how these men wanted to kill him. Then he recalled Nicodemus explaining how they might desire to harm anyone who supported Jesus' teaching. A chill ran down his spine suddenly and the hair on the back of his neck and on his arms rose. Knowing that he was in trouble, fear for his family filled him. Nicodemus had seemed very clear about this one thing: profess any belief in the prophet's teachings and you will be thrown out of the synagogue.

Simon's only thought was, therefore, to protect his mother and father as he replied as matter-of-factly as possible, "The man they call Jesus made some mud and put it on my eyes. He told me to go to Siloam and wash. So I went and washed, and then I could see."[10]

"And when did this marvelous thing happen?" the scribe asked, his voice dripping with sarcasm.

"Yesterday, about the sixth hour," Simon responded.[11]

The man from the well said, "See? See? I told you."

There were more murmurs. Some of the scribes were grinning, obviously pleased that this "Jesus fellow" had defiled the Sabbath. Again!

The inquisitor smiled cruelly at Simon. "Well then, where is this man?" he demanded.

"I don't know," Simon replied truthfully.[12]

The scribe raised his hands to stop the crowd's chatter, and they quieted immediately. "You will come with us," he commanded loftily, "and explain this *thing* to the members of the Ruling Council." He spat out the word "thing".

Simon asked, "Right now?" He could not keep his voice from quivering, which annoyed him greatly. How he hated to let on that he might be afraid!

The cruel scribe obviously detected the fear in the "blind man's" voice and enjoyed it, because he grinned at him with the look of a predator eyeing its prey. Embedding his finger in Simon's chest, he replied, "Yes! Right now!"

It sounded more like a curse than a command.

Anger flared in Simon's breast, searing away his fear. "I need to get my cloak." The scribe crossed his arms over his chest majestically and nodded. Simon grabbed his mother and father and pulled them back into the house.

---

[10] John 9:11.

[11] The sixth hour was probably around noon.

[12] John 9:12.

"If they ask you, Mom, or you, Dad, about how all of this happened, do me a favor. Say you know nothing. Let me do all the talking, please."

"Why?" They both asked, looking alternately from him to the crowd and back, trembling with fear.

"Because you know what might happen if the Pharisees do not like what I have to say."

His mother began to weep, and he embraced her. His father took his outstretched hand solemnly and nodded. Then the "blind man" allowed himself to be led quietly away by the crowd, many of whom had begun to argue loudly and vehemently among themselves as to what this might mean and as to who this "Jesus fellow" really was.

When they got to the palace and went into the council chamber, Simon was placed in the center of a semi-circular amphitheater with four tiers, in the lowest of which sat twenty-three men with the high priest Caiaphas at its center, sitting in the president's seat. Nicodemus was sitting to Caiaphas' right about two seats away. He nodded his head slightly at Simon as he entered—an expression of apology it seemed—and Simon nodded back. In the second tier there were another twenty-three and another twenty-three in the third and then a final two on the top tier. Seventy-one total. They sat from Simon's left to his right and from top to bottom in order of increasing age and importance of position, with the youngest and least important scribe sitting on the left at the very top.

Simon was outraged. Here was the entire Sanhedrin, meeting to harass him because someone had done a wonderful thing for him, and he, Simon, had had the temerity to proclaim it to the whole world. Well, at least to his immediate neighbors, Simon thought, as a chuckle bubbled up in this throat. It was that same someone who, by his teaching and by his miraculous signs, had clearly challenged the Pharisees' authority, which, if the ruckus at the temple were any indication, they hated to the core of their souls.

A thought suddenly came to Simon: Jesus had also proved that He *was* the Son of God. Who else could heal a man born blind? Simon felt a wave of fear rush through him, but it was fear for these foolish, evil men. For they were clearly going to use this meeting to gather evidence against Jesus, using as a pretext the fact that this "thing" had been done for him on God's very own holy day. How ridiculous these men seemed to him! How petty! How sad!

Now when he had first entered the council chamber Simon had been white with fear. His outrage suppressed that awful emotion, however, and something wonderful seemed to pour into him and calm his heart. All of a sudden it mattered not in the least to him what these men might decide. All he knew was that he had been healed. He wanted to continue to shout the Good News to the world. With all his heart and soul, Simon wanted to see this Jesus again. Rage welled up in him that these corrupt, vicious men, Nicodemus and a few others excepted, would have the temerity to judge the very Son of God. No indeed! He did not care in the least what these men did to him personally. He just wanted to see Jesus again so that he might worship Him.

When the clamor died down, Caiaphas looked around and started the meeting, saying, "We have the required quorum of twenty-three. We admonish the clerks to keep careful records of this proceeding; for by it we intend to establish that a grave crime has been committed here." There were many murmurs of affirmation.

Simon's outrage flared to intense anger fueled by utter contempt. Presumption was always supposed to go to the innocence of a man, according to their own traditions as well as to Roman law. Yet they had already proclaimed Jesus guilty. *Yes, indeed,* thought the beggar, *He was guilty—of performing a tremendous act of mercy and kindness. A grave crime!* He gnashed his teeth at Jesus' accusers.[13]

Caiaphas raised his hand, and the murmurs stopped. He stared at Simon for a moment before asking how he had received his sight, and Simon told him what he had been telling everyone for the past two days.

One of the men to the right of Nicodemus shouted, "This man is not from God, for he does not keep the Sabbath." He was referring to Jesus, of course, and about half of the council agreed, some of them repeating his words.

Simon grunted scornfully, thinking, what better way to serve God than to heal on His own holy day?

Nicodemus turned away from staring at Simon and asked the president, "How can a sinner do such miraculous signs?"

Simon's admiration for this man's courage and uprightness increased ten-fold as shouts of outrage from some of the other Council members greeted this reasonable question.

Caiaphas raised his hand again to silence the room, and it became quiet instantly. He leaned forward, narrowed his eyes at the "blind man" and asked, "What have you to say about him? It was your eyes he opened."

---

[13] The words of the participants in what follows are more or less quoted from John 9: 16 – 34 with a few modifications to aid the narrative.

Simon straightened his shoulders. He said with a firm voice, "He is a prophet." He wanted to add "and clearly the Son of God—our Messiah" but thought better of it. Some shouted they did not believe that Simon had really been blind. Others snickered at the man's impudence.

The scribe who brought Simon here from his home said, "Why don't we get his parents here? They will tell us."

Fear filled Simon again, but he said nothing as Caiaphas waved away several armed men who quickly left the building. Meanwhile Simon was ushered to the side and forced to sit between two more heavily armed men.

Many of the council members left their seats and milled around, talking quietly; some clustered in little groups, others stood two by two; but all of them glanced over at Simon from time to time. Nicodemus and a few other men of honor had started to approach him, but Simon waved them off with a slight motion of his hand. His friend nodded understanding. At Nicodemus' urging the men all turned away to engage others in conversation. It took about thirty minutes before the frightened faces of his mother and father were thrust before the council. They were standing arm in arm, quaking with fear. Simon's heart went out to them as they looked over at him with terribly forlorn expressions, and he prayed to God that they would heed his admonition and claim ignorance.

After the men had retaken their seats, the president pointed at his parents and then at Simon and asked, "Is this your son? Is this the one you say was born blind? How is it that now he can see?"

Jonah glanced at his son briefly. Simon nodded slightly, and Jonah responded, "We know he is our son and we know he was born blind." He looked over at his son again, who shook his head slightly. "But how he can see now, or who opened his eyes, we don't know for sure. Ask him. He is of age; he will speak for himself."

Simon breathed deeply and smiled at his father and then at his mother. But the two elderly people bowed their heads and began to weep. How he wanted to go to them and comfort them! Of course he could not. Rather, he set his chin and stared up defiantly at the high priest.

Caiaphas, for his part, was not stupid. He could see what was going on, and truth be told, he found himself admiring a man who had the courage to stand alone in front of a body that had what amounted to life and death power over him; to defy them like this without flinching. What was it about these followers of Jesus, the high priest wondered? They were impertinent at least; arrogant at worst. But none of them could be cowed. What was it about them, anyway?

Nevertheless, Simon's uncompromising attitude kindled hot anger in Caiaphas. He turned to face the "blind man" and summoned him a second time to sit before them. As Simon's guards roughly grabbed his arms and raised him to his feet, the elderly couple was ushered out of the room. Simon was deeply touched by the look on their faces as they craned their necks to keep eye contact with him as long as they could, before the cold stone walls separated them.

When Simon had taken his place back in the middle of the semi-circle, Caiaphas stood and pointed at him, making himself as menacing as possible. He shouted, "Give glory to God. We know this man is a sinner."

Simon shuddered. He knew the Scriptures well enough to know that the high priest had as much as threatened to have him stoned to death by saying, "Give glory to God."[14] But Simon did not care that they wanted to stone him, though he knew that the worst thing they could do under Roman Law was to throw him out of the synagogue. Putting people to death was reserved for the Roman authorities only. Nor did he care about the synagogue anymore because of these men's shameless hypocrisy.

Setting his jaw and staring defiantly at the high priest for a moment, Simon said, "Whether he is a sinner or not, I do not know." *Although I do have my opinion,* he thought, hating the high priest and his associates in this travesty more every second. "One thing I do know. I was blind, but now I see!"

This stopped them. There were many murmurs from the crowd. Even some of the worst of them were forced to nod in agreement with the answer. Nicodemus did everything he could to hide a smile as he beamed with admiration for his friend. He stole a glance at several of his godly colleagues, who were smiling also. Catching Nicodemus' glance, they also beamed back at him their admiration for Simon.

Caiaphas hated that answer because it was so very simply the truth, and he was too distracted to notice the byplay between Nicodemus and the others. He sat down heavily, his jaw rigid with anger, but he continued to squirm in

---

[14] See Joshua 7 for the story of how the LORD chastised His people for violating His order not to take anything of value from Jericho. Apparently the phrase "Give glory to God" is a paraphrase of Joshua 7: 19 where Joshua is speaking to Achan: "... give glory to the LORD, the God of Israel, and give him the praise. Tell me what you have done; do not hide it from me." When Achan admitted his guilt, and at the LORD's direction, the man and his whole family were stoned and everything they owned was burned and the ashes buried.

his seat for a moment. He looked right, then left, and then with an angry and frustrated voice he asked, "Tell us exactly. What did he do to you? How did he open your eyes?"

Enjoying himself now, especially enjoying the high priest's obvious frustration, Simon responded in a mocking tone of voice, "I have told you already and you did not listen. Why do you want to hear it again?" As Caiaphas squirmed more, Simon smiled slyly, adding, "Do you want to become His disciples, too?"

Outrage rained down on the "blind man" with shouts of "dirty beggar," "swine eater," "insolent fellow," and "He's not good enough to be a Jew. Maybe he's a Samaritan in disguise," or "I bet he's not a Jew at all but a gentile sinner," and the like. Simon looked over at Nicodemus and saw that he had his hand over his mouth hiding a broad smile as he watched his outraged colleagues spit and splutter. Simon smiled too as he turned his face back to the high priest.

Caiaphas raised his hand, and when they had quieted he said angrily, "You are this fellow's disciple! We are disciples of Moses! We know that God spoke to Moses, but as for this fellow, we don't even know where he comes from."

Simon looked around at them all. He then looked them up and down. His voice dripping with contempt, he replied, "Now that *is* remarkable! You don't know where He comes from, yet He opened my eyes." This stopped them for a moment. Some hands stroked beards; others went nervously to foreheads. There were a few nods, which were quickly squelched by an angry glance from the high priest. Only Nicodemus continued to smile. "We know that God does not listen to sinners," the beggar continued.[15] "He listens to the godly man who does His will. Nobody has ever heard of opening the eyes of a man born blind. If this man were not from God, He could do nothing."[16]

Caiaphas stood suddenly and spat at him, "You were steeped in sin at birth; how dare you lecture us!" Most of them shouted concurring obscenities at him.

A few blushed, however. Shaking their heads sadly at their ranting colleagues, they looked down at Nicodemus, who, by a slight motion of his hand, indicated that they should leave. This they did quietly as the rest of the

---

[15] See, for example, Proverbs 3:32, 11:20, 15:8 – 9 and 15:26, which are just a few verses which demonstrate the truth of Simon's statement.

[16] See John 5:19 and John 8:28 where Jesus confirms this Himself.

men rose and shouted at each other and then at Simon, waving their fists at the "blind man", who watched all this with a placid smile.

Caiaphas, seeing that this man did not fear them, became insanely angry. He rose and pointed the sharp finger of judgment at him. "You, Simon, son of Jonah, will no longer be allowed to assemble with us. You are a non-person in the eyes of our God. Now GET OUT!"

Simon left quickly, their angry shouts following him out of the room.

He went immediately to his home and told his stricken parents what had happened. He told them that he needed to leave their home so as not to endanger them. They wept bitter tears, but he consoled them, saying, "Mother, Father, don't weep for me. Consider what God has done for me." He waved his hand in front of his eyes.

"But, son, we cannot bear to lose you." They both embraced him, still weeping.

"I know. I will come by from time to time and look in on you. Please, I'm okay. I can't explain why I feel so good about all this, but I do. It's as if something incomprehensible has filled me with peace and joy. I certainly can't explain it, but, well, it has."[17] With that he got his bag, packed the few things he owned, and left his weeping parents standing in the door of their house, arm in arm, waving at him.

He was weeping too as he headed toward Artemis' home, who, because he was a Greek, could not have cared less about the Jews or their synagogues or their Law. Simon knew that his friend would not be afraid to take him in. Simon stopped weeping and began to give thanks to the LORD for what He had done for him and for having given him this faithful friend.

As Simon rounded a corner he bumped into someone. For his head had been bowed and he was not looking where he was going. He apologized without looking up and turned to continue on his way when a familiar voice said, "Simon, son of Jonah, where are you going in such a hurry?"

Simon started and turned and looked into the kindest pair of eyes he had ever seen. The young man had His hands out to him, and Simon rushed into His arms. Jesus embraced him. "I heard about what happened," He said. "I have been looking for you."

Simon could not believe it. Why would God's Son ever waste His time looking for him? Suddenly, certain words of the twenty-third Psalm came to mind: "Surely goodness and love shall pursue me all the days of my life and I

---

[17] See Philippians 4:7.

147

shall dwell in the LORD's house forever."[18] Certainly this Son of God was the very God of Abraham, Isaac, and Israel, come to them in the flesh.[19] Now he knew beyond doubt what this verse meant, that God would pursue His servants with goodness and love, as Jesus had pursued him. How wonderful it was!

Chills going up and down his spine, his heart expanding with joy and his breath quickening, Simon responded, "LORD, I don't care in the least. Since you healed me, well, I've had such peace in my soul that I can't explain."

Jesus, understanding his reaction, asked, "Do you believe in the Son of Man?"

Suddenly a group of Pharisees came along. They had obviously been looking for Jesus. The "blind man" saw Jesus look over at them sadly.

Simon said as loudly as he could, to make sure they all heard him, "Who is He, sir? Tell me so that I may believe in Him." He knew the answer, but wanted the Pharisees to hear it for themselves.

Still looking over at the Pharisees, Jesus said to the "blind man", "You have now seen him; in fact he is the one speaking with you."

Simon then fell down at Jesus' feet and worshipped Him.[20]

After a moment, Jesus extended His hand and helped the no longer blind man to his feet.[21] The Son of God then turned to the crowd that was gathering. With a sad voice He said to Simon's persecutors, "For judgment I have come into this world, so that the blind will see and those who see will become blind." He extended His hand first to Simon and then to some in the crowd.

The men at whom He pointed became red-faced with anger. One of them asked with a sneer, "What? Are we blind too?"

---

[18] Psalm 23:6, paraphrased. The Hebrew word translated as 'follow' in the NIV has the sense of one being actively pursued as one might hunt for a precious possession that has been lost.

[19] See Genesis 32:28 where God renames Jacob, Israel.

[20] This conversation between Simon and Jesus is recorded in John 9:35 – 38. Some verses have been paraphrased for the sake of the narrative.

[21] During this account, John repeatedly refers to my character, Simon, as "the blind man". I believe he did this on purpose to emphasize that those who were blind will be made to see, but that those who think they can see are really blind, as Jesus says in the following dialogue with the Pharisees.

Jesus replied sadly, "If you were blind you would not be guilty of your sin; but now that you claim you can see, your guilt remains."[22]

With that the LORD and God of creation in human flesh walked off with Simon, His arm around His new disciple's shoulder, shouts of outrage following them both.

---

[22] The conversation between Jesus and the Pharisees is from John 9:39 – 41.

The End of Intellectual Achievement

If anyone else thinks he has reasons to put confidence in the flesh, I [the Apostle Paul] have more: circumcised on the eighth day, of the people of Israel, of the tribe of Benjamin, a Hebrew of Hebrews; in regard to the law, a Pharisee; as for zeal, persecuting the church; as for legalistic righteousness, faultless. But whatever was to my profit I now consider loss for the sake of Christ.
(Philippians 3:4 – 7)

I [Paul] thank Christ Jesus our LORD, who has given me strength, that he considered me faithful, appointing me to his service. Even though I was once a blasphemer and a persecutor and a violent man, I was shown mercy because I acted in ignorance and unbelief. (1 Tim 1:12 – 13)

Author's note: I have found that a big stumbling block for me in my walk with the LORD was my own pride of intellectual accomplishment. This is not an uncommon problem for many Christians, I think. This story speaks of someone else who had that same problem.

There was a dungeon in Rome during the reign of Claudius Nero, the Roman Emperor, in which were caged many enemies of the Empire, whether imagined or real. In one such cell there was an aged and tired man awaiting his execution, which must come any day. Despite this, Paul, the great Apostle of the Gospel of Jesus Christ, reclined on his cot, hands behind his head, breathing easily. For Death gave him no fear at all. Rather, he looked forward eagerly to it, for he had been poured out completely in his service to his LORD; he had fought the good fight; he had finished the race and kept the faith; and he knew that there was a great crown waiting for him.[1]

He found solace in this: that there was nothing left that he could do. He was old, tired, bent and beat up from the abuse of several decades of service. Paul raised his arm and counted the scars from the stoning at Lystra; then he counted the scars on his back—there were almost two hundred.[2] And he laughed quietly. He also took comfort that his sons in the faith, Timothy and

---

[1] 2 Timothy 4: 6 – 8.

[2] See Acts 14: 19 for the account of the stoning; and 2 Corinthians 11:24 for the number of stripes Paul received in the LORD's service.

Epaphras, among many others whom he had left behind, would carry the torch for him; that they, led by the Spirit of Jesus, would shepherd the flocks he had sired. He knew that they would carry the Gospel to the ends of the Empire, and that their sons and daughters in Christ would continue to proclaim the LORD's Gospel to every creature under heaven, as the LORD had promised him so long ago.[3]

Despite all this, the old saint still harbored regrets; try as he might to bury them in the LORD's mercy and forgiveness, which had been lavished on him so many years ago.

Paul stared at the ceiling and reflected on his life before the LORD took hold of him. How sad it had been! The image of his old teacher staring into his face on the day he had persuaded his fellow Pharisees to murder Stephen came to him, and tears welled up in his eyes. He could remember that evil day and the many that followed—days filled with murder and mayhem, all by his very own hand!—as if they were yesterday. Paul recalled with vivid clarity the day they brought Stephen, one of God's greatest saints, before the Jews' Ruling Council. The day was especially hot, as were many tempers in the Sanhedrin council. Though it was several decades earlier, Paul could see the council's chamber in his mind as if he were standing there now.

The priests and Pharisees paced the Sanhedrin's council chamber angrily. The meeting had long since dissolved into chaos, and the men, all seventy or so of them, were out of their seats. Voices were raised; hands waved around wildly; and through the cacophony no one could hear what anyone else was saying. A shout silenced them, however, and they looked around to see that it had been Annas, their high priest, standing in their midst, his hands raised. They turned and waited for him to speak.

He said quietly, "I know, brothers, that this obnoxious sect they call the Nazarenes is proving hard to stamp out." There were many loud murmurs of agreement.

A voice from their midst shouted, "How about that guy they call Stephen? There are men who say that he speaks against our Law and against Moses. They say that he has declared the Law null and void, and that the way to righteousness is through belief in this Jesus fellow, whom they call the Christ.[4] The people are up in arms over this. If we let this go unchallenged, our authority will be called into question."

---

[3] Colossians 1: 23.

[4] "Christ" is the Greek word for Messiah.

151

There were many more loud murmurs of agreement.

The voice was that of a young man, a new addition to their number. His name was Saul and he was from Tarsus in Cilicia. He was well respected because he was a student of the great teacher of the Law, Gamaliel, who was one of the most respected remembers of this Ruling Council and who had brought him in personally. Of course, the young man would never admit publicly that he had heard Stephen speak, and that his accusation that Stephen spoke against the Law and Moses was false. Yet he knew that if the Council could be convinced of this and then went after Stephen and put him to death, they might be able to deal with this Nazarene sect once for all. He was glad to see by their expressions that they all shared this desire. Well, all except for his teacher, apparently, because Gamaliel was frowning at him, as if he actually knew that Saul was lying about Stephen.

Nevertheless, the young man, emboldened by the looks of the others, said, "I thought we had done with the ones they call Peter and John, but every time we threaten one of them it seems another one takes their place. And now we have this ... this ..." he finally managed to splutter out the name, "... Stephen fellow to deal with."

"Saul, Saul, please control yourself," Gamaliel said, looking around the room. "Remember that if this Nazarene sect is of God, we cannot stop them. If not, then they will fail."[5] There were many concurring nods.

Recalling the last time his teacher had used this argument, young Saul became furious. For the first time in his life he went against his teacher. "You, my teacher, of all people know what Moses said to the people of Israel:

> 'If a prophet, or one who foretells by dreams, appears among
> you and announces to you a miraculous sign or wonder, and
> if the sign or wonder of which he has spoken takes place,
> and he says, "Let us follow other gods" (gods you have not
> known) "and let us worship them," you must not listen to the
> words of that prophet or dreamer. The LORD your God is
> testing you to find out whether you love him with all your
> heart and with all your soul. It is the LORD your God you
> must follow, and him you must revere. Keep his commands
> and obey him; serve him and hold fast to him.' "[6]

---

[5] Acts 5:34 – 37.
[6] Deuteronomy 13:14.

Many hands stroked beards and chins, their owners frowning in agreement.

Rabbi Gamaliel looked around at them sadly, his shoulders slumping.

Energized by their encouraging stares, looking around at them all, Saul said, "You yourselves have heard how Jesus of Nazareth claimed to be God." The young Pharisee made a face as if he had eaten something vile. "How ridiculous is that?" he spat out. "Well, I say that these men are servants of the devil, not God's own servants. And you, my teacher, are responsible for letting the others go.[7] Now look what we've got. Not only are this obnoxious Peter and his scruffy followers doing these evil things, but others are sprouting up, this Stephen being but one of many." There were hisses and angry growls.

"Well, then, my son, what do you propose?" Gamaliel asked, defeated. As the old teacher looked at the grim faces around him, there seemed to be no one who might listen to reason.

Gamaliel was sorry now that they had put Jesus' followers and apologists, these Nazarenes, out of the synagogue. How he wished Nicodemus were here! At least he could help. He always seemed to be able to sway them. For the first time the elderly rabbi wondered whether they had been right to crucify Jesus. Maybe he had been the Messiah after all. Whether he was the Messiah or not, Gamaliel was not so sure that his followers were servants of the devil. With that thought, fear rose in him. *What if God were with these men?* he wondered. This admonition from God came to him suddenly, " '... if any nation does not listen [to my servants and repent], I will completely uproot and destroy it,' declares the LORD."[8] *Suppose these men were God's servants. Then that curse would come down on all our heads,* he thought, his fear intensifying.

Saul answered him, "I propose that we hunt these Nazarenes down, root them out of their houses and put them to death, man, woman, and child, as the LORD commanded Joshua when he put to death all the pagan hordes—a divine judgment of the LORD our God." There were many murmurs of approval. Saul turned to his teacher and said, "I propose that we start with this Stephen. Make an example of him."

This was greeted by a few concurring shouts.

---

[7] Acts 5:38 – 40.

[8] Jeremiah 12:17. Gamaliel has supplied the words in brackets which are clearly implied by the passage.

The old teacher replied sadly, "My son, think what you are saying. What if you are wrong? If they are really our God's servants and we do not listen, then we will have sinned against God and He will punish our nation. You know God's curse as well as I."

This stopped the grumbling for a moment, and many heads came up suddenly. Saul, with an arrogant grimace, said, "You mean the curse from the prophet Jeremiah? That was made when our people worshipped idols and angered the LORD our God thereby. Everyone knows that! So it does not apply to us." Many nodded sagely, for an idol—that is, something carved out of wood or stone or forged out of metal—had not been seen among the people for over five hundred years.

Saul took his eyes off his teacher and turned around slowly to address them all. "Listen, all of you. If we allow these evil men to flourish, the curse of Moses, which has been spoken in your hearing, is clear. Certainly Jesus, who claimed he was equal with God, was a liar. We all know that. Therefore he must have come from the devil and God is testing us, as He said He would. Clearly these obnoxious men are calling the people away from the one God to worship a demon. This can only be the work of the devil." There were many more murmurs of approval.

Annas raised his hand, and they all turned to him. "I agree with our young colleague here." Smiling, he turned to the old teacher. "Rabban Gamaliel, you have taught this young man too well, it seems. I think he has bested you." He laughed and they all, except for the one addressed, laughed with him. When they had quieted, the high priest said, "Let us arrest Stephen and bring him before us." As they turned to congratulate themselves, he raised a finger, his eye on Rabban Gamaliel, whom he feared as much as he respected him. They stopped and looked at him, their mouths still partially open. "But let us see what he has to say."

"Then we'll stone him to death," a voice shouted out of the crowd over their angry growls, which turned to shouts of agreement amid much laughter.

Through gulps of laughter, the high priest said, "Well, if that is merited."

Saul interjected, "There is no doubt in my mind, my lord, that when this blasphemer gets done speaking, our decision will be quite easy." Seventy heads nodded while one old man sat heavily on a stone bench, his head bowed, supported by the palm of his hand.

"Very well. Let's get this guy and see what he has to say." Annas put his finger to the side of his nose and thumped young Saul on the back. "And then we'll stone him." All the men in the chamber, except one, again shouted concurrence.

"Well then, it's settled," the high priest said. He looked around at them all briefly. "Look, it has been a long day, the sun is about to set, and we are all hot and tired. Let's wait until we meet again, and then we will interview this man." Seeing that they all agreed, the high priest called several men over and instructed them to search Stephen out—though he would not be hard to find, just follow the trail of miracles (laughter)—and on the morning of the fifth day, bring him here. The men saluted and ran off. Everyone else began to file slowly out of the chamber.

As Saul turned to leave, he felt a tug at his shoulder, and he turned to see the wizened old face of his teacher staring up at him. Suddenly it registered that he was at least a head taller than this shriveled old man. This man whom he had always regarded as being like a god was not quite so impressive now. No. Now he seemed old, worn out, and if truth were told, useless; for had he not stood up for the followers of this Jesus before? How Saul hated that Nazarene blasphemer Jesus! How he hated his followers. How, suddenly, did he hate this old man, who was looking him intently in the eye. The arrogance of pride flared up in Saul's heart, and he despised that look in his eye, which he took to be one not merely of displeasure but of rebuke. And pity!

Saul gritted his teeth and said contemptuously, "What is it, old man?"

The old teacher recoiled as if he had been struck. *Old man, is it?* he thought. *How far is this arrogant young man prepared to go in his quest? For what? Vengeance? If so, against whom? Against me? What have I done?* The old priest continued to stare sadly at him.

After a moment, Gamaliel said, "My son, please allow me one last plea, if not for what I am to you now, which I can see by that look in your eye is next to nothing, but for what I once was, upon a time not so long ago." His voice had trailed off and his eyes went to the floor.

Saul softened because there was a tear in his teacher's eye. The young Pharisee found himself regretting his insolence, but not too much, as he said quietly, "Of course, my teacher. Of course. Here, let's sit." He led Gamaliel to one of the stone benches and they sat side by side.

Something tugged at Saul's heart, deep conviction that he had terribly wronged this humble man. He began to wonder what he was doing. Why this hatred? How had he dared insult his teacher this way? But he could not find the answers to these questions within himself, as his teacher continued to stare kindly and sadly into his eyes.

Gamaliel nodded and smiled. Saul had the slimy feeling run through him that his teacher had read his thoughts. The elderly priest placed a trembling hand against the young man's cheek. "You know, my friend," this stung Saul mightily, "that you are the best student I have ever had?" Saul dropped his eyes and raised his hand to his cheek. Gamaliel retracted his own hand. "Of all the students of the Word, you are the very best I have ever seen. Your fluency with Greek, Hebrew, Aramaic, even with that hateful language of our occupiers, is amazing. Your encyclopedic knowledge of the scrolls is second to none, myself included." Saul looked away briefly. "Oh yes!" Gamaliel exclaimed, gladdened at seeing humility flash briefly in Saul's eyes for the first time that day. "And your ways, always living in the very strictest compliance with our Law, have been exemplary." Saul sniffed and wiped his eye. "I would bet, if I were a wagering man that is ..." The old rabbi chuckled and nudged his student playfully. Saul chuckled too. "... that if God Himself came down and examined you, He would have a hard time finding fault with how you have comported yourself with respect to following our rules and upholding our traditions." Saul bowed his head.

Then the old man thought, *But with all that intellect; with all that knowledge; with all that training; with all of your faultless ways—with all of it—where is it leading you? To murder!*

"I am worried for you, my son. Where are you going with this vendetta of yours? What is the purpose? You know as well as I that if these men are not of God, then God Himself will dispose of them. Suppose, on the other hand, ..." Saul bridled, "... I know, my son, I know what *you* think. Your zeal for the righteousness of God is to be commended, as always." The old man hated himself for the flattery, but he was desperate to make an impression on this young man, whom he loved like a son. "I beg of you, Saul, think again. Suppose they are from God. Think of the judgment you may be calling down upon yourself. Think of the judgment you may be calling down on our nation."

The old teacher felt a tug at his heart; maybe he had overstated Saul's danger a bit. Surely if these men were from God, then Jesus was the Messiah and by murdering Him they had already called a terrible judgment down on themselves; and this young man was not guilty of that. Still, the old rabbi hoped that he could somehow get through that brick wall of hatred his favorite pupil, no, his favorite son, had erected around himself. He looked hopefully up at Saul, wishing that he might relent. It was so very sad that he saw nothing there but the fires of hatred shining brightly in the young man's eyes.

Saul replied, "I know that what you say is true, Abba." Gamaliel could not help the tears that came to him. Saul, seeming not to see those tears, said, "And I intend to be the agent of God's justice here. I believe these men are from the devil. Look at how they disregard our holy law. They even say that it is not necessary anymore. That righteousness comes through the worship of this Jesus, whom they call the Christ. What could be plainer? How can anyone who knows the Law of our God and all of His admonitions to follow it, support such blasphemous behavior? Does the LORD not say through Moses that anyone who willfully disobeys the LORD has blasphemed His Name?"[9]

The old man nodded sadly.

"Well then, I intend to be that justice."

Gamaliel was utterly defeated. Normally he would have said, "May the LORD be with you." But he could not because as he looked into that unholy fire burning in his son's eyes, he knew that the LORD was *not* with him. He patted Saul on the knee, got up silently and walked away slowly, shoulders slumped, weeping. Weeping for his son.

The old teacher had become convinced just then that these men, Peter, John, James, and the rest of them, including this young man Stephen, whom they were about to murder, had been right to say that the Jews had crucified their very own Messiah, their very own LORD. Feeling the awful weight of this sin on his shoulders, Rabbi Gamaliel headed slowly back to his house, where he vowed to get on his knees and repent of that awful deed with all his heart. After this, he planned to search out the Nazarenes—maybe their leader Peter, or James, Jesus' brother—to speak with them.

Gamaliel stopped just before leaving the council chamber, however, and looked around. Suddenly, all of this meant nothing to him. He had just come to realize that it was all a show, all a demonstration of men's pride rather than of the true and humble submission to God's will that the LORD demanded.

Taking one last look back into the chamber, seeing the angry eyes of his son following him, the old man said a silent prayer to the LORD his God, asking forgiveness for himself, for his people, and most of all for his son Saul. Though Gamaliel could not possibly have known it, the LORD heard his righteous prayer, at least where the angry young man was concerned.

As Saul watched the old man hobble away, his contempt for him rekindled. He wondered how one such as Gamaliel, the greatest teacher of his day, could be so blind to the obvious. To give up the Law, to give up everything he (Saul) had worked so hard to achieve, and to which he had devoted his whole life, heart, mind and soul, was outrageous.

---

[9] See Numbers 15:30.

Saul also looked around at the council chamber of the Sanhedrin and ambition rose like bile in his throat. He focused on that first row and thought how he wanted to sit at the right hand of that center seat. And he vowed to do anything he could to get it one day. Anything at all. If it meant putting a few blaspheming Jews to death to do it, well then, so be it. After all, had not the LORD said that blasphemers should be put to death? So it wasn't murder. Having convinced himself of this, Saul stomped out of the chamber and went searching for a few reliable men whom he could trust. He had a task for them to perform, and he knew that they would do it gladly—well, if the price were right. But he had plenty of money, so that should be no problem.

A few days later, early in the morning of the fifth day of the week, the Sanhedrin gathered in their council chamber. Seventy-two members were present, but there was one notable absence, a certain old teacher. Nevertheless, tension filled the air of the room. Saul and two men were seated near the center of the semi-circle near where the accused would stand and be questioned, while the members stood in little groups chatting quietly, constantly glancing from Annas to the door through which the accused would be led.

The high priest raised his hand, the chamber became quiet, and everyone took his seat. Annas looked up at the guard. "Bring in Stephen," he commanded.

Two burly armored men came through the special door from the cells where prisoners were kept, grasping the arms of a little man, maybe one half their height, as if he might suddenly bowl them over and turn and run. Many sneers greeted their prisoner, who appeared quite young because he was still pink-cheeked. There were some murmurs of surprise, as well; for this question occurred to many: how was it possible that this person, not more than a boy, really, could be the cause of all of this trouble? Not so sure of themselves now, they looked around at one another as the guards led the young man to the center of the semi-circle and left him standing there, alone.

The high priest looked over at Saul and asked, "Are your witnesses ready?"

Saul motioned to one of the men he had hired. The man stood, stared at the high priest and pointed at Stephen. "This fellow never stops speaking against this holy place and against the Law. For we have heard him say that Jesus of Nazareth will destroy this place and change the customs Moses handed down to us."[10] He then pointed at his friend who was still sitting beside Saul, and the man nodded eagerly. Neither man looked at Stephen, who continued to stare intently into the eyes of the high priest.

Annas, made uncomfortable by the young man's stare, turned and looked around at his colleagues. He noted that Gamaliel's seat was empty. This bothered him, but he would never have admitted why to himself. He turned back to the young man and asked, "Are these charges true?"

Stephen opened his mouth, and an amazingly sonorous voice poured out the words, "Brothers and fathers, listen to me!" The men were startled by its depth and rich timbre. Many, in their fantasies of meeting a great prophet, say, Moses or Elijah or Jeremiah, had imagined speaking with him and hearing a voice like this answer them. Some had imagined that such a voice must have come from the burning bush on Mount Horeb.[11] Suddenly they weren't so sure what they were about. Saul, sensing that they had begun to waver, became intensely angry.

Stephen began, "The God of glory appeared to our father Abraham while he was still in Mesopotamia, before he lived in Haran ..." and he recounted to them the story of how Abraham left his home and came to this land of theirs; how their most revered patriarch *believed* the promises of God and had Isaac as a result; how he became Israel's father through God's covenant of circumcision; and how this land of theirs was promised to them because of Abraham's faith.

The young man went on to tell them the story of Joseph's sojourn in Egypt, which came about because he was sold into slavery by his *jealous* brothers. Stephen's emphasis of the brothers' jealousy caused the doubts about this man that had started to fill the members of the council to fade. Seeing this, Saul grinned. The young man then recounted to them how, through God's provision and Joseph's great faith, the whole country of Egypt and their own people were saved from a terrible famine in the land.

He recalled his people's history in Egypt, about how they came to be its slaves and how God raised up a great prophet, Moses, to deliver them. As he told them about the incident of the burning bush, the look in his eye and the tone of his voice testified to his high regard for Moses. With this, some of his inquisitors' doubts were rekindled, and Saul became angry again.

---

[10] Acts 6:13 – 14. See Acts 6: 13 – 7:60 for the Biblical account of the trial and stoning of Stephen.

[11] See Exodus 3: 1 and following for an account of Moses' conversation with God in the burning bush.

Their doubts were quickly put aside, however, when Stephen was careful to point out to them that, "This is the same Moses whom they had rejected with the words, 'Who made you ruler and judge?' even though he was sent to be their ruler and deliverer by God himself ..." They knew full well what he was implying; for they said the same thing to Jesus of Nazareth. Some actually squirmed in their seats as they recalled this. Saul grinned at the looks on their faces.

Undaunted by their angry stares, the young man recited all the miracles with which God delivered his people from their slavery in Egypt. Angry murmurs rose as Stephen went on to refresh their memories as to how, despite all of God's gracious provision for them, despite all the miracles Moses did in their midst, still they grumbled and complained and rejected him and their God again and again, even making for themselves a golden calf.

Stephen had warmed to his subject now; his eyes were flashing and his voice echoed throughout the room, drowning out the council's angry murmurs.

Brimming with accusation and reproach, Stephen now recounted how all through their history they had worshipped idols and rejected their God, despite the many prophets the LORD had sent to them. All during his testimony, the young man made his case by quoting liberally from the writings and prophets. Many of the priests and Pharisees were astonished at his erudition. Saul gnashed his teeth at this because these men admired learning and might be persuaded by his victim's keen arguments.

But any concern Saul may have had evaporated when Stephen pointed around at them all and cried out, "You stiff-necked people, with uncircumcised hearts and ears! You are exactly like your fathers. You always resist the Holy Spirit! Was there ever a prophet your fathers did not persecute? They even killed those who predicted the coming of the Righteous One. And now you have betrayed and murdered Him—you who have received the law that was put into effect through angels but have not obeyed it."[12] Saul smiled as everyone shouted at the young prophet. Saul wanted to shout too, but for joy, when Stephen, with his eyes now turned to heaven, said, "Look, I see heaven open and the Son of Man standing at the right hand of God."[13]

With this, the Ruling Council covered its ears and leapt to its feet. It poured out of the benches and rushed at Stephen. Yelling and screaming curses, it dragged him out of the city to the valley of Ben Hinnom and there it

---

[12] This closing statement is quoted from Acts 7: 51 – 53.

[13] Acts 7:56.

stoned him to death. Meanwhile Saul had taken the men's cloaks—for they had not wanted to be hindered by them. While they did this, Saul laughed joyously as the young man sank to his knees and then fell on his face and died.[14]

After this, Saul, with the concurrence of the council, went on a rampage. With many armed men at his disposal, he went from house to house in the city and dragged suspected followers of the Nazarene out of their homes and put them in prison. Many were murdered before they made it to their cells. Many died due to mistreatment in prison, and fear of Saul of Tarsus spread among the Nazarenes so that, except for Jesus' original followers, they left Jerusalem and scattered throughout all Judea and Samaria.

Maddeningly, this obnoxious sect, referred to by its followers as the Church of the Way, began to spread to the outlying districts, and its numbers grew greatly with each passing day. Saul was forced to go into the furthest reaches of Judea and Samaria, even up as far as Damascus, to persecute these followers of Jesus.

Saul went in to Annas and complained. "This is driving me crazy. The more we kill them, the more they multiply. They are even starting to pop up as far away as Syria, and the sect has taken a foothold in Damascus now. How is it possible?"

The look on the young man's face and the whining tone of his voice seemed funny to the high priest, though he too was concerned about the maddening propensity of these followers of Jesus, who had called himself the Christ, to multiply no matter how much the Jews tried to wipe them out. Nevertheless, Annas was becoming increasingly concerned about Saul's tactics. Not that the high priest had any ethical objection to them, mind you. Rather, he feared that this young man might be getting too powerful. Keeping this concern to himself, however, Annas said, "So what can I do for you, my son?"

"My lord, give me letters to all the synagogues in Damascus. Instruct them to look for everyone who is a follower of Jesus and to point them out. Make sure it is clear that I have permission to arrest them to bring them back here where we can deal with them properly."

"Of course, my son."

Annas readily agreed to this request because he had begun to fear Saul's bloodthirstiness. He was also starting to think that maybe this young Pharisee

---

[14] Acts 7:58.

might be a little too dangerous to be allowed to wander freely around with so many armed men. The high priest wondered if Saul might not be a liability to them all. He wondered how long it would take for Saul to turn on them if they happened to disagree with his tactics, for example. As the high priest's fear of Saul intensified, he considered denouncing him to the Romans so that they would be forced to deal with him.

With these thoughts in mind, Annas quickly wrote the letters Saul had requested. But once the young man left him, he went to the Roman governor of Judea and had a long talk with him.

Meanwhile, Saul set out for Damascus. Everyone knows that on the way he met Someone who had a few words with *him*, and several days later, Saul found himself lying on a cot in the house of a man named Judas, on a street named Straight, in the city of Damascus.[15] He was blinded and he was changed. All of the hate, the murder and the blasphemy had been seared out of him in one tremendous act of mercy. He had not eaten or drunk anything for two days; but he could not have eaten had they tried to force food down his throat. And he began to pray:

> "O Sovereign LORD, what have I done? In my foolish pride, fueled by my ignorance and wrongheaded zeal, I have murdered your servants. Like all my people before me, I have murdered your messengers. With my lips I honored you; but how far from you was my heart? Oh yes, I too, had an idol in my heart. It was myself.[16] How impressed I was by my own wisdom and knowledge; by my own accomplishments; by my own righteousness! How many visits did I make to that great harlot, Pride?
>
> "How I wish I had listened to my old friend, father and teacher on that day. But no, I was too full of myself; too full of my own wisdom. I was so foolish. What was the end of all that knowledge and wisdom? What was the end of all my accomplishments, of all that intellectual achievement of which I had always been so proud? Hatred! Murder! Blasphemy!

---

[15] See Acts 9 for the account of Saul's meeting with Jesus and then of his sojourn in Damascus.

[16] Saul is referring to the admonition of the LORD against harboring idols in one's heart that comes in Ezekiel 14:3.

"Yet you, O LORD, in your wonderful grace and mercy saved me, though I certainly deserved to die for what I have done. It's too wonderful to contemplate, too awesome to understand. Now I am blind. But if you were to restore my sight, I would devote my heart and soul to do everything you instruct me to do."

As he breathed out this last vow, Saul had a vision of an elderly man named Ananias coming to him, placing his hands on his eyes and restoring his sight. He then finished his prayer by saying, simply, "Oh thank you, Lord Jesus. Thank you."

After that day, Saul, the murderer, eventually changed his name to Paul. He was appointed an apostle of the LORD by the grace of God, and he set out to do as he had vowed. He served the LORD faithfully for many decades, evangelizing the known world and planting churches throughout Asia Minor.

Paul stared at the ceiling of his cell and reflected on his life before the LORD his God took hold of him. The image of his old teacher staring into his face on the day he decided to murder Stephen came to him for what must have been the thousandth time. Tears ran down his cheeks now, cascading rivers of remorse. That he had had the temerity to abuse his friend, his father, this devoted old man who had loved him and had nothing but Paul's own well-being at heart, crushed him with grief. Those kind eyes kept boring into his consciousness on the screwing points of the words, "Think, think!" Paul had thought all right; he had spent his whole life thinking before that day; but the gist of his thoughts, fueled by his pride and arrogance of knowledge, had been worse than excrement. Where had all that thinking, all that knowledge, all that observance of the Law led him after all?

Paul gazed at the ceiling, hoping that his old teacher might be in heaven with the LORD, hearing him as he said, "I am so very sorry for the way I treated you that day, my dear, dear friend. So very sorry. Forgive me."

Somehow, Paul knew that old Gamaliel had forgiven him long ago, and he rolled over and went to sleep.

After note: As I reread this story, it occurred to me that a reader might think I wrote it to denigrate Paul the Apostle, probably the greatest Christian of all time. I certainly did not! His work for the Kingdom in service to the Lord Jesus Christ speaks for itself.

As noted at its beginning, this story is based on Paul's own testimony as well as what Luke tells us in the book of Acts about the life Paul lived prior to his meeting with Jesus on the Damascus road. Paul was clearly a very smart guy and a model Pharisee. But Paul confesses that all the knowledge he had gained and the righteousness that comes through following the Law were as rubbish compared to knowing the Lord Jesus Christ. (See Philippians 3: 4 – 10.) Paul confesses that knowing about God as he did, is not the same as knowing Him personally.

We can see that the life he lived was typical of godless intellectual before he yielded to the saving Grace of God. And such godless religious leaders have been known to do horrific things in service of their own pride and human wisdom; see for example the Spanish Inquisition of the fifteenth and sixteenth centuries.

A Wealthy Young Ruler

Jesus looked around and said to his disciples, "How hard it is for the rich to enter the kingdom of God!" The disciples were amazed at his words. But Jesus said again, "Children, how hard it is to enter the kingdom of God! It is easier for a camel to go through the eye of a needle than for a rich man to enter the kingdom of God." (Mark 10: 23 – 25)[1]

Author's note: Not only does the worship of the idol of intellectual accomplishment present a barrier to accepting the LORD's gift of salvation as we just saw. So does the worship of wealth. But this story shows that God can conquer all things.[2]

A wealthy young man named Joseph—who, despite his youth, was influential among the Jews because he was a righteous man, and because he was also the ruler of a small district in northern Judea—had just finished his sumptuous afternoon meal when Antonius, one of his servants, entered and stood near the door, breathing heavily. Hearing him enter, Joseph looked up. Seeing the young man's heaving breast, he waived him over.

Antonius ran up to him, knelt at his feet and kissed his hand. "Master, that fellow you are interested in, Jesus of Nazareth, is traveling not far from here. It is said he is heading up toward the lake in Galilee. I have heard talk that he has passed through Sychar, Lord, and I have come to inform you, as instructed."

Joseph's breathing quickened, as did his beating heart. *Jesus is here!* he thought. *How I want to meet him!* But, not wanting to let his servant know how excited he was, he said as nonchalantly as he could, "Well done, Antonius. Well done." His young servant beamed at the praise.

Joseph stood slowly. "Get the chariot, Antonius. I must go see this man, Jesus. I have a question to ask him." The young man eagerly ran off to do his master's bidding.

While the young ruler waited, he began to pace.

---

[1] The story of the wealthy man is told in Mark 10: 17 – 25 and also told in Luke 18: 18 – 25. It is Luke who identifies the man specifically as a ruler. Scripture does not identify him by name or inform us where he came from, however.
[2] See Mark 10:27.

Now the room was quite large, and Joseph could pace a good number of steps before turning and reversing course. Also, the ceiling was high and the floor and walls were made of a finely polished pink marble. Therefore his steps echoed loudly. As he paced, two of his servants followed him with anxious eyes. If you looked closely you might have seen their lips moving as they counted his steps. It was a rule among them, though self-imposed, that after one hundred steps they would call out to him and offer him something to drink or eat, lest fatigue get the better of him. This had always amused Joseph because he kept himself physically fit; but he allowed them this, for he knew that they did it because they loved him, as he loved them.

That was why when he motioned to one of them, the young woman hurried over to him, bowed low, her palms flat on the floor in front of her. "Yes, my master," she said, her eyes glancing upward and then quickly returning to the floor, "what may I do for you?" It was Ruth, Antonius' wife.

"Ruth, bring me Elias the priest, please. I'd like to speak with him."

The young woman ran off quickly to do as she was bid. About half an hour later, she came back into the dining room followed by a very old man. When the old priest had stopped and looked up with kind smiling eyes into those of his lord, Ruth bowed and left them. The other servant left as well.

"And, my young master, how are you today?" the old man asked as the young man took his hand, laid his forehead against it and then kissed it before looking into his eyes. When Joseph had let his hand go, the old priest caressed his cheek because he loved this young man to distraction, as if he were the son he had lost many years ago to sickness.

Taking Elias' wrinkled old hand in his own, Joseph said, "Rabbi, I must ask you something."

"Certainly," Elias replied, glancing over at the table where the wine was.

Joseph chuckled. "I'm sorry, my friend," he said, placing a hand gently on the rabbi's shoulder and turning him toward the table. "Here, let's have some wine." The old man smiled brightly as he was led to the table and helped into a chair. Ruth, anticipating this and having already entered, hurried up to them, grasped a flagon, and poured both of them a goblet of wine, starting with the priest. Then, at a look from her master, she bowed and left them again.

The young ruler smiled at his teacher. "I have been troubled lately, Elias," Joseph said, stroking his chin. "This rabbi, Jesus of Nazareth, you have heard of him?"

Elias nodded, all seriousness now. He had heard of Him all right, and word was going around that the Ruling Council, of which his master was an influential member, was trying to find a way to put Him to death. Because Elias loved Joseph, he did not want Jesus' blood on his son's hands.

Truth be told, the old rabbi had eagerly followed Jesus' career for some time now. Elias had heard Him speak on the mountain some months ago—though he had never mentioned this to his young master—and he believed that He was indeed the Son of God and their Messiah come to save them. Therefore, he had put his faith in Him on that day. Oh yes! The old rabbi had known instantly who He was. Nothing he had seen since contradicted this. For Jesus had healed a man blind from birth. He had raised Jairus' young daughter from the dead.[3] And there had been a man named Lazarus, who was raised, but only after he had been dead for four whole days! Only God could do that. No, indeed, Elias thought, he certainly did not want Joseph involved with the evil men in Jerusalem who wanted to kill the very Son of God. How he hated the hypocrites in the council!

Seeing the steely look in his teacher's eye, Joseph said, "I see you have heard about what our rulers in Jerusalem have been saying about the Nazarene and what they have started to plan." The rabbi nodded. "Well, let me assure you, I will have none of it." The old man exhaled so loudly with relief, Joseph put a finger to his lips and turned his head aside briefly to hide a smile. He knew then what the priest must have been thinking about the danger he would be in if he were part of the plan, and Joseph loved him for it.

Serious again, the young ruler said, "But I have a question I want to ask him. He is close by, you know." No, the priest did not know. He sat up, his eyes widening with interest. "Yes, I can see that you have been following him too." Elias' eyes narrowed. "You know, they say that this Jesus fellow is the Son of God." Joseph shook his head in disbelief, but the old man blushed. With a chuckle Joseph leaned forward and put a hand on Elias' forearm. "Really? Do you believe them?" The rabbi's eyes went to the floor. Intrigued, Joseph said light-heartedly and confidentially, "Don't worry. I won't tell anyone your little secret." They both laughed quietly, but Elias a bit nervously because of his fear of what the Ruling Council might do to them both if their interest in Jesus' teaching were ever found out.

After a moment or two, the young man assumed a contemplative air and looked around the room, the rabbi's eyes following his. Joseph turned back

---

[3] See Mark 5: 22. Jairus was the ruler of a synagogue near Capernaum.

to his teacher. "Tell me, Rabbi Elias, as you look around you, what do you see?"

The rabbi sighed loudly again and then looked around the room slowly. When his eyes came back to rest on his young student, Elias said, "I see a room filled to the brim with wealth. Gold goblets and silver plates and bowls; beautifully crafted tables, chests, and chairs made of the finest hard woods and lacquered and polished until they gleam. I see Greek and Roman vases of the most exquisite quality. If I could see through the walls I would see ten other rooms like this one." He paused dramatically. "Yes, my son! I see a palace made of the finest polished stone, and tending it, an army of servants of all ages. Beyond that, I see grounds with stables for horses and chariots. I see barns holding an abundance of grain and many large vats of new wine. And then there are many large gardens meticulously maintained." The young man nodded with each sentence.

The old man's eyes narrowed as he touched the young man's wrist. "But above it all, I see the owner of all this." He waved his other hand around at the room. "A young man of great authority in Judea, who is well-loved by all who live here. I see servants who rush eagerly to fulfill his slightest wish. Not because they fear him. No, not at all! But because they all love him more than they could ever express otherwise because he loves them too and shows it by treating them like his closest relatives." The young man blushed and lowered his eyes modestly. Smiling with love for him, Elias continued, "I see a godly and humble man who fears the LORD and walks in His ways; who loves Him, and tries to serve Him with all his heart and all his soul, which, I would guess, he has succeeded in doing, almost without fault."[4]

Joseph bowed his head and murmured humbly, "Please, Father, no."

But the old priest nodded and contradicted him. "Yes you have, my precious son. Yes you have! And I see someone who has always given lavishly of his wealth, not only to the work of the temple, but also to the care of the poor, the sick, and the weak. I see a man of towering generosity and goodness." He paused again. "Yes, my lord. This is what I see." He stared at the blushing young man for a long time, nodding and smiling at him.

The master of the house cleared his throat and said haltingly, anxious eyes glancing around the room because many of his servants were listening, "Please, Rabbi Elias. Please! You're embarrassing me."

---

[4] See Deuteronomy 10:12.

He was right. The servants were listening! But he could not see that they had tear-filled eyes and were shaking their heads "no", as if to say, "No reason to be embarrassed, Master, because everything he said was true." O those eyes of theirs! Shining with admiration, emphasizing the point by as much as shouting, "And how we love you for it!"

Old Elias chuckled at his son's discomfort. "So, tell, me young lord," he said, "what is the question that burns in your heart that you must fly off this instant to ask it?" Rabbi Elias had just heard the chariot pull up noisily, and through the wide arched door that led outside, he could see its anxious young driver staring at his master with eager eyes.

Joseph turned his head and motioned—a moment please—to the young horseman, who nodded acknowledgment.

Then he too chuckled as he turned back to his teacher. "Well, Rabbi, does it not say in the Writings, the Psalms and the Prophets that great wealth is a sign of God's blessing? Does not all this indicate that I have pleased my God *by my righteous life,* as you put it?" He said that with a self-deprecating tone of voice and laughing. "And that I will therefore be taken into glory to be with the LORD?"

The old priest nodded slowly, his mouth forming into a thin straight line and his eyebrows narrowing under a furrowed brow. He understood his student's reference to the Psalms.[5] Elias stroked his beard slowly and stared intensely at Joseph, thinking, *So, he is troubled about his eternal future. He wants to be sure that he will go to rest in the bosom of Abraham when he dies.*[6] But as always, the old priest was slow to answer such a weighty question, and as he sat and thought about his answer, the young man squirmed impatiently.

After a long moment, the rabbi raised his head and said, "Well, let's see." He raised his eyes to the ceiling as he began his answer. "It is certainly true the LORD has said that great wealth is a blessing from God and that it can come because a man leads a righteous life. For example, the LORD God

---

[5] There are many Scriptures that indicate that wealth is the sign of the LORD's blessing. Rabbi Elias was thinking of Psalm 112: 1 – 3. See also Proverbs 8:18 and Proverbs 10:22, among other verses. As to being taken into glory, Elias understood that Joseph had made an oblique reference to Psalm 73:24: "I am always with you [,LORD]; you hold me by my right hand. You guide me with your counsel, and afterward you will take me into glory."

[6] Resting in Abraham's bosom was the Jew's metaphorical reference to going to heaven to live with their LORD.

has said through Solomon that if we honor the LORD with our wealth, He will bless us with more wealth. I can see that this has happened in your home, my lord."[7] The young man indicated wordlessly that he recognized the reference. Then Elias cited many other Scriptures that implied that God blessed the righteous with great wealth. There was Job, for example; and everyone knew that Job rested in the bosom of Abraham. And Abraham himself was also very wealthy, as all the patriarchs had been as well as King David. "And as the Psalm you quoted indicates," Elias concluded, "it is certainly true that God has reserved a place in heaven for the righteous when they die."

The old priest stealthily watched his student's eyes throughout this discourse, and he saw that Joseph seemed to be relieved somehow.

"But, young man, I think there is more to it than outward signs."

Joseph slumped back in his chair.

The rabbi raised a finger. "Yes, I think so, now that you mention it."

The young man again squirmed impatiently, narrowing his eyes as if to say, "Mentioned what? I mentioned nothing of the sort."

Reading Joseph's frustration, Elias smiled. "Well, I guess I'm about to mention it, then."

The young lord's slight motion of his hand expressed his not-too-well-hidden desire that his teacher get on with it.

Amused, the priest sat forward and looked deeply into his beloved son's eyes. His eyes narrowing, Elias said, "You see, my son, after Asaph says, 'You guide me with your counsel, and afterward you will take me into glory,' he then says, 'Whom have I in heaven but you? And earth has nothing I desire besides you. My flesh and my heart may fail, but God is the strength of my heart and my portion forever. Those who are far from you will perish; you destroy all who are unfaithful to you. But as for me, it is good to be near God. I have made the Sovereign LORD my refuge ...' "[8]

Joseph leaned forward, staring eagerly at Elias.

With raised finger the old priest said, "Yes, indeed. I think we must put being near to God above all things *in this world*. And if something gets in the way of that ..." His voice trailed off as he glanced around at the opulence surrounding them. "Well, we need to deal with it." He sat back, nodded a few times and stroked his beard, waiting for his beloved son's response.

The young ruler looked around him, considering all his possessions. Certainly he had not let this get in the way of being near God. Had he?

---

[7] Proverbs 3: 9 – 10.
[8] Psalm 73:24 – 28a.

Becoming impatient with the old man's knowing stare, he began to wring his hands. *Would you stop staring!* he thought irritably as the old rabbi's eyes shone brightly and relentlessly at him, but with a light that penetrated into Joseph's innermost being and illuminated a certain place hidden deep in his soul.

Joseph rose abruptly, and Elias rose slowly. The young ruler was angry now, but he did not know why. He wanted to shout at the old man that all this—his eyes glanced involuntarily around at the room—meant nothing at all to him. But he did not shout, for as he stared into his teacher's kind and loving eyes, his heart calmed, as did his hands. Rather, he smiled and embraced his teacher warmly. He noted that some of his servants, who had started into the room, sensing his displeasure, had retreated again, and he wanted to laugh. But he did not.

He held the rabbi away from him by the shoulders and smiled into his eyes. "I think I know what you are saying, my father. I appreciate your candor. That's why I love you so, you know." The old man's eyes moistened as he covered his son's hands with his own and patted them gently. "But let's see what Jesus says," Joseph concluded.

Rabbi Elias nodded, admiring his young student. He smiled again as he considered him. No hypocrite here. Not at all. Here was someone who truly hungered and thirsted for righteousness, for the righteousness that would bring him into that Glory the Psalmist referred to. But Rabbi Elias also knew from the Prophets that the truly righteous man must live by his faith.[9] Not by finding comfort and justification through works and deeds—or by the blessing of wealth—but by putting his faith in God.

The old rabbi had always known this, so he knew what Jesus would say to his young lord. He hoped that his beloved son would put away anything that entangled him so that they would meet again in the hereafter, standing joyfully in the presence of Jesus, their LORD and God. How Elias hoped that would happen, as young Joseph embraced him again and then turned and left.

After this the wealthy young ruler rode out eagerly to find Jesus. But when he got to the lake in Galilee, he found that the young rabbi had left the day before and was heading south toward Judea. Frustrated, he rode like the wind, and the next day he did find him. For there was a large crowd gathered near the Jordan river, opposite the Judean village of Bethabara, and Joseph knew that that must be where Jesus was. He had his driver stop some

---

[9] Habakkuk 2:4.

distance away, and he quickly dismounted his chariot. He motioned that his driver should wait as he left him to see what was going on.

After nudging his way through the crowd, Joseph saw that they had gathered around but at a respectful distance from a plain robed young man of average height and average looks, who was speaking to them all, turning around slowly.

I can see that he likes to make eye contact with his audience. I like that, Joseph thought. *But I would have expected him to be taller or more impressive somehow.* Joseph had to admit he was disappointed that Jesus was not at least six cubits tall or that fire did not come from his mouth or eyes, as he had imagined. "Childish foolishness," the young ruler said to himself with a chuckle. As he continued to scan the crowd, he took note of several other young men who were with the young rabbi, and who, Joseph thought, must be the disciples everyone was talking about.

As Joseph got closer, a young couple was presenting their little daughter to Jesus, but one of the disciples rebuked them for bothering the Master. Jesus' expression became stern as he took the giggling little girl in his arms. He looked over his shoulder at the disciple and said to him, "What are you thinking? It's all right. Let the little children come to me!"[10]

The young disciple who had spoken deflated instantly and bowed his head, scuffling his feet nervously. His master glared at him for a moment, increasing the poor young man's discomfort noticeably.

Then Jesus turned His face to the child, who was maybe four or five years old. She giggled and put several of her fingers in her mouth. When He smiled at her, she giggled more and squirmed with shyness. He sat down on a nearby boulder and set her on His lap. He whispered something into her ear, and she yanked her fingers out of her mouth, looked down at them, and laughed heartily at herself. Then she rose up and gave Him a peck on the cheek, still giggling delightedly. Jesus threw His head back and laughed loudly with pleasure, while the little girl stared around at all of their smiling faces, clearly proud of herself. Even the disciples were laughing, the one embarrassed young man especially loudly.

Jesus looked up and around at them all. When His eye lighted on the young ruler it stopped. He stared into Joseph's eyes for a moment and

---

[10] This is a paraphrase of Mark 10: 13 – 14. Scripture never reveals who specifically among the disciples rebuked those bringing the children to Jesus. But later I've named Peter as one of the offenders because of his seeming tendency to speak before thinking.

smiled. The young man thought he might faint with joy and embarrassment as all other eyes lighted on him also.

Turning back to the crowd, Jesus repeated, "Let the little children come to me." He looked back at the offending disciple again. "Do not hinder them, for the kingdom of God belongs to such as these." Turning again to stare at Joseph, He continued, "I tell you the truth, anyone who will not receive the kingdom of God like a little child will never enter it."[11] They all murmured with astonishment, and Joseph felt uncomfortable, but he could not say why.

Jesus set the little girl down on her feet and kissed her. This time she whispered something in His ear, and He laughed again. She put her arms around Jesus' neck and hugged Him, after which He picked her up again, stood, and handed the giggling child to her very embarrassed but very proud parents. As Jesus turned to go, He turned back quickly to look at her. She pulled away abruptly because she had put a finger in her mouth again; but she yanked it out quickly and squealed delightedly at being caught. And everyone laughed as the crowd moved off to follow the young rabbi. As they walked, Jesus embraced his young follower, hugged him and whispered something into his ear. The young man smiled.

Joseph, not to be denied, ran up to Jesus and fell on his knees in front of Him, stopping Him abruptly. Jesus looked down at the young man, took his hand and brought him to his feet.

Then the wealthy young ruler asked, "Good teacher, what must I do to inherit eternal life?"[12]

"Why do you call me good?" Jesus answered, looking around at them all. "No one is good—except God alone." The young man blushed furiously and nodded an apology. But Jesus smiled. Knowing Joseph's heart, He had compassion for him. Looking deeply into his eyes, Jesus added in a quieter voice, "You know the commandments: 'Do not murder, do not commit adultery, do not steal, do not give false testimony, do not defraud, honor your father and mother.' "

Joseph sighed, relieved that Rabbi Elias had been wrong. With bright eyes, he replied, "Oh yes, Teacher, all these I have kept since I was a boy."

Jesus nodded, loving him. "There is still one thing you lack." The young man's heart fell, as if the smiling eyes of his old friend Elias were staring at him rather than Jesus' eyes. Joseph got the strange feeling that this young

---

[11] Mark 10:14 – 15. The interplay between Jesus and Joseph is, of course, fictional.

[12] The following conversation is from Mark 10:17 – 21, modified slightly to allow for the flow of the story.

rabbi had heard his conversation with his friend. As the young man's heart beat rapidly, Jesus said, "Go! Sell everything you have and give it all to the poor, and you will have treasure in heaven. Then come and follow me."

What?

Joseph recoiled as if he had been struck. In that moment, he realized that the thought of selling all his possessions was horrible for him. He did not think he could do it. His eyes staring at the ground, he turned and walked slowly away from his Saviour. But as he did, he could feel Jesus staring at his back, and he could all but imagine the sad look in His eyes. It was then that he realized that the old rabbi had been right: his possessions were an entanglement.

Joseph stopped briefly, however, when he heard Jesus say, "How hard it is for the rich to enter the kingdom of God!" There were intakes of breath. Joseph looked back, and he could see by the amazed looks in the disciples' eyes that they had thought the same thing he had: a Jew's great wealth was a sure sign of his salvation. The young ruler began to weep when Jesus said again, "Children, how hard it is to enter the kingdom of God! It is easier for a camel to go through the eye of a needle than for a rich man to enter the kingdom of God."

In response, all his disciples murmured at once, "Who then can be saved?"[13]

With that the young ruler turned and ran weeping into the woods. He did not hear Jesus say in response, "With man this is impossible, but not with God; all things are possible with God."[14] Nor did he see Jesus looking after him longingly.

Despairing, Joseph wandered through the woods for some time. When his driver found him, he waved him away. Antonius went dejectedly back to his chariot to wait and worry about his weeping master.

Joseph was thinking, *All my life I've followed the Law. I've done everything possible to gain righteousness in the eyes of God, as my father did before me. And as the LORD God has said in the Scriptures, my family has been blessed with power, wealth, and a good name.[15] Why, at the age of twenty-eight I was an influential member of the Ruling Council—almost unheard of. That certainly was an act of God, if nothing else was. But what the LORD has now made clear to me through Jesus, who must be His Son, is*

---

[13] Mark 10: 23 – 26.

[14] Mark 10:27.

[15] See Proverbs 3: 1 – 10.

that all this time what I was doing was considering my possessions as evidence of God's salvation. This means that I was really relying on my own righteousness to get me into glory.

Joseph's head was bowed and he was wiping a tear from his eye when he heard the crack of a branch behind him. He turned angrily around, expecting to see Antonius. He had opened his mouth to shout at him when he saw that it was Jesus standing there. He fell to his knees before the LORD and wept bitterly.

Jesus stooped down, raised Joseph to his feet, took his head and brought it down to His shoulder as the young ruler wept.

After a few minutes, Joseph looked into Jesus' eyes, and as he did, everything Elias said came back to him. It's not about what you own or about how you got your wealth or even about your righteous works, but it's about what you put your trust in and in whom you believe. In that moment he understood what Jesus had told him, and he placed his faith in Him.

Joseph stayed in Jesus' arms for a long time, weeping, but now for the bittersweet joy he felt.

A Wealthy Young Ruler (Epilogue)

Then Jesus said to his disciples, "I tell you the truth, it is hard for a rich man to enter the kingdom of heaven. Again I tell you, it is easier for a camel to go through the eye of a needle than for a rich man to enter the kingdom of God." When the disciples heard this, they were greatly astonished and asked, "Who then can be saved?" Jesus looked at them and said, "With man this is impossible, but with God all things are possible." Peter answered him, "We have left everything to follow you! What then will there be for us?" (Matthew 19:23 – 27) "I tell you the truth," Jesus replied, "no one who has left home or brothers or sisters or mother or father or children or fields for me and the gospel will fail to receive a hundred times as much in this present age (homes, brothers, sisters, mothers, children and fields—and with them, persecutions) and in the age to come, eternal life. (Mark 10:29 – 30)

Author's note: One of my readers, who provided many valuable comments on an early draft of this book that did not have this story, suggested that A Wealthy Young Ruler ended too abruptly. "What did Joseph do? Did he sell his stuff?" she wondered. Well, Nichole, here's my answer. Note that this story is entirely fictional: Scripture never tells us what happened to the wealthy young ruler.

After weeping for a good long time on Jesus' shoulder, Joseph knelt before Him and said, all earnestness sounding in his voice, "I hear and obey, Lord. Surely it will be done as you have commanded." But he was wondering how.

Knowing what was in his heart but also knowing how devoted to Him Joseph had been his whole life, the LORD embraced him once again, and then turned back to join His disciples.

As Joseph stumbled back to his chariot, he realized that selling his possessions wasn't going to be so easy because he had grown used to the life of riches and wealth and power. He also thought that if there was only himself to consider, it would be a lot easier, but he also had dozens of servants and their families who depended on him. What would happen to them?

Joseph also had responsibilities to his nation as a member of the Ruling Council. In his eyes it might be only him and Nicodemus and a few other honorable men who stood between Jesus and the other Pharisees who wanted to put Him to death. Who would replace him? Joseph shuddered when he recalled that there was a young Pharisee waiting to get a seat on the council. Joseph's abdication would provide him the opportunity. The Pharisee's name was Joshua, same as Jesus' name, ironically, and he was no friend of His. Again and again this violent young man had said how much he wanted to gain a seat on the council so that he could help silence Jesus once for all.

Antonius saw his master coming and, seeing that Joseph had been weeping, became alarmed. Jumping down to meet Joseph, he bowed low to him and asked, "My lord, what has happened? Are you all right?"

Joseph was touched by his concern. Looking back to where he and Jesus had stood, and then turning back to his servant and motioning for him to rise, he said, "Yes, Antonius. Everything's quite all right. I heard what I came to hear, but it was a hard thing."

"Is there anything I, no, we," he waved his hand around indicating the entire household of Joseph's servants, "can do for you?"

Crinkling his brow, stroking his chin, and looking deeply into Antonius' eyes, he said, "Well, maybe there is." The young man's eager eyes shone with gladness. Laughing a little at Antonius' expression, the young ruler said, "You can help me break the news to the others." He paused and sighed deeply. Meanwhile, Antonius squirmed with anticipation of what he might say. "We have to go back and arrange to sell everything I own."

The young servant recoiled as if he had been struck, which in fact he had, by the pounding fists of anxiety and sorrow. *Sell **everything**?* Antonius wondered. The images of his wife and four-year-old daughter, plus the images of the other men and women who served in Joseph's household and their dozens of children—he counted mentally at least one hundred of them—came rushing to his mind. What would *they* do? What would *he* do? Though his master treated them like his own family, they were still his slaves. They had no rights at all. He knew that Joseph would do everything he could to find them new employment and with a kind master, but that was little solace because the young servant sincerely believed there could never be another master as good and kind to them all as Joseph was. And he was right.

Though Antonius understood what a hard thing this was for his master, he could not stop himself from asking, "But what will happen to the rest of us?" Quickly realizing how selfish this sounded, Antonius dropped to his knees. "Of course, master, I know that you will take good care of us. I didn't mean to …"

Joseph motioned him to silence. Then he took the man's hand and again brought him to his feet. "I certainly know what you meant, and I'm touched.

Don't worry, Antonius. By the grace of the LORD our God, I will find you and the others and their wives and children a good employer. There are many who would gladly take you into their homes. Rest easy on this, my friend."

Antonius blushed at the endearment. That this wonderful, kind man of tremendous wealth and power considered him, a lowly bond-servant, a friend touched him more deeply than he could have said. To express his love for and devotion to his lord and master, he went to one knee before him, took his hand, kissed it and laid it on his head.

"Come, come, Antonius," Joseph said, weeping again, but this time from the warmth of love he felt for this good young man and his family, "we will find you and your wife and your daughter a good employer."

"I know you will, my master," the young man replied softly, looking into his eyes. "I know you will." Nevertheless, Antonius could not keep sharp-toothed doubt from gnawing at his insides.

"Good!" Joseph replied, taking Antonius' hand. Motioning to the chariot, he said, "Well, we'd better get back. I have some arrangements to make, and *you* have some sad news to impart to the household."

Joseph chuckled at his little joke and Antonius joined him, though reluctantly. For that thing eating at Joseph's servant was growing in strength and he hated himself for it.

With that, they climbed into the chariot and started the journey back to Arimathea, Joseph's home city. It was dark when they arrived at Joseph's house.

"It's been a long trip," Joseph said. "Go, get something to eat. Then tell the servants what we must do. Try to make them understand that they will all be taken good care of. Will you, my friend?"

Antonius nodded sadly as he turned to lead the horses back to the stable.

On entering the house, Joseph saw that Elias was waiting for him. At first, the old rabbi smiled for joy at the sight of his son. But when he saw Joseph's expression, his smile faded rapidly to be replaced by a frown of deep concern.

"What is it, my son? Did you see Jesus?"

"Yes, Father, I did." He sighed, staring at the ground. When the old rabbi held out his arms to him, Joseph fell into them and wept.

"So, my son, I see that He answered your question."

"Yes He has," Joseph replied, not taking his head off his friend's shoulder.

"Were you surprised?"

Lifting his head, the young man said, "No." He wiped a tear from his eye and smiled bravely.

"Well then, what do you plan to do?"

Looking around at his lavish surroundings, Joseph said with a shrug, "Sell it all, I guess."

The old man felt tremendous pride in Joseph well up in him in that moment because he instantly understood what a heroic effort that answer had required. Surveying the room, Elias also understood, as his son did, that there was more than these "things" to consider. He also saw in the young man's eyes the concern he harbored for his household.

It was difficult in this day and age to find work for people, much less to find them surroundings as good as these. Maybe even impossible, the old man thought. Hard and cruel masters were easy to find. Very easy, indeed. For one *lepta* you could probably buy twelve such, and for a *denarius*, a thousand. (He chuckled quietly at his little joke.) But good, kind and caring masters such as this young man were few and far between. The few Elias knew of had all the help they could possibly use, mostly because they had taken in anyone who came to their doors until there was literally no more room for anyone else. Putting his son's head back on his shoulder and stroking it tenderly, he thought, *My son, you will have to make some very hard choices.*

Meanwhile, Antonius had gone to the servants' quarters to inform them of what had happened. Groans and sobbing greeted the news, as he expected, but not in the way the young servant would have predicted. After the other servants had gotten over their shock, they responded, "Our poor master. Sell all his property? Give it to the poor? What will he do? How will he live?" after which they looked at each other, tears flowing. As they hugged and comforted each other, one of them suggested taking an "offering" to help the master live. There were many shouts of concurrence, the loudest coming from Antonius' wife, Ruth.

Take an offering to help the master live? Antonius was dumbfounded. What were they thinking? What was Ruth thinking? Where was her concern for the well-being of her own family, and all these others for their families as well? Apparently these stupid people did not realize what was at stake here. That thing gnawing at Antonius' insides worked feverishly now.

After a long moment, ravenous doubt, having eaten its fill, spewed this out of the young servant: "Have any of you thought what might happen to us?" Everyone stopped talking suddenly and stared at Antonius as if he had just dropped a large clay pot on the floor, loudly shattering it.

"What about us?" Ruth responded softly. Everyone looked at Antonius with expressions that clearly said, of what importance can that possibly be? Or, how could you even think of yourself at a time like this?

Burning with humiliation, Antonius mumbled, "I dunno. I was just thinking ..."

"Just thinking what, my darling?" Ruth interrupted, softer still.

She didn't sound angry, but she had that look she got when she was disappointed, and her husband really hated that look of hers just now.

Stroking his cheek tenderly, she said, "Master Joseph has never thought of himself before thinking of our welfare, has he?"

Amid loud murmurs of agreement, Antonius mouthed "no", tears welling up and blood rising to his cheeks and forehead.

Shaking her head for emphasis, Ruth continued: "Why, I'll bet the first thing he said to you was, 'Tell the others not to worry. They will be well-taken-care-of.' Am I right?"

Her husband sullenly mouthed "yes."

"Since we know that Master Joseph would take the very last bit of food out of his mouth and rip the very last strip of clothing off his back to make sure we were taken good care of, what question can there be?" Ruth looked around the room at them all and they all shook their heads slowly, Antonius gradually emulating them.

Turning away from her red-faced husband, but grasping his hand and holding it tightly, Ruth said to the others, "Let's go get Rabbi Elias. We need him to help us figure out how to help Master Joseph."

This was met with a loud chorus of "Yes, let's do it!"

Turning back to her husband, giving his hand a little squeeze and then nestling it against her heart, Ruth asked, "Is that all right, my love?"

"Of course, my treasure, it's all right," he choked out. He lifted her hand to his lips and kissed it tenderly. "I feel so ashamed."

She said, "I know you do, my love. We all know you do." Everyone murmured sympathetic understanding.

"There's no need *get* Rabbi Elias," came a loud voice from the entrance to the servants' quarters.

They all turned to see the old rabbi standing there, smiling. Had he had a thousand years to form the thought and then another thousand to translate it into words, he probably could not have expressed how proud he was of these good people—his people, God-fearing sons and daughters of Abraham; and how proud and thankful and humbled he was to know that he belonged to them, heart, mind and soul.

"I heard everything. I can't tell you how pleased I am. And I think," he pointed at the ceiling, "there's Someone Else whose pleased as well." He nodded vigorously with the words "Someone Else" to make his point. They all bowed their heads to hide their embarrassment. But they smiled at each other from beneath hooded brows: to get such a compliment from this man was very high praise!

"Joseph is already on his way to Jerusalem," Elias said. "He has contacts there that will help him dispose of his assets at a reasonable price. Since he expects that that price will be in the thousands of talents of gold, he has left instructions that you should all get the equivalent of one year's pay per person." They gasped, their eyes wide, looking around at each other. The old priest added, "I mean every person!" Pointing first at the men, then at the women and then at their little ones, he added, but slowly for effect, "That means men and women, sons and daughters."

They were stupefied.

"He will also meet with the Roman Consul there to start the process of manumission. All of you will be free."

Hugging each other tightly, but not taking their eyes off the rabbi, they began to weep.

"Oh, and there's one other thing," Elias added, affecting an off-handed matter, as if it were the littlest thing possible.

They looked around at each other, their mouths open and a funny expression on their faces that might have been interpreted as, "What more can there possibly be?"

"He is arranging with a representative of the Roman governor to buy all of you your citizenship."

What? They were already citizens of Judea.

"Not of Judea," the old priest added hastily. "But *of Rome!*"

Some sat down slowly. Those not able to find a chair, a box, or anything else to sit on, slid down to the floor and sat cross-legged. A Roman citizenship could cost thousands of *denarii*.[1] It also provided absolute freedom to go anywhere in the empire, to work anywhere, to own property and to vote, if you were actually in Rome. Most of all, you were protected from injustice in other countries by Roman law. How wonderful!

---

[1] In Acts 22:28 a Roman commander testifies that he paid "a big price" to purchase his citizenship. Unfortunately no one seems to know exactly what that might have been, so I made a guess.

Seeing their astonished but grateful expressions, the rabbi raised a finger and cautioned, "But it will take some time, of course."

They responded with expressions of mock seriousness. Of course. Then they started to laugh—so it will take some time. Who cares? The rabbi was confused at first. But when he understood why they were laughing, he laughed with them. They all hugged each other, they danced, and they laughed until they could hardly breathe.

When they had calmed down and had finished wiping the tears from their eyes; when they all had had a chance to catch their breath; when they had had a chance to again reflect on what their master was doing for them, they looked at each other, nodded, and then they turned to the rabbi.

When Elias saw the expressions on their faces, he knew immediately what they had in mind. Up until that time, if you had asked him whether he could possibly have loved these fine people more or been more proud of them, he would have sworn (if he were a swearing sort of person, that is) that he could not. After a minute into of discussing their plan, however, that conviction flew out the door, and the rabbi felt his heart swell to the point of bursting with admiration for them.

Over the next several months the manumission papers came in, immediately followed by their citizenship papers, and then they put their plan into motion.

Meanwhile, Joseph had resigned from the Ruling Council, to many astonished shouts of "No, don't do it!" He had also been selling off his lands, one hectare at a time. He also sold the animals; the art, furniture and other treasures in the house; the house itself and finally the land on which it stood.

One thing he did not sell, however, was the family graveyard, which consisted of several tombs carved into a rock cliff. That was not really his to sell, since his mother, father and other siblings were buried there. And he would have had to get permission from his elderly uncle Festus, a very powerful man in his own right. But Joseph hated him because the old man was miserly to the nth degree and very cruel, someone from whom Joseph had vowed never to ask anything.

Nor did he sell the clothes off his back, although he had started to do that too, until his friend Elias convinced him that he had more than satisfied Jesus' command.

For his part, the rabbi oversaw the collection and distribution of the proceeds. Every synagogue in Judea got a very large sum of money with strict instructions to use it to help widows, orphans, the lame, halt, and blind. This caused quite a stir throughout the country. Needy people flocked to

Judea. It turned out that the proceeds helped over ten thousand needy people: some to find work; some to pay off debt and redeem their children out of slavery; others to get housing; still others to get medical attention.

Once the deed was done, Joseph went off in search of the LORD Jesus. It did not take long to find Him. For the LORD God in the flesh had also heard of the young ruler's deeds and had come looking for him. He found Joseph kneeling on the shore of the lake in Galilee, praying.

Joseph had his back to Him, and with the undulating sea murmuring quietly along with him and being so completely focused on his prayer, he did not hear the LORD coming. It was therefore with no little surprise and shock that the young man responded to a slight touch on his shoulder and then a friendly hand laid lightly on his forearm.

Joseph shot to his feet and opened his mouth to greet the LORD, but no words came out. His lips moved without making a sound. When he started to get back on his knees before Him, Jesus took him by the hand and embraced him warmly. Joseph began to weep, but for the overwhelming joy he felt as the LORD his God held him in His arms. He also recalled what Isaiah the prophet had said about Him:

> See, the Sovereign LORD ... tends his flock like a shepherd:
> He gathers the lambs in his arms and carries them close to
> his heart ...[2]

When Joseph opened his eyes and looked over Jesus' shoulder he saw that Jesus' disciples were there. They were pointing at Joseph, muttering among themselves. They also had strange expressions, as if they were discussing something that astonished them, something they found hard to believe. He knew, though he could not have said how, that it wasn't because Jesus was giving him His special attention by embracing him. No, it was for some other reason.

Jesus let Joseph go and held him out at arm's length. "Are you wondering what they are saying?"

Jesus jerked His head backward a little toward his disciples, and Joseph nodded, wiping his eyes with the backs of his hands and then wiping his nose on his sleeve.

---

[2] Isaiah 40:10 – 11a.

"If you will recall that day we met, and I told you to sell all that you had, they," another slight motion of His head toward the disciples, "didn't think it would ever happen. They argued about it for weeks after."

Chuckling softly, Jesus looked back over His shoulder and smiled at His friends, and they smiled back, bowing their heads and scuffling their feet, as if they had just been taught yet another lesson.

"But you know what, my son?" Jesus said. Joseph shook his head, his mouth opening a little, anxious anticipation seeming to ooze from every pore. "Because I have known you from before the creation of the world, I knew that you would do this very hard thing. You know why?" No, in fact, Joseph did not. "Because you loved me. Because you have loved me your whole life." Joseph bowed his head, blushing, silent, not knowing how to answer.

But the hair on the back of Joseph's neck and along his forearms began to bristle as this thought flashed through his mind: *Of course I have known Him. I never called Him by the name Joshua (God Saves) specifically, but I have always known Him as my Saviour. I had certainly known and loved Him as the God of my fathers, the God of Abraham, Isaac, and Jacob. As the God who loved His people and considered the sons of Abraham and Isaac His treasured possession. The very same God who brought Israel out of the land of Egypt, gave them the Law and then sent His prophets to them.* It was this God Joseph had certainly loved, honored, served and worshiped with all his heart, mind and soul his whole life; and it was this same God in the flesh who was now speaking to him. During the few seconds it took for these thoughts to course through Joseph's mind, his mouth had fallen open slightly, and he had begun to drool.

"So, are you ready?" Jesus asked, chuckling again.

Joseph was startled out of his trance-like state. Ready? Well, he really didn't know, but he guessed he was as ready as he'd ever be. Wiping the moisture from his chin, Joseph nodded.

Smiling warmly at him, Jesus extended His arm. Joseph quickly stepped into His embrace, and the LORD said, "Well, then, let's go."

Jesus, still with His arm around Joseph's shoulders, turned and went on His way, quickly joined by His disciples.

For their part, the twelve greeted Joseph warmly, introducing themselves and welcoming him to their fellowship. Joseph immediately recognized some of them. Peter, especially, from that time he had first met Jesus and He had rebuked Peter about letting the little children come to Him.

As they walked, the disciples could not get enough of talking about what he had done, and asking him questions such as "How did you do it?" and "What was it like?"

Well, the questions came mostly from one disciple in particular, who seemed to do most of the twelve's talking for them. Always having been a leader, Joseph immediately grew to like this young man very much, and he wanted to be the best of friends with him, as well as close brothers.

For the next several months, Joseph followed Jesus everywhere, eating and sleeping with Him and the disciples. He was constantly amazed at Jesus' teaching and by all the wondrous things He did: healing the sick; casting out demons; even raising the dead. It was so amazing! Joseph especially loved how Jesus castigated the Pharisees, most of whom Joseph hated because of their hypocrisy and the mean-spirited way they ruled over the people.

This made Joseph realize that the thing he had missed most was not the easy life: the luxuries of wealth, the fine foods and wines he had enjoyed from the time he was a boy. Rather, he admitted to himself after much thought, that it was the power he had had as one of the Ruling Council. But now he could not imagine going back to that, though he did have friends there, men whom he admired, men of honor.

Nevertheless, the evil that controlled that awful body was beyond the reach of these few good men. Joseph came to understand in that moment that Jesus' kingdom would not be like any earthly kingdom. It would certainly not be filled with evil men and hypocrites and liars, political opportunists of the lowest sort, the very sons of evil.[3] No, indeed. In Jesus' kingdom there would be love and mercy and compassion and, most of all, justice for its people. The young disciple loved the thought of it.

During these months, they had traveled extensively through Galilee, Samaria and Judea. But they had, interestingly enough, spent very little time near Joseph's home of Arimathea.

It had been six months since Joseph accepted Jesus' offer when they turned toward Arimathea (finally!), and the young ruler realized how much he had missed his beloved father, that is Rabbi Elias, and his friends, that is his former servants. Since he had left Elias to manage all his affairs, he had not had time to personally see to his friends' well-being, and he was anxious to see for himself how they were doing. Of course he did not doubt for a minute that Rabbi Elias had done everything he had asked of him and

---

[3] See Revelation 22:14 – 15.

probably much more. Still, Joseph was anxious to see them all again. He hadn't realized until this day just how much he had missed them and how much he loved them.

The saddening thought came to him that they might no longer be in Arimathea. Freed now and citizens of mighty Rome, they could have scattered to the ends of the Earth. Many might have gone to Rome itself to see it in all its glory. Personally, Joseph had never liked Rome. It was too crowded; there was too much poverty and want in the midst of splendor; it was dark and bestial beyond belief in its sexual behavior; and its entertainment was bloody and cruel—savage even! All in all, not much to his taste. Though he wished his friends well, he hoped that some might have stayed in Judea. In Arimathea.

It was about the sixth hour of a beautiful day as they entered the city. Jesus turned to his disciples and said, "Go, my friends, and get us something to eat." As Joseph began to follow them, Jesus laid a hand on his arm and said, "Not you, Joseph. I want to speak with you."

The young man said, "Certainly, Lord." He watched his other friends turn away and head to the market section of town. Once they had turned a corner, he turned back to Jesus and asked, "Yes, Master?"

"Let's go sit over there."

They walked over to a decorative fountain, a marvel of Roman engineering, its waters spilling out of the mouths of the statues of the Roman gods, Jupiter, Mars and Quirinus—who stood back-to-back, looking outward toward the city. It then ran down over the beautifully sculpted forms of some lesser gods and down into a pool with a low marble wall. There many people sat, some to refresh themselves, some to chat, and others simply to enjoy the bright warm light that beamed down on them through the high blue sky above. Puffy white clouds also glided silently by, chased along by a playful breeze that whooshed here and there among the buildings and through the stone-paved streets.

Jesus stared at His friend for a moment. For such a long moment, in fact, that Joseph started to fidget, his hands going to his face, then to his lap, and then clasping themselves tightly, coming to rest finally between his thighs.

Smiling now, Jesus said, "I want you to leave us and go back to the Ruling Council."

What? Joseph was struck dumb.

"I know. You're confused."

Joseph felt like shouting, "Confused? You bet." He kept silent, however.

Looking away from him, as if He were peering into the very depths of Creation itself, Jesus said softly, "Maybe you can talk some sense into them. The leaders of the Jews are taking their nation down a terrible path that will lead to its utter destruction."

This brought to Joseph's mind the following passage from the prophet Jeremiah:

> This is what the LORD says about this people: "They greatly love to wander; they do not restrain their feet. So the LORD does not accept them; he will now remember their wickedness and punish them for their sins." Then the LORD said to me, "Do not pray for the well-being of this people. Although they fast, I will not listen to their cry; though they offer burnt offerings and grain offerings, I will not accept them. Instead, I will destroy them with the sword, famine and plague."[4]

Jesus gazed at Joseph as if He could read his thoughts. He said, "I want you to be my witness to them." The LORD sighed deeply and then said, "And there is one service I want you to perform for me." At this Joseph perked up, his eyes eager. "But not now. You will know when the time comes." Joseph's expression fell into the confused state it had been before.

"But, Lord, how can this be? I don't have any property. You have to have property to be on the council."

Jesus frowned, as if He were surprised; as if He had not realized the impossibility of the command He had just given. This reaction enforced Joseph's thoughts to this effect, especially when Jesus nodded, still frowning.

The LORD then said, stroking His beard, looking at Joseph through narrow eyes, "Hmmmm. I guess you're right. How can this be?"

Joseph's eyes went wide with wonder. He clearly had no idea.

Smiling now, Jesus looked around at the crowd, as if He were searching for someone. "Let's see. Maybe our answer is approaching." He pointed into the crowd.

As Joseph's eyes followed the direction Jesus' finger was pointing, he saw Rabbi Elias and his whole family, meaning his former servants, coming toward him with big smiles on their faces. It was as if they had suddenly

---

[4] Jeremiah 14:10 – 12.

materialized out of nothing. To say that Joseph was astonished would be a terrific understatement.

And these people were pointing at their former master and then turning to the rabbi and laughing, their hearts obviously overflowing with joy. All the children who were old enough to stand on their own, some of whom had just been learning to walk when Joseph left them, came running up to him, shouting, "Master Daddy! Master Daddy!" That's what they had always called Joseph, and it had never ceased to touch him.

But not nearly as deeply as it did today as they danced around him, their arms out to him, their little faces beaming with smiles bright as the sun above. Joseph knelt down to hug them and embrace them all, laughing and crying at the same time, their delighted giggles drizzling down on him like a soft refreshing rain.

Tears of joy running down his cheeks, buried in the loving embraces of "his" children, Joseph looked up at Jesus, clearly puzzled by what was happening, a question forming silently on his lips.

But the LORD did not immediately respond to Joseph's implied question because at that moment the adults had arrived, their hands out to him, their joy-filled voices calling out to him. Still holding a little girl in his arms, Joseph embraced her mother and then her father, and then, after returning her to them, he embraced all the rest, one at a time. What tears flowed then! What sobs of joy! What glad hands caressed the young man with love and affection! What warmth, what caring was expressed by everyone's gleeful but tear-filled eyes.

Well, it quite surpasses one's ability to find words to adequately express what was happening there.

When Joseph had finished, he looked around for his friend, Elias. The old priest had just finished embracing Jesus, and they were smiling into each other's eyes. Jesus said, laughing, "Well, old friend, how long has it been since we last saw each other?"

"Much too long, Master. Much too long, indeed!" They embraced again.

It brought tears to Joseph's eyes to see that his old friend Elias loved the LORD as he did.

When they had finished, Jesus turned to speak to the crowd. But He found that everyone had fallen to one knee, their heads bowed, their palms flat on the ground. Even the children were kneeling; though the littlest ones fidgeted mightily to escape the tight hold their mothers and fathers had on them. They were, rather, straining toward Jesus, at whom their eager eyes and bright smiles now beamed.

Smiling at these little faces, Jesus said, "Please rise, my friends."

They all did.

Then the adults all came up to greet the LORD, though shyly, many blushing for the pleasure they felt when He spoke to them and embraced each of them. There was not a bit of shyness in children, though, who, when they had managed to break out of their mothers' tight grasp, ran up to Jesus and crowded around Him, arms upraised, giggling loudly.

Filled with joy, the LORD Jesus sat and took each of them on His knee and spoke to them briefly, and then, after kissing them on their little cheeks and foreheads, set them down again. They then ran with delighted squeals back to their parents, some of them hiding shyly behind their mother's skirts, yet keeping their eyes glued on their LORD and Saviour.

Several other men approached Him. They were all members of the Council whom Joseph knew to be men of honor. One in particular, whom he greatly admired, was Nicodemus, who took the LORD's hand and then embraced Him, as did the other men. Joseph, filled with wonder, glanced at Nicodemus and then at Jesus, his eyes asking the question to which he could not manage to give words.

Jesus, seeming to ignore him, turned to Rabbi Elias. "Well, my friend, is it done?" Elias nodded. Jesus looked around at Nicodemus and the other men, and they all nodded too.

Joseph, bursting with anxiety, asked, "Lord, could you please tell me what's going on here?"

Jesus and the others laughed. All of them laughed, even the little children, who all looked like they had some wonderful secret to share and obviously wanted to shout something at him. But they were restrained by their parents' cautioning looks and extended index fingers, wagging back and forth, saying, in effect, "Don't you dare."

Jesus motioned to Nicodemus, who came forward and said to Joseph, "My friend, we have secured your seat on the Council. It took some gentle persuading." He glanced first at Jesus and then at his colleagues who nodded, and then said, "But we got it done. So, welcome back!" He took Joseph in his arms and held him tightly.

Squirming free, Joseph said, "How can this be? I don't have any property."

Elias said, "Oh, didn't we tell you?" He laughed a big belly laugh at Joseph's annoyed expression.

Antonius came forward and laid a calming hand on his master's arm. "Master, we have something to tell you."

Not calmed in the least, Joseph said, "I'm no longer your master, Antonius." He looked around at them all, obviously perplexed by their smiling, knowing looks. Joseph shouted at them all, "Would you please let me in on this little joke of yours?"

Antonius replied, "We all went to your uncle Festus and told him what you had done for us."

Joseph scowled around at them all. He and his uncle had not spoken for years. Joseph had never ceased to thank God that he had inherited a small fortune from his father, Festus' only brother, so that he would not have to go crawling to his uncle for money as all of his cousins did regularly. And he had always thanked God—he glanced over at Jesus, who was staring at him—that He had given him success in all that he had undertaken, and that He had allowed him to amass a great fortune on his own.

In fact, as Joseph was selling all of it, it had come to him that the reason he was given this fortune—which had meant being free of his cruel uncle's grasp, irritating the old man no end, much to Joseph's great satisfaction—was to do precisely what the LORD had commanded him: give it to the poor. And by the grace of God (he glanced at Jesus again, who nodded), it had helped thousands of people.

Reflecting on this, anger burned in Joseph. He would have cut off both arms and legs before going to his uncle for any type of help. Now he had heard that his servants—his ungrateful servants, it seemed—had done this for him.

"What?" he cried as they all looked at him, but not at all affected by his black turn of mood. They continued to smile, rather, which made him angrier still. "What did you say?" he repeated, glaring at them.

Elias stepped forward and commanded, "Calm yourself, my son." This stopped Joseph's rampaging anger as suddenly as a hard yank on the reins would have stopped a stampeding horse. The rabbi then turned to Antonius and said, "Go on, my son, finish what you started."

Trying his best not to smile, though he understood fully his master's anger, the young man continued. "We did not ask him to *give* us anything, Master." Joseph opened his mouth to speak, but because of a stern glance from the rabbi, he shut it again. "Rather, we offered to sell ourselves and the rights to all of our citizenship papers to him."

Joseph's mouth dropped open and he felt his legs going weak. "What?" he mouthed.

He did not notice the children or many of the adults giggling in the background because he was busy looking around for a place to sit. He might have fallen on his face, had not Elias and Jesus taken his arms and led him to the wall of the pool where he sat slowly, not taking his eyes off his friend and former servant.

Joseph asked weakly, "Why?" He then mouthed the words "hundreds of talents" to himself.

Antonius' wife Ruth approached and came to rest on her haunches before him. Looking lovingly into his eyes, taking his hand and holding it next to her heart, caressing his cheek with the other, she said, "Because we love you more than our own lives. For all the wonderful things you did for us. For who you are. For how much our children love you." There were some bashful little giggles in the background as Joseph looked into the children's smiling faces.

The adults all murmured agreement, and Elias had to turn away because his eyes had filled with tears, and he didn't want to distract his son just now. He did wipe his eyes several times with the sleeves of his robe and then with the palms of his hands when the cloth got too damp to be of any further use.

"We told your uncle," Ruth went on, "that we would give the money to you, well to Rabbi Elias, here, so that you ... and your friends ...," her eyes flicked over to Jesus, "would have a place to stay when you came back through town. We wanted you to have a home to come to and people there who loved you, so that the burden of your service to our LORD might be a little lighter."

Joseph said through his tears, "I don't know what to say. And I am so sorry for doubting you." As he looked at everyone, they, tear-filled eyes and all, motioned a "you don't have to say anything, nor do you have to apologize" back at him.

"Wait, Master, you haven't heard the best part," a little voice said to him. It was Leah, Antonius' and Ruth's little daughter. All the children giggled and murmured, "Oh no, Master Daddy! You really haven't!" to much laughter from their parents and the others, including One Other who had tears in His eyes too.

"Your uncle was quite surprised, needless to say," Ruth continued.

"Dumbfounded," said one voice. "I think he almost passed out," said someone else. Another shouted, "Thunderstruck's more like it!"

Joseph nodded in agreement.

"Well, actually no," Ruth said.

Joseph mouthed "What?"

"No, not thunderstruck so much; rather, he wept. You see, back then, when he heard what you were doing, he *was* dumbfounded at first. He said that he could not believe what he had heard."

There were many "really dumbfoundeds" mumbled in the background.

"But when one of his money lending buddies came over to confirm what was happening, he began searching all over Judea, Samaria and Galilee to find 'this Jesus fellow' as he put it." Ruth lifted a hand toward Jesus and continued, "Who had, as Festus put it, 'caused his nephew to sell all he owns'. Your uncle had gone with the idea of reporting our LORD to the Romans, thinking that He might be a charlatan."

There was much laughter. Jesus laughed with them when they pointed at Him and mouthed the word "charlatan", mocking Festus' manner.

"But when Festus found our Lord Jesus ..." Ruth glanced over at the LORD, who smiled warmly at her, causing her to blush. "... well, ah ... ah ... and listened to Him for a while, he said he felt so ashamed of what he was, he knelt before Him and begged His forgiveness, which of course he got immediately."

Everyone looked over at the LORD.

"But that wasn't all he needed, you see," Ruth added, and Joseph nodded, though he didn't see at all. "He wanted to beg for your forgiveness too, Master."

Joseph mouthed, "Unbelievable!"

"Yes, Master, truly unbelievable." She had been talking around to them all, but she turned to Joseph and stroked his cheek again. "But there's more. He also told us that he could not bear to be parted from his wonderful nephew for one more day. He said he was aching to come to you, my master, to beg your forgiveness."

Joseph was even more astonished, if it were possible.

"Yes, Master, it's true!" they all said, in unison. Joseph nodded dumbly.

"Then he said that he would rather just give us the money to set you up in a household of your own, rather than buy us for you," Ruth continued.

"And you took it, of course."

"Well no, in fact."

"Why on earth not?" Joseph had risen a little off the wall when he said this, but he sat back down as Ruth laid a hand gently on his shoulder.

Chuckling a little at his expression, Ruth responded dryly, "Despite the fact that your uncle had had an obvious change of heart, we did not want to have him give *us* money. We've always loved you more than words could express; so we wanted to give you our most precious possession—after our undying love, our undying gratitude, our devoted service, of course—we wanted to give you ourselves, our very lives. This is why we said, okay, you can give us money, but only by buying our lifelong indenture and then giving us to you, Master Joseph, as a gift—along with a nice house with plenty of room for all of us and all the rest, you understand."

Ruth had added that last part so matter-of-factly, Joseph laughed. Then they all laughed, including Jesus.

When they had quieted a bit, Ruth said, "So he bought us out, citizenship and all, signed the papers bequeathing us to you, and then gave us his blessing. But as we were going out to find you a nice place to live ..." They all murmured, "Nice place" nodding their heads enthusiastically. "... he asked us to wait." Looking around at them all, and then back at Joseph, Ruth said, "He wanted to propose something. He asked us to ask you, Master, no, rather to beg you ..." She got on her knees, causing Joseph to blush a deep red and to take her hand to try to make her stand, though she would not. "... to make his home your own and allow him to make you his sole heir. Poor old man. He was obviously lonely, and he is in very bad health, as it turns out. He told us that he had always known that no one ever really loved him— that they hated him, in fact. But he hadn't cared. He said that he enjoyed watching them crawl to him for money, and that it had always chafed at him that you wanted no such thing from him. But all this changed when he believed in our Saviour here and received Him into his heart. And sensing that he was close to going through that one-way door to eternity and wanting to make amends to you, he made his request."

"What did you say?" Joseph said, taking her hand and standing up, bringing her to her feet as well.

"That we would ask you. So here we are, asking you." She giggled and swatted him playfully on the forearm, amused at his obvious embarrassment.

Looking over at Jesus, recalling His injunctions about forgiveness and all the rest and suddenly longing to see his uncle, Joseph said, "Of course we can do this." They all cheered. "But," he said, and they quieted suddenly, "I sure wish you had all kept your freedom. Not that I won't love having you with me, you understand. I've loved you like my own family my whole life." They mouthed "We know" at him. "But not to be free. Doesn't it bother you?"

Putting a hand to his cheek again, Ruth said, "Serving you makes us free. We know that you will do anything and everything necessary to keep us safe, well fed, and all the rest. We know that you will educate our children and then set them up as you have done before. Just the fact that you love us this much is enough for all of us." They all murmured agreement. "Besides, where would we go? We have no family except each other. All of our relatives either live far away or are slaves themselves." Waving a hand toward her friends and family, she said, "No, we want to stay with you. That is, if you'll have us."

Looking over at his Sovereign LORD, Joseph suddenly understood how one could still serve a master as a bondslave and yet be a free man. He said, "Of course. I can't imagine not having you." They all cheered again. Then they all embraced him, Jesus included.

After receiving Jesus' blessing and then bidding Him farewell, Joseph went with his family to his uncle's house with a proud and happy rabbi in tow. Finding a very anxious old man waiting for him, Joseph took him in his arms and asked Festus' forgiveness for hating him, which the old man waved off.

After many joyful "how good to see yous," Festus began to talk of his nephew's glorious future as his sole air and ruler of Arimathea. He could seem to talk of nothing else, not letting his nephew get a word in edgewise. So Joseph let him go on and on, alternatively holding his hand and then embracing him, and they spent the rest of that night in joyous reunion. After this, Joseph, along with his servants, moved into the house, and they all lived out their lives there; except, that is, for the children, whom Joseph indeed had educated and then sent off, free men and women and citizens of Rome, but only after finding them suitable husbands or wives and setting them up in houses of their own.

Not long thereafter, Festus died, and Joseph inherited an estate twice as big as the one he had sold, and he became ruler of all Arimathea. From which lofty position, Joseph also fulfilled Jesus' command that he be a witness for Him among the rulers of the Jews, which he did honorably and well. It is sad to say, however, that despite this, the evil ones won out—in accordance with the eternal plan and will of Almighty God—and crucified Jesus. It was then that Joseph performed the other service that Jesus had mentioned. But let's let the Scriptures themselves reveal what that was:

> [The day Jesus died on the cross] as evening approached, Joseph of Arimathea, a prominent member of the Council, who was himself waiting for the kingdom of God, went boldly to Pilate and asked for Jesus' body. Pilate was surprised to hear that he was already dead. Summoning the centurion, he asked him if Jesus had already died. When he

learned from the centurion that it was so, he gave the body to Joseph. So Joseph bought some linen cloth, took down the body, wrapped it in the linen, and placed it in a tomb cut out of rock. Then he rolled a stone against the entrance of the tomb.[5]

And the rest, as they say, is history. And what a truly marvelous history it has been!

---

[5] Mark 15:42b – 46.

Rules, Rules, Rules

The LORD says: "These people come near to me with their mouth and honor me with their lips, but their hearts are far from me. Their worship of me is made up only of rules taught by men." (Isaiah 29:13)

[The LORD says:] "Who is it he is trying to teach? To whom is he explaining his message? To children weaned from their milk, to those just taken from the breast? For it is: Do and do, do and do, rule on rule, rule on rule; a little here, a little there." (Isaiah 28:9 – 10)

Since you died with Christ to the basic principles of this world, why, as though you still belonged to it, do you submit to its rules: 'Do not handle! Do not taste! Do not touch!'? These are all destined to perish with use, because they are based on human commands and teachings. (Colossians 2:20 – 22)

All of us have become like one who is unclean, and all our righteous acts are like filthy rags; we all shrivel up like a leaf, and like the wind our sins sweep us away. (Isaiah 64:6)

Author's note: This story is about what happens when overly religious people create for themselves idols of righteousness and then put their own pride in these idols ahead of God's righteousness. The church depicted here is NOT the typical Christian church. But there have been some like it. There is an important message from God here. I hope everyone who reads this hears it.

Pastor Jim Richards, kneeling by his bed as he always did, finished his nightly prayer with these words: "O Lord, how I desire to meet you face to face. I have prayed this prayer every day since I was a little boy. I have eagerly sought to obey all your commands and teachings. I have done everything I know to live a righteous life. Come and let me see you that I may know that you are!"

After this, he crawled into bed next to his sleeping wife. He kissed her, whispered into her ear that he loved her, cuddled close to her, and closed his eyes. It was about eleven o'clock on a Saturday evening.

At two o'clock Sunday morning Pastor Richards was still awake. He had been unable to get to sleep because there was a storm brewing at his church. It had been brewing for some time, and he knew that during the service this morning it would likely break in great hostile waves over his congregation.

How he hated these disputes; they seemed to come one after another. And most of them were so incredibly petty. What time should evening service be? Should we have two services on Sunday or one on Saturday night instead? What Sunday school curriculum should be chosen? And on and on.

But this one was going to be serious.

One of the church elders and one of Jim's closest friends, John East, admitted that he occasionally drank a glass of wine with dinner; he also admitted going to a bar occasionally for business meals. (Actually, he had admitted that he went to restaurants to meet his out-of-town colleagues, who generally sat at the bar and that he had *even had a drink* with them.) One member of congregation had seen him sitting at the bar of one of the town's finer eating establishments, and the gossip had quickly spread throughout the church. That revelation had roiled the congregation no end, for his church denomination had long considered any alcoholic beverage to be a tool of the devil, and they believed that anyone who drank alcohol in any form must be Satan's devoted servant. Even Pastor Jim had preached this; and with the utmost integrity, at least in his own mind, because neither he, nor his father and grandfather nor anyone in their families had, as far as he knew, ever tasted a drop of the stuff. (Not counting, of course, the many modern medications that contained alcohol and were taken internally; but that was for only medicinal purposes, after all.) And they had taken pride for generations that this validated how righteous they were before God.

But that was not the end of it. For shortly after this, John had written a letter to the elder board that had set the entire church aflame. He had posited that the drinking of grape juice instead of wine at communion was a direct violation of the LORD's command to take wine, and that by doing this, the church was bringing judgment on itself. And he had had the temerity to cite the Apostle Paul's admonition to the Corinthian church concerning violating the communion table.[1] What a commotion that had caused!

Unable to sleep, the Senior Pastor of the Southside Christian Faith Church crawled out of bed and went quietly down to his study to pace and think.

Pastor Jim, as he was called by his congregation, had known John East his whole life and had turned a blind eye to his drinking habits because he had always been a responsible drinker. If such a thing were possible, that is.

---

[1] 1 Corinthians 11: 26 – 32.

This was a point they discussed many times and had agreed to disagree upon, though always in the kindly spirit of brotherly love.

This had been made easy for Pastor Jim by the LORD his God because John was also a fruit-bearing servant of the LORD and as God-fearing and firmly grounded a saint as Pastor Jim had ever known. Everyone in the church family had respected John for this, though many had not known about this "tendency of his to drunkenness" as some of the members put it.

Despite John's history of devoted service, Pastor Jim had gotten over a hundred angry letters demanding that his friend be thrown out of the church. All of them had cited this admonition from that same letter to the Corinthian church: "But now I am writing you that you must not associate with anyone who calls himself a brother but is sexually immoral or greedy, an idolater or a slanderer, *a drunkard* or a swindler. With such a man do not even eat."[2] They had all emphasized the same words.

Pastor Jim frowned. All those letters had been awful, virulent, hateful. He had thought his people were more loving, more understanding; and he wondered where all that godliness had gone. It was like a fire had swept through his congregation and burnt away their love, as if it had been but a mere façade made of wood, hay, or straw. Pastor Jim wondered what John must have been thinking when he wrote that letter. John had known full well the tenets of the church, which contained, among other things, a very strict injunction against being "given to drunkenness".[3] How, then, could they possibly agree to drink wine at communion?

Pastor Jim raised his eyes to the ceiling. *Well, some of this is my fault,* he thought. He had always been taught that God had said that drinking was a sin, and he had overlooked that in favor of his friend. Now the church was caught in this firestorm. How awful!

How Pastor Jim dreaded going there today! For the first time he could remember, he dreaded being with God's people. He sat and stared at the walls of his study for a long time that morning, praying. He begged God to intervene and show him what he must do both with the controversy over the communion table and with his friend's qualifications to be a member of the church, much less an "overseer" as the Apostle Paul had defined the term.[4]

At the very hour that Pastor Jim had gotten out of bed to go down to his study, Bert Jones, the proprietor of Bert's bar, a humble establishment

---

[2] 1 Corinthians 5:11.
[3] 1 Timothy 3:3.
[4] See 1 Timothy 3:1 for Paul's definition of an overseer.

situated on Southside Street, about three blocks from Pastor Jim's Church—or "the Big Church", as Bert's customers generally referred to it—was preparing to close his doors for the evening. He had been wiping the bar down, pulling out the last of the glassware from the dishwasher, putting away the last of the fruit and wiping the bottles and putting them away. But he had kept a sharp eye on his most pitiful and needy customer, Sam Smith, whose head hung low over a shot glass that was still half full of liquor, and who was weeping quietly.

Bert stopped to consider this poor sad man for a moment, and as he did so he also started thinking about himself.

Bert knew that he was a sinful man. He knew that he needed salvation. But he did not know how to get it. He had tried that Big Church down the street—once—but after the sermon, which had been based on a certain passage in the New Testament, his conviction that God could never love him was confirmed.[5] He had felt awful, especially after the preacher had condemned everyone to hellfire who drank alcohol and those who sold "that damnable evil" to its very lowest depths.

Bert Jones shuddered.

Nevertheless, since that day, he had kept a Bible on the bar, and it was always open, many times to that very same passage. His customers had started to call him "preacher Bert," because when they got tipsy or out of hand, he would read them that passage, plus some others about the evils of drunkenness. They would laugh, of course, because he was preaching to them against a backdrop of bottles, all containing strong liquor. They pointed down the street and said, "Hey Bert, if you're not careful you'll be just like them!" They laughed harder at the terrific joke they had made at poor Bert's expense. *Yep,* Bert thought, *I guess I'm a hypocrite too.*

But he was not nearly as needy as poor old Sam.

Sam knew he was sinful! Oh yes he did, for he had confided this to Bert every time he came in, especially on those Sunday afternoons while looking longingly at the "Christians" as they passed by the bar on their way home from the service at the Big Church. He would laugh scornfully and tell Bert how he had been a Christian once: how he had read the Bible every day, prayed his heart out, gone to Sunday school and to worship service every week, tithed his income, served on committees, gone on mission trips. Why,

---

[5] Pastor Jim had preached that day out of Luke 21: 34 – 36.

he had even thought about becoming a missionary once. Sam would shake his head sadly at that and murmur, "Me? A missionary? What a joke that was!" He'd take another swallow of liquor, and then he would tell Bert how that all ended when he lost his wife and kids in a car accident. "Drunk driver, don't you know," he was careful to add. Then he would laugh bitterly as he took another swallow. Sam might then belch loudly and laugh at that too! After one of these confession sessions, Sam would invariably look down the street and say, "Tried to come back several times. Tried the Big Church." But he would shake his head sadly, and Bert knew why.

It was about 2:30 on this eventful Sunday morning that the tired sad bartender went over to Sam and touched him gently on the wrist. "Sam, old buddy, we're closin' up now. You need to get home." Sam looked up at him through bloodshot eyes and nodded.

Bert wondered whether Sam was really drunk, for he had had only one shot and had been staring at that for hours. Bert knew that if he was, it wasn't from his bar because after that sermon, he never let his patrons have more than three beers or two shots of strong drink or glasses of wine without eating something. If they appeared to be tipsy, he cut them off and called them a cab; he would certainly not let them drive away, though most of his customers lived within walking distance. Or if they came in already drunk he would not serve them.

Now the Southside was not a nice neighborhood, and most of his customers were hard cases like Sam, who also lived nearby. Therefore Bert had worried that he might lose business. But strangely enough business had picked up. People seemed to understand that Bert cared for them. At least, he cared enough not to let them get so drunk they would endanger themselves or someone else, and they must have appreciated that. Well, Bert concluded, at least one good thing had come out of that awful experience at the Big Church.

Try as he might, Bert could not understand them "over there". He looked down the street. What was wrong with a drink once in a while? For Bert had started to read his Bible after that Sunday morning, and he could find nothing in it that declared drinking in and of itself a sin. Even Jesus drank wine and so often apparently that His enemies called Him a drunkard.[6] Of course there was a lot of warning in the "Good Book" about getting drunk, Bert would

---

[6] Matthew 11:19 and Luke 7:34.

have admitted to anyone who asked. But having an occasional drink and getting drunk were two different things—at least as far as Bert could tell from his experience.

(Bert had laughed once when he stumbled across a passage in one of the books of the Old Testament that told how God himself required a drink offering of fermented drink—one in the morning and one at night—from His people, the Jews.[7] For he had been thinking that even God takes one now and then. He had paused and looked at the ceiling before continuing the thought, *Well, considerin' this awful world the LORD has to deal with, I don't blame Him.*)

Bert's thoughts were interrupted when Sam said, "I got a gun, Bert." This froze the blood in the bartender's veins. He looked over fearfully at Sam. "Yep. Got a gun," the poor man repeated. He then added ominously, "Don't think I can stand it anymore."

Bert bent over him. "Whaddya mean, Sam? Whaddya mean?"

Sam did not answer. Rather, he got up slowly and quietly left the bar, Bert's troubled eyes following him. The shot glass was still almost full.

Bert could not sleep that night. Visions of Ol' Sam putting that gun to his head or into his mouth and then pulling the trigger troubled him. So the bartender got up early and went over to the bar to do some cleaning, though this morning he was thinking of going over to visit Sam, to make sure he was okay.

As Bert worked, he looked up at the empty streets from time to time. Since he was usually at the bar on Sunday mornings, he would always find himself looking longingly at the people, all nicely dressed as they headed for the Big Church. For they used an empty lot next to his bar to park their expensive cars. It was too early yet, though, so he went back to his work.

Around nine o'clock Sunday morning, cars filled with worshippers and many on foot began to pass Bert's place. As always, the bartender stopped to watch them file by.

Suddenly his head went up, for the pastor of the church, Reverend Jim Richards—he would never ever forget his face or his name!—went by, stopped briefly, looked through his window, and then went on, quickening his step. Bert chuckled at that. For the pastor passed his place on the way to or from the Big Church several times every week, though until a few days ago he had been careful to cross the street before passing. *As if we got the*

---

[7] Numbers 28:7.

plague, or somethin', Bert had always thought. But over the past week or so, the reverend had come right by his place; sometimes he had looked at the window, as he did this morning, as if he were looking for someone.

One evening, a couple of days ago, Reverend Jim had even stopped, approached the door, but then quickly turned and continued on his way. It amused Bert to recall how his customers, who had been watching this little drama, cheered the man on like they were at a sporting event, urging him to come in—as if he could have heard them anyway—and then moaned loudly and sarcastically and raised their glasses in salute when he walked away. Bert recalled how it had been Sam who had laughed and cheered the loudest.

Yet a strange look had then come into Sam's eye when the reverend had not come in. What was that look, Bert wondered? Could it have been disappointment? Why, the thought had never occurred to him before. Had Sam been disappointed, really? Suddenly Bert was not so sure but that Sam might have been hoping for Reverend Jim to come in. Bert wondered whether if he had, he could have persuaded the pastor of the Big Church to come over to talk to Sam. Maybe the reverend would have been able to comfort him in his pain. Wasn't that what these "men o' the cloth" were for, anyway?

No, not this man! Bert concluded harshly. All this man could see, probably, was the bottles, not the need their contents answered, as poorly and awfully as they did. What was that passage again he had read a few days ago? It went something like—Bert looked at the ceiling—something like: "Give beer to those who are perishing, wine to those who are in anguish; let them drink and forget their poverty and remember their misery no more."[8] Bert was sure that Reverend Jim had never read that passage. How could he have? For Sam was indeed in anguish. Maybe, come to think of it, he *was* perishing.

Suddenly Bert had to go over to Sam's! He slammed down his towel, grabbed his jacket, and rushed out of his bar, not thinking to lock the door behind him.

Now as Pastor Jim walked slowly along Southside Street, he was greatly troubled. What might happen today, he wondered?

He chanced to look up briefly as he passed the bar. How he hated the place. Surely it was but a den where demons and devil worshippers gathered. At least, that's what his daddy and granddaddy had always said of places

---

[8] Proverbs 31:6 – 7.

such as this, and he believed them. Jim shuddered. He had always been so careful to cross the street to keep himself as far away as possible from this evil place. But for the past week or so, he had been moved—was he really moved?—to pass closer by. He could not understand it. It was as if something or Someone were calling to him to go into that place. But that could not possibly be the case. Everyone knew that such places were off limits to the truly godly. And what might happen if one of his congregation saw him come out of there?

Nevertheless, there had been this undeniable urge, this incessant voice in Pastor Jim's ear, to go into that place. But why? Could someone be in trouble? Well, the church mission was always open. Certainly everyone "in there" knew about it, for this place was on the church's mailing list, and they posted flyers nearby all the time. If someone needed help they could darn well walk three blocks, couldn't they? Pastor Jim stopped briefly to stare into the window as he had for several days now. Seeing that the bar was empty, he walked quickly on, again immersing himself in the trouble facing him a few yards down the street. He had not gone twenty yards when all thought of the bar and of its trouble had evaporated from his mind.

About 11:30 am, there were loud shouts and many screaming voices coming from the church as the trembling bartender came slowly up the steps and walked timidly into the foyer. The voices were so loud Bert could hear them from the street below. Nevertheless, white-faced with fear, he came in, looking for someone to help him. He needed someone to go over to visit Sam. Right away!

For he had run over to Sam's little apartment, and he had pounded on his door, calling to him. But Sam had shouted at him to go away. Bert had pleaded with him to open the door, but Sam would not. Rather, he kept saying, "I got a gun, Bert." And "Can't stand it anymore." Bert became afraid for him. He did not want to call the police because he was afraid that they might kill Sam. The authorities did not have much tolerance for local residents having firearms; especially those who had a reputation for drunk and disorderly behavior, with which epithet they cynically labeled anyone who was a known patron of Bert's establishment. No, indeed, he did not want to get Sam killed. So the only place he could think to go was the Big Church. And why not? Their flyers, which filled his mailbox every week, very annoyingly by the way, had said that help for the needy could be found there.

So, despite his fear, as if he were propelled by an invisible hand, Bert had come here, hoping to find someone to help.

Now, as Bert entered the foyer of the church, he could see that the entire congregation was in the big room straight ahead with the stained glass windows and long wooden benches, and they were shouting at each other. Nevertheless, still urged forward, Bert stepped up to one of the wooden doors and looked in carefully, only to see many hands and voices raised in anger. There, up in front on the raised platform, was Reverend Jim, standing red-faced behind the podium next to another man, against whom all the invective was being shouted, apparently.

Pastor Jim raised his hand and said over the shouts, "Please, brothers and sisters, let's let John speak. Please."

One voice answered angrily, "Who is he to dare to lecture us about defiling the Lord's Table? He's a drunk and has no business even standing up there with you, Jim." There were many loud shouts affirming this righteously indignant sentiment.

When the shouting had abated somewhat, the man addressed said, "Since when is taking a drink the same as being drunk?"

Bert nodded absentmindedly as he continued to look around, hoping that he might attract someone's attention. He really needed someone in a hurry! But everyone was too busy waving his hands toward the podium and shouting vehement answers to the man's question. Bert could also hear a lot of Scripture being quoted, much of which he recognized. But from what he'd read, and from the way it was said, it did not seem to answer the question at all. Rather, it seemed only to affirm one's reason for being indignant.

"And who's lecturing whom here?" the man standing beside Pastor Jim continued, now yelling to make himself heard over their shouts. This question raised the noise level considerably more. The man then raised his hand, the shouts abated slightly, and he said, "I don't mean to lecture anyone. I apologize if I have been lecturing. I have merely suggested that we take a serious look at the issue." But with this plea, the angry voices resumed, louder than ever.

Suddenly, someone turned and saw Bert, who brightened noticeably. Bert said, "Can I...?"

The man interrupted him, "You're the bartender aren't you?" Bert nodded slowly, wondering how this man, whom he could not remember ever meeting, knew his profession. "Can't you see that we're busy here?"

Bert nodded agreeably but insisted, "But, I need ..."

The man angrily interrupted, "We all have needs, buddy. Come back later! The mission opens to *drunks* at three o'clock." He then turned angrily away and started shouting again.

Bert wiped a tear of shame and humiliation from his eye, turned and left quietly. He did not notice Pastor Jim staring after him.

Bert the bartender hurried back to Sam's place. Just as he got to Sam's door, he a gun fire. Taking no care for his safety, he put his ample shoulder to the door. Since he was about six feet six inches tall and weighed well over three hundred pounds, he broke it down easily. On entering, he saw Sam on the floor, bathed in a pool of his own blood, his brains scattered over the wall. The gun was still in his hand. Bert knelt and wept bitterly, thinking that if he had not bothered with *them*, knowing what he knew about *them*, Sam might still be alive.

Much later that afternoon, as the sun was setting, a greatly unsettled pastor walked slowly down Southside Street. It had been so awful back there. He turned to look over his shoulder at the church, its windows now darkened. *Like many hearts,* Jim thought bitterly. They had resolved to throw John out of the congregation then and there, no ifs, ands or buts, using Scripture to justify this awful action of theirs, of course.[9] It was certain that the issue of the communion table would never come up again; and that was too bad. For as he thought about it, Pastor Jim had come to the conclusion that maybe John had a point. Who were they, after all, to nullify God's command by their own traditions?[10]

Pastor Jim passed by the bar again. But this time there was no voice urging him to go in. *How strange,* he thought. *Every day, every time he had passed it this past week, there had been that nagging voice. But not now.* He wondered why. Perversely, he went up to the door, took a deep breath, and entered.

What he saw was a small dark room stuffy with smoke. It had what looked like wood paneling along the walls, but the wood, if that was really what it was, had long ago lost any of its natural luster because cigarette smoke had completely blackened it. Its ceiling had also been painted black, but whether by real paint or by the same smoky paint on the walls, Jim could not be sure. It was extremely ill lit, many of the overhead lights being burnt out. Most of whatever light there was in the room seemed to come from the bright purple-red "Beer Meister" neon sign hanging over the front window that reflected its light back into the room. There were several small square tables in the center, each with four high-backed, flimsy wooden chairs, all of them empty. The bar on his right was a long, dingy and well-scratched

---

[9] See footnote 2 above on page 198 above.
[10] See Mark 7:8.

wooden counter with eight stools, all except one of them occupied, and a brass foot rail. Behind it was another counter out of which several beer taps rose. There were also many bottles on it, and dozens more standing on several shelves attached to the wall behind it, which itself was covered by a mirror. There were several ceiling lamps shining down on the bottles, which reminded Jim of illuminated tombstones. To his left were several booths, all empty, with seats obviously in need of repair as foam protruded from several large rips in the green plastic upholstery. On the back wall was a calendar displaying a scantily clad woman, bending forward tantalizingly and displaying a good deal of cleavage. To the left of the calendar was a large sign with "Restrooms" written in white letters on a black background and with a large gold arrow pointing to the left toward a small hallway.

Pastor Jim thought, *Yep! Dark, seamy, smelly, just as I expected.* He was half surprised that there was not a dead body lying on the floor somewhere in here. He had found himself looking around suspiciously for one, strangely enough, though he could not have said why. But he quickly caught himself and turned back to the bar.

The men sitting at the bar were all looking at him. He noticed that their eyes appeared bloodshot. *Yep,* he thought, *they are all sullen and drunk,* also as Jim had expected. Without any change of expression or even acknowledging him, they turned back and stared down at their drinks. But they weren't drinking. Jim noticed something else: occasionally, one of the men would wipe at his eye; another might sniff; and then they would embrace and pat each other on the back. Were they weeping? Suddenly the place had the air of a funeral parlor. Well, funerals he could handle. The Reverend Jim Richards approached the bar slowly.

When he had gotten near enough to place his hands on the bar, the enormous bartender came up to him, inclined his head respectfully and asked, "May we help you, Reveren' Richards? Are you lost?"

The pastor was startled that the man knew his name. "No, sir," he replied. "I'm sorry for disturbing you, but I've been wanting to come in for some time." This assertion was met with several sarcastic chuckles and a few grunts. Jim wondered why.

The bartender said, "Well, Reveren' Richards, we couldda used you earlier today."

The Reverend Jim Richards felt a chill run through him. He said defensively, "We were busy today."

The bartender's jaw tightened noticeably. "I know, Reveren'." He waved a precautionary wave at a few of his customers who had been regarding the

Reverend Jim Richards with no little hostility. As they slowly and sullenly turned back to their drinks, Jim wondered why they might harbor ill will toward him, fear and anxiety steadily rising in his soul.

Sensing his discomfort, the bartender leaned forward and said, "Don' worry 'bout them." He pointed at his customers. Jim let out a relieved breath. "You're a lot safer in here, I think, than we are over there." He pointed down the street.

Reverend Richards felt anger rise in him. *How dare they?* was the first thought that came to him.

Understanding Jim Richards' expression, the bartender said, trying to be placatory, "I don' mean to be offensive, Reveren' Richards."

Jim relaxed again and smiled graciously. "How do you know my name?" he asked.

The bartender said, "Went to your church once, Reveren'." He paused, sighed and added, "Well, twice, axually," more to himself than to his guest.

Reverend Richards could not believe his ears. He did not remember ever seeing Bert, and he had a great memory for names and faces, especially faces as big and imposing as the one staring down at him.

Seeing disbelief register, Bert said, "Name's Bert Jones. Went 'bout six months ago. Even filled out one o' those little cards you got behind each seat in there." He added, clearly annoyed, "Been on your mailin' list ever since."

Reverend Richards suddenly recalled that Bert was indeed on the church mailing list; he had always wondered why. He said, "Well, I hope you enjoyed the service," for which he immediately felt terribly stupid and ill-mannered.

The bartender smiled. "Well, I ain't never went back. Well, for services that is. That might tell you somethin'."

Of course it did.

Reverend Richards suddenly understood how the hypocritical Pharisees must have felt when Jesus confronted them. Then he wondered why that thought had come to him. He tried to think back to any message he might have preached six months ago. As he looked down at the bar and rubbed his chin, still wondering, but more about his awful feelings than about his past sermons, he noticed a Bible sitting some way away from him—on the bar! It was a really big one with big letters that lay open easily.

When he looked up in bald-faced astonishment, the bartender chuckled. "Read it ever' day, Reveren'." The Reverend Jim Richards was too amazed to speak. Bert picked it up, set it carefully before the dazed pastor, and turned deftly to a passage in the New Testament. "You pro'ly recognize this here."

Reverend Jim read these words from the LORD Jesus Christ, " 'Be careful, or your hearts will be weighed down with dissipation, drunkenness and the anxieties of life, and that day will close on you unexpectedly like a trap. For it will come upon all those who live on the face of the whole earth. Be always on the watch, and pray that you may be able to escape all that is about to happen, and that you may be able to stand before the Son of Man.' "[11] His head shot up. As he looked into the bartender's knowing eyes, he suddenly recalled the fiery sermon he had preached. He recalled especially how his heart had burned with righteous indignation concerning drunkenness that day.

Then the thought struck him, *What did I do to this man?*

Bert nodded forcefully at that look in Jim's eye. He said, "That trap slammed shut on someone today, Reveren'." He sniffed and looked away, wiping a tear from his eye and shaking his head slowly.

The Reverend Jim Richards' heart began to beat quickly as the memory of that certain voice urging him to come in here became like a jackhammer pounding on his brain. "What?" he said softly, staring at that passage, his eyes boring a hole in it.

"Yessiree. Had a customer named Sam." Bert then told Jim everything about Sam he knew, and as he did so, the Reverend Jim Richards' eyes moistened. Bert had not yet told Jim about the tragic events of the day, however, when he concluded, "Yep, Reveren', he was a real sad case." He paused and sniffed again. "But we get a lot of 'em in here, don't ya know?" Jim certainly did, though that thought seemed gratuitous and patronizing just now.

Pointing at the Word of God, Bert nodded. "Well, that's what this here book is for."

Jim looked down dumbly at the book with which he was so familiar, as if he had never comprehended a single word of it. Dumbstruck, he looked up at the bartender, his eyes wide.

Bert said, "When they get a little too drunk or rowdy, or when they get sad an' weepy, I find a passage in here and read it to 'em." Looking around at the sorry souls seated at the bar, he said emphatically, "And since I'm bigger 'n most of 'em, they don't dare object." The bartender chuckled at the looks he got from his customers, who raised their glasses, a confirming salute, and took a swallow. He turned back to the Reverend Jim Richards and

---

[11] See footnote 5 on page 199 above.

said without a bit of irony adulterating the tone of his voice, "You'd be amazed at what happens; how it seems to calm 'em down." The reverend did in fact realize, to his shame, that he would truly have been amazed.

"So what happened to Sam?" Jim asked, his voice quivering, suspecting he knew the answer and fearing with all his soul what he might hear. It then dawned on him why he had been looking for a dead body earlier.

The bartender's head snapped back, his look hardened and he sighed heavily. "Sam killed hisself today."

The Reverend Jim Richard's quivering hand went to his forehead, his elbow resting on the bar. It was then that he recalled seeing this man at his church today, the continuing echoes of that voice commanding him to come into Bert's Bar now like thunderous explosions in his mind. A chill ran through him. He could only recall having had such a feeling once before: when his father had caught him in a bald-faced lie. Now Jim knew there was another Father who might be angry with him, and he shuddered.

So completely engrossed was Jim by that feeling still freezing his heart, he only dimly heard the bartender say, "Came to your church today again, Reveren' Richards, hopin' to get someone to go over and visit Sam. He was still alive then. I know because I was standin' outside his door when he killed hisself, after I got thrown out …"

The Reverend Jim Richards' head shot up. "Thrown out?" he said softly. He had tears in his eyes now, and his chin quivered, both his hands and knees shaking also. He found himself yearning to get on those knees of his and talk to Someone, to beg for forgiveness, to beg for peace of mind—peace that he feared he might never again be granted in this life.

"Well, Reveren', not thrown out 'xactly," the bartender relented. But then his voice got hard again as he added, "Just tol' to come back later when the mission *for drunks* uz opened. Three o'clock I believe it is. Too bad ol' Sam killed hisself about one o'clock. Awful rude of him not to wait, don't ya think?"

The Reverend Jim Richards looked up into eyes as hard and cold as stone, grinding anger having polished them to a fine brightness—accusing, relentless, penetrating, convicting. Those awful eyes! All the Reverend Jim Richards could manage to do was mouth the words, "I'm so sorry …"

"Sorry's not goin' to cut it, Reveren,'" the bartender interrupted with a growl, pounding a gigantic fist on the bar, causing every bottle and glass to clash and ring loudly. And his customers flinched, astonishment and fear radiating from their expressions. "Sorry's for cowards, scoundrels … ne'er-do-wells, I guess is what you fancy folk might like to call it." Bert looked at the ceiling a moment, took a deep breath, and then gazed down at the reverend, an awful smile crossing his face, the others smiling darkly as well. "Why, now as I think on it, Reveren', sorry's for the likes o' us." He thumped his chest for emphasis, after which he gathered up his Bible and turned his back on the weeping, quivering man and went back to his customers, who sat slowly down, mumbling angrily among themselves.

Reverend Jim also imagined that they were shaking out their jackets at him as if they were ridding their persons of some awful thing that clung to them; nor would he have been surprised had they also brushed the dust off the soles of their feet as well.[12]

Now they may actually have intended to give Jim this impression, though we'll never know. What they did do, in fact, was turn their backs to him, still mumbling things about this man who had had the gall to "do them such a big favor" as to come in here now that poor ol' Sam was dead. This was followed by words spat into their glasses like "hypocrite", "holier-than-thou", "self-righteous", "too good for anyone else", and other hurtful things that the Reverend Jim Richards would never have thought anyone might say about him.

Jim staggered away from the bar and its grieving patrons, out the door and to his car. He got slowly in and stared over the steering wheel into empty space for the longest time.

When he got home, he ignored his wife's waiting arms for the first time in his marriage. Rather, he went directly to his study and closed the door quietly. He then got on his face before the LORD and begged for forgiveness. After several hours, knowing that the LORD had indeed forgiven him, he got up.

Pastor Jim realized that for the first time in his life, he had not asked to meet his God and Saviour face to face. Suddenly a voice—a clearly audible voice—spoke harshly into his ear, saying, "You didn't ask the question." Jim didn't know what to say. The voice said again, more forcefully this time, "You *did not* ask the question!"

Trembling with fear, the stricken man of God got back on his knees and prayed his standard prayer, the words now like sawdust in his mouth: "O Lord, how I desire to meet you face to face. I have prayed this prayer every day, ever since I was a little boy. I have eagerly sought to obey all your

---

[12] See Matthew 10:14.

commands and teachings. I have done everything I know to live a righteous life. Come, and let me see you that I may know that you are!"

That same voice, unmistakably weeping now, said, "I came to you today, Jim Richards, but you threw me out." The image of a giant burly man, standing at the entrance to the church sanctuary, a pleading look on his face, came suddenly to Jim. The weeping voice repeated, "Yes, indeed, I came to you today, seeking your help for one of my children, and you threw me out." Then it was silent.

The Reverend Jim Richards never prayed that prayer again.

Redemption

With what shall I come before the LORD and bow down before the exalted God? Shall I come before him with burnt offerings, with calves a year old? Will the LORD be pleased with thousands of rams, with ten thousand rivers of oil? Shall I offer my firstborn for my transgression, the fruit of my body for the sin of my soul? He has showed you, O man, what is good. And what does the LORD require of you? To act justly and to love mercy and to walk humbly with your God. (Micah 6:6 – 8)

Author's note: All was not lost in the last story, awful as Pastor Jim's sin was. See how God can work a wonderful salvation even out of the most seemingly desperate circumstances. All we have to do is repent of our sin and accept God's forgiveness and then do as He instructs us.

Pastor Jim Richards, still weeping, got off his knees, sat slowly down on a chair in his study, and cradled his head in his hands. "What have I done?" he cried out. "What have I done?" He raised his eyes to heaven and cried again, "O my precious Saviour, what have I done?"

There came a soft knock at his study door. He did not hear it at first, but eventually he called out, "Come in, Evangeline."

A perky pretty redhead with sparkling eyes opened the door slowly and peeked in. "Honey, are you all right?" she asked softly, sticking her head a little way further into the room. When she saw his puffy tear-stained face, his expression of utter sadness cried out to her, and she ran and knelt in front of her husband. "Oh, Jim, my darling, what's wrong?" He looked up at her, pain radiating from every pore. She took his hand and urged him down toward her.

Yielding to her gentle loving touch, he got down from the chair, knelt before her, put his arms around her and held her. He had never held her as desperately as this before, and this made her afraid. Her fear soon became overwhelming sorrow when he laid his head on her shoulder and sobbed for a long time, saying over and over, "Eve, I've sinned against God. Such an awful, awful sin."

When Jim could finally manage to control himself, he told his wife what had happened. As he sobbed out his story, her expression went from unbelief, to anger, to overwhelming shame, and then to deep sorrow and regret. There were many exclamations like, "Oh, no, Honey!" and "That just can't be, Jim," and "How could that have ever happened, my love?" Eve had begun to weep also, as if she personally had sinned her husband's awful sin against those poor men at Bert's Bar and against the unfortunate man who had taken his life.

Truth of the matter is Eve knew that she had in many ways. For in that instant she came to understand that she, too, had harbored a self-righteous holier-than-thou spirit in her heart. She recalled one of the most moving parables in the Scriptures, wherein Jesus tells of a Pharisee and a tax collector who come to the temple to pray. The LORD then describes how the Pharisee comes in with his face raised pridefully to God and thanks Him that he is not like murderers, adulterers, and all sorts of other awful people—even like this tax collector. Jesus leaves no doubt that the Pharisee justified this prayer in his mind because he was obviously so much more righteous than everyone else. But then Jesus tells how the tax collector never dares to raise his face to look up to heaven nor to even approach the altar, but pounds his breast and cries out for mercy because he is such a miserable sinner. Jesus also leaves no doubt in the minds of his audience whom God justified that day.[1] Now she knew how that Pharisee felt. But oh, how so much more did she also know what the tax collector must have felt. Oh, so very yes, indeed, did Eve know!

Wiping her eyes and smiling at her husband, Eve said, "Honey, Darling, you need to go back there." Her head jerked a little in what she supposed to be the direction of Bert's place. "You need to beg their forgiveness." Seeing her husband's expression, she pleaded, "Oh, please, Jim, please do this hard thing. Please!"

She had seen that her husband was taken aback at first. She might have even read his mind. For his first thought was, *There's no way I'm going back there.* But then, after confessing his weakness to God, Jim's expression softened. Eve's shoulders relaxed and she held her arms out to him.

He came into them and said, "You are so right, my precious treasure. You are so very right."

Another few moments passed as they comforted each other quietly, holding each other closely, finding that wonderful ability to freely share their souls and let their love—love given to them by the LORD their God—fill them with relief, healing and, amazingly, joy.

---

[1] See Luke 18: 10 – 14. Tax collectors were lower than the scum of the earth to the Jews, especially because many of them were also Jews who used their position of authority to rob and oppress their own people.

Jim leaned back and stared into his wife's eyes. "You know, Eve, how I thank God every day, almost every waking moment that he gave you to me." She blushed deeply, incredible happiness and love for her husband flooding into her at the sound of those words. "Well, I do," he continued. "I can't imagine life without you. I can't imagine what I might have become without your wise counsel to help me, and your incredible love to sustain me."

Laughing and saying, "Oh, go on with you", Eve drew him back to her and held him tightly, thanking her God as well for the good and righteous man He had given her.

They eventually got up and sat next to each other on a little sofa. Pastor Jim Richards put his arm around his wife's shoulders and drew her head down to his shoulder. He said into her hair, "Not only do I need to go back to Bert and his friends, by the grace of Almighty God, we need to straighten out the church. To try to see ourselves as God must see us." He mouthed the words, "How awful that must be. So very awful!"

"How are *we* going to do that, my love" Eve asked, looking into her husband's eyes. She had a smile also, maybe laced with a little irony, as indicated by her emphasis on the word "we".

Chuckling, Jim said, "Well, I really did mean, our Lord Jesus first and then me. If He'll let me, of course." Eve solemnly mouthed the words "Of course", causing him to break into laughter. "You're teasing me, aren't you?" She nodded, love like a shooting star streaking across her expression, the glint in her eyes its shining trail.

All seriousness now, Eve asked, "So how?"

"How what?"

"How are *we* going to straighten out the church?" She pointed at the ceiling as she asked the question.

"Well, by God's all-knowing grace, of course," he replied with a chuckle, drawing laughter from her. "I'm going to get on the phone to each elder and tell them we must meet. Tonight, if possible. That it's an emergency. And it really is!" Eve loved the steely glint her husband got in his eye when he had decided to do a hard thing that could cost him personally but that must be done nevertheless.

Feeling heavy fatigue weighing on her shoulders and sliding slowly and painfully down her back, Eve looked up at the face of an old grandfather clock that stood near the study door. It said four thirty (a.m.). Since she was a little girl she had always imagined that it really was an old grandfather nodding down at her, each motion of its imaginary head done in time with the heavy tick tick tick of its heart. Just then the half-hour chime sounded.

214

Eve had always loved its hardy baritone voice, so appropriate for a gentleman of its advanced years.

Looking again at the clock, she nodded in respect of its timely advice. Chuckling at the pun she had made in her mind, she said to her husband, "Darling, look what Grandpa is telling us."

Jim looked over at "Grandpa." He loved that she always called it that.

"I think it's time we try to get a little sleep, don't you?" Eve said, motioning toward the stairs. Jim yawned widely and nodded slowly.

Eve stood and held out her hand. He took it, but as he felt her relax, he yanked on it suddenly. Eve lost her balance and, shrieking delightedly, fell face up into her husband's embrace. Jim lowered his face to hers slowly. Her laughter subsiding, she started to admonish him, saying "Hey, what are you do…" but the words did not make it out because he had covered them with a passionate kiss.

"Oh my," Eve said, squirming with the desire his kiss had awakened in her. "I thought we were sleepy," she said with a dreamy voice.

"We are. Really, really sleepy." Jim smothered her laughter with another kiss, which, if it were possible, was more passionate than the previous one.

"Oh!" she said breathlessly.

Eve said nothing more as her husband lifted her up, stood her on her feet, took her hand and then led her up to their bedroom, not taking his eyes off her until he carefully closed the door behind them. It must be said that daybreak came too soon for her liking, and they had to get up because they heard their children rustling around in the kitchen, looking for something to eat.

Still in his pajamas, Pastor Jim went straight to his study. He called every elder, some of whom he woke from a sound sleep, and asked them to make time to come to an urgent meeting that evening. When they asked why so urgent, he said that he would tell them when they were all assembled. To those who showed reluctance, he piqued their interest by adding that he'd found an awful sin in the church that they needed to deal with as a body. That got their attention in a hurry, though they would have been astonished beyond words had they known that he was talking about their sin as well as his.

After Pastor Jim had finally talked to the last of them, still feeling somewhat dubious about this approach, he mumbled, "Well, it was necessary, I think. And it was true." Nevertheless, he prayed to his God, hoping that He was not displeased with this method. Which He was not!

Pastor Jim ate, kissed his children as they headed off to school, and then, when they were out of sight, kissed his wife as passionately as he could. Once Eve had caught her breath, she murmured, "My, my, darling, do we need to go back up?" pointing absentmindedly toward the stairs.

"No, Treasure. We can't."

Eve's shoulders slumped a little.

Chuckling at her expression, Pastor Jim said, "Sorry, Eve, but I'm going to the church. I'm going to go into the sanctuary, stand before my God and pray. Then I'm going to get on my face before Him and pray. I plan on going to Bert's after my meeting with the elders, and I'm already trembling with fear. I need God's guidance. I need the words to ask their forgiveness. I also want that unfortunate man's forgiveness. I'm going to ask God to ask him to forgive me."

Eve caressed Jim's cheek, saying, "I'm sure everything will be all right. Of course He'll forgive you." She had obviously meant God, rather than the dead man.

Not bothering to correct her, Jim said, "I hope so, my love. I really hope so." He really did mean the dead man, and this thought bothered him because nowhere in Scripture are we commanded to, or was it even suggested that we pray for the forgiveness of those whom we had wronged to the point of costing them their lives. Nevertheless, he was going to do it anyway. God knew where Sam was, after all, and would relay that message to him. Somehow, though Jim could not say how, he also knew that Sam was in Heaven with the LORD Jesus, which seemed to make it all right to do this thing.

Now as is its wont on occasions like this, obstinate Time ground along especially slowly on this sunny Monday, as if it too were outraged and was personally punishing Jim for what he had done. Every minute seemed to the pastor of Southside Christian Faith Church like an hour. Each hour seemed like a day. As he looked up again and again at the Sanctuary clock, it felt like the eternal Watch Keeper was pouring increasing amounts of dread into his heart.

When four thirty struck (finally!), Pastor Jim got slowly to his feet because his awful burden weighed heavily on him. He dusted himself off and hurried, as best he was able, to his office to type out what he planned to say to the elders, who had agreed to meet him at seven o'clock. He thought there'd be more than enough time to prepare. Strangely enough, however, this contrary adversary, which till now had seemed to be plodding along in heavy spiked boots—up and down his back and through and through his raw grieving soul—now donned mythical Mercury's winged shoes and proceeded to race along as if there would be no tomorrow. Before Jim Richards knew it, the elders began to come into the church office.

As they entered, all had the same question on their lips, asked in a clearly irritated tone of voice, "So what's the big emergency that couldn't wait a week or so until our next meeting?" But when Jim looked up at them, his expression killed any further questions before they were uttered. Their faces got somber. They sat quietly and stared at their senior pastor, not taking their eyes off him. They remained silent until every one of them arrived.

It was Spencer Norman, the most respected of them, who asked quietly, "Okay, Jim. What's up?"

Jim looked around at them all for a long time, and then began to tell the story he told his wife. At first, they were outraged. The name of Bert's establishment had barely left the Reverend Richards' lips when someone had the temerity to ask angrily, "What have we to do with those drunks down there?" pointing toward Bert's Bar. There was more grumbling until Someone, by His Spirit speaking to their hearts, told them to stow the false righteousness, get off their high horses and take what their senior pastor said seriously.

Thankful that they had quieted down, Pastor Richards plowed resolutely on, his face crumpling into tears, sobs coming to him from time to time, his expression showing clearly the quiet desperation his soul felt, the awesome shame he endured, the abject sorrow that filled his heart; and above all, the tremendous anger he harbored at himself, and at them just now, for reacting as they had, though he had to admit that they could not have helped it—yet.

As Pastor Jim continued, one by one, they too began to feel shame. They all eventually broke into tears when Jim relayed to them what the LORD had said to him earlier this morning. What a change in their hearts and expressions happened then! Some got on their knees, clasped their hands, lifted their eyes to heaven and cried out for God's mercy and forgiveness. The others, still seated and supporting their foreheads in their hands, also prayed earnestly. It was not too long, however, before they all got on the floor and then on their faces and prayed that God would forgive them, that He would show them the way to make amends, to Him first, but as importantly, to Bert and his friends.

When they had finished, they got up slowly off the floor, sat slowly down in their chairs and looked around at each other, barely able to see because of the tears filling their eyes. It was Spencer Norman who, with a quivering voice, asked, "So, Pastor Jim, what are we going to do?"

Sighing heavily, Jim replied, "By the grace of God we're going to fix this!" He pointed toward the sanctuary, and they all said a loud Amen. "But right now, I'm going to go over to Bert's bar, get on my knees in front of him and any customers he might have there, and beg their forgiveness." The men could not get out of their mouths fast enough the desire to come with him, each of them to do likewise. Their pastor, smiling, loving these men with all his soul, said, "Not tonight. None of you get the pleasure." They laughed, though a bit nervously. "This is for me, and me alone, to do tonight. However ..." Their eyes shot up, their expressions eager. "... God will certainly make a way for all of us, including the entire congregation, to make amends to these poor men, who love each other as much as *or more* than we love those in our congregation." They nodded. Jim, sighing again, said, "It shames me to say this, but I believe with all my heart that we could learn a little about love from them." Every man blushed as the Spirit dwelling within him assured him that what His servant Jim said was true.

The meeting broke up around nine o'clock. When Jim had ushered the last man out he sat briefly at his desk and stared at the document he'd written. How utterly banal it seemed to him now, for Bert's steely expression and his words "Sorry's not going to cut it, Reverend," bore deeply into his mind, into his heart—into his very soul. He smiled sarcastically. "Reverend" he humphed out, his shoulders humping up and his hands balling into fists on his desk. "How inappropriate a title is that?" he said, looking at the ceiling.

Jim got up slowly, got his jacket and headed toward Bert's Bar. It seemed that he got there in an instant, and he wondered whether Time really was conspiring to punish him. Or maybe just to humiliate him beyond his ability to endure. Refusing to give in to the Evil One, who was working with all his might to keep Pastor Jim from his task, he looked in the window. It seemed to him that nothing had changed. The same men, as far as he could tell, were sitting at the bar, in their very same seats, and Bert was wiping a glass while talking to them. Well, one thing had changed a little. Bert wasn't really talking to them; rather, he appeared to be reading the Bible to them and they were staring at the book as he did.

It took Bert a few seconds to notice Pastor Jim standing at the window. When he did, he stopped reading and his expression hardened. The men at the counter all turned to see what had caught Bert's attention. When they saw who it was, they made it clear, with a dismissive wave of their hands, that Jim was not welcome. He did not blame them. Normally, he would have fled as fast as he could. But he had a mission to fulfill, and he was determined to do it.

Jim opened the door slowly and came in, his head bowed. There was some grumbling that caught Reverend Richards' ear as he approached the bar, such things as, "Didn't get enough of lordin' it over us before?" or; with a smirk, "Has he come to save our souls?" or "Who does he think he is, anyway?" and such like. The comment that stabbed at Jim most was, "I wonder what ol' Sam wouldda thought o' this high and mighty man comin' in here now, after all's been said an' done?"

Seeing the expression on the Pastor's face and sensing something in Jim Richards' manner, Bert said to his customers gruffly, "Quiet! Your makin' yourselves out to be just as high and mighty, I reckon." This stopped them cold. Several heads came up suddenly and a few eyebrows were raised. Some turned back to their guest, but they offered no apology. Bert said, "I think Reveren' Richards here has somethin' to say to us."

"I'll bet he does," came a comment from a man sitting nearest the Bible, which was on the end of the bar nearest Pastor Richards.

"One more word out o' you, Spud, an' you're through here for the rest of the night," Bert commanded.

This was said to a gnarly, skeletally thin old man with a chiseled jaw; hawk-like eyes that peered out at you from beneath a bony brow and bushy gray eyebrows; a beard of gray stubble covering a sharp jutting chin; and a mouth that bowed sharply downward at both ends, giving the impression that if a smile had ever had the temerity to try to bring some light to that stern dark countenance it was quickly and ruthlessly extinguished. The old man was also wearing an old sailor's cap, a threadbare pea coat, a red and white striped tee shirt and faded jeans. He had stared longest and hardest at Reverend Jim, and he had made it clear what he thought of this man "comin' in here on his high horse like he was better 'n us or somethin'." Nevertheless, he mumbled an apology to Bert and lowered his head to stare into his shot glass, no doubt avoiding the Bartender's steely glare as Bert gave him a stern nod of his head, his lips formed into a thin line.

The bartender turned to back Jim, who had come to stand near the Bible. "Well, Revern' Richards," he said, "it's quite a surprise seeing you. How may I ..." He stopped, looked at his friends, and then continued, "... *we* be of service?" Some sarcastic exhalations of breath let Reverend Jim know their feelings about this turn of phrase.

Jim stammered, "I ... I ... just wanted to come here and ... and ..." He swallowed hard, and looked up into Bert's eyes, a plea that the master of this establishment might honor his offer by showing some encouraging gesture, something, anything that might help Jim say what he had come to say.

To his surprise, and very great relief, Jim got precisely that when Bert's eyes softened and he said quietly, "Come Reveren' Jim, we're all friends here. It's a rule o' the house that anyone carryin' a large burden must leave it at the door; or iffn' they can't do that, then they can deposit it on this here shoulder." He patted his own massive shoulder. "An' I'll carry it for them an' then dump it into the trash when I clean the place up later."

How humbling this was! Here was a man whom Jim and his church had wronged terribly, whose friend they had as good as murdered by their self-righteous hatred and smallness of heart and mind, who was offering help and love in return. And to carry his burden! Amazing! This passage from the Proverbs came instantly to Jim's mind: "If your enemy is hungry, give him food to eat; if he is thirsty, give him water to drink. In doing this, you will heap burning coals on his head, and the LORD will reward you."[2] And those coals burned so very intensely on Pastor Richards just now. It had been commands like this and others in Scripture that he had made the basis of his life's walk with Christ because it had been the very foundation of Jesus' ministry while He walked among us. And here was one whom his congregation had treated like the dirt under their feet living this out. How humbling, indeed!

"Thank you, Sir," Jim mumbled, tears flooding his eyes. Doing his best not to weep but not succeeding very well, Jim continued, "You, Sir ..."

"Call me Bert, Reveren' Richards. My dad ain't here just now," he chuckled, placing a hand gently on Jim's shoulder to comfort him.

Jim replied, "And ... Bert ... please call me Jim. I don't think I deserve the other."

"You got that right!" It had come from Spud who was smiling darkly at the weeping man.

Bert pointed at the offender and said, "One more time, Spud, and you're outta here for a month."

"Geesh, Bert, just jokin'"

"This ain't no time for jokin', you got that?"

"Sorry, Bert." When Bert nodded toward Pastor Jim, an unmistakable command, the man complied with "Sorry, Reveren'." Bert glared at Spud for the longest time.

After which he turned back to Pastor Richards and urged, "Go on, Jim, tell us what it is that's troublin' you."

---

[2] Proverbs 25:21 – 22. See also Romans 12:20 – 21 and Matthew 5: 43 – 48.

Swallowing hard several times, sniffing, wiping his eyes with his hands and then with the sleeves of his shirt, Jim said, "I can't tell you all how terribly sorry I am for the way you, Bert, were treated by me and my congregation."

By this time all heads had turned toward Jim. Most expressions had softened as well. Even Spud seemed to be moved by Jim's confession of regret and sorrow.

Jim looked at each of them and said, "How we treated all of you." He looked at the bartender, who nodded encouragement. "I've come to ask ... no, to beg for your forgiveness. All of you here and anyone else who knew Sam."

Bert sniffed and wiped his eyes. "Rev ... I mean Jim, we know you weren't to blame for Sam's death. But I guess I jist wish you had been able to help him when he needed the help." Tears trickled down the big man's cheeks, as he wiped his running nose with the back of his hand.

Barely able to say the words, his mouth quivering, Jim said, "I know, Bert, I know." Jim began to lose his balance, but Bert hurried around the bar and helped him to a stool—ironically, the one next to Spud; the one where Sam had always sat. Jim breathed out a "thank you" between quiet sobs. He felt an arm go around his shoulder. Looking up, he saw that it was Spud's arm. Jim put his hand on top of his and nodded a "thank you" at him. Whereupon, Spud emptied his glass in one mighty swallow, lifting it to Jim in salute. Jim smiled and squeezed his hand in response.

Several minutes passed. Then Jim Richards asked, "Have Sam's remains been claimed yet?"

Surprised, Bert said, "Why no, Pastor Richards. He ain't. They've got him at the morgue and they're tryin' to find next o' kin. Don't think he has any, though, at least none that'll claim him."

"Oh? Why not?"

"His wife an' kids were killed in a car accident some time ago."

"What an awful shame!" Jim breathed out heavily. "They were his only living relatives?"

"No, Pastor Jim, they weren't."

Jim shook his head, not comprehending.

Bert said, "Nope. His folks is still alive 'sfar as I know." The bartender swallowed hard, as if he were battling something awful that wanted to rise out of the depths of his soul, to lash out again at the weeping man staring into his eyes. It took Bert a few seconds to get control of this thing, which was overwhelming consuming anger and hatred. Doing his best to control the tone of his voice, to keep it even, level, non-threatening, non-judgmental, Bert continued, "Nope. They're all what you might call good Christian folks."

Jim's head shot up. "What?"

"Yep, Reverend Jim. At least, that's how they think o' themselves."

Jim had stood partially at the mention of "good Christian folks", but he dropped heavily back onto the stool, a hand to his forehead, mouthing the words, "You mean, O God, that there's more?"

"Yep, there is, I'm afraid," Bert said. "Ya see, when Sam lost his family, he was overwhelmed with grief. He became a real hard case, no question. Wouldn't accept help from anyone, at least that easy 'Oh, it'll all be all right' type of help that many folks, be they Christian or not, are willin' to offer. Ya know, Reveren', the kind that really can't be bothered with pourin' their own souls into someone, even if'n it means gettin' a little dirty in the process. All the while, though, what was really happenin' was that he was screamin' for help from someone who'd listen to him rant and rave, but who knew that once that had played itself out, they could reach him. Eventually he took to drinkin'. He lost his job. Started to visit prostitutes. Even spent some time hooked on cocaine."

His forehead on the bar, Jim moaned, "How utterly awful." Tears were pooling up on that bar now as the enormity of what he had done hit him again. He absolutely knew what Bert would say next, because he had seen people he knew and loved do the very same thing with a wayward daughter or son or loved one who had strayed off God's righteous path for whatever reason. Yes, indeed, Jim knew very well.

"You see, Pastor Richards, his folks disowned him and threw him out o' their lives. Called him all kinds o' awful names. Stood right in this here bar, almost next to the place you're sittin', and tol' him never to darken their doorway again. Said he was the devil's spawn, son of Cain and all kinds o' things like 'at." Bert glanced over at his customers. "I think you were all here then, 'ceptin you, Spud."

That excellent gentleman said with a swift up and down movement of his head, "And they ought'r be d...d glad that I warn't here, 'acause if I hada been, they'd been layin' face first on the floor, a bottle or two broke over their heads."

None of Bert's customers really took this threat seriously because Spud was known to utter such tremendous but dubious assertions on a regular basis, and he was also known for being the biggest hearted man on earth, who possessed a keen sense of justice and was easily outraged by its lack of faithful application. Many thought that the reason he uttered such things was to vent his anger, rather than to act upon it. Nevertheless, they all mumbled agreement with the sentiment he had just expressed, though carefully, lest Bert take offense and likewise break "a bottle or two" over their heads to express *his* displeasure.

Staring at the heated angel of wrath sitting at his bar, Bert said, "Don't take Spud too seriously, preacher."

Jim nodded understanding, thinking that if he'd been here that night he most likely would have considered a similar remedy for such despicable behavior by people who presumed to carry the Name of God prominently displayed for everyone to see.

"Well, after that we never saw them again. Sam called 'em a few times. At least, that's what he said, but they wouldn't return his calls." Sighing deeply, Bert concluded this sorry tale: "And, well, Reverend Jim, the rest, as they say, is history. An' such a sad history, indeed!" There were loud murmurs of agreement around the bar.

"Do you know where they live, Bert?" Jim asked.

"Sure as ... um pardon me, pastor. Sure do!"

"This is what I propose." Jim's voice had suddenly firmed up; his jaw had tightened and there was a glint in his eye that Bert recognized, considering a similar glint Bert had had in his own eye after his conversation with Jim Richards last evening. "Let us bury Sam, me and my family, meaning the whole Church congregation. All at our expense, of course."

There were many surprised remarks uttered with wide eyes: such things as, "Of course? Well, that's nice" and "Poor ol' Sam gets a proper Christian burial?" and other such sentiments.

"We'll have a gravesite burial, say, Thursday," Jim continued. "We'll pay for the preparation of his body. There'll be lots of flowers. Maybe even a picture of him taken at a better time in his life. It'll be real nice." Bert's grateful eyes filled with tears again. "Then we'll have a memorial service on Sunday. Everyone will be required to attend the memorial, though I don't think I'll have to twist too many arms. There might even be a huge crowd at the cemetery."

Bert's customers looked around at each other, clearly pleased.

Weeping with gratitude now, Bert tried to speak but could not. Jim put a hand on his shoulder. "Don't say anything." Bert took his hand and shook it many times. Then each of the men at the bar got up, approached Pastor Jim and shook his hand too, saying how nice this was and how happy Sam'd be to know this.

"There's one more thing, though." Their heads shot up. Uh oh, here's the catch-22, their expressions seemed to say. Chuckling a little, Jim said, "You give me Sam's folks' address and number, and I don't care if they live in Timbuktu, they'll be at Sam's memorial service. I will see to it personally." The bar whistled with disbelief.

Spud piped up with, "Whoa, that's real nice o' you pastor! But where the .... uhm... ah ...is this tims-berk-too place anyway?"

They all laughed.

Jim said over their laughter, "Well, I'm not quite sure, but it might as well be next door." They laughed harder, and slapped Jim on the back.

After this, Jim spent the next hour talking with the men, asking them about themselves. They seemed genuinely pleased that he took a sincere interest in them and were not reluctant to tell him whatever he wanted to know. Now he understood why many men resorted to strong drink, for their stories were uniformly sad. His heart went out to them that night. Later, after he got home and greeted Eve properly—who seemed anxious to get upstairs, but for what reason, Jim wondered out loud to her, he could not possibly understand (which got a dark blush, a girlish giggle and a caress from Eve)—he went into his study, got on his knees and prayed for many hours that God would open a door for these men to step into His loving arms. He also prayed that the LORD his God would make good on his (Jim's) promise to get Sam's folks to come to his funeral. This posed no trouble, however; because after Jim had told them about Sam's death and then had a good heart-to-heart talk with them for a few minutes, their weeping and keening repentance filled the room.

Pastor Jim Richards got the first answer to his prayer concerning the salvation of the men at Bert's establishment a few days later. He had just gotten off the phone with the funeral home to check the preparations for Sam's funeral when there was a knock on his door. He said, "Yes, Julie, what is it?"

A young and pretty secretary came in. "Pastor Jim," she said, "there's someone here to see you."

"Who?"

She smiled slyly but did not answer. Rather, she extended her hand. Onto that hand latched one of the largest hands Jim had ever seen, but so very gently you would have thought this petite young woman had just donned a glove of the finest velvet. She tugged a little on the hand, and quietly and humbly, with head bowed, Bert came into Jim's office. He nodded gratitude at the young woman. Julie nodded a reply and reluctantly accepted her hand back. Then she left quietly, but not before laying a hand on Bert's forearm, smiling a bright smile of encouragement at him. The young woman shut the door softly behind her.

By this time Jim had shot up out of his chair and was standing in front of the obviously embarrassed man. Jim felt like he was standing in front of a mountain. Because Jim's office was not large, Bert seemed to fill it completely, making him all the more imposing. Smiling broadly, looking up into his eyes, Jim took his hand. "Bert. What a wonderful surprise! Here. Come. Sit."

His eyes shining and a few streaks running down his cheeks, Bert allowed himself to be led to a sofa. He sat and Jim sat next to him.

When the giant began to sob softly, Pastor Jim's voice softened. "Is there something wrong, Bert? Anything I can do? Just ask and I'll do whatever I can." When Bert did not answer, he asked, "Is it one of your friends? We can go down to the bar right now, you know."

Jim made to rise, but Bert placed a hand gently on his forearm. Jim sat back and waited for the bartender to speak. But now his soul was stirring mightily in him; this only happened when his God was speaking to him. Right now it was as if the LORD were shouting with glee, though if you asked Pastor Jim, he could not have put into words why he got this impression.

Bert sniffed. "Pastor Jim," he choked out, "I came to ax you a question."

"Sure, Bert." The big man looked over at Jim's desk, at the Bible he kept there. Jim said, "Should I?" motioning toward the Book.

"I don't know, Pastor. You know that I have one of those at the Bar. You know that I read it from time to time."

Jim replied softly, "To your friends. Yes, I know." His heart was pounding so loudly now he wondered whether Julie might be able to hear it.

"Not just to my friends Pastor." Jim's eyes widened. "No. I've been readin' it myself for about an hour or so every night after I close. Almost got all the way through it," he added, a gleam of pride showing in his eyes. Throwing off any pride he might be feeling, however, Bert the bartender continued, "Well, there's a few verses that have caught my eye recently." Jim reached over to get the Bible, but Bert said, "Not yet, Pastor Jim. Not yet." Jim sat back and took Bert's hand. The big man did not pull away. "Well these verses go, 'Come to me, all you who are weary and burdened, and I will give you rest. Take my yoke upon you and learn from me, for I am gentle and humble in heart, and you will find rest for your souls. For my

225

yoke is easy and my burden is light.' You know that it's Jesus as is sayin' that." Yes, Jim nodded, thinking of the reference.[3] "And there's another un that says, 'I am not ashamed of the gospel, because it is the power of God for the salvation of everyone who believes: first for the Jew, then for the Gentile. For in the gospel a righteousness from God is revealed, a righteousness that is by faith from first to last, just as it is written: "The righteous will live by faith." ' "[4] Jim nodded again. "Ya see, Pastor Jim, I been burdened mightily by my wickedness. You know what you said way back then."

"Please don't go back there, Bert. I didn't mean to..."

Bert interrupted, "I know you didn't, Pastor. But you were right, at least about what's in a man's heart. And this guy Paul's always talkin' about this Jesus and what He done for him. Well, Pastor ..." Bert stopped, looked away briefly, wiped his eyes and continued. "Well, I'd like to come to know this Jesus Paul's allas talkin' about. I think I might like Him, though I don't know that He'd like me all that much." Jim opened his mouth to speak, but Bert interrupted again. "Yes, Pastor, I know Jesus loves me. That's what He keeps on sayin' and that's what His disciples kept sayin' too. And I really believe Him, Pastor."

"I know you do, Bert. I know you do." Jim patted Bert's hand gently. Jim marveled that this man had memorized so much Scripture without any prompting, except, of course, from the Holy Spirit. He was also giddy with joy that God Himself had shown Bert the path to salvation, though he did not seem to realize it yet.

"Trouble is," Bert went on, "I don't know that He'd *like* me all that much." He sighed, looked down at the floor. "But mebbe that's because I don't like myself all that much." He looked back up into the sunlight streaming into the office from a large window. He said softly, as if he were addressing the light itself, "Mebbe that's why."

Just then, Jim became keenly aware of that light. Watching Bert, Jim imagined that a strange glow surrounded him, reflecting off his tear-streaked face, making his eyes shine more brightly. For the Pastor of Southside Christian Faith Church it was as if the very finger of God were touching the struggling man.

"So, Pastor, what must I do to be saved?" Bert pounded his chest, startling Jim. "To get this wickedness cut outa me." Flattening his hand over his heart now, he added, "To get a heart that's right with God? How, Jim?"

---

[3] Matthew 11:28 – 30.
[4] Romans 1:16 – 18.

After mouthing a silent prayer of thanksgiving to the One who has extended His hand of love to all sinners, no matter what they've done, Jim explained how a man could be saved.

Bert's eyes went wide when he heard the phrase, "just confess your sins and invite Him into your heart and receive Him and you will be saved." The bartender said, "Geeze, Pastor Jim. I kinda did that last night." It was Jim's turn to be surprised. "Yeah. I got on my knees last night and axed Jesus to have mercy on me, because I'm poor an' wretched an' needy, as it says in that their book o' yours." He pointed at Jim's Bible.

"Looks to me, Bert," Jim replied, once he had done marveling at the power of God to bring men to Himself without any help, "that that's your Book too."

Bert looked at the Bible for the longest time and then said, "You know what, Pastor Jim. You're right!"

Bert laughed and slapped Jim on the back, but apparently a little too roughly, because it knocked Jim forward a little. He had to clear his throat to respond. "Ulp ... well then, I guess I am." They laughed together for the longest time.

They had been talking for around an hour when someone knocked quietly. "Please come in," Reverend Richards said, getting to his feet.

Julie came in with a bright smile. "I hate to disturb you two ..." She cast a shining eye briefly at Bert. "... but, Pastor Jim, you've got a meeting with the local Christian Youth Organization. Since you've cancelled twice, I thought maybe you'd like to keep it this time. Or ..." She blushed.

Jim laughed. "Or tell them myself why I can't come a third?" Julie nodded, laughing with him. "Sure. I'll be on my way in a minute."

Satisfied, Julie left them, but not before flashing another bright smile at Jim's guest.

Jim Richards turned to Bert and said, "I'm sorry, Bert, but I have to go. Now, since you already have a Bible and are obviously reading it, I don't have to worry about that. But you really have to find a church that suits you. One of the most important things in your life from now on will be to form ties to your brothers and sisters in Christ."

Bert nodded, smiling broadly.

Jim opened his Rolodex and thumbed through it briefly. Finding a card, he said, "Here's the number of a friend of mine, runs a good Bible teaching church not far from here."

Looking puzzled, Bert said, "But Jim. I don't want to go to no other church. I want to come here. That is, iff'n you'll have the likes o' me."

Tears welling up in him, Jim said, "Of course. How wonderfully kind of you after all we..." He stopped, looked away and wiped an eye with his hand.

"After all what, Pastor Jim?"

Jim raised an eyebrow.

"It was because o' you that I got that there Bible", Bert continued. "It was because o' you that I started to read it. It was because o' you that I'm here right now. All because o' you, Jim."

Rendered speechless by this confession, which was quite an accomplishment on Bert's part, considering that Jim was a preacher, the Senior Pastor of Southside Christian Faith Church embraced his big friend, gratitude filling his heart to overflowing. When he could manage, he said, "I claim none of the credit. It was God working in you who did this wonderful thing. Nevertheless, that was, yet again, very kindly said, and I appreciate it more than I can say."

Bert took Jim's outstretched hand and shook it once.

Sniffing and wiping his nose with an index finger, Reverend Richards said, "Well, this church will be a much better place with you in it." Jim looked down at the card and said, "Ol' Jerry will never know what a loss his church has just suffered." He tossed it on his desk and smiled at Bert.

Who turned beet red. "That was a very nice thing to say, Pastor." Bert then said, "Well, I've got a place to run, and you've got a meetin' to go to, so I'll see ya on Sunday."

"You sure will, Bert. Go with God and I know that God will go with you."

They embraced again and Bert left. A second or two later, Jim heard Julie shriek delightedly and say, "Oh, how wonderful for you!" Pastor Richards wondered whether a hug or two had punctuated Julie's exclamation.

And wonderful for us, Jim thought. *Yep, Bert will certainly be a wonderful addition to the family.* He had a definite spring in his step as he headed out of the church.

To tie together the remaining threads of this story, the gravesite and memorial services for Sam went off wonderfully well. Then the entire congregation greeted Bert the first Sunday he attended and apologized profusely to him, no one more so than the man who had yelled at him that awful day. Bert was gracious and forgiving, much to their joy. Jim Richards also got to know Sam's folks quite well, and they eventually came to worship with his congregation.

And God continued to answer Jim's prayer, for over the next several weeks, one by one, Bert brought his customers to church with him and eventually led them all to know Jesus Christ as their LORD and Saviour. During this time, Jim never ceased to marvel at how good God was, and the following Psalm became a keystone of his faith from that day on:

> Shout for joy to the LORD, all the earth.
> Worship the LORD with gladness; come before him with joyful songs.
> Know that the LORD is God. It is he who made us, and we are his; we are his people, the sheep of his pasture.
> Enter his gates with thanksgiving and his courts with praise; give thanks to him and praise his name.
> For the LORD is good and his love endures forever; his faithfulness continues through all generations.[5]

Oh, and there's one more thing. A few weeks after the last of Bert's friends had been baptized, as Jim lay sleeping, he had a dream.

> In it he found himself in a place of awesome beauty. It was full of light, and angels by the thousands and tens of thousands were singing the sweetest music. As Jim stared at it all in wonder, the light coalesced into the likeness of a man. Slowly the man's body firmed up and His face took on features, the one most notable being His eyes, which burned brightly, like flashes of lightening. Jim saw that He was wearing a shining white robe with a gold sash draped around his shoulder and down around his waist, that his hair and beard were as white as snow, and that His feet shone like molten bronze. One hand, in which he held what appeared to be seven stars, He had extended out partially toward Jim. Jim looked and saw that another man, also dressed in white, was standing next to the LORD Jesus, who had wrapped His other arm around his shoulders. Then the other man vanished.

---

[5] Psalm 100:1 – 5.

As Jim sank first to his knees and then fell face down before the LORD, he was thinking, 'The other must have been Sam.'

The LORD God of all Creation touched him on the shoulder. "Rise, son of man," said Jesus. Then the LORD said to him, "Well done, thou good and faithful servant."

Jim wept for joy.

He woke to find his wife stroking his arm, asking why he was crying. When he told her, she wept for joy too. For the rest of his days, Jim Richards was the happiest man alive.

When Doom Comes to the Ungodly

[The LORD] said to [Ezekiel], "Have you seen this, son of man? Is it a trivial matter for the house of Judah to do the detestable things they are doing here? Must they also fill the land with violence and continually provoke me to anger? Look at them putting the branch to their nose! Therefore I will deal with them in anger; I will not look on them with pity or spare them. Although they shout in my ears, I will not listen to them." Then [Ezekiel] heard him call out in a loud voice, "Bring the guards of the city here, each with a weapon in his hand." (Ezekiel 8:17 – 9:1)

Author's Note: It seems to me that we all tend to take the love and grace of God for granted. We forget that He is not only the God of love and creation but also the God of wrath and destruction, and that He will bring justice to the earth. The above passage concerns the destruction of Jerusalem during the days before the last remnant of Israel was carried off to Babylonian captivity. But the LORD has also said, "[If] any nation does not listen [to my word and repent], I will completely uproot and destroy it ..." (Jeremiah 12:17). And, as is made clear later in chapter 9 of Ezekiel, the principal agents of this destruction will be the LORD's own angels. Should we who live in a nation defiled by abortion and grotesque sexual sin not take this warning to heart?

It was a hot day, this ninth day of the fourth month in the eleventh year of the reign of Zedekiah, King of Judah. Asa, son of Isaac, ran like the wind through the streets of Jerusalem toward the Temple. He was only six years old, but he could run fast, and he was running now for dear life.

His mother had sent him to fetch his father Isaac because their neighbor Kenan had decided to go to the priests of Baal to offer his little daughter Miriam to the flames. The siege by Nebuchadnezzar's army had lasted for almost two years now—the Babylonians were at the gates, food was scarce, the people were afraid—and Kenan had hoped that offering his daughter to the demon Baal might entice him to bring relief to the city. But Asa's mother Ruth, who worshipped the God of Abraham, knew that this would be detestable in the eyes of the LORD, and that it would add one more offense to the mountain of offenses her people had already piled up before Him. She hoped that Isaac could persuade the little girl's father not to do this awful thing. Asa was also running extra hard because he loved Miriam; they had been playmates their whole lives, and he did not want her to die.

231

As Asa neared the temple he stopped suddenly. There was a man standing at the base of the steps, dressed in the whitest linen robe Asa had ever seen, holding a writing kit in his hand. The shining man was looking up at the temple and then at the people as they went into and out of the gate, and he shook his head sadly as he wrote on his tablet. Every once in a while, however, he would stop writing and touch the forehead of one or more of those who passed by—men, women, and children—and after the man touched them, a bright six-pointed star glowed on their foreheads. Asa noticed that they all seemed to be weeping, their heads bowed, as if they were mourning what they had seen in the temple. The little boy rubbed his eyes because none of these people seemed to notice the man as he did this, though he was standing right in front of them. Nor did they seem to notice that glowing mark on each other's foreheads. Asa rubbed his eyes again.

But the boy quickly forgot about the glowing marks as the urgency of his mission came back to him. He looked up to the temple gate to see if he could see his father, who normally would have been there, yelling out the prophesies of Jeremiah the prophet, of whom he was a devoted disciple. But Asa did not see him. Forgetting completely about the white-robed man in his urgency to find his father, he ran past him and up to the gate.

He called out for his father but could not find him. He rudely stopped some of the passersby to ask if they had seen him. Those who did not growl out obscenities at him and push him away said that they had not. After several more attempts, the frustrated child sat down on a low stone wall near the gate and began to cry. How he wanted to save Miriam! What would become of her if he did not find his daddy? Then he thought, *It will be all my fault if she dies.* He cried harder.

He felt someone touch him on the forehead. He looked up and there, squatting down and looking him in the eye, was the same white-robed man. He had the kindest eyes Asa had ever seen, and they were the bluest blue the boy could have imagined. Fascinated, Asa stopped crying. Wiping his eyes with the heels of his hands, he asked with a quivering voice, "Have you seen my daddy, Sir?"

Before responding, the man brushed a strand of hair away from his little eye and smiled and Asa leaned into his gentle touch. "Yes, Asa, son of Isaac, whom the LORD loves," the man said. "Do not be afraid, because your father is with your mother, Ruth, even as we speak. They are also beloved of the LORD your God."

Asa felt like jumping for joy; his eyes got wide and he smiled the biggest smile he could manage. "Oh, boy, that's such good news!" he exclaimed. But then he could not decide what exactly the white-robed man had meant. What did it mean that he was beloved of the LORD?

The man laughed. "Yes, it is good news, indeed." But his face became grim as he looked back over his shoulder and out into the city. "But there is bad news too."

Asa's face crumpled in tears. "Oh no, they can't let Miriam die."

The man turned back to the child and touched his wrist to get his attention. "No, your friend Miriam, daughter of Kenan, will not die. Even now she has taken refuge in your home; your parents are withholding her from her father. But Kenan and his wife will indeed die before the next sunrise, as will all who have bowed their knees to the detestable thing." Asa sucked in his breath as his joy over Miriam turned immediately into fear for her parents. The shining blue-eyed man went on, "Even now we are gathering to do the LORD your God's bidding."

Asa saw that six more men had come to stand at the base of the temple steps. Asa stood and looked down at them. They had grim faces and they were frightening to behold. In their hands they held swords, but not of iron or of any other substance Asa had ever seen; rather, they seemed to be made of red light, the color of blood.

The man laid his hand on the boy's shoulder. "You must go to your father and mother. Tell them that before the second watch is completed, the Babylonian hordes will break through the wall.[1] Then the killing will begin." Asa shuddered again as the man put his head next to his and pointed at a man who had that glowing spot on his forehead. "Do you see that?" Asa nodded. "Only people with that mark will escape with their lives, though their homes and all they own may be destroyed."

Asa turned to the man and tears began to roll down his cheeks again. He asked, "Will my daddy and mommy live, sir?"

The angel said, "Yes, they and you shall live, as will your friend Miriam. Because you have told her about your God, she has believed and has been saved. She owes you her life. But her mother and father will not live." He looked down at his tablet, sadness filling his expression. Then his voice took on an awesome sound like the sound of a thousand rushing waters. "Nor will many thousands of others—men, women, children—who will die without mercy before the sun rises again on this city." The angel had stood as he said

---

[1] The twelve-hour night was divided into three four-hour watches, the first starting at sunset, which was generally around 6:00 p.m.

233

this, and he was now glaring down at Asa from the awesome height of the very sky itself.

At the change in his voice and at the sudden fearsome aspect of his being, Asa became frightened of him for the first time, and he bowed down with his face to the ground. When he could find his voice, he said, "I'm afraid. Please don't hurt me, Sir."

The voice softened. "Of course I won't hurt you, little one. Because of your faith you have nothing to fear from me or from these men." They nodded grimly as the mighty angel pointed at them, Asa's eyes lighting on them.

"Who are you, then?"

"I am Gabriel, and I have been sent to you directly from God. Now go! Quickly!"[2] Asa got up and began to run. But as he ran, the angel's words came reverberating into his ears as if they were raining down on him from the very depths of the heavens: "Tell your father and mother not to go out tonight after sunset. Tell them what I have told you. Tell them that the LORD their God has decreed that your house will not be touched. All who stay there will be safe from the swords and arrows of the Babylonian horde, and from us as well."

Asa's little bare feet became like whirring wheels as he ran through the dusty streets toward his home.

In his urgency, Asa had decided to take the short route through a district in the city his mother had told him to avoid. It was the place were the shrine prostitutes, both male and female, and the priests and priestesses of the detestable pagan gods Baal, Chemosh, Marduk, Molech, the Queen of heaven, and Ashtoreth lived, and where they carried out many of their detestable worship practices. As the boy ran, men embracing men and women embracing women shouted after him, "Hey, little boy, stop. Where you going? We've got something for you." But Asa did not stop, of course. Until he inadvertently thudded into a man who grabbed him by the shoulders and lifted him, kicking and squirming, off his feet and held him tightly. He dangled Asa in midair.

"Hey, don't you look where you are going?" the man breathed into Asa's face.

---

[2] The identity of the man (angel) with the writing kit is never revealed in Ezekiel 9.

His breath was so rancid with the smell of drugs and alcohol Asa felt like gagging. Struggling and kicking at the man, Asa said, "I've got to get home. My daddy's waiting for me."

"Is he now?" the man said with a leer. He looked over his shoulder as his male companion approached him and put an arm around his waist. Then they laughed as they both leered at the kicking, squirming little boy. The man bent his head to his companion; kissed him on the lips and then said to him, "See what I caught. Think what great entertainment he would make this evening."

"No!" Asa shouted. "The Babylonians are coming tonight, and everyone without the mark will be slaughtered. And you don't have the mark."

They laughed into his grim little face. The first man said, "What mark is that, you little slug? When we get done with you, you won't care about any marks, let me tell you."

The laughing men were just about to take the still squirming and kicking boy into a nearby building when they stopped suddenly, their laughter dying on their lips. Blocking the entrance was Gabriel, whose expression was frightening—his eyes glowed blood red and his face shone with a terrible light. So frightening was it that even Asa, who was glad to see him, was afraid.

When the angel motioned toward the ground, the men set Asa down gently. When he looked down at Asa and jerked his head to the side, Asa ran.

The boy chanced to look back and saw that Gabriel was just then sheathing one of those flaming swords; and where the two men had been standing, there were now two quivering, headless bodies on the ground, blood squirting in torrents from their severed throats.

As people gathered around them, Asa stopped briefly. He could see them looking first at each other and then at the sky, as if the men had been slaughtered by some invisible thing that had landed among them for an instant and then had flown back into the heavens. When they pointed at Asa, the little boy took off running again. As he ran he could hear screams coming from that district. He had heard this horrid sound before when the Babylonians had defeated some of their men outside the city gates—they had been the sounds of people being mercilessly mowed down. This time, however, he did not look back.

When Asa got to his tiny two-room home his mother was sitting at a table with Miriam in her arms, and the little girl was crying on his mother's shoulder. Her father Kenan had gone into the district of Baal to get some help, to bring men back with him to wrest his daughter from Isaac's house so that he might offer her in the fire. But he had not come back and his daughter missed him. In her innocence and love for her father, she did not understand what he had decided to do with her.

Asa was covered with the dust and grime of the city street and he was gulping for air. His mother held out her other arm to him and he came over to her. She said, "Where have you been, you little dust ball? Your father has been looking all over for you."

The little girl looked up as she said this. Seeing her best friend, she stopped crying and smiled a tear-streaked smile at him.

Asa came into his mother's embrace, still gulping for breath, and took his friend's little hand in his own. He climbed onto Ruth's lap and snuggled next to Miriam. Staring at the glowing mark on his mother's forehead, he said, "I went to the temple just like you said, Mommy. There was a man there named Gabriel."

Asa's stare at his mother's forehead was so insistent, she crossed her eyes trying to look up at her own forehead. Realizing how foolish she must have looked, she asked, "What are you looking at?" Miriam giggled.

Asa giggled too as he squeezed Miriam's hand and smiled at her, glad to see that she also had that glowing mark. He touched his mother's forehead. Still gulping for breath, he said, "Gabriel said that all those who have that mark will survive tonight when the Babylonians come." He then told his mother everything the angel had commanded him. He did not tell her that he had disobeyed her and gone into the forbidden place, though.

Miriam was still wondering what all this meant when Isaac came back into the house. Her husband's eyes were still on the streets as he entered and said sadly, "I did not find the little one, Mother, nor did I find Kenan ..." He was interrupted by a shout from his son, who leapt off his mother's lap and ran into his daddy's arms. Isaac gathered his son up in his arms and said with a relieved laugh, "There you are. We were so worried. A rumor has been spreading that tonight the Babylonians will enter the city. Everyone is gathering what little food and water there is."

"Why did you do that, Mouse?" he then asked, using his pet name for his son, because Asa had touched his forehead.

"Because you have the mark, Daddy."

When his father looked over at his mother, she extended a hand toward her son. Asa told his father everything the angel had commanded him.

With a grim face, Isaac set his son down and glanced at his wife and the little girl, who had laid her head again on Ruth's shoulder. He squatted down in front of them and said, chucking Miriam under the chin, "I'm sorry,

Princess, but I could not find your daddy. It seems he has disappeared in the district of Baal."

Asa could not resist saying, "Gabriel put two evil men to death there today, Daddy. Then he and six other men started putting a whole lot of people to death there." Reacting to his mother's angry stare, he said in a small voice, "I'm sorry, Mommy. I was in such a hurry to get home I forgot not to go through there."

As he told her what had happened, she threw her arms up in exasperation. Then she set Miriam down and held out her arms to her son, who melted into them. Holding him tightly to her breast, weeping, and rocking him back and forth, she said, "How many times have I told you not to go into that awful place? Satan and his demons live there, don't you understand?"

"Yes, Mommy. I'm sorry," the little boy answered, his voice muffled by her arms' tight hold on him.

Ruth's fear gave over to joy and she held him even more tightly to her. "They almost got you. But I'm so glad you are safe, Precious. So very, very glad!" She looked knowingly up at her husband.

Isaac silently gave thanks to the LORD that He had protected his son from a fate worse than death at the hands of the devil's servants. Then his hands started to tremble because his master, Jeremiah, had predicted that the Eternal I AM, the LORD, out of his righteous anger, would bring disaster on His people. *Were the goings on in this awful place the start?* Isaac wondered. Perspiring profusely now, he sat down slowly next to his wife. "Well, if there are people dying in the district, maybe they got ..." he did not need to finish the sentence, as his wife wordlessly indicated that she understood.

Asa said, "We must not go out after the sun sets, Daddy. That's what Gabriel said."

"Gabriel?" Isaac had not really focused on the name until now. "Did you say Gabriel?"

"Yes, Daddy. I think he was an angel, though he looked like a man. He had blue eyes, though, and his robes were so white they almost blinded me."

Staring toward the door, Isaac said softly, "So it has begun. The very angels of God are among us. Heaven help the city." Then he looked up to the ceiling. "No, not heaven. Especially not heaven. For the LORD our God has turned from His love for us and now His terrible anger will rain down on us. Who will survive, if the LORD's anger burns against us? Who?"[3]

He had begun to weep, but Asa slid out of his mother's arms and put a hand on his knee. "Don't be afraid, Daddy. Gabriel said everyone with the mark will live. We all have the mark, and we must stay indoors. The LORD himself will protect us against the slaughter." Miriam had come to stand next to the boy. He opened his arms to her, and she snuggled close to him and nestled her head on his shoulder. He said, using his favorite nickname for her, "Don't worry, Mi. It will be okay, I'll protect you."

Isaac laughed, pride for his son filling him. His wife, also proud of her son, embraced both of the children and said, "So will the LORD, my darlings. So will the LORD."

That night, during the second watch, as the angel Gabriel had said, the Babylonian horde broke through the wall and their troops stormed into the city. Immediately, they set fire to the buildings, including the temple of the LORD and Solomon's palace, and they cut down people without mercy as they ran through the streets.

Inside Isaac's home, four people huddled close together as the screams of the dying echoed through the streets. They were praying to the LORD when there were shouts right outside their door. Isaac quickly got up and peeked out through a crack in his door and saw two soldiers standing a few feet from the house. He heard one of them say in Aramaic, "Look at how the people are falling. We have barely even touched the city and already over five thousand have died. What's going on?" Then the other answered, "I don't know, but there's something with us here. People are falling like flies and we haven't touched them. And it's gruesome—men old and young, women, children, even babies in their mother's arms, dying horribly." They turned and ran away from the grisly scene, taking no notice of Isaac's house.

Isaac took his family in his arms. "The LORD said this would happen and now it has. I hope my master is safe."[4]

They stayed in Isaac's embrace until the sun rose the next morning.

The city was deathly quiet, and the air was filled with smoke and the foul smell of burning flesh as Isaac cautiously opened his door and peeked out again. He dropped his arms and gasped as the door swung open wide. The street was littered with dead bodies: men, women, children, babies, all gruesomely slaughtered and left bleeding in the dust.

---

[3] See Jeremiah 16:5 – 7.
[4] See Lamentations 2:17.

That very same morning Isaac's master, Jeremiah the prophet, was sitting on a ruined wall near the temple. As he surveyed the corpses of the dead which littered the streets and then looked up to see the flames still licking at the ruins of what Solomon had built, these words came to him:

"How deserted lies the city, once so full of people! How like a widow is she, who once was great among the nations! She who was queen among the provinces has now become a slave. Bitterly she weeps at night, tears are upon her cheeks. Among all her lovers there is none to comfort her. All her friends have betrayed her; they have become her enemies. After affliction and harsh labor, Judah has gone into exile. She dwells among the nations; she finds no resting place. All who pursue her have overtaken her in the midst of her distress. The roads to Zion mourn, for no one comes to her appointed feasts. All her gateways are desolate, her priests groan, her maidens grieve, and she is in bitter anguish ..."[5]

In the next few days, during the twelfth year of Zedekiah, King of Judah, which was by our reckoning the year 586 B.C., the Babylonian army gathered up all the people with the glowing marks, except for the poorest among them, and led them off to the city of Babylon, as the LORD had commanded. Isaac and his family, including Miriam, also went into captivity; but they prospered there along with their faithful brothers in the LORD, as He had promised through Jeremiah.[6]

It is now a year in the not too distant future from our current day, and we find ourselves in a large city on the West Coast of the United States, a city well known for its progressive liberal thought, a beautiful city, called by many the Paris of the West. It is a city noted for its museums and theater, for its great music and world renowned dining establishments. It is a city to which people come from all over the world to marvel at its great beauty. It is truly a city of light, or so its proud residents claim.

Well, though it is conceivable that one might find some light here, it would not happen on this day, for dark clouds of concern had gathered over it. Yes, even over the entire country. For the war in the Middle East was not

---

[5] Lamentations 1:1 – 4.
[6] Jeremiah 29: 4 – 14.

going well, nor was the one on the farthest East Asian shores. Many of our fine young men and women had died, and everyone was marveling that "such a backward people" could defeat division upon division of our powerful, some had said invincible, army. Now these "backward fanatics" threatened to bring our war down around our own heads. How could this have happened, everyone wanted to know?

The streets were largely empty of pedestrian traffic, nor was there much vehicle traffic, as little Antoine ran along the sidewalk, trying to find his father, who had gone to the local abortion clinic to talk his wife out of letting the monsters in that place murder their second child.

Antoine's mother had told him to stay home and wait for his father because she would be back in a few hours. But when his father got home and the boy told him where his mother had gone, he had not even bothered to shut the door behind him as he ran out of their little apartment and into the street. So Antoine had run after him. After all, it was only a few blocks, and what harm could there be? At least, that's what Antoine told himself, even though his parents told him to never go out alone.

"Why, Mommy? My friends play out there all the time."

"Because I say so," his mother, Raythina, had said.

"But why?" Antoine whined.

She took him in her arms and set him on her knee. "There are men out there who ... well ... who might want to hurt you."

"Why, Mommy?"

She breathed out an exasperated sigh. Staring into her six-year-old son's eyes, she said, "Well they just do, that's all. Don't go axing dumb questions. Stay off the streets!"

As Antoine ran he recalled the fear in his mother's eyes; but he was not afraid. He was a big boy and could take care of himself.

As he rounded the corner, he came upon the building that housed the clinic. He slowed to a walk and stared up at it in awe. The little boy had always been impressed by this building because it was made of fine marble and was gleaming white, with columns in the Doric style, supporting a massive stone portico.

If Antoine had been a little older and had studied the history of the Middle East, he might have thought of this as a temple of some kind, for it certainly looked like the temples they built over there. And though he could read the words carved into the portico above the columns, "Equal Rights for All," he would have had to be much older to consider the awful irony of those words. And it might have occurred to him that it should go on to say,

"... for All, except for the helpless unborn that are murdered by the thousands here in this place."

Of course, Antoine had no such thoughts as he stood staring up at it. Nor, because of his youth and innocence, did he think it strange that a barbed wire fence surrounded it, nor that there were usually many armed guards standing outside. Had he asked, however, he would have been told that it had been a place of tremendous contention for many years, and that people gathered outside its doors daily to protest the slaughter that went on inside its walls, despite its lofty sayings about equal rights.

But there was no crowd here today as Antoine approached the building; nor were there any guards. Rather, there was one lone man dressed in what looked like a very white bathrobe. He had gold sandals on his feet and his hair was bright white. Antoine had never seen anyone like him, so he stopped and stared at him.

He saw that the man had a pouch slung over his shoulder, that he was holding what looked like a tablet and that he was writing on it. The man's head came up suddenly, and he looked across the street. Antoine's eyes followed his. He saw a billboard across the street facing the building. On the billboard was an animated action feature. As the little boy and the man stared at it, the image of a grim-faced man materialized out of a blue background. He pointed a finger at the building and opened his mouth and then words streamed across the front of the billboard in large white letters: "Over fifty million murders. Stop abortion now!" This message was repeated every fifteen seconds or so.

Then Antoine heard the blasting sound of a radio coming from below the billboard. He turned and saw three young men walking along beneath it. One of them was carrying a large Walkman on his shoulder right next to his ear. Antoine turned away from the billboard figure to stare at the radio because the voice coming out of it was shrieking, "The Associated Press has just announced that terrorists have detonated a nuclear device in the middle of New York City. There is no word yet on the number of casualties, but there are reports that it was a hydrogen bomb with the yield of ten or so Hiroshima bombs." The voice paused for a moment. "Oh my God," it screamed. "Another bulletin has come in. Terrorists have detonated similar devices in Chicago, Washington D.C. and Philadelphia. There is no word on whether our government has escaped." There was a brief pause, and then the announcer cried, "Now word has come to us that Air Force One was still on the ground. No contact has been made with the President or his cabinet."

Suddenly, the voice was replaced by the obnoxious sound of the civil defense warning system. Then there were the words, "This is not a test. This is not a test. Our Homeland Security forces have been put on full alert. It has just been reported that our enemies in East Asia have launched several missiles at the West Coast of the United States. Get off the streets! Get off the streets! Do not panic!"

Then Antoine heard another voice say, "And casualties from the nuclear attack in the east are thought to number in the millions as the cities of New York, Washington, Philadelphia, and Chicago lie in ruins. The attacks seem to be spreading to other eastern cities. Now Boston reports that ..." but the sound faded. *It must have been a car radio,* Antoine thought, because a car had just passed him and turned a corner.

But now all the cars were coming to a stop and their drivers could be seen turning frantically at the dials of their radios.

Meanwhile, the young men across the street looked at each other, sat the radio down on the sidewalk and sat down beside it. Two of them embraced and kissed passionately as a man and woman might embrace and kiss each other. Another voice came echoing through the streets that all attempts to destroy the Korean missiles had failed.

Now Antoine could hear from one of the car radios the panic-stricken announcer shouting, "They don't understand why nothing seems to be working. Everything is breaking down. All our military communications satellites seem to be out of order. The missile defense system has been compromised, it seems. There have been reports of the missiles being launched but blowing up inexplicably before they reach their targets. It's as if someone or something is sabotaging it, along with all our other defense systems."

Antoine looked over at the man in white, who turned to stare back at him with the bluest eyes Antoine had ever seen. As the man turned and looked up into the sky, the sun was setting and there were no clouds. Antoine turned to look also, his eyes following the angel's. Overhead were several vapor trails, one of them starting to bend downward. As it continued to descend toward the city it reflected the rays of the setting sun, and it became a long, blood red streak, stabbing down at him. When the little boy looked back at the man who was writing on his tablet, the man stopped writing and shook his head grimly at him.

Antoine's blood froze.

Afterward

My God & Saviour is a collection of short stories based on my understanding of God's nature as a Person and on the principles of my Christian faith. Many of these stories came to me as I meditated on God's word and on its application to my life.

Most of them are based on Biblical events: for example Gabriel coming to Mary to tell her that she will soon bear the Son of God. These stories came to me as I imagined myself watching these events unfold; as I imagined watching the characters interact with God, usually in His incarnation as Jesus—or with His angels or with His enemies—as the characters struggled to serve the LORD. On the other hand, some of these stories are what one might call parables. They are fictional and they contain a single point of instruction, generally about what it means to be a Christian and to faithfully serve the LORD our God.

To enhance a reader's understanding of each story, it is introduced by one or more verses of Scripture, which are quoted to illustrate the story's point or to provide the source of its inspiration. There is also a personal note from me describing my motivation for writing it.

Finally, though I wrote these stories for the reader's entertainment, it was also my hope that he or she would find in them some spiritual instruction. My hope is that they will make each reader who knows our LORD Jesus Christ think about his/her faith; about what it means to be a Christian. My fervent hope is that the messages in these stories will inspire all readers to try to attain to a better knowledge and understanding his/her God and His ways.

Lightning Source UK Ltd.
Milton Keynes UK
UKHW040218240223
417572UK00001B/43